LAND OF
FRIGHT

Collection VIII

JACK O'DONNELL

Welcome to Land of Fright™!

Land of Fright™ is a world of spine-tingling short horror stories filled with the strange, the eerie, and the weird. The **Land of Fright™** tales encompass the vast expanse of time and space. In the **Land of Fright™** series of books you will visit the world of the Past in Ancient Rome, Medieval England, the old West, World War II, and other eras yet to be explored. You will find many tales that exist right here in the Present, tales filled with modern lives that have taken a turn down a darker path. You will travel into the Future to tour strange new worlds and interact with alien societies, or to just take a disturbing peek at what tomorrow may bring.

Each **Land of Fright™** story exists in its own territory (which we like to call a **terrorstory**.) Some of the story realms you visit will intrigue you. Some of them may unsettle you. Some of them may even titillate and amuse you. We hope many of them will give you delicious chills along your journey as you struggle to survive in the trenches of World War I, take a taste from a mysterious cup of tea, encounter alien life forms on planet Saffire, and visit many more odd places.

First, we need to check your ID. **Land of Fright™** is intended for mature audiences. You will experience adult language, graphic violence, and some explicit sex. Ready to enter? Good. We'll take that ticket now. **Land of Fright™** awaits. You can pass through the dark gates and—Step Into Fear!

Readers Love Land of Fright™!

"Some truly original stories. At last, a great collection of unique and different stories. Whilst this is billed as horror, the author managed to steer away from senseless violence and gratuitous gore and instead with artful story telling inspires you to use your own imagination. A great collection. Already looking for other collections... especially loved Kill the Queen (God Save the Queen)." – Amazon UK review for **Land of Fright™ Collection I**

"Fantastic science fiction short that has a surprising plot twist, great aliens, cool future tech and occurs in a remote lived-in future mining colony on a distant planet. This short hit all the marks I look for in science fiction stories. The alien creatures are truly alien and attack with a mindless ruthlessness. The desperate colonists defend themselves in a uniquely futuristic way. This work nails the art of the short story. Recommended." – Amazon review for **Out of Ink (Land of Fright™ #26 – in Collection III)**

"I am a fan of the Land of Fright series and have found the horror found in the stories diverse and delightfully bizarre. This tale amp's up the gritty to 11. The barbarian warrior king in this short story is a well written, fearsome, crude and believable beast of a man. This story is not for those offended by sex or violence. I was immersed and found it great escapism, exactly what I look for in recreational reading."- Review for **The King Who Owned The World (Land of Fright™ #50 – in Collection V)**

"The thing I like about the Land of Fright series of short stories is that they are so diverse yet share a common weird, unusual and original vibe. From horror to science fiction they are all powerful despite of their brevity." - Amazon review for **Snowflakes (Land of Fright™ #3 – in Collection I)**

DEDICATION

To all the brave readers who are still adventuring into the weird world of Land of Fright™ with me!

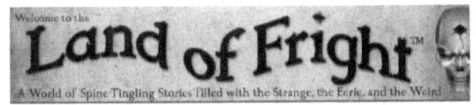

LAND OF FRIGHT™ COLLECTION VIII CONTENTS

TERRORSTORY #71
IN THE TRENCHES

1917
The Great War
Northern France
In the Trenches

Robby, you should be thankful for your disability. It is not your fault that your poor eyesight and gimp leg prevented you from being here. This is a wretched war and we are stuck in this wretched trench fighting for our wretched lives. Everyone is so unclean. Filth is everywhere. Your fastidious nature would most likely have driven you mad if you were here.

There is no respite from the odious release of urine and fecal matter. There are times a soldier must make do with a hole dug in the muck. When we move into a different trench we don't often know if we are stepping in malodorous mud or someone's fetid refuse. I can think of no other area on earth where the conditions are so deplorable. One section on the far end of the trench we currently occupy has been designated a latrine, but most of the men don't make it that far. They are either too tired, too listless, or the painful urge comes on so suddenly and so strongly that there is no time to make it to the latrine area.

The ground in the trenches never seems to dry out. The mud isn't anything like any mud I've ever experience elsewhere, even in the woods behind our house after a heavy rain. It has some weird life of its own. It sucks at your boots as if it wants to pull you down into the earth to become part of it. Shell-fire can dissolve a man's body into sludge, disintegrate a man into a muck that blends invisibly into the muddy ground at our feet. I know this is a horrible thing to think, but sometimes I do feel like I'm trudging through the remains of many a man's soul as I move through the trenches, and their ghostly fingers are pulling at my boots.

I really could use a good cuppa right about now. Chamomile, lemongrass, good old-fashioned black tea, it doesn't matter what kind. I just want to smell it wafting up out of the cup. That's all. I don't even need to drink it, though that would be wonderful as well. I just want to get a whiff of the sweet aroma.

That's it. Just to block out the smell of too many men confined in too tight of a space, if only for a few seconds.

All my love to you and Mother.

- Verne.

Robby, we lost another man last night. It was Ferguson, a skinny fellow. Used to be a cook, he said. Famous for his bacon and cheddar omelets in his home town. Oh, for a single strip of fresh crispy bacon! He's just gone. There's no trace of his body. He either ran out towards the German lines and was riddled to pieces by Jerry machine gun fire or he was blown up by a land mine in no man's land.

Or an artillery burst might have quite literally blown him to shreds.

Before I got here, I feared the German machine guns the most. One of the boys who has a zealous habit of studying weapons told us the Jerry machine guns had a sustained fire of 450–600 rounds per minute, giving those wretched Huns the ability to cut down attacking waves of our troops like a scythe cutting through wheat. But contrary to popular belief, machine guns are not the most lethal weapon in this war to end all wars. That dubious distinction goes to the artillery.

The German artillery was fierce during the night last night, making the ground shake under our muddy boots incessantly. It was as if a five-hour earthquake ravaged the ground beneath our feet, making the walls of our trench tremble with each shudder-inducing explosion. The bursting shells made the air bellow around us like an angry thunder god screaming at the top of his lungs. You cannot understand the effects of an endless artillery barrage unless you experience it. It's a relentless assault on all your senses. Your entire body shakes, your ears ring, the acrid smell of explosives fills your nose, the taste of ash and mud and smoke coats your tongue. You try to close your eyes to at least shield that one sense from the assault, but your fear refuses to let them stay closed. It doesn't matter if you haven't slept for twenty four hours and your body and your mind are desperate for sleep - no man can sleep through a barrage like that.

Ferguson might have just cracked and went over the top by himself. I've seen it often enough that it doesn't surprise me anymore. Men do crack under the incessant strain. Good men. They just reach a breaking point and something pushes them over the edge, whether it's one more shell burst, one more explosion, or seeing one more good man standing right next to them get shredded by shrapnel into bits and clumps of human flesh. I understand it. I'm afraid of that feeling because I do understand it. I pray that day never comes where I feel compelled to join them in their madness.

Don't tell Mother about Ferguson because she'll just worry about me more.

All my love to you and Mother.

- Verne.

Robby, you can tell Mother there is someone here with us who is doing quite well in the trenches. Maybe this story will bring a smile to her lips. We call him Tubby. He's an orange-haired cat who is having a field day with all the rats. I swear that every time I see him, he's put on a few more pounds and his belly has gotten bigger and rounder. He seems very content to stay near us. It's quite amazing that all the artillery barrages haven't scared him away. He might be just as scared to leave the trenches as we are. He'll sit on the trench boards (we sometimes are able to line the floors of a trench with wood planks to try and keep our feet dry, if we get lucky enough to find some spare planks) and just absently lick at his paws and groom himself. We don't have to feed him at all. He does quite well on his own. Sometimes, he does demand something from us, though. He'll just sidle up next to you, look up at you with his soulful green eyes, and just meow and paw gently at your hand. He just wants to be pet. He gets pretty insistent when the mood strikes him. Sometimes, the men have no patience for him and shoo him away, but most of the time the men will give in and give Tubby a little scratch behind his ears or under his chin. He's all purring and content after that.

That reminds me, Robby, how is your sweet Rebecca? Is she still making you purr? Or was it the other way around?

All my love to you and Mother.

- Verne.

Robby, in your last letter to me you said you wanted to know what a typical day was like in these wretched trenches. I can honestly say no day is typical because something new always seems to be happening, but there are some things that do happen on a recurring basis.

We start the daylight hours with a Stand-To-Arms. We're on high alert for a German attack because they'll often happen right before sunrise. If no attack from the Jerries comes, we'll stand down a half hour after dawn. We'll get a bit of breakfast, grabbing whatever bits of stale bread we can get our hands on. Sometimes we get shreds of dried-out meat, but our main meal is often just a watery stew filled with few vegetables and tiny clumps of meat. The food is always cold. The biscuits are always hard and they have no taste. Dreadful, but we can't let ourselves starve.

We'll spend the rest of the morning cleaning mud from our boots with our bayonets. Then we dry our boots out as best we can, and try to dry out our feet as best we can as well. I know of some men who purposely left one of their wet boots, or even both, on for days because they actually wanted to get trench foot. It's their one way ticket back home — and for some of them they've decided it's worth losing a foot for. What a wretched state of mind those pitiful blokes must be trapped in to act in such a cowardly way.

Then we'll clean our weapons and fix any part of the trench that needs shoring up. Then we'll have a bit of food. We call it dinner even though it's barely past noon when we eat. Then we try to get some sleep. Most men are lucky to get a few consecutive hours of sleep in a day. Then we Stand-To for about half an hour before dusk, readying ourselves for a night attack. If no attack comes, then we spend time on patrols, keeping watch, digging more trenches or widening the trench we're in, or laying down barbed wire on the top of the trenches.

And, of course, in the middle of our daily routines the Germans will often lay down a barrage of artillery fire to keep us all on edge. And we do the same right back at them. If there is a moment of quiet in all this madness it barely lasts more than a half hour.

Time for me to see if I can grab a few winks of shut-eye.

All my love to you and Mother.

- Verne.

Robby, I know I've been promising you more details about the men I'm fighting with, so here's a little bit about Dutch. Dutch is a big burly fellow, well-traveled. He spent some time in Africa before the war, studying the wildlife, mostly birds I think. I think he is the smartest one out of all of us, but I think that acute intelligence has caused him some timidity. His brain calculates all the possible outcomes of a situation and that often leaves him paralyzed with indecision. He is not very good at judging between possibilities. He gives all outcomes equal weight in his mind when clearly some outcomes have much greater odds of occurring than others. He'll volunteer to man the periscope for hours upon end, keeping his face glued to the little viewfinder that lets him peer out of our trench towards the German trench without getting his head blown off. He doesn't like being surprised so he doesn't want to risk not being one of the first to know if the Jerries are launching an over-the-top attack.

Another one of the soldiers fighting in the trench with us is descended from an Indian tribe from the United States. His mother was part Cherokee, I believe he said. His father runs a small pub near Wales. He's an odd fellow. Not a drinker, but he enjoys a good pipe when we can get our hands on some tobacco. He is very quiet, almost somber, except when he is telling us about Indian lore and regales us with many fascinating trickster stories his father and grandfather told him when he was growing up. He always performs his assigned duties without fail and without griping about it. Somehow he got stuck with the nickname Cheeky, probably from somebody too lazy to say Cherokee correctly. Anyway, Cheeky's what we call him, and he doesn't seem to mind. In fact, nothing seems to ruffle Cheeky. I think he's got a soft spot for Tubby because he always lets Tubby lie down on his chest when he's trying to sleep. I've never seen him push the cat away, no matter how tired he might be. I like Cheeky. I don't talk to him much, but I'm glad he's with us. He helps pass the time with the wonderful stories from his Indian heritage.

All my love to you and Mother.

- Verne.

Not much is happening today, Robby. Even the Germans are quiet. They stopped the artillery shelling late last night, but I can still hear the bursts ringing in my ears. I think the Jerries do that on purpose. They must know how long the ringing in our ears lasts because every time the ringing is about to disappear from my head, they drop another hellfire burst of artillery shells right on top of us.

They are feeding us hard biscuits and corned beef in a can. Same old story every day. The food is never warm. Even the muck they are calling pea soup is served up cold.

Swifty, our squad's dog, caught a big rat in the trench today. Yes, we have dogs with us. We use them to send messages up and down the trenches. They are quite hearty fellows, those dogs. They can deliver a message much faster than any man can. We let Swifty eat that big fat rat all on his own. None of us are in the mood to start eating rats. At least not yet, even though we all feel like we are on the verge of starvation at all times and constantly crave more meat. Don't fret, we'll find a way to keep going. We always do.

Oh, and don't worry about Tubby. He and Swifty get along swimmingly. Sometimes they'll even sleep cuddled up right next to each other.

How is Archibald? I hope he is still playing baseball. He was always so very good at it. I know it isn't very popular in England right now, but I have a feeling it will catch on.

All my love to you and Mother.

- Verne.

The rats fed well again yesterday, Robby. We don't know why but they seem to treat the corners of men's mouths as a delicacy. They chew on the edges of their lips as they sleep. They somehow know which men are the weakest, which men are too tired or too ill to fend them off in the dark of night. Gorsach, one of our lead scouts, awoke with both corners of his mouth wet with blood. The flesh was tattered at the corners, with little bits of loose skin barely still attached to his mouth. He's sitting with his back against the mud wall of the trench today, picking at the tiny strips of flesh around his mouth, sometimes trying to put them back in place on his lips, sometimes pinching them off his face to get rid of them as if he were picking lice off his flesh.

Oh, the lice, Robby. They are vile little vermin. Feeding on the scalps of diseased and dying men. What other of nature's creatures are so vile? None, I say. The little buggers are about the size of a sesame seed and can move very fast. The itchiness they cause on a man's scalp is extreme. I've seen grown men scratch their heads so hard they do more damage to themselves than the lice could ever do. Just the thought of the little vermin crawling through your hair and feeding on your blood is enough to make all your skin crawl and your entire body itch. Some afternoons, that's all a man does is pick lice out of his hair and out of his clothes.

Well, I'm off to play cards with some of the boys. It's one of the few amusements we have left.

All my love to you and Mother.

- Verne.

Robby, we had a terrible fright yesterday. The mustard gas alert was given and we all scrambled to find our gas masks and put them on. We've all heard enough horror stories about what happens to men exposed to mustard gas, so we take this warning very seriously. The skin gets inflamed and itches and these horrendous yellow blisters erupt out of a man's flesh. Several men have gone blind from direct exposure to the gas burning out their eyeballs. Some men have choked to death because the gas blisters their lungs and suffocates them. I can't imagine a more horrible fate than to feel your lungs blistering inside your chest. Makes me afraid to take a deep breath sometimes when I think about it.

The gas masks are horrendous contraptions. I feel like my head is trapped in a fish bowl when I have it on. It made me feel horribly claustrophobic wearing that dreadful thing over my face, and my field of vision was greatly limited. I felt bad for Dutch because he couldn't find his gas mask. He either left it in the last trench we were in, or he lost his mask somewhere along the way as we moved to our new holding position. He blames himself for losing it, and we all nodded our heads at him and sympathized with his plight, but there was something in Dutch's eyes, just a hint of an accusatory glare that made me wonder if someone else was to blame. I hope we don't have a despicable thief in our midst. We need to trust each other with our very lives. For someone to sow seeds of distrust amongst us would be a terrible crime.

Luckily, the alarm was called off hours later. Our trench had not been targeted. But rumors are swirling about that a trench on the far eastern edge of the battlefield had been targeted and several men had been killed by it. I cannot say for certain whether that is true. A lot of rumors spread amongst the men and a vast majority of them turn out to be false, or they become so greatly exaggerated in the telling as they spread that they are clearly overblown.

Our current orders are to hold this trench at all costs. And that's what we'll do, Robby. Please keep writing. Your letters renew my strength and conviction that we are here fighting a noble fight for the good of all mankind.

All my love to you and Mother.

- Verne.

⚜

The smells of the trench are especially horrid today. There's no wind to give us any fresh air or any relief from the stink. Forgive me, Robby, for thinking such untoward things, but I try to imagine your sweet Rebecca in her pretty yellow dress smelling of daffodils and sunshine whenever the wretched smell of too many men in too confined of a space assaults my nostrils. Please give her a kiss on the cheek for me if I may be so bold to ask that of you.

All my love to you and Mother and Rebecca.

- Verne.

⚜

Tea! We found a tin of tea, Robby! My heart soars. Quite melodramatic, I know, but you can't understand the joy such a simple thing brings when your every waking hour is filled with misery and fear. I'm going to enjoy a cuppa right now, so forgive my letter for being so short.

All my love to you and Mother.

- Verne.

Robby, it's amazing how quickly the overall mood in the trench can change. It only seems to take one man to change it. I never suspected it would be Cheeky. He's the part Cherokee Indian fellow I told you about earlier. As I told you before, he is usually quiet, keeps mostly to himself, but for some reason he went a little mad yesterday. That's the fairest way to describe his actions. He went a little mad. What makes what he said even more nerve-wracking is that his episode wasn't triggered by any German artillery blasts, or any machine gun fire, or any close combat with the Jerries. He looked genuinely terrified, and this was from a man who charged a German machine gun nest a few months ago and single-handedly killed three Jerries by himself with the hunting knife he always carries with him. He gutted one of the Huns, and slashed the throats of the other two. He was covered in blood when I saw him afterwards, but there was no fear in his eyes, just grim resolve in his tight jaw. That's it. Not fright, just resolve.

Now you know, Robby, that I'm not much of a religious or spiritual man. I don't believe much in ghosts and spooks and spirits. Or angels or demons. But I found out that Cheeky believes in them. He believes very deeply in the world of spirits. We all found that out when he told us about the dark demon he saw flying above the trench. He said at first he thought it was an evil spirit the Cherokee call the Raven Mocker. A supernatural beast greatly feared by the Cherokee. He said this dark spirit robs the sick and the dying of their heart by ripping it out of their chest with its sharp talons and eating it. It takes to the air in a fiery shape and pierces the night sky with a bloodthirsty cry as it begins its hunt. But then Cheeky said the thing he saw in the night was no raven. He isn't sure what it was, but it definitely unnerved him. He said it was a demon bird of some sort, a bird with black feathers and a wingspan eight to ten feet wide. He said its head appeared to be bald and it had a long, curved beak. He said he saw it circle our trench a few times, then it dove down into no man's land and he lost sight of it. He thinks it's a demon spirit embodied in a giant bird. And that it's hunting us.

Dutch thinks it was just a big vulture scavenging for the rotting flesh of our dead brother soldiers decaying in no man's land. But Cheeky was adamant that it was no ordinary bird he saw. He said it was big, far bigger than any bird he's ever seen. He said its feathers were blacker than the night. That's how he could see it. How can something be blacker than the night, Robby?

And now other men are coming forward saying they heard the sounds of flapping wings in the night. Even Sergeant Preston says he heard the flapping sound. He first thought it was just some tattered regiment flag blowing in the wind, but now he's altered his story. Now he says the flapping sound was too heavy to have come from a mere fluttering flag.

We're all a bit on edge now, Robby. Even me. I'm going to try and rest now, but I doubt the blissful ignorance of sleep will comfort me for quite some time.

All my love to you and Mother.

- Verne.

The dogs are going mad. They are barking and growling and howling despite us commanding them to stop. They are good dogs, well trained, with good discipline. But we cannot get them to stop. They clearly know something that we do not. Even Billingsley, the lanky fellow who feeds the dogs, cannot calm them.

I do not have time, or the energy, to write anymore, Robby. The last few days in the trenches have been quite harrowing. I will fill in the details when I can.

All my love to you and Mother.

  - Verne.

I understand now why the dogs were barking so vociferously. We found Teddy's body. You know him, Robby. He went to school with us. Teddy Jacoby. The one who always got the lead in the school play.

I know you are of a delicate nature, Robby, but I must tell you what we all saw.

His body was chewed. That's the best way I can describe it. Teddy's body was chewed on like he was just some piece of meat. Some parts of him were eaten right down to the bone. His face was gone. His chest was torn open and his heart was missing. We identified him by the boots that were still on his feet. He had the biggest feet in the whole regiment, so his boots were very unique to him, specially tailored to fit him. Something chewed him, Robby. Something chewed him up and ate parts of him.

Do not speak to Teddy's mother of this. Just tell her he died bravely in battle. He died a hero fighting for what is right.

All my love to you and Mother.

- Verne.

Robby, I remember writing to you that lice were the most vile of nature's creations. But now I must retract that declaration, for there is another creature even more vile, even more dangerous. No man here has ever seen this beast before in their lives, but there are now half a dozen sightings of this monstrosity that is now tormenting us.

Cheeky still fervently believes we are under attack by a demon, a demon in the guise of this horrible winged beast. A demon in vulture form.

Dutch now thinks it is some mutated form of a black vulture. He says black vultures are the largest kind of vulture and the largest bird of prey. They are entirely black with very broad wings and a short, slightly wedge-shaped tail. He says they are commonly found where we are now fighting, but he's never heard of them growing so large. He believes the poisonous gases both sides have used in this wretched world war have befouled the creature, turning it from a scavenger of the dead and the dying to a hunter of the living. Us.

If we didn't have enough to worry about with the Jerries wanting to kill every single one of us, now we have another enemy to fear.

All my love to you and Mother.

- Verne.

We heard screams last night coming from the German trenches. They are only about a hundred yards or so away from us. It must have been an awful scream for it to travel to our ears. This thing seems not to care which side it feeds on. You would think I might get a feeling of grim satisfaction from the Jerries being brutalized by this beast, but all I feel is pity for those poor soldiers, even though our sole mission here is to kill each other.

I'm tempted to run, Robby, but I have nowhere to go. There are nests of German machine guns in front of us, and officers determined and ready to shoot deserters on sight behind us. I am no coward, you know that. But the nights fill me with such an immense fright that I fear my legs may move of their own accord and drag me into no-man's land. I truly wonder if it would be better to be blown to smithereens by a land mine or wait here and suffer an attack from that thing. I don't want to be eaten alive, nor do I want this horrid beast to feed on my corpse if I should perish here.

Your letters give me the strength to carry on so please continue to write to me.

All my love to you and Mother.

- Verne.

Robby, it came again. In the night. It took Billingsley. I'm sure of it. He was no coward. I would bet my life on that. He didn't crack. He didn't run. Something took him. Maybe this winged beast has the strength to carry a man off, I don't know. But Billingsley wouldn't run. He wouldn't abandon his brothers-in-arms. And he wouldn't abandon Swifty and the other dogs. He loved those mutts. He just wouldn't run.

I'm tempted to allow myself to get trench foot to be rid of this place. Losing a foot is far better than losing one's sanity. Or one's life.

All my love to you and Mother.

- Verne.

Please don't judge me, Robby. A man can be driven to do… vile things when his very life is threatened. We haven't had food delivery in over two days now. Every man here misses our daily rum ration, even though it was thick and dark and barely a full swallow. Talk of this demon bird has reached deeper into the rear echelon and we have heard many of the men tasked to re-supply us have suddenly come down with dozens of excuses as to why they are unable to return to the front. Many of the men in the trench with me are getting desperate. Some of them have given up. It's a nerve-wracking sight to see the light in a man's eyes go out when despair has overwhelmed his desire to live.

The light has gone out in Cavendish's eyes. The man is an expert at close-quarters combat and can kill a man with the handle of a knife, let alone its sharp blade. But now his stare is empty. There appears to be no life left in him. He sits in the mud and just stares at his wet boots. I'm sure trench foot has set in. He hasn't cleaned his feet in days. He is just letting his toes rot inside his saturated boots. We tried to encourage him, but he gave us no response. I know this may sound horrible, Robby, but we are just leaving him alone. No one will sit near him anymore. Because we know he is going to be next.

All my love to you and Mother.

- Verne.

It took Cavendish last night. I only feel relief that it wasn't me or Dutch or Cheeky. If that demonic monstrosity can take Cavendish, then it can take anyone. The three of us have made a pact to watch out for each other. There is a brotherhood between us that cannot really be described. The only other person I feel a stronger connection to than the one I feel towards them is the connection I feel towards you, dear brother. How is Mother? I know I am supposed to tell you to tell her not to worry, but that would be a lie. Tell her to worry, tell her to worry for all of us.

I am writing this during the sweet brightness of day. We don't close our eyes at night any more. Not for any longer than a blink. We all try to grab what sleep we can during the day, but the Germans have renewed their shelling during the day, so grabbing more than fifteen minutes of sleep at a time is quickly becoming an impossibility. Everyone is on edge. Everyone is terrified. I have never seen anything like it. Several of the men are talking about leaving the trench and running away, despite knowing they will most likely be executed for cowardice. They don't care. They would rather face a firing squad than remain trapped in the trench with whatever ungodly beast is hunting us. Please don't share that part with Mother.

All my love to you and Mother.

- Verne.

I saw it, Robby! It is a vulture. A vulture with a man's eyes! How can that be? If I received such a missive I would most surely think the sender had gone mad. Yet, I know I am not mad and I have seen this beast. There's both a cunning and a madness in those eyes. Something human, but not human. An inhuman intelligence. It watches us, assesses us. It knows who is weak. Its eyes are streaked with a yellow film and Dutch believes the mustard gas has seeped into its brain. As if it's not enough to have a vulture demon hunting us, we are now faced with a giant vulture demon tainted with additional madness induced by the horrors men perpetrate upon each other.

The black-winged beast is taller than a man when it rises up to its full height. It can't open its wings wide when it's in the trench because the trench walls are too narrow to allow it to spread them fully open. But I have seen it use its wings like a shroud. The cursed vulture enveloped Mickelson in its big black wings, and then he dropped dead with a ragged gash ripped into his neck. It uses its sharp beak to attack a man's throat, puncturing through flesh with a murderous strike. Yes, I called it murderous. For I don't think it's just an animal hunting for food. There's an element of sport to its attacks.

We are trying to stay strong, but every man here is terrified. We cannot go forward because the Germans have machine guns and mortar fire lined up on the open ground that separates our trench from theirs. Anyone who tries to set foot on that no-man's land is either ripped to shreds by machine gun bursts or blown to bits by expertly targeted mortar fire. We cannot go back because our orders are to hold the line at all costs. What I had told you before still holds true now - anyone who leaves the trench and flees back to the command post is deemed a coward and is immediately put before a firing squad.

All my love to you and Mother.

- Verne.

⋙⋘⋙◉⋘⋙⋘

I'm afraid, Robby. There is a dark shadow circling over our trench. I can feel the flying demon's shadow crossing over me every time it circles. I can feel its chill penetrating me. I think it's circling over me. I think it's my turn next. Yes, your big brother is scared out of his wits.

Even that fat cat Tubby seems to be avoiding me, as if he can smell the stench of death upon me. I tried to pet him to soothe my own nerves, but he hissed at me and raced away. That cat has never hissed at me before.

I know you and I were not always praying men and Mother berated us for not going to Mass regularly like good Catholics, but I need both of you to pray hard for us now, Robby. Pray for all of us. Pray as if my life depended on it because I truly believe it does.

All my love to you and Mother.

- Verne.

⊰⊱✿⊰⊱

Cheeky has given me a glimmer of hope. He remembered a tale his grandfather had told him when he was a boy. Perhaps Mother's prayers helped him to remember for my sake, I do not know. But his memory of the tale certainly has come at a very opportune time for me. It was the story of a young Indian warrior being chased by a demon bear. The warrior nicked his finger with the tip of his arrow and smeared blood along the arrow's head. The warrior shot the arrow as far as he could and the demon followed it, chasing the scent of the warrior's blood, giving the clever warrior time to escape.

I don't have a bow or an arrow, Robby, but I have this letter and an envelope. And blood from my wounds. I took a bullet in my left arm last week. I didn't tell you because I knew you wouldn't be able to keep that from Mother.

Forgive me for what I am about to do, but I am afraid. I don't want to die here. I don't want some demonic beast to feed on my corpse and send my soul straight to Hell. I'm too afraid to let that happen. I have suffered enough. Tell Mother she raised us well. Tell her I believe. Tell her she was right all along. If I survive this, I will go to Church with her every Sunday just as I should have done.

Robby, you once wrote to me wishing you could feel the excitement of being in a life and death situation. If you are reading this letter, your wish has been granted. Forgive me, brother. Protect Mother as best you can. I have faith in you. Be strong. You must

24

now watch the skies, Robby, watch the skies and listen. If you hear the flutter of heavy wings, take heed. If you see a dark shadow circling over you and you feel a chill creeping deep into your bones, steel yourself Robby, steel yourself for a fight.

All my love to you and Mother. I will pray for you.

- Verne.

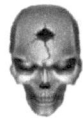

TERRORSTORY #72
TEA TIME

William Luskerett stared at the carved wooden sign sitting on a round table positioned just inside the entrance to the booth. It was one of the smaller booths at the expo, sandwiched between a steampunk clothing booth to the right and a large action figure booth to the left. He had to admit he liked the name carved into the wooden sign. It gave him pause and brought a little smile to his lips.

Eternatea.

The woman manning the tea booth was pretty, her face bright and cheerful. She had some cute dimples when she smiled, and she smiled a lot as she assisted other customers who were patronizing her booth. She had shoulder length brunette hair, a pert nose, and full lips colored in a soft shade of red. Her hazel eyes held something deeper within them, a wisdom, a cunning. He wasn't sure. They gleamed like a cat's eyes gleam in the dark, even though the booth was adequately lit. "Hello, William. Are you looking for something special?" she asked him as she took a seat on a small leather-covered stool positioned in the corner of the booth.

William was attending the first annual Pop Entertainment Expo, looking for collectibles, comics, graphic novels, original artwork, movie memorabilia, really anything that struck his fancy. At first he wasn't sure if the folks in charge of the expo realized their acronym would get a few juvenile giggles, but after he saw quite a few people proudly wearing their *'I Love PEE!'* shirts and baseball caps, or proudly displaying their *'I Love PEE!'* bling buttons, he realized it was more a stroke of twisted genius than anything else. There were other booths at the expo selling weird candy from Japan and a few food carts selling stale churros and dried-out hot dogs, but there weren't many other food or drink vendors as a whole at the expo. The tea booth really stuck out to him.

He was faced with such a simple decision, really. Go into the booth and see what the woman was selling, or don't go into the booth and continue wandering around the convention. "Just browsing," he replied as he crossed the threshold of the Eternatea store booth and entered her world, not realizing how much his life would change because of it. And then he paused to look at the woman, scrunching up his forehead as he gazed at her. "How did you know my name?"

She pointed at his chest, indicating the Pop Entertainment Expo badge clipped to the lanyard that hung around his neck. "I saw it on your badge," she said.

William glanced down at his badge. The badge was backwards, his name hidden from view on the opposite side of the badge. Perhaps it had gotten twisted and she had seen his name on it as he had entered her tea booth. He shrugged it off.

He slowly meandered through the booth. He had switched from coffee to tea several years ago because coffee was wreaking havoc on his stomach. Just a half of a cup of coffee was enough to send him straight to the bathroom. Tea didn't have the same effect on his stomach so he was still able to at least enjoy some measure of caffeine. The shelves in the booth were stocked with some of the typical tea varieties you find in any grocery store, numerous black teas, some green teas, many herbal teas. He turned to look at the woman watching him from her stool in the corner of the booth, then tilted his head back towards the booth's entrance. "I like the name. It caught my attention."

She nodded. "Thanks. I had a hard time deciding on that one. I considered Universitea, not like a college university, more like the universe Universitea. Then there was Immortalitea, Deitea, and Divinitea." She paused. "Eternatea had a nice ring to it, I thought."

William nodded. "Good choice."

She gave him a soft smile. "As you can see, we have all kinds of tea. You can open any of the jars you like and take a whiff." She waved her arm towards the rows of shelves that lined the booth. "I sell them by the ounce, half pound, full pound. However you like."

William studied the shelves. They were filled with dozens and dozens of clear glass jars, each one containing a different variety of crushed tea leaves, the labels on the jars indicating what strain of tea was contained within. "You have any of that lapsang souchong?" he asked her. "I had that one time and it was really tasty. It had a very unique flavor. Kind of smelled like a campfire."

She nodded her head, smiling knowingly. "Some people call it '*that smoky tea*.'"

He nodded. "It reminded me of all the times I used to go camping with my dad when I was a kid," William said.

"I do have some of that." She pointed down to the second shelf nearest the bottom on the back wall of the booth. "It's a black tea from a mountain region in the Fujian province in China. The leaves are smoke-dried over pinewood fires. That's what gives it that distinctive smoky flavor."

William walked over to the shelf she had just indicated, and bent down to grab the jar labeled *Lapsang Souchong*. He raised the jar up to look at its dark leafy contents. "Is it good for you?"

She smiled again. "All of my teas are good for you." She pointed to the jar he held in his hand. "Lapsang souchong improves your heart health and reduces the risk of cardiovascular disease."

"That was pretty definitive," he said. "Aren't you supposed to say it *may* improve my heart health and it *may* reduce my risk of getting cardiovascular disease."

She shrugged. "It will."

He flipped the tiny latch on the jar he still held in his hand and opened the lid. The smoky smell immediately wafted up to his nostrils. It was a strong, bold smell, but he loved it. It really did have a campfire aroma to it.

"Legend has it that during the Qing Dynasty an invading army unit occupied a tea factory filled with fresh leaf awaiting manufacture," the woman said. "The villagers took back the factory after a bloody battle, but the invading army set it ablaze before they retreated. The villagers were able to salvage some of the tea and still bring the tea to market. The smoky flavor created a sensation and lapsang souchong was born." The woman paused. "Out of destruction comes rebirth into something new."

"Interesting," William said. He took another sniff at the contents, then looked over to the woman. "Do you drink it?"

She shook her head. "It's a fine tea, but a bit too earthy for me."

He cocked his head quizzically.

"It's a very bold tea. Masculine, you might say. A little too burly for me. For some reason, it reminds me of smoked bacon. It's the perfect tea for men who drink whiskey, puff on cigars or their pipes, and sit around a blazing fire pit talking shit."

He closed the lid and latched it back shut. He handed the jar to the woman. "I'll take half a pound."

The woman nodded as she rose up from her stool to take the jar from him. She moved behind a small partition where a small table was set up where she weighed and bagged the tea.

William watched her for a moment - she really was quite pretty - then turned to peruse more of the teas that lined the walls of the Eternatea booth. The booth probably had over a hundred different types of tea, if not even more than that. And every one of them supposedly had a positive benefit. Every one was recommended by some study or the other. This one will fight inflammation and stimulate the immune system. This one leads to improved sleep quality and fewer symptoms of depression. This one has antibacterial, anti-inflammatory, and liver-protecting effects. This one helps prevent stomach ulcers and relieves indigestion or constipation. The list of conditions the teas would cure went on and on. You would have to drink twenty gallons a day to consume them all.

There were several rows of various herbal teas positioned on the shelves on the back wall of the booth. He silently read the labels as he moved closer to them and let his gaze roam over the jars. Chamomile, ginger, rooibos, echinacea, sage, hibiscus. He saw several types of peppermint tea on the back wall and felt a momentary distaste swirl in his stomach. He had a great dislike of peppermint. It was supposed to have a positive effect on digestion, help relieve nausea, cramping, spasms and stomach pain, but every time he tried peppermint tea it only seemed to aggravate his stomach even more.

He turned away from the rows of herbal teas and let his gaze wander amongst the jars positioned on the right wall of the booth, the wall not visible until you stepped into the booth itself. One brand of tea really captured his attention. It wasn't in a clear glass jar. In fact, it was the only tea available in the entire booth that wasn't in a jar. It was sealed within a small cardboard box about two inches long and two inches high. He stopped in front of it and just stared at the box for a few moments. It was just a plain white box with ornate lettering. Eternatea was the name inscribed on the box. Must be the house brand, he mused. And then he gaped at the price. Two hundred dollars. He looked back over at the woman standing behind the low partition finishing up his order. "Two hundred dollars for a box of tea?" he muttered, but saying it loud enough for the woman to hear.

She shook her head. "It's not really a box of tea," she said. "There's only one tea bag inside of it."

He turned to face her squarely, then just stared at her for a moment. "One tea bag?"

She nodded. "One tea bag."

"Two hundred dollars for one tea bag? That's gotta be one helluva tea."

She nodded again. "Oh, it is. It is."

He looked over at the little white box of tea again. Eternatea. "Why is it so expensive? What's in it?"

She shook her head. "That's a trade secret."

He frowned. "Don't you have to reveal the ingredients to your customers?"

She shrugged. "I don't force anyone to buy it."

He was quiet for a moment. "Have people actually bought it?"

She was quiet. "Most people wouldn't understand it," she finally said.

He squinted at her response. He wondered how someone would understand tea, but he didn't ask the question. He was again quiet for a moment. "What does it do? Does it have some kind of magical healing properties or something?"

She pointed towards the name on the box. "Gives you a glimpse of that," she said.

He looked at her, then looked back at the white box, again reading the name silently to himself. He looked back to the woman. "It gives you a glimpse of eternity?"

She nodded.

"You ever try it?" he asked.

"I wouldn't be here if I did." She shook her head. "I'm too timid still. I'm afraid of it. I'm not ready for it."

He frowned. "Ready for what?"

She finished bagging up his order and stood silently near her payment terminal.

He frowned at her. "Come on, what's in it?" he asked as he moved to the counter to pay for his lapsang souchong tea purchase.

"Let's just say some of the ingredients are not from here," she said, taking his offered credit card.

"Not from here?"

"From this planet," she said.

Whoa. Her reply made William freeze for a moment. What the hell did that mean? These kinds of shows did sometimes attract some of the lunatic fringe, he knew, but this woman seemed very level-headed. But then again, he thought, looks could be deceiving. She could be a genuine nut job for all he knew, despite how pretty and sweet she appeared. "Are you kidding me?"

She shook her head. She swiped his card through the card reader positioned on the table behind the partition.

"It's from an alien planet?" he asked. He glanced back at the white box, then back to the woman.

She shook her head again. "I didn't say that," she said. "I just said it's not from here." She handed his credit card back to him, then lifted up his order, holding the bag out to him. "Here's your lapsang souchong." She smiled sweetly at him, displaying her cute dimples again; her hazel eyes gleamed. "Enjoy."

William couldn't stay away from the Eternatea booth. It wasn't like him to be so indecisive, and he didn't like that feeling. He circled the tea booth half a dozen times, pretending to look at the action figures still safely tucked away in their protective casings in the booth next store, or feigning interest in buying some steampunk clothing in the other booth next to the tea booth. What the hell could be in a bag of tea that made it worth two hundred dollars? Some kind of weird drug? Was it all just a publicity stunt to get people to talk about it?

He still had about five hundred bucks of spare change in his wallet, so it wasn't about the money. He could spend two hundred dollars easily on some old comics, or some autographed artwork, or some collectible statuettes, or some movie memorabilia. Was he really going to spend two hundred bucks for one cup of mysterious tea?

How could he not?

Talk about instant buyer's remorse. What a damn idiot. Two hundred bucks for a single serving of tea. He could have gotten an original EC Tales from the Crypt comic for that much. But he did have to admit he was jazzed by the whole thing. Was he just telling himself that to justify his purchase? He didn't know. It didn't matter. Because it did jazz the heck out of him. He couldn't stop thinking about it.

William glanced over at the passenger seat as he drove down the highway on his way back home. His two tea purchases were buried inside the bag that rested on the seat, nestled at the bottom between two collectible monster statues from Ray Harryhausen's movies.

Was he really going to go home and drink some strange concoction whose ingredients were a complete mystery? It could be some kind of poison for all he knew.

⋘⋙

William stared at the little white box. He was seated at his kitchen table, pondering the strangeness of the Eternatea he had purchased the day before at the expo. He turned the box over in his hands, giving it a little shake. He could hear the tea bag shifting slightly in the box.

He thought about what the woman who had sold him the tea had told him about its proper preparation. He should let the tea steep for four minutes. And then he would have only five minutes to drink it. After that, the tea would lose all of its properties. "What properties?" he had asked her. But she had only given him the same damn cryptic smile she had given him earlier when he had first asked about what ingredients were in the tea. He had asked her if she could at least tell him how many ingredients were in the tea. She had quickly responded to that question.

"Forty-two," she had said.

He had smiled at her answer. Forty-two. The secretive tea had forty-two ingredients, an obvious play on The Hitchhiker's Guide to the Galaxy. The number 42 is, in The Hitchhiker's Guide to the Galaxy by Douglas Adams, the "Answer to the Ultimate Question of Life, the Universe, and Everything." The answer had been calculated by an enormous supercomputer named Deep Thought over a period of 7.5 million years. It was part of the joke that no one was able to say what the actual question was.

William opened the white box and stared into it. There it was. A single tea bag supposedly filled with forty-two secret herbs and spices and who knew what other alien additives. The mesh pouch was in the shape of a tiny pyramid with a small Eternatea label attached to the thinner top portion of the pouch by a thin string.

He raised the small pouch up to his nose and sniffed at it. It had no smell. None at all. He wasn't sure how that was possible, especially if it supposedly contained forty-two ingredients. He sniffed at it again. No aroma. He gently squeezed at the pouch, crinkling the ingredients together, trying to force an aroma to be emitted. Still no smell.

His teapot whistled, blowing out a thin blast of white steam, momentarily startling him. He could have just microwaved a cup of water to heat it up, but he felt this tea deserved to be made the old fashioned way. He turned to look at the stove, watching the thin column of water vapor spray out of the spout. The water was ready. But was he?

He rose up from the table and went to the

cupboard. He knew which cup he would use for it. It wouldn't be the coffee cup he got from Disney, or the one from Universal, or his Nightmare Before Christmas cup, or his old Spider-Man coffee cup. It would be the plain dark red coffee cup, the one Deidre, his fourth wife, always liked to use. This would be the first time he used it since she had died from her lung cancer. It just seemed right to him to use that cup for this. He grabbed the dark red coffee cup from its place in the far right corner on the top shelf, then closed the cupboard. He set the cup down on the marble counter next to the stove, turned the flame off, and fetched the bag of Eternatea from the kitchen table.

He placed the tea bag into the empty cup, then grabbed the teapot. He stared into the cup for a moment, staring at the tea bag. He tried to picture Deidre's face but some reason all he could bring forth in his mind was the face of the woman from the Eternatea booth. He felt anxious, almost nervous, a feeling that was rare to him, a feeling that he didn't enjoy feeling. And then he tilted the teapot, pouring the hot water over the pyramid-shaped diffuser bag.

The aroma hit him immediately and he quickly set the teapot back down on the stove as his head felt like it was starting to spin on his neck. He bent over, gripping the edges of the marble counter tightly with both hands to steady himself. The scent wafting up from the dark red coffee cup was overwhelming. It was smoky and sweet and bitter and sour and earthy and fruity and acidic and burly all at the same time.

And it was fucking amazing. Just the smell of it was intense. Almost erotic. His entire body tingled ever so slightly with a weirdly delightful sensation. If just the aroma of Eternatea had this effect on him, what the hell would actually drinking it do to him? His brain felt like it was speeding up, his thoughts racing through his head with amazing speed, but he was still able to keep up with them all. Is that what Eternatea did? Acted like a mega caffeine rush? He grabbed the cup handle with shaking fingers and slowly moved over to the kitchen table. He still felt a little lightheaded and dizzy. He needed to sit down.

He set the coffee cup down on the kitchen table and sat. And immediately did a double-take as he stared at the once formerly plain white Eternatea box that now was covered with words and images. It was as if the words and images had been drawn on the box in some invisible colored ink and the act of creating the tea, perhaps due to the wafting vapors rising out of the cup, had revealed the hidden images and words. There was a picture of a swirling galaxy on one side of the box now, and a sentence on the other side of the box. He picked up the box and read the newly revealed sentence. "Taking a drink of Eternatea is like kissing God."

William frowned. What was God to him? Some cranky old man with a thick white beard Who demanded obedience? That was the image that had been ingrained into his head ever since he was a child. It was hard to shake it. He certainly didn't want to kiss Him. He didn't want to mope around in flowing robes and pay homage to Him for all eternity. That would bore the fuck out of him. He wondered if all the same things would occupy his thoughts in the afterlife. How could they? He would have no need for food, for sleep, for money. What the hell was he going to do for Eternity? And if the same sorts of things that occupied his time on Earth had no bearing in the afterlife, then what was the point of it all? If the same rational type of thinking existed in the afterlife, then so be it. But if it didn't, then the whole point of good and evil, of living a good life, of living a meaningful life, made no difference whatsoever.

A beautiful woman as God was much more appealing to his psyche. Not some old wrinkled hag, but a vibrant, young woman. Not too young, but not too old either. Someone who looked like she was in her thirties or early forties. Someone with a mature look to them, but someone not starting to age too much around the eyes or the corners of her mouth. Of course, She would have no age, really, but if She did take on a physical form, that would be the one he preferred. Just like the woman in the Eternatea booth who had sold him the tea. He paused, bringing up her face again in his mind, thinking of her shining brunette hair, her delicate nose, her full red lips. And those gleaming golden brown eyes of her. He quickly pushed aside that thought. That was just ridiculous. Wasn't it?

He turned his thoughts away from the mysterious woman who had sold him this mysterious concoction. Were there worlds to conquer in the afterlife? Were there things he could take? He enjoyed taking. That's what he did for his entire life. He took things. He collected things. Houses. Cars. Businesses. Women. Money. He took them all. But it was never enough. He always wanted more. What if there was nothing to take in the afterlife? No businesses to conquer. No women to conquer. What would he do then?

The aroma wafted into his nostrils. He felt a tingling in his head, but he didn't know if that was a real feeling or if he was just imagining it. Did that even matter? What was real or what was imagined? Would the afterlife be just a world of thought? A world of pure imagination. Would he find himself alongside Charlie in the great chocolate factory of Willy Wonka?

He stared at the pool of dark liquid in the cup. Was that a galaxy he was staring at now within the cup? Or was it just the light and the oils in the tea-infused brew playing tricks on him?

Just a taste. He only needed to take one taste. He grabbed the small label that was attached to the thin string that was connected to the tea bag and lifted the tea bag up out of the water, then lowered the tea bag back into the hot liquid. He felt a rush of fascination as another galaxy seemed to manifest itself within the liquid, another swirl of colors whirling about within the cup. Was he looking into the heart of the universe? Was he about to take a drink out of the very universe itself? The swirling, shimmering colors moving within the darkening liquid entranced him.

He thought about the creation of the universe. According to physics, all of the matter and energy present now in the universe had existed in some form at the moment of the Big Bang. And since matter could not be created nor destroyed, everyone's atoms were once something else. A body of matter cannot disappear completely. It only changes its form, condition, composition, color or other properties, and turns into a different complex or elementary matter. Even the particles and molecules and atoms making up his human body were once part of something else, and upon his death his physical body would decay and his atoms would transform and become something else.

The atoms of the ingredients in Eternatea were also once something else. He paused at the thought. Or were they? Perhaps they contained some of the original particles that existed at the beginning of the universe. Was that what the secret ingredients were comprised of? Perhaps there were some particles that still existed that never underwent any transformation at all. Perhaps there were particles that existed at the beginning of time that still retained their original properties. And perhaps those particles were in the very tea he was brewing.

He somehow instinctively knew the four minute steep time was up. He lifted the tea bag out of the cup, somewhat surprised by how incredibly light the tea bag felt, and set it down on a plate next to the cup. He froze for a moment as he stared at the tea bag. There were no dark trails of moisture leaking out of the bag onto the plate. In fact, there appeared to be no moisture at all leaking out of the bag. The tea bag was empty and flat. All of the ingredients had dissolved away into the cup.

He stared back at the dark liquid, at the swirling colors twirling within the tea. Just a taste. That's all he needed. He knew he had only a few minutes to decide. If it cooled, the woman had told him, it would lose its potency and drinking it would have no effect on him. Could he not taste it? Could he just walk away from it and never know the answer? It would plague him until the end of his days, whenever that might be.

Was he really just a jumble of neurons firing inside a spongy gray blob encased in a hard skull? Is that what he truly believed deep inside? That somehow he, as a living human being, had come to be out of nothing? What if the tea really did what the woman had intimated it might do? What if it took those neurons, took that electrical energy, and transformed them into something greater? What if they unlocked his mind from his skull and let his thoughts roam free in the vast cosmos? What if the mysterious elements in the tea did release his very consciousness back into the universe from whence he had come?

He was always very good at being decisive, at simply making a choice and going with it. So many people were plagued with indecision, tormented by running various simulations in their heads about what may happen if they made one choice over another. He never let that become a problem for himself. He just made a decision and went with it. Sometimes, they were horrible decisions with terrible outcomes, but that was okay. He'd rather live with those mistakes than be wracked with incapacitating indecision. But yet he still could only stare at the dark liquid in the cup, a mysteriously fascinating dark liquid that appeared to be teeming with stars.

He thought of the conversations he had back in his college days, when he and his roommates and their gang of college friends would get stoned and try to figure out the meaning of life. Some of them had unwavering faith in their religious beliefs that no logic could ever shake. Some of them were very decidedly nihilistic and believed life had no meaning whatsoever and it was pointless to even try and make sense of it. Others were existentialists and they believed that, through a combination of self-consciousness and the freedom to choose one's own path that comes from free will, they could construct their own meaning within a world that intrinsically had none of its own.

And then there were the absurdists. Of which William was one. He had Albert Camus, the father of Absurdism, to thank for that. Camus rejected that any meaning to life existed, at least in relation to humanity, and sought to point out the absurdity in the human search for meaning in life despite the fact that life was meaningless. In philosophy, 'the Absurd' referred to the conflict between the human tendency to seek inherent value and meaning in life and the human inability to find any in a purposeless, meaningless or chaotic and irrational universe.

Camus saw Sisyphus as the absurd hero who lived life to the fullest, hated death, and was condemned to a meaningless task. In Greek mythology, the legends tell of Sisyphus who defied the gods and put Death in chains so that no human needed to die. After finally capturing Sisyphus, the gods decided that his punishment would last for all eternity. He would have to push a rock up a mountain, then upon reaching the top, the rock would roll down again, leaving Sisyphus to start the task all over again.

That's just how William felt. Every time he started to read a new book, or watch a new documentary, or watch a new movie that promised a deep revelation about the nature of humanity, or dig deeper into world philosophies, he felt like he was just on the verge of getting a true meaning of life — but then the book would end, the documentary or the movie would fade to black, the philosophy would reach the zenith of its teachings, and he would be right back where he started - continuing to search for some form of meaning even knowing full well that he would never find it. Death would come and the great answer to the meaning of life would remain the absurd answer of forty-two.

He thought more about the nature of absurdity. The absurd man demanded certainty above all else, and recognized that he could only be certain of the absurd. The only truth about himself that remained constant was his desire for unity, reason, and clarity, and the only truth about the world that seemed certain was that it conformed to no obvious shape or pattern. Living as if you are never going to die, but knowing full well that you will die someday -- that was the pinnacle of absurdity.

True believers in mainstream religions either never believed that the world lacked inherent meaning, or they chose to stop believing it because the reality of a universe with no meaning was too empty and sad. William couldn't surrender to any particular religion. He couldn't just give in to one supernatural belief and let that be his answer. He knew that would be doing a dishonesty to himself.

The very nature of human consciousness brings forth the realization that you will one day die, and there is nothing you can do about it, no matter how long you try to prolong it. William remembered reading about a study that found the brain shields humans from existential fear by categorizing death as an unfortunate event that only befalls other people. Not too many decades ago, death was more of an everyday occurrence that everyone had some involvement with, but now the ill and the aging were hidden away in hospitals and nursing homes and all that death that normally occurred in everyone's lives was buried away out of sight. Very few people actually encountered death as it happened.

William thought about some of his younger employees, about what he observed regarding how they lived their lives. The young in particular saw death as a problem for other people. Sorry, they were too busy to die right now, thank you very much. They had work to do, text messages to send, social media accounts to update, TV series to binge watch, things to buy online, parties to attend. They were way too busy to even think about dying right now. They were running on a treadmill of denial that ultimately went nowhere. They were all Sisyphus, all pushing their own personal rocks up the hill only to have to start all over again. Hell, it wasn't even that. To him, they all seemed to be pushing their own personal rocks without a final destination even in mind.

William straightened up in the chair and stared down into the coffee cup. What appeared to be another swirling galaxy rotated slowly in the cup, the billions of stars and planets that comprised the galaxy shimmering with hundreds of different colors. His thoughts again shifted to the nature of the universe itself, of what it contained. Recent studies he had read now estimated the number of galaxies in the universe to be two trillion galaxies. Two trillion galaxies in the observable universe. Not planets. Not solar systems. Entire galaxies. Two trillion of them. Of which the Milky Way galaxy was only one. One of two trillion. It was a number so big that it was impossible to wrap his head around.

And to top that off, the Milky Way galaxy was estimated to be the home of at least 100 billion alien planets, possibly more. It was a staggering number. And then when you multiplied 100 billion planets per galaxy with the two trillion galaxies estimated to exist, the number became mind-numbingly huge. One might as well say there were an infinite number of planets in the universe. And some God-being supposedly created them all? And He only put the creatures He created in His likeness on one of these planets?

The white Eternatea box caught his attention again. William read the sentence again that he had seen appear on the side of the box. "Taking a drink of Eternatea is like making love with the Goddess." But then he paused. Was that what it had said before? No, the sentence had clearly changed. How was that possible? How had the sentence on the box changed? Had his thoughts made it change? Did it somehow react to his own wishes and desires? He stared at the word Goddess. He immediately thought about the woman who had sold him the tea. The more he pictured the memory of her face in his mind, the more beautiful she became. He really should have at least gotten her name. Or was that her name? Was she the Goddess of the universe? Had she come to the tiny planet humans called Earth just to find him?

He put his hands around the mug, feeling the warmth of the cup seep into his fingers. Eternatea. Was that what was floating in the cup? Was that what Eternatea was? Was it truly eternity in a cup? Would it destroy time? Would it put him in a state of timelessness? He knew while he was alive he would never know what lay beyond life's threshold. Was it nothingness? Would he simply cease to exist? Or would this mysterious blend of tea truly give him a glimpse of eternity? He thought it was rather funny that there was a time limit to the potency of a mysterious drink that might bring him into a state of timelessness.

Perhaps the forty-two secret ingredients in Eternatea would accelerate the speed of his expanding consciousness, expand his thoughts faster than the speed of light. Would it expand his mind to the outer reaches of the universe? If the universe was expanding as most scientists believed, then what was the universe expanding into? What was beyond the edge of the universe? Maybe Eternatea would take him beyond the end of the universe. Maybe he would be the first conscious being to ever reach it. Maybe he could stake a claim.

He knew his time was running out. He had to make a decision, and he had to make it quickly. Every muscle in his body tensed up; he felt an intense tightness gripping the back of his neck.

Maybe the Goddess was there waiting for him. He glanced at the white box and saw that the image of the swirling galaxy was now gone, replaced by an exquisite portrait of the beautiful woman from the Eternatea booth. His eyes lit up at the sight of her. And her golden brown eyes gleamed back at him. Could it really be that simple?

By all the gods of humanity, he understood now. He bolted upright in the chair. There was an endgame. There was a purpose. It was to find Eternatea and drink of its immense power. That was it. That was the endgame. So simple. So clean. So easy to understand. To expand his mind to the edge of the universe and kiss the sweet lips of the Goddess of Eternatea with his thoughts and make mental love with her.

William felt an immense feeling of relief flood through him. All the muscles in his body relaxed and his entire body tingled as if he had just orgasmed. He had done it. He had reached the end. He had pushed the rock to the top of the hill and the rock remained in place.

He smiled and raised the cup up to his lips.

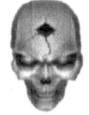

TERRORSTORY #73
THE BLACK COFFIN

Sheridan Creek, Kansas
1884

Wayne Johnson stared at the black coffin, his eyes filling with dread. "Who's that for?" He was a beefy man with short dark hair. He wore a tan shirt and dark brown trousers lined with suspender buttons around the waistband. His brown boots were covered with splatters of mud and dust. A thick mustache covered his upper lip, curving down towards his chin on either side of his mouth. Wayne was a turpentine farmer, extracting the resin from pine trees that was used in the production of many types of paints and varnishes. His pine trees were having a hard time in the Kansas climate as pine trees were not native to the region, but he was doing the best he could and still turning a slight profit. No matter what he did, he could not get the smell of pine out of his clothes, nor even out of his nose; everything smelled like pine to him now.

The black coffin sat in the middle of the dusty street that was the only main thoroughfare that ran through the small town of Sheridan Creek, Kansas. The coffin was positioned a few yards outside the swinging doors that led into the saloon on one side of the street and half a dozen yards from the new telegraph office on the other side of the street. The six-sided black box rested atop a wooden bier comprised of two criss-crossing vertical slats of wood on each end that formed an X, and two horizontal slats that were fastened along the tops and bottoms of each X. A single stabilizing slat of horizontal wood ran from the bottom of one X to the other, connecting the two sides.

"Not for me," Buddy Renoy said, answering Wayne's question. Buddy wore a double-breasted brown canvas vest that matched the brown canvas trousers he was wearing. His black shoes were freshly polished, practically gleaming in the sunlight. His tobacco tin was stored in its customary place in the upper right pocket of his vest. He had just come from the barber so his face was clean shaven, his tanned skin smooth. He was an employee of the Lukas Telegraph Company, working as a telegraph operator, so the mysterious coffin was quite visible through the windows of his place of employment. The coffin had drawn him to it, just as it had drawn Wayne and several other townsfolk.

Wayne looked over at Buddy. "How do you know that?"

"It's too short. I wouldn't fit," Buddy said.

Wayne sized up the coffin again, taking in the widened upper portion where a corpse's head and shoulders would rest, his gaze moving down the body of the coffin as the box narrowed until his gaze rested on the tapered bottom where a corpse's feet would go. He glanced over and sized up Buddy. Buddy was right. His tall, gangly frame wouldn't fit into the coffin.

"Doc Greer said he didn't order it," Wayne said. "Anybody just die?"

Buddy shook his head. "Not that I heard. Nothing came over the telegraph and nobody came in to send a message to any next of kin." He looked at the coffin for a moment. "Maybe it's for Grace Nally. She's been sick for quite a spell."

"Grace?" Wayne shook his head immediately. "It's too big for her. That'd be a waste of some good wood."

Both men stared silently at the black coffin. The black surface didn't appear to be painted; the very wood it was comprised of was a deep black in color. There were no markings on it but for the white cross that was visible on the upper portion of the coffin. The white cross appeared to be part of the black section of wood that comprised the coffin's lid, as if the white cross had appeared naturally within the black wood itself. There were no indications of who made it or where it had come from.

"Maybe somebody's already in it," Buddy said.

Wayne nodded his head towards the coffin. "Be my guest."

Buddy remained where he was. "Anybody see someone put it there?" he asked.

Wayne shrugged. "Just showed up."

"Just fell out of the sky, huh?" Buddy said.

Wayne shrugged again. "It just showed up." He pointed past the coffin to the telegraph office several yards away. "Don't you sit right there, right inside the window?"

Buddy nodded. "I do when I'm working. I wasn't working today."

Several other townsfolk gathered near the two men, everyone staring curiously at the black coffin. Sheriff Daniels pushed his way through the gathered crowd. He was dressed in his tan sheriff's uniform, his badge pinned to his left breast, the silver metal polished and gleaming in the sunlight. His brown beard was neatly trimmed, speckled with just a hint of grey. He stopped near Wayne and Buddy. He tipped his hat towards Wayne as they glanced at each other.

"Sheriff," Wayne said in way of greeting.

"Wayne," the sheriff said in reply. "Buddy."

"Morning, sheriff," Buddy said.

"What have we got going on here?" the sheriff asked.

"Don't know," Wayne said. "It just showed up here. Nobody saw anybody put it there. It was just there this morning."

The sheriff frowned. He moved up to the black coffin and stared at it for a moment.

The crowd of onlookers slowly moved forward, as if being drawn to the coffin by some undeniable pull.

Eleanor Johnstone, the local schoolmarm, looked on with nervous trepidation as the sheriff stood over the coffin. She was a handsome woman, dressed in a flowery dress that reached down to her ankles, her brown hair tied into a bun.

Sheriff Daniels reached down and opened the lid. The brass hinges that connected the lid on one side of the coffin creaked ever so slightly as the sheriff raised the lid.

The coffin was empty, its interior lined with a layer of pristine white cloth.

The sound of fast approaching hooves pounding against the dirt street caused the entire crowd to look up in unison at the rapidly approaching man on horseback. The rider was a well-known hunter and trapper named Houston Smith. A body was sprawled across the horse's back, the body lying in front of Houston on the animal. "Get the doc!" Houston shouted. "Somebody get the doc!"

Two young boys raced off down the dusty street to get doc Greer.

Houston tugged on the reins and pulled the horse to a sharp stop near sheriff Daniels. The horse whinnied and pranced about; Houston fought to keep the animal under control, spinning the horse around once before getting the beast to be still. "Somebody get the doc. Walcott's hurt. He's hurt bad."

The sheriff looked up at Houston as the man shifted in the saddle. His long wild hair and thick beard hid most of his face, but Daniels could hear him puffing hard. "What happened?" the sheriff asked.

"We were out trapping and he slipped off a ledge," Houston said between heavy breaths. "He took a

59

pretty bad fall. Hit his head pretty hard."

"I think he's dead," someone said from the crowd. It was Bertram Cyrus, the town's only dwarf. He did odd jobs around town, using his short height to his advantage for those jobs that required a strong hand in confined spaces. He had a head full of curly brown hair and a full beard that he had a habit of stroking.

The sheriff glanced down at Bertram, then looked towards the ever-growing crowd of townsfolk that had gathered. He said nothing.

Eleanor pointed to the motionless man lying prone over the horse. "He isn't blinking," she said, aghast at the sight.

The sheriff bent down to get a better look at Walcott. Bertram and Eleanor were right. Walcott had the stare of a dead man, his eyes open and glassy.

Houston hurriedly dismounted and joined the sheriff. "No," he muttered as he stared at his friend. "No." He lifted Walcott's head up. "Come on, Wally. Stay with me."

Walcott didn't respond.

Buddy stared at Walcott's motionless body for a long moment, then turned to look at the opened coffin, then shifted his gaze over to Wayne.

Wayne met Buddy's stare, then turned to look at the black coffin. He looked back over to Buddy, his eyes widening slightly. "You don't think..." He let his words trail off, keeping his voice low.

Buddy didn't say anything.

Walcott's body was a perfect fit for the black coffin. When the six pallbearers lifted the closed coffin off the bier, there was no sign of the coffin stand, no markings in the dirt, no indentations, no indication that the bier had even been there. Someone speculated that the bier was some newfangled invention created by those city folks in the East and that it had folded itself up inside the coffin as the pallbearers had raised the black box. No one else had a better explanation, so that became the accepted answer.

They buried Walcott the trapper in the cemetery on the hilltop on the far outskirts of town. Besides a few parting words spoken for the recently deceased, no one said a word.

Wayne rushed into the saloon, pushing hurriedly through the swinging doors, his face flush, his eyes slightly manic. His gaze sought out Buddy, who was playing poker at one of the tables on the left side of the saloon. He quickly moved to his friend's side. "It's back."

Buddy frowned at him.

"The coffin," Wayne said. "It's right outside."

Buddy quickly put his hand of cards face down on the table and moved outside with Wayne. Half a dozen men who had been in the saloon and one of the working girls followed them out into the street.

A black coffin sat in the street, sitting in the same spot the prior black coffin had occupied.

"It looks just like the other one," Wayne said, feeling the need to keep his voice down in the presence of the black box.

"Anybody in it?" Buddy asked.

"I didn't look," Wayne said.

"You tell the sheriff?" Buddy asked.

Wayne shook his head. "He went to Red Rock for some supplies. He'll be back tomorrow."

Buddy pursed his lips. He turned his attention back to the black coffin. "Seems a bit shorter than the last one," Buddy said. He moved closer to the coffin, hesitated for a moment, then reached out to raise the lid.

The coffin was empty, its interior lined with the same pristine white cloth that had lined the previous black coffin.

Buddy lower the lid back down. He glanced over at Wayne. "Looks about your height," he said. He casually took out his tin of tobacco from his vest pocket and pinched off a piece to put between his cheek and gums.

"Like hell it does," Wayne shot back, his voice raised. "Seems like you'd be a good fit for this one."

Buddy stepped back away from the coffin, keeping his gaze on the rectangular box, sizing it up. "No, it's not for me. It's too wide."

"Who's it for then?" Wayne asked.

Buddy shook his head and shrugged, then spit some dark tobacco juice out of the side of his mouth.

They decided not to wait and find out.

The first man to go at the coffin was Inglemir Johansson, a big, burly Swede who had moved to Sheridan Creek about a year ago. He took his blacksmith's hammer to the black box. But the hammer just seemed to bounce off the closed coffin lid, leaving no mark at all, no indentation, no scratch, not even a slight scuff mark. The strong repelling reaction caught Johansson off guard, knocking him back a few steps from the black coffin.

The big Swede re-gripped his hammer and went in for another strike, bringing his full power to bear on the blow, delivering his strike using the power of his thick shoulder and his mighty bicep and his muscular forearm. The repelling force of the coffin seemed to feed off the strength of Johansson's swing, growing stronger the more might the blacksmith put into his blow.

For his third strike, Johansson gripped the hammer with both hands and raised it high above his head. With a snarl emanating through gritted teeth, he brought the heavy hammer down, but that only resulted in the big Swede being knocked flat onto his buttocks. The hammer hit the dusty street next to him, jarred loose from his beefy hands.

The second man to go at the coffin was Wayne. He poured kerosene all over the black box. The liquid pooled on the ground beneath the coffin, running down its black sides. For good measure, Buddy opened the coffin's lid so Wayne could pour the last remaining portion of kerosene in the container into the coffin. Wayne lit a match, striking it on the back of his boot. He stared at the flame for just a moment, then tossed it into the open coffin.

Flames erupted outward from the coffin, sending a wave of heat washing over the gathered crowd. Everyone took a few steps back away from the coffin. Some townsfolk gasped at the sight and at the warmth biting at their cheeks, while others gasped at what was *not* happening. The kerosene burned, but the coffin itself did not burn. The white fabric that lined the interior of the coffin did not turn brown, did not crisp into black ashes. The coffin itself did not succumb to the flames either. It was as if the kerosene never actually touched the coffin nor its interior, as if the flammable liquid was floating in its own layer of space above the coffin. The kerosene burned itself away in a matter of moments.

The black coffin remained unharmed.

No one said anything. What they had just witnessed should not have been possible, yet it had occurred right before their eyes.

Then they brought in the horses. Two of the biggest work horses they could find. They tied the animals to the legs of the bier, each animal attached by a thick rope to one of the slanted pieces of vertical wood that comprised the bier's X-shaped sides. Once the ropes were secured, Buddy and Wayne gave each horse a slap on their hind quarters, shouting a "Hyaah!" to get them moving. The horses bolted forward, but quickly came to a dead stop as the thick ropes grew taut.

Buddy gave the horse nearest him another slap on the hind quarters and the muscular animal strained and tugged and snorted, clawing at the ground as it tried to take another step forward.

After several minutes of intense straining, the horses stopped trying to go forward. No slapping hands, or commanding voices could get them to move, as if they instinctively knew this was a lost cause.

The black coffin sat immobile in the middle of the street.

"Step aside. Step aside." The slurring voice

belonged to Eli McField. He had his six-shooter out of its holster, waving it haphazardly before him as he stumbled through the crowd. One side of the suspenders for his pants that should have been hooked up around his shoulder dangled loosely at his side. His rotund belly was too big for his soiled shirt and his belly button was visible along with a patch of his flesh above his waist. To the surprise of no one in town, he was already drunk even though it was barely past noon. Eli was a rag picker and his occupation fit his appearance. His self-proclaimed job was to go through all the garbage in town and sort through it to see if anything could be put to re-use.

"Put that away, McField," Wayne said. "You're going to hurt somebody."

McField swiveled his head towards Wayne, his head bobbing slightly up and down as he turned it. "The only thing I'm gonna hurt is that bloody coffin," he said, his words slurred. "Everybody stand back."

Wayne started to move towards McField. "Don't do it, Eli," he warned, picking up his pace.

McField ignored Wayne's warning. He raised his gun, sliding his finger over the trigger. "Take that you spooky son of a—" and fired at the coffin. He never did finish his sentence because the bullet bounced right back at him off the side of the coffin and penetrated his big belly with a wet smacking sound, puncturing his liver, and ripping a two inch hole in his back as it exited his body.

To the surprise of no one in town, Eli McField was a perfect fit for the black coffin

Wayne woke up to a blessed sight. Rather, it was the absence of something that brought him great joy. He ran towards the saloon, a huge smile splitting his face. He reached the area between the saloon and the telegraph office and did a little jig right on the spot that had brought so much dread to the town.

The black coffin was not there. After six days of hellish torture, was the torment finally going to end? Yesterday, the coffin had come for Grace Nally as she finally succumbed to her long illness. Everyone feared who would be next. Wayne stopped his little dance to think about that for a moment. Did the absence of the black coffin really mean no one was going to die today?

He looked up to see Buddy coming down the wooden plank sidewalk that lined the north side of the street. Wayne fingered the gun at his waist. Would it even matter if he took a shot at Buddy? Would the bullet even hit him if he had a clean bead on Buddy's head?

Wayne started to draw his weapon from its holster. Could he fire point blank into Buddy's heart and somehow not kill him? But then he caught himself. The shot might not kill Buddy today, but he could still be wounded. It could take days to die from a gunshot wound. He pushed the gun back into its holster and moved his hand away from the cool metal. Where had that mad idea come from? He shook his head, as if trying to shake the crazy notion from his thoughts. He then realized he was still standing in the spot the black coffin occupied when it mysteriously just appeared in town. He hurried out of the spot, stepping quickly away from it as if he had just spotted a rattlesnake at his feet.

The relief felt by the townsfolk of Sheridan Creek, Kansas was very short-lived.

Sheriff Daniels came up and put a comforting hand on Bertram's shoulder. Several other townsfolk were already gathered around the latest black coffin to appear in the street. Wayne and Buddy were already walking away from the coffin as the sheriff approached, this particular black box holding no more interest for them.

Eleanor felt an immediate release of the fear gripping her heart when she saw the dwarf standing nearby; the little man stared forlornly at the small black coffin. Thank God. She slowly lowered her hand from her mouth and slowly straightened back up. She pressed down on her petticoat, rubbing her hands along the fabric. Bertram was a good fellow and she had no quarrels with him, but she felt no pity for him. She only felt immense relief that she was safe.

"Anyone measure it yet?" Bertram asked, his voice soft. The dwarf glanced around the gathered crowd.

The undertaker, Lucius Cornwall, nodded his head, a loose piece of measuring tape dangling down from his hand. He was a young handsome man, dressed in a dark suit, immaculately groomed, his thin mustache trimmed to perfection. The mysterious appearances of the black coffins had made Lucius extremely nervous at first, as he felt as if they might threaten his position, but after he realized there was nothing he could do about them appearing out of nowhere, he just went about his job as usual preparing the dead for burial — minus the part about having to build a coffin for the recently deceased. "Three feet nine and one-quarter inches," he said to Bertram.

Bertram was quiet for a moment. "I'm four feet and two-thirds inches," he said, still speaking softly. He absently stroked at his beard.

The undertaker glanced down at the dwarf. "What?"

Bertram glanced about the gathered crowd. "I'm four feet and two-thirds of an inch," he said, speaking louder. "It's not meant for me."

Several townsfolk started mumbling to each other, their voices growing louder as more and more people joined in. "Who's it for?" someone asked. "He said it was three feet nine and one-quarter inches?" another voice said. "Who's that short? Nobody in town is shorter than Bertram."

Eleanor Johnstone's eyes widened; her hand moved back over her mouth, her body recoiling in horror, her face contorting with fear, her other hand protectively going to her stomach as a nauseous feeling roiled inside of her. The black coffin was sized to accommodate a smaller body than normal, but everyone was assuming it was still meant for one of the adult folks. No, it couldn't be. She stared at the black box, her mind still trying to wrap itself around what it all meant. The box was too small for a man or a woman, even too small for the only dwarf in town. How was this happening? Eleanor couldn't contain her overwhelming fear any longer. "The children!"

she shouted. "The children!"

"It's not for my Bobby," a woman in the crowd shouted. "I measure him every morning. He's four feet one inches today. Thank the Lord!"

"My Abigail is four feet three and three quarters inches," a man called out from the crowd. "It's not for her." He took off his cowboy hat and whipped it around his head. "It's not for her!"

The sheriff glanced over at Eleanor. "Did you measure Wyatt today, Mrs. Johnstone?"

Eleanor straightened up, forcing herself to project a calm demeanor. "I did not."

"Well, you better get it done," the sheriff said to her.

Eleanor did not move.

"Eleanor?" the sheriff prompted.

Eleanor remained still, staring at nothing. Then, she turned her head slowly to face the sheriff. "What if I don't want to know?"

"We all need to know. You know that, Eleanor."

Eleanor steeled her gaze, looking sharply at the sheriff. "You need to know if my child is going to die today? Is that what you are telling me, sheriff?"

"Now, Eleanor. That's not how we all agreed to handle this. We need to stay calm."

Eleanor straightened her back. "I never agreed to any of this."

"Now you know the town voted and that's how it has to be. We all agreed to measure our heights and let everyone else know what they are." The sheriff was quiet for a moment. "You need to go measure Wyatt and come back and tell me his height," he said, keeping his voice low so only Eleanor could hear him. "I know that boy is still growing, so you got to measure him every day, Eleanor, every day."

Eleanor re-appeared on the street hours later. Most of the townsfolk had departed the scene, moving on to deal with the business of the day, so only a few people were near the coffin as she approached. She never moved her gaze from the coffin, not even when Annie Brothman wished her a good day as she walked slowly past her. Eleanor was dressed in her finest schoolmarm dress, her hair neatly tied up in a bun. There was a calmness in her face, almost a serenity.

She reached the coffin and raised its lid. There was no hesitation in her actions, only firm resolve.

"Eleanor, what are you doing?" a woman's voice nearby asked.

Eleanor knew it was Annie calling out to her, but that didn't matter. She pushed the lid all the way up on its hinges until it remained open without her help. She raised one of her booted feet and hooked it up over the side of the coffin.

"Eleanor, stop!" Annie cried out.

Eleanor heard the rustling of feet quickly approaching her. She redoubled her efforts to clamber into the coffin, gripping the hard wooden sides, pulling her other leg up and in to the coffin. It wasn't a graceful motion, but she managed to get herself into the coffin. Her body was too tall for the interior, but that didn't deter her. She pulled up her legs, folding them towards her chest to take up less space in the coffin, and hunched her shoulders slightly. In this position, she was fully within the coffin and the lid could be closed. Death wasn't going to take her Wyatt. Not if she could help it!

She reached up for the edge of the coffin lid to pull it closed, but a strong male hand gripped the edge of the lid right next to her hand. She glanced up to see sheriff Daniels looking down at her with grim eyes.

"No, Eleanor," the sheriff said.

"Leave me be, sheriff," Eleanor said, her voice taking on the stern tone of a school teacher well accustomed to being strict with her students and fully expecting them to obey her words.

"I can't do that, Eleanor," the sheriff said, keeping his hand firmly gripping the edge of the coffin lid.

Eleanor glowered at him. "Yes you can, sheriff," Eleanor said. "Remove your hand and let me be." She maneuvered her body in the coffin, as if trying to show the sheriff she was a good fit for the black box.

The sheriff was quiet for a moment. He lowered his voice to barely above a whisper. "This isn't meant for you, Eleanor."

Eleanor turned her head sharply to stare up at the sheriff. "And how do you know that, sheriff? Are you the one who put it here?"

The sheriff slowly shook his head. "Now, Eleanor, you know I have nothing to do with this… coffin just showing up here."

"Then how can you speak to who it's for?" Eleanor asked. "Or why it's even here?"

The sheriff was quiet.

"Maybe it wants a sacrifice," Eleanor said. "Did you ever think of that? Maybe it wants me to do exactly what I'm doing to save my boy."

The sheriff rubbed the back of his free hand

across the stubble on his cheek, but still said nothing.

"If it needs to feed on death," Eleanor said, "then it can feed on mine."

"Nobody ever said anything about it needing to feed," the sheriff said.

"It's here for something, sheriff. It's here for somebody's life. It can take mine. Then maybe it will go away for good and never come back."

The sheriff was again quiet, thinking. He glanced about the street, noticing the gathered crowd. He looked back down into the coffin, his fingers still gripping the edge of the lid, and leaned in closer to her. "I could just drag you out of there," he said.

Eleanor's gaze snapped to his eyes and a thick growl of words gushed out. "Don't you dare!" Her eyes narrowed to even thinner slits. "Don't you damn dare do that!"

The sheriff pulled back slightly, removing his hand from the open coffin lid. "Okay, okay. You can stay in the damn thing." The sheriff was quiet for a moment, thinking. Then he glanced back down at Eleanor. "How you gonna eat?"

"I'll bring you something, Eleanor," Annie said. "Some bread and some apples."

"Thank you, Annie," Eleanor said, truly grateful for her friend's gesture.

Annie nodded back to her. She looked over at the sheriff to see a frown of disapproval darkening his features, then turned and headed away down the street.

"And a chamber pot," Eleanor called out to her.

Annie turned back to nod at Eleanor, gave the sheriff a soft smile, then turned away to head towards her house on the end of the street.

The sheriff watched Annie for a moment, then returned his attention to Eleanor. There was clearly a question on the end of his tongue, but he was reluctant to speak it. Finally, he gave in and spoke it aloud in a soft voice. "Where's Wyatt?"

Eleanor looked up at him. "He's taking a nap. Maisie is watching over him."

The sheriff was again quiet for a moment. "What do you want me to tell him when he wakes up?"

Eleanor was quiet for a moment as she thought about her reply. "Just tell him I love him."

Later that afternoon the lone street of Sheridan Creek was bustling with activity. People walked along the sidewalks going about their business. Horses moved up and down the street. A carriage clattered past, its occupants staring curiously at the black coffin sitting in the middle of the street as they moved by it. Everyone who knew better avoided even looking at the coffin, nervous of its mere presence, let alone of the obsessively determined woman who was lying in it.

A wrenching cry suddenly filled the air, coming from the far end of the street. Eleanor sat up in the coffin, looking towards the sound of the commotion. Several men on horseback struggled with their horses, the animals dancing about in chaos. Several people on foot raced towards the scene. One man bent down on one knee, glancing down at something in the street. He slowly turned his head to look directly at Eleanor.

Eleanor started to scream.

"What happened?" the sheriff asked Maisie.

Maisie shook her head. "I was just tryin' to keep it a secret for a little while." She was a dark-skinned woman, lean and fit with a gentle rounded face and soft, gentle eyes. "He asked me where his Ma was, and one of his little friends who had come over to play told him she was sitting in the coffin in the middle of the street. I tried to shush that boy but I was too late. Wyatt heard him clear as day. He just raced out the door and ran into the street right in front of those horses. There's nothing them men could've done. He ran right under their hooves." Maisie closed her eyes as tears streamed down her cheeks.

Sheriff Daniels put a comforting hand on Maisie's shoulder.

"Why?" Maisie looked up at sheriff Daniels, her face wet with sorrow. "Why him?"

The sheriff shook his head. "I don't know, Maisie. I don't have the answers."

"Wyatt was a fine young gentleman." Maisie wiped several tears off her wet cheeks. "I loved that boy."

Sheriff Daniels nodded. "We all did."

"I heard you got yourselves a creepy coffin right in the middle of the street in this town," the visitor said as he moseyed up to the bar in the saloon. He was dressed in a two-piece suit with a black bow tie and a white vest. A gold ring glistened on one of his fingers. The newcomer was trying to present an image of high esteem with his polished appearance, but his rough use of language belied his standing, giving off the impression of a coarse man of newly acquired wealth. He glanced over his shoulder, looking towards the street, then glanced back to Wayne and Buddy who were standing at the bar sipping whiskey. "But I thought it was just some tall talk. Why don't somebody just move it?"

Buddy shrugged. "Part of the town's charm." The tone of his voice was filled with a sad melancholy.

"Kinda eerie, ain't it?" the newcomer asked. "Anybody know who it's for?"

Wayne hesitated for a brief moment as he cast a furtive glance at Buddy, then just gave a slight shrug. "Death just comes," he said, his words an admission of defeat that all the others present in the saloon understood. "Ain't no rhyme or reason for it sometimes. It just comes. Can't fight it. Can't trick it. Can't plan for it. Can't plan against it. It just comes."

The visitor glanced outside at the dark box sitting in the middle of the dusty street, part of the black coffin visible under the bottom of the saloon's swinging doors.

Buddy scratched at his grizzled beard, then looked back to the newcomer and stared at him, as if suddenly seeing him for the first time. His droopy eyes widened just a touch. "Say, 'bout how tall are you?"

"Six foot," the visitor said.

"Exactly?"

The visitor frowned at Buddy. "What?"

"I mean, is that exactly how tall you are?" Buddy asked. "No inches, half inches, quarter inches?"

"I guess about six feet and one inch, really. If you needin' me to be so exact and all. That's what my tailor told me at my last fitting last month. Don't suppose I've grown much since then, right?" The visitor grinned.

Buddy broke out into a big smile of his own, straightening up from his slouched position over the bar. He slapped Wayne on the back. "You hear that, Wayne? Six feet and one beautiful inch." Buddy looked to the newcomer and sidled a step closer to him. "Welcome to town, big fella," Buddy said with a drunken grin. He glanced around the saloon with his bloodshot eyes, beaming the other occupants a sloppy smile. "Drinks are on me today, boys!"

A hootin' and a hollerin' rose up in the saloon and the whiskey flowed heavily in fountains of shimmering liquid gold.

"You fellas always so friendly to newcomers?" the visitor asked, moving his gaze from Buddy to Wayne.

"Didn't use to be." Buddy downed the rest of his whiskey in one gulp and set the glass down on the bar, motioning to the bartender for a refill. He glanced outside towards the coffin, then looked back at the newcomer, trying not to be too obvious about sizing him up. "But I think we're going to learn to be a lot friendlier," he added. Buddy raised his refilled whiskey glass and clinked it against the newcomer's glass. "That'll keep travelers and homesteaders comin' in at a good clip."

"I reckon so," the visitor said, nodding as he spoke.

Buddy moved behind the newcomer as the visitor started to down his shot of whiskey, drew his gun, and fired point-blank at the back of the newcomer's head. The visitor made no sound as he collapsed in a heap, quite dead before he even hit the saloon floor.

His shot glass bounced off the wooden planks that comprised the floor, the spilled amber of the whiskey mixing with some of his spilled dark red blood.

Buddy stared down at the man's corpse as blood and brain matter seeped and oozed out of the gaping hole in his skull. A whisper of smoke emanated from the barrel of his gun. "Six feet and one beautiful inch," he said.

Everyone in the saloon was quiet, all staring silently at Buddy. No one had moved.

"Same size as Wayne," Buddy said, speaking to everyone in the room. "Same size as Wayne."

Slowly, one by one, the rest of the patrons in the saloon raised their glasses in salute to Buddy and gave him a respectful nod.

Buddy brought his gaze back to Wayne.

Wayne raised his shot glass to Buddy, spilling a bit of the whiskey onto his hand as he did so. Perhaps he had spoken too soon. Perhaps there was a way to fight it after all. He looked out through one of the saloon's windows at the black coffin that sat in the dusty street, his defeated eyes filling with a new hope.

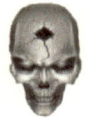

TERRORSTORY #74
FOREST OF FEAR

Seeing Joanie Huffman entering his convenience store erased the last ten years of Lawrence Malroney's life. Something about her mere presence sliced through his brain to cut away the last decade as if it had never happened. He was suddenly back in high school, watching Joanie walk towards him in the school hallway. There were other bodies in the hallway, but none of them were in focus. There was a soft haze over Joanie's face in his mind, as if his brain had always had put in a filter over her to smooth out any imperfections that might be present in her skin; it couldn't have been a better set up for her inside his mind than if she was a Hollywood starlet milking the camera for her close-up.

Sure it had been about ten years since he had seen her last, but she had a face he would never forget. And those eyes. Those fucking sky blue eyes of hers. Holy shit. It wasn't fair that Joanie was the only person he knew who had them.

It was like she had made herself as perfect as she could be before she entered the store, dressed in form-fitting faded jeans that cupped her buttocks and a light pink blouse that did not hide any sign of her ample breasts. Beyond her bright blue eyes, a pert nose that was absolutely the perfect size for her face was positioned in exactly the right place on her face. Her lips were red, not cherry red, but nearly that red; they looked moist as if she had just applied a fresh layer of lipstick. A subtle layer of make-up gave her facial skin just the hint of a glossy sheen. She truly looked like she could have been a beauty queen movie star or a glamorous high fashion model. She even had the dark mole of a beauty mark just above the right side of her upper lip.

But then suddenly the painful feelings and realities from Lawrence's past were whipsawed to the front of his brain. He raised an arm and pointed a slightly shaking finger at Joanie. "Hey," he said, his voice cracking just a little. "You can't be in here."

Joanie looked over at him, her expression a little

dazed, as if she were a bit out of it and distanced from her surroundings. "Oh, hello," she said. "I didn't see you there."

"You can't be in here," Lawrence said again.

Her face still remained somewhat blank as she stared at him. She glanced down at the name sewn with white thread into his red Malroney Market uniform shirt. Lawrence. And then her head jerked back up and her bright blue eyes widened just a bit. "Oh, shit." She was quiet for just a brief moment, shuffling her feet. "Hey, Lawrence. I didn't recognize you for a second."

Lawrence put his arm down and slowly shook his head back and forth. "Come on, Joanie. You can't be in here."

She stared at him for a long moment, as if contemplating some big decision. Then, she just shrugged, brushing off his concern with an exaggerated wave. "It doesn't matter anymore. None of it fucking matters."

Lawrence stared at Joanie. He wondered how she saw him now. He certainly wasn't the super awkward skinny kid she had encountered in eighth grade, then got to know all too well in high school. He had bulked up a bit since high school, tried to keep himself fit. Kept himself clean. Kept his brown hair short in front and trimmed straight in the back. Kept himself relatively neatly groomed. Well, not perfectly, but he let no more than a few days' growth of stubble sprout on his face between shavings. He absently scratched at the two-day stubble on his chin.

"I guess you *were* the only one who really cared about me," Joanie said to him, her voice soft, full of a lonely sadness.

He opened his mouth several different times to speak, but each time he was about to say something he stopped himself. Why the hell would she say something like that to him? Didn't she know that all he needed was just a tiny spark of hope to rekindle the... feelings he had for her? Finally, he forced himself to be calm. "Look, I was young. I was awkward." He straightened his shoulders. "I already told you I was sorry a hundred times." He paused for a second. "Okay, I'm still awkward," he admitted, his shoulders drooping slightly forward as he spoke. "I was smitten. You were a goddess to me." He looked away from her, hanging his head like the kid who never got picked to be on anybody's team.

"Smitten," she mused. "That's a fun word." She seemed to roll it around in her head before saying it again. "Smitten." She paused and raised her finger. Joanie always had a bit of a smirk behind her eyes in high school, like she was privy to some secret knowledge about you and she wanted you to know she knew all your secrets; she had lost none of that mischievous sparkle with age, but there was something new behind that sparkle, something darkly sad. "But there's your use of the word *were*." She slowly lowered her hand and hung her head to mirror what he had just done with his head. "I don't even have that going for me anymore."

An enormous surge of dread gushed up inside of Lawrence with the force of a fountain of black oil geysering up out of a newly-struck well. Why was she here? Was she drunk? She was acting a little loopy with the floppy head wags and the slightly exaggerated body movements. He felt an uncomfortable squirm of anxiety snaking across his shoulders and his stomach muscles tightened like a freshly dead spider's legs reflexively tighten when its exposed abdomen is poked. Of all the places she could be in the world right now, why here? With beauty like that, she should be walking in a runway show in Paris and strutting her stuff. Or she should be waving her arms about and kicking her slender legs up and smiling her dazzling smile in a pro football cheerleader outfit. Or she should be making the fancy poses of a highly paid fashion model, tilting her head and flashing her dazzling smile for the cameras.

"What are you doing here?" he asked.

"I'm sure not here for three-day-old hot dogs," she said, flashing him a crooked smile that was still dazzling despite her half-hearted effort.

He didn't smile back. "Come on. What are you doing here? Really." he asked.

Joanie looked towards the thick forest visible beyond the large window that covered nearly half of the front of the convenience store, then looked back to him. She said nothing.

He glanced out the window of the convenience store at the darkly shadowed expanse of trees that made up Shadow Forest. It was so close physically, located just beyond the store's parking lot, yet such a far distance away mentally. At least for him. Others, not so much, he knew. For others, for those with an ominous black cloud swirling amidst their thoughts, the bleak essence of the dark woods was much closer mentally than physically; all they had to do was enter the forest and their physical state would soon mirror their mental state. They were already dead in their own minds, so why not match up their physical bodies to boot?

Lawrence turned back to look at Joanie. All the old feelings from high school had never gone away; they had just lain dormant for the right opportunity to resurface. And her presence, the sight of her, the intoxicating aroma of her nearness, threatened to flare up those old feelings with the force of a volcanic eruption. "Is that really why you're here?" he asked.

She shrugged.

"No," Lawrence said. "Not you." She was the prom queen. She was so smart, too, always in the top of the class. Head of the cheerleading squad. And she was so fucking beautiful with her perfect cheekbones and soft chin and sensuous mouth. And those damn mesmerizing sky blue eyes. If he looked like her, he'd be masturbating twice a day just looking at himself in the mirror.

"Why not me?" She put on a mock frown. "Can't a girl fall apart?" She pointed to a drink machine behind the counter. "But I could use a slushie first. You got that blue flavor?"

Blue wasn't a flavor but he didn't think it appropriate to correct her in the moment. "Yeah, sure. What size?" He nearly bit his own tongue after asking the question. What the hell difference did it make what size?

"Small is fine," she said casually.

He grabbed a small plastic cup, filled it with the blue raspberry slushie mix, stabbed the frozen mixture with a straw, and handed it to her, very careful not to brush his fingers against hers in the handoff. She took the offered drink, then patted at the pockets of her jeans. "Shit, I don't have any cash on me."

He raised his hand. "That's okay. It's on the

house."

She was quiet for a moment, then took a sip of the blue slushie. "Thanks. I would tell you I was good for it…" She glanced outside at the dark woods in the distance, then looked back to him. "But it's not much good where I'm going…"

Are you sure you want to go in there? The question burned on his tongue, but he didn't speak it aloud. He had vowed to himself never to interfere again. Not after what had happened the last time he had tried to prevent someone from killing themselves in Shadow Forest. The guy had nearly blown his head off. If the guy's gun hadn't jammed, he wouldn't be standing where he was today. Lawrence took that as a pretty damn strong sign to stay out of other people's business. But it made Lawrence Malroney's heart ache thinking about what Joanie Huffman was about to do to herself, so he wasn't sure if he would even be able to uphold his own vow to himself.

He was quite certain the forest hadn't been like this when his great grandfather had first opened Malroney's Market over a hundred plus years ago. Even as few as twenty years ago, Shadow Forest had been a camping ground for families and adventure seekers and all manner of outdoor types. Now it was the last stop for people on their one-way trip to death's door. Now the thick growth of trees that comprised Shadow Forest was just a gloomy mass of towering trees that blocked almost any light from entering it. Now Shadow Forest was just a home for Death itself.

He looked out the front window of his convenience store at the old faded sign visible near a gap in the dark trees. **No Trespassing. Greenbrook**

Nature Preserve. A suicide prevention hotline placard was shoved into the dirt right near the entrance to the single path that led deeper into the green and brown gloom. Hell, it wasn't even really named Shadow Forest. That's just what everybody called it now. The Greenbrook Nature Preserve was dead. Long live the Shadow Forest.

He had thought about selling the place numerous times, but the prospective feelers he had put out over the years had not yielded a single interested buyer. Not one. The thought of just closing up the convenience store and walking away from it didn't sit right with him. His great grandfather had worked so hard to get it started and keep it going. And then his daughter took over, then Lawrence's dad took over, and then Lawrence took it over after him. He felt an obligation to keep it going. He had told himself it would just be for one more month, then maybe he would think of closing it up. But one month turned into two, which turned into ten, then into thirty. After a while, he just stopped thinking about selling the store or closing it up.

It was kind of morbid to think that some of his best customers were only hours away from their self-inflicted deaths. Some of them would just dump hundreds of dollars on the counter and tell him to keep the change. Hell, one guy left him over three grand one time, said he didn't have any use for it anymore so Lawrence might as well take it; all the guy bought was a 100 Grand candy bar, which in of itself was somewhat amusing in a very morbidly grim way.

Most visitors just bought a bottle of water or some other drinks, some snacks, maybe a candy bar. He didn't know why they bothered, but that's what they bought. Maybe it was because they still clung to a glimmer of hope that something would change in their life over the next few hours that would save them from themselves. He didn't know. He never asked why people bought what they bought. He just did the transaction and let them be on their way.

But this was Joanie Huffman. His Joanie. He couldn't prevent himself from trying to stop her.

"Don't go in there," Lawrence said.

"Why not?" Joanie asked. She slurped on her blue slushie.

"Because you won't come out," Lawrence said.

She nodded a lazy nod. "That's exactly why I'm going in."

He was quiet for a moment. "Is it that bad?"

She shrugged. "My time's up." She slurped on her drink.

He looked at her quietly for just a moment. Just stay out of it, he admonished himself. It's her business, not yours. But he couldn't keep silent. "Why rush it? It's gonna get us all eventually."

She shrugged again. "Why not now? I've got nowhere to go but down." She lowered her head.

Lawrence tilted his head slightly at her, softening his voice. "Come on, it can't be that bad."

She was quiet for a long moment, holding her head down. "You don't know, do you?" she finally asked. "You haven't heard?" Joanie slowly raised her head and stared him straight in the eyes with those piercing sky-blue eyes of hers. "Of all the people I expected to know my every move, you don't even know." There was a genuine sadness in her voice.

Lawrence frowned. "Heard what?"

Joanie dug into her jeans and pulled out a scrap of

folded-up paper. It looked like a clipping from a newspaper. He frowned at the oddness of it. He didn't see many people reading actual newspapers anymore, let alone people clipping out stories. He took the offered folded scrap of newspaper, unfurled the piece of paper and instantly recognized the picture of the woman featured in the clipped article. She was a few years younger in the photo, but it was still Joanie. He was sure of it, especially since the beauty mark on her face matched up with the mark on the woman's face in the photo.

"Jesus," Lawrence muttered under his breath as he read the headline of the article. He wasn't much for reading newspapers, or even keeping up with current events online, and he had stopped following what was going on with any of his old classmates, even Joanie, years ago, so the news had never reached him. "You had a baby," he heard himself mutter.

"Yep, that was me. Took real good care of her," She nodded with a grossly violent toss of her head up and down up and down, grossly exaggerating the word '*real*' with a very long drawl. "That was me. I just left her there. How is that even fucking possible?" She pursed her lips and tilted her head from side to side. "Sure enough, I did it."

"Were you… did you go… to jail for that?"

She pumped her head up and down. "Oh, yeah, I was in jail. Got out for good behavior. Ha!" She pumped her free hand up and down, the sudden motion nearly spilling the slushie she clutched in her other hand. "What do you think about that? My good fucking behavior got me out of jail." She shook her head. "Nobody gave a damn about that baby's life. Not the courts. Not the justice system. Not even me."

Lawrence stared down at the wrinkled newspaper clipping again. The headline sent a shiver down his spine. "***Infant abandoned by mother dies in hot car.***" He read the article and felt a surging wave of pity overtake him. She hadn't meant to let the baby die. She thought she had dropped her off at the daycare before going to work, but she hadn't. The baby was sleeping peacefully quiet in the backseat of the car, so she didn't even notice her when she got out of the car. Funny how the mind can play tricks on someone like that. It was something she had done so often, so routinely, that her brain just filled in the gap for that day. It didn't matter to the judge what her explanation was, what her excuse was. Her poor child had died under her care.

Joanie's reason for entering Shadow Forest was a pretty powerful one. Lawrence wondered what other thoughts had so occupied her mind that she forgot about her child. Was she worried about getting fired? Was she caught up with texting on her phone? Fretting over not having enough money to pay her bills? Maybe she was thinking of sneaking off and cheating on her husband? No, that wasn't fair. He was just making up scenarios in his head. He didn't even know if she had ever married. Or maybe she could be a widower. He felt a guilty, odd burst of hope at the thought of any would-be husband of hers being dead.

The door entrance bell jangled and Lawrence glanced up to see Joanie Huffman walking out of the store. He opened his mouth to shout at her, but no sound came out. She paused just for a second to toss her blue slushie into the garbage can just outside the door, then headed for the entrance to Shadow Forest.

Was it right to save someone who would be living

with eternal despair and endless guilt for the rest of their lives? Could anyone really get over that? Would time even matter? Lawrence wondered. Would time even heal that kind of wound? Should he even call this one in to the cops? What if he didn't? What if he just let her go and left her to die completely alone?

Within moments, the forest had swallowed Joanie Huffman up as if she had never existed at all.

"Yea, though I walk through the valley of the shadow of death, I will fear no evil: for Thou art with me; Thy rod and Thy staff they comfort me," Lawrence muttered. He always loved that phrase, but never truly thought he'd actually use it himself one day. He laughed a grunting laugh after muttering the religious words. "Yeah, right." He was scared shitless. He was fearing evil big time.

He stood at the edge of the gloomy forest, staring into its darkly-shadowed interior. He was still dressed in his jeans and his red Malroney Market uniform shirt. The convenience store was several dozen yards behind him, the CLOSED sign pressed up against the glass door. The Glenbrook Nature Preserve sign and the suicide hotline placard were just to his left.

He had promised himself never to go into the woods. He had been afraid of Shadow Forest as soon as his little brain was able to understand what fear was. Plus, his father's horror stories did not dissuade him from holding on to his absolute fear of the Glenbrook Nature Preserve. Those eerie tales filled with glowing-eyed monsters and savage cannibals and rabid wild animals still gave him a flash of chills if he really thought about them hard enough.

Take a final stroll in the Finito Forest, he thought, mentally going through the forest's twisted nicknames given to it by some of the locals. Tiptoe along the trail of the Terminal Trees. Walk through the Waste Yourself Woods. Follow the blood-soaked path through the Forest of Fear. Embrace the shadow of death in the Shadow Forest.

What the fuck am I doing here? Lawrence wondered. She never wanted anything to do with me, he thought. She had a fucking restraining order issued against me, and here I am about to go into the scariest place on the entire fucking planet Earth just because Joanie Huffman is in there?

He remained where he was on the edge of the forest. A tightness squeezed at his shoulder blade, resurfacing the pain in his upper right shoulder from an old tennis injury he had suffered in high school. He knew it was nervous stress causing the pain, but that knowledge did nothing to prevent the pain from radiating throughout his entire right shoulder area.

The forest was quiet, but somehow that lack of sound only added fuel to his anxiety. There should have been sounds of birds twittering, animals moving through the brush, insects making noises insects make, but there were none of those. He glanced down at his feet, not quite sure if he was willing them to move and they weren't responding, or if he was willing them to stay put and they were obeying. Regardless, they weren't moving.

Others had gone into the forest and had come back out, police officers in particular going in to try and retrieve corpses at the behest of victims' families, so he knew he could still leave the dark swath of trees once he entered the forest. But no one had come back out unchanged. They might have not been harmed physically, but no one had remerged from the forest unscathed in their minds. It didn't help matters that they never found a full corpse to bring out. Sometimes, they only found bits of bone, or a skull, or a half-chewed leg, but they never retrieved a full, recognizable corpse from the forest. Ever. Even the police officers were affected by the forest, and some now outright refused to go back in there.

Can your mind be scarred, he wondered? Can your very thoughts get permanently scarred? Can you stop your silly questions and go save Joanie Huffman and be her hero? At least for a few minutes?

"Fuck," Lawrence Malroney said and stepped into Shadow Forest.

Shadow Forest was oddly and eerily silent as Lawrence moved through the tall trees. No buzzing or fluttering of insects picked open a hole in the silence. No howling of animals broke through the wall of quietude. No cawing of birds shattered the tranquility. No creaking branches put any ripple in the stillness. There was no wind. None at all. Even the sounds of his own footsteps seemed strangely dampened, as if the sound waves had to battle their way through some thick dark invisible ether to reach his ears.

Lawrence looked down to his left to see a lone gym shoe resting askew on the forest floor. He felt a nervously unpleasant tingling creep its way up his spine. He glanced around the area but saw no corpse, saw no skeletal remains. Just the shoe. Someone had somehow lost their shoe in the forest but had probably just kept walking. What the hell difference did it make if they lost a shoe when they knew they were going to be dead in a few hours?

He pictured Joanie stumbling through the forest in one shoe. He saw her trying to do her best to ignore the brambles and jagged-edged ground cover that bit into the soles of her feet, but not quite able to stop the little grimaces from forming on her face. That sad, beautiful face. That achingly, fucking amazingly beautiful face that he could just stare at for hours. He felt himself falling into the obsessive state that plagued him so ruthlessly in high school, and he knew he should force his thoughts elsewhere but he couldn't. Because he didn't want to. He just wanted to think about her, think about seeing her, think about being close to her, think about... touching her. If only just to slide his hand slowly, adoringly, across her smooth cheek. Just once. He had never touched her their entire time together in high school. Not once. Not even an accidental bump in the hallway. He didn't want his memory of their eighth grade encounter to get pushed aside by some clumsy accidental meeting.

He cursed himself for being such an awkward fuck. He could've just asked her out for a date instead of creeping about and staring at her like some sick puppy with a pathetically low level of self-esteem. Sure, she might have said no, but at least she would've thought him a little more normal instead of the creep she filed a restraining order against. He had never thought of himself as one of those crazy guys he saw on TV stalking women, but lo and behold a woman was scared enough of his behavior to issue a restraining order against him. How long did a restraining order last? he wondered. He thought it was only for a few years, but couldn't remember for sure. The first one had scared him enough that he felt like it was permanent. That would be a great irony if he was arrested for violating a restraining order while trying to stop Joanie from taking her own life.

He glanced about the forest. What was it about this place that drew in hopeless people ready to forfeit their own lives? People came from all over the country, sometimes even from other countries. That's how strong the allure of the forest was to some desperate people. It was a magnet for despair. Yeah, he profited from it by selling some Shadow Forest souvenirs in his convenience store. So what? At least he was a friendly face. He didn't hassle anybody. He just let them go about whatever it was they were doing. It wasn't his fault the forest became what it was. His family's store had been there first, dating back to the late 1800's when it was an old-fashioned general store. Sure, the store had been updated and modernized several times since then, but the main structure still had been there long before Shadow Forest got its dark name.

Lawrence kept moving, walking slowly, deliberately taking one measured step after the next. He saw other remnants of people's last possessions as he walked through the forest, abandoned shoes, torn clothes, empty beer bottles, shattered liquor bottles, rusty syringes, scraps of food packaging, numerous flip phones, some modern smart phones, even a few ragged-edge paperback books. It was so quiet, so damn quiet. And everything seemed to have a weird haze over it, like some cryptic fog layer was spread from the forest floor up to the tops of the trees, washing over everything to give it just a slightly diffused glimmer. The fogginess reminded him of the filter his brain had put over the memory of Joanie's beautiful face, but this filter wasn't meant to enhance the forest's beauty; it existed just to make it damn creepier.

The oppressive atmosphere in the woods only made him want to turn and run away from its insidiously foul air as fast as he could. He found it hard to believe that others accepted its dark embrace, welcomed its bleak promise of relief. Did the trees whisper to those people? Encourage them to do the dark deed? *Welcome, you've finally made it to where you belong. Join us. Spill your blood and let our roots drink it. Become one of us. You can rest now. Finally, you can breathe that last big sigh of relief and just rest.*

Then Lawrence felt a tingling sensation creep up the back of his neck. He felt his gaze being pulled upwards and he glanced up to see a row of crows perched on a branch, the dark birds staring down at him. They were about thirty feet off the ground, all sitting motionless along the same branch, their dark wings folded against their black bodies, their beady eyes all focused directly on him. A murder of crows. That was what a gathering of crows was called. A murder. There was a keenness to their stares, a knowing, an understanding of what this gloomy wooded place meant for those two-legged creatures who stumbled through its murky interior.

One of the birds suddenly took flight, the crow swooping down towards him. It flapped its wings furiously as it neared him, somehow managing to hover in front of Lawrence. The crow stared directly at him, looking intently into his eyes. Then, the black bird cawed loudly, a screeching cry that scared the shit out of him.

"What the fuck!" Lawrence shouted, startled by the bird's outburst, stumbling back a few steps and nearly tripping over a fallen branch.

The black bird rose back up into the air, rejoining the murder of crows still perched on the branch.

A short, chopping laugh made Lawrence spin about sharply.

"Ha," a mangy-haired man said, laughing at Lawrence's startled face. He was wearing a heavily-soiled, faded police uniform. A name badge was still pinned over his left breast, the name McCorver etched into the metal. McCorver was in his late forties, stern-faced, his faded uniform looking just a bit too big for his body as if it used to fit him in days long past but no longer did.

"What the fuck, man?" Lawrence stared at the guy nervously, doing a quick scan of his hands and body to see if he had any kind of weapon on him. He was still wearing his weapon's belt, but there was no gun in the holster. There was a baton stuck into his belt, but the cop did not seem intent on wielding it. His face was pale, as if his skin hadn't seen the sun in months, maybe even years. His hair was long, running past his shoulders, matted with dried leaves and mud. Lawrence looked at the man's corroded name badge. McCorver. The name seemed familiar, but Lawrence couldn't remember from when or where.

"They did the same thing to me the first time I came here," McCorver said. "They know you're not here to end it."

"How the hell do they know that?" Lawrence asked. He fought to still his wildly beating heart. The pale cop had really put a good scare into him.

"If you was going to end it, that crow would have pecked some of your face off to help you get started," McCorver said. "I saw that happen. Last time I seen them one of them birds got a chunk off some dude's cheek. Just ripped it right off with its beak." He made a gross gesture of chomping down on something and whipping his head wildly back and forth like he was some feral animal shaking its intended kill to death.

Lawrence scowled. "What?"

The pale officer stopped his wild head shaking, looked at Lawrence, then shrugged. "They just know. Fucking animals can sniff out that kind of shit. Just do your best to ignore the crows. If you fuck with them, they remember. And their offspring will remember. Don't know how they do it, but they pass that shit along to their damn chicks." He tapped at his head. "Crows are damn smart, man."

Lawrence said nothing.

McCorver nodded. "And if you think those are smart, wait till you see the big guy."

Lawrence scowled at the man. "The big guy?"

The pale officer nodded, with a bit more enthusiasm this time. "Yeah, the big guy." He waved his arm about, indicating their surroundings, the dark trees, the gloom. "The one who rules this place."

Lawrence froze for just a second, trying to digest what the cop had just said, then threw his hands up in a protective gesture. "Whoa, whoa. Wait a fucking minute, man." He squinted at the pale guy. "The one who rules this place? This place has some kind of fucking ruler? Like some kind of fucking king?"

The pale cop just laughed and started to move on, heading away from Lawrence.

"You really a cop?" Lawrence shouted after him.

McCorver stopped and turned back to face him. "No, I just dress like one on TV." The guy burst out with an hysterical staccato burst of laughter, as if he just told the funniest joke he had ever heard in his life. He turned away and started to move off again.

"Wait! Who are you? What are you doing in here?" Lawrence shouted after him. "I need your help."

The guy raised up a pale skinny hand. "Looking for strays."

Looking for strays? What the fuck did that mean? Lawrence watched him in silence for a moment; the guy clearly had mental issues. But then Lawrence took a quick step towards the retreating figure, raising up his hand. "Hold on, man! Let's stick together. I'm looking for somebody, too. We can look together."

"You're going in the wrong direction," the pale guy shouted back without turning around to look at him.

Lawrence watched the pale, baggy-uniformed officer walk away until he vanished into the dim gloom in the distance. "Well, that wasn't creepy as shit," he muttered out of the side of his mouth.

⋘⋖●⋗⋙

Lawrence looked back over his shoulder, but the convenience store was long gone, no longer visible. All he saw were thick rows of dark trees, each tree now suddenly taking on a human-like shape, each one becoming a personification of a lurking stranger danger as what little sunlight had been able to pierce the thick canopy above was now starting to fade. The oddball pseudo-cop he had encountered earlier was nowhere in sight, either.

He looked back towards the old trail, which was now barely more than a thin scuff mark a few feet wide, and kept moving. He thought of shouting out Joanie's name but the very thought of breaking the silence filled him with dread. If this place was filled with ghosts, he wanted to draw as little attention to himself as possible.

He spotted a yellow tent up ahead to his right. Someone had actually set up a fucking tent in Shadow Forest. As if they were thinking about ending it all but still gave themselves just that little inch of hope that maybe something will happen that will make them change their minds. Or was that tent just their personal mausoleum? Could be, he thought. Maybe they just wanted to hide from the world and close their eyes and never open them again. He stopped on the makeshift path as he drew level with the yellow tent; it was set up about five yards off the path on his right. The tent looked big enough to maybe sleep three people side by side. He wondered if there was more than one person dead in there.

And then Lawrence saw a shadowy shape move within the tent. He had thought it was just some weird trick of the fading daylight that made one part of the yellow tent seem so much darker than the rest, but he soon realized it was no trick of the light. There was something moving in the tent. Something alive. Something rather large.

"Son of a bitch," Lawrence said, exhaling the words through clenched teeth and a tight breath.

He started to walk again, trying not to make a

sound but his footsteps and the branches cracking under his weight now roared in his ears. He felt his chest tighten. It was hard to breathe. He wanted to look back but his fucking neck decided to stop working; it would only face straight ahead. He glanced down at the forest floor, thinking about picking up a tree branch and using it as a makeshift weapon, but he had no desire to touch anything in this place. He'd rather face whoever, or whatever, it was with his bare hands than hold a piece of this cursed forest in his fingers. His heart pounded in his chest. Had he really seen something in that yellow tent? Was it following him?

Then he saw Joanie up ahead. She was standing motionless in the middle of the trail, not even moving her head. He saw several crows perched in branches just above her; the dark feathered birds just stared at her, not moving at all, just keeping their beady eyes focused directly on her. He thought they all looked like they were ready to pounce at any moment and dive-bomb Joanie's face and peck away at her flesh with their hard beaks. He wanted to yell out to her, to warn her, but his fucking mouth wouldn't open. His lips stay clamped shut.

He quickened his pace and reached Joanie before the birds could launch their strike, moving around her to stand before her. She glanced up at him and his heart broke again. Tears were streaming down her face, the weird hazy fog of the forest making the droplets glimmer on her cheeks. He stood near her, still not touching her.

She looked away from him. "How can I go on?" she sobbed. "The memory of my daughter will never leave me, ever. Not for all eternity." She covered her face with her hands. "Oh my God. Not for all eternity."

He let her cry. He reached into his pocket and pulled out the newspaper clipping she had shown him but had forgotten to take back. He thought about giving it back to her, but then crumpled it up and tossed the balled-up chunk of paper into the woods where it vanished amidst a pile of leaf and branch debris. She would never get better if she had that constant reminder always in her face.

After a moment of soft sobbing, Joanie calmed herself, then angrily wiped at the tears muddying the make-up on her cheeks. She looked up at Lawrence. "Why are you here?"

"I came after you," Lawrence said.

"Why?" She wiped at her cheeks again.

He was quiet for a moment before answering. "You know why."

"No, tell me."

He answered immediately. "Because I love you, Joanie, you know that. I know I'm creepy and weird but I would never hurt you. Ever."

She hung her head. "Just let me die, please." There was no hope left in her tone, not even a hint of energy. She had given up, but was too tired to really fight him off.

He was quiet for a long moment. "How are you going to do it?" he finally asked, his voice soft, gentle.

She looked up groggily at him, her eyes streaked with red lightning bolts of deep misery. "What?"

"How... how are you going to... do it?"

She shrugged. "I've got pills."

"Did you take them already?"

She gave a barely perceptible shake of her head.

"Not yet."

"What kind of pills?" he asked.

"I don't know." She waved her hand impatiently. "Some opioid shit. I stole them from my neighbor's house. She's always stoned on them. Gets 'em by the truckload from that quack doctor in town."

"Can I see them?"

She dug into her front right jean's pocket and pulled something out, opening her palm to show him about a dozen white pills.

Lawrence was quiet for a long moment. "Umm, those are generic ibuprofen."

"What?" She glanced down at the white oval-shaped pills in her hand, then looked up at him. "Are you sure?"

He nodded. "Yes. One hundred percent." They weren't ibuprofen, but it was the first thing he had thought of.

She laughed a disgusted laugh. "I can't do anything right." She tipped her palm and let the white pills fall to the dark green forest floor.

He watched as more tears gushed out from the corners of her eyes. Those fucking amazing sky-blue eyes. He ached to touch her, to pull her to him, to comfort her, but his arms remained plastered to his sides as he watched her cry.

A loud crunching sound caused Lawrence to turn, and time froze for just the briefest of milliseconds, but it was enough time for Lawrence to get a full-on look at the big guy, the ruler of Shadow Forest. The ruler of Shadow Forest had a rat-like face but with a flattened snout tipped with moist black nostrils, its face covered in grey fur. Its glistening eyes appeared multi-faceted like a fly's eyes, the oily surfaces giving off a kaleidoscope of color. Its plump lips looked like they were made of living worms. It had a sleekly muscular, wolf-like body, covered in dark grey fur, with two legs ending in large, dark-grey-fur-covered paws. Its arms and hands appeared somewhat human-like, but devoid of any hair. What looked like stunted wings that seemed just decorative and not really functional were visible protruding from its fur-lined back.

Lawrence saw the creature's hands were covered in smooth, human-like flesh just a split second before one of those hands smacked painfully hard into his face with a powerful, stinging strike. The blow knocked him flat on his back. He hit the ground hard, grunting forcefully as the air was knocked out of his lungs; a piece of branch dug painfully into his back.

Lawrence shook off the pain, moving quickly to a sitting position, and looked over to see the creature standing before Joanie, staring at her. Then it did something quite foul and disgusting. It sprayed Joanie with some pungent liquid coming out of its mid-section. It moved its waist slightly back and forth and up and down, as if Joanie's body was a wall and it was trying to cover every inch of it with its putrid paint.

The big guy finished its task and turned its attention back to Lawrence, who was still sitting somewhat stunned on the ground, still somewhat in shock over what he was witnessing; his cheek flared with pain where the creature had struck him. The creature moved over to him on its two furry legs and stared down at him. It leaned down closer to Lawrence and Lawrence could see a million reflections of his own terrified face reflected in the creature's multi-faceted eyes. The creature shrieked an unearthly shriek at him, then rose back up and bounded off into the forest.

Lawrence didn't move for a long moment, remaining on the forest floor, staring off in the direction the creature had gone. Then, he regained his senses and quickly clambered to his feet.

Joanie still stood in the path, just as motionless as before. He thought she looked just as shocked and stunned as he felt. "I'm losing my fucking mind," she said.

He didn't say anything. His cheek continued to throb from where the creature had struck him.

"What the hell was that thing?" She glanced down at her soiled blouse and wet jeans. "Did it just spit on me or something?" She looked over to Lawrence. "Did that fucking thing just puke all over me?" She sniffed at her arm, then frowned heavily, scrunching her face up tight. "God, that's foul!"

"I don't know," he said. The odor coming off of her was thick and musky and quite pungent. Now was probably the best time to hug her and comfort her, he thought, but the stench of what the creature sprayed on her was immensely foul, keeping him at an arm's length from her. The odor was really quite horrendous. "We need to get the fuck out of here," he said.

She nodded. "What the hell was that thing?"

Lawrence shook his head. "I have no idea. It wasn't human, that's for sure."

They headed back out of the gloomy forest. Lawrence wasn't one hundred percent certain they were going the right way, but he did recognize a few of the discarded remnants he had seen earlier on the forest floor, so he felt pretty confident they were moving in the right direction. But now there was movement all around them. There were more crows in the trees now, all of them watching them, flying from tree to tree, growing in numbers, all of the black birds keeping pace with them. In the far distance on either side of them, he was pretty certain wolves were paralleling their movements as well, their numbers also growing. Much closer to them than the wolves, rats scurried along the forest floor, also obviously following them, also growing in numbers.

What the fuck were they doing? Lawrence wondered. He quickened his pace and Joanie matched his speed, both of them beyond ready to exit this accursed place.

The animals continued to trail them, paralleling their movements to exactly match their pace.

Then up ahead they both saw the outline of the convenience store in the distance. Without saying a word to each other, they both broke out into a run, racing towards the edge of the forest, sprinting towards what they both thought was going to be safety.

"What is this place?" Joanie asked, taking in the twin bed, the refrigerator, the sink nearby, the glass-walled shower stall on the far end of the room.

"I live here," Lawrence said.

"Under the store?"

Lawrence nodded. "Makes it so much easier to

open and close."

"So you own the store?" Joanie asked.

"Yeah, one hundred percent. My great grandparents started it back in the late 1800's as a general store. We just upgraded it over the years to make it more modern. I took it over when my Dad died a few years ago."

"That's pretty cool."

He looked at her with the hint of a frown.

"Not that your Dad died, I mean. Jeez. That you run it, I meant."

He nodded, giving her a soft smile. "Yeah."

They stood awkwardly in silence, looking sheepishly at each other, then looking away. The silence lingered and the awkwardness thickened.

"Hey, remember that time in eighth grade when we played spin the bottle?" Lawrence asked, desperate to break through the deepening silence between them.

Joanie was quiet for a moment, clearly trying to remember, but not succeeding. "Ah, sorry, but I don't."

"Oh," he said, clearly crestfallen. He'd been replaying that kiss in his mind for a dozen years, but he wasn't about to admit that to her now. Especially because that encounter was clearly not even a blip on her memory radar.

"Why are you asking that?"

He shrugged, trying to be casual but looking stiff and awkward instead. "Because I cheated."

"You cheated?"

"I stopped it with my knee and forced it to point at you."

"You did?"

He nodded.

"Did you... kiss me?" she asked, her voice hesitant.

That was the ultimate blow to his heart. She couldn't even recall if they had kissed or not, while the memory of her mouth pressed against his still made his lips tingle with the ghostly remembrance of it. Lawrence pointed to the shower in the back of the room. "I think you need to get cleaned up. No offense, but you really stink. I've got some freshly laundered sweatpants and some t-shirts you can wear." He pointed to a pile of folded clothes on a nearby table. "Anything in there is clean. I just washed them."

Joanie looked over at the clear glass door that let into the beige tile-lined shower. "Kind of right out there in the open, isn't it?"

At first, Lawrence frowned at her question, then he realized what she was talking about. "Oh, shit. Yeah, sorry. It used to have a frosted door, but it got a crack in it and it was cheaper to get a clear replacement." He shrugged at his own excuse. "I can throw a blanket over it or something."

Joanie was quiet, then threw her hand out dismissively. "Ah, fuck it. I was going to kill myself a half hour ago." She grunted out a laugh. "What the fuck difference does it make now?" She started to unbutton her wet pink blouse.

Lawrence quickly stepped away from her, nervously clearing his throat. "Hey, I'll go up into the store and see what kind of snacks I got." He looked over at the stairs that led back up into the store. He slowly started to move away from her. "Just come up when you're ready." He pointed to a clothes hamper near the washer and dryer combo on the far side of the room. "Just throw them in the hamper over there."

She smiled softly at him and unbuttoned another button on her soiled blouse. "One of those wrinkled three-days-old hot dogs sounds pretty delicious right about now."

He nodded. "Okay, but they're always fresh. One hundred percent fresh. Just so you know. I don't let them sit for three days."

She smiled and unbuttoned another button on her blouse.

Lawrence smiled awkwardly back at her, continuing to walk backwards away from her. His feet hit the bottom of the stairs and he nearly tripped over himself, but then quickly turned to face the sanctuary of the stairs and bound up them.

Lawrence suspected something was deeply wrong when he saw the crows circling the convenience store. He stood near the convenience store window, staring through the glass up into the sky. First off, since when do crows circle like vultures? But that's exactly what they were doing. There must have been twenty or thirty of them, all slowly circling above the store.

He should have known something else was severely wrong when the five wolves came padding up to the edge of the forest, eyes ablaze with a feral heat. There was a clear leader of the pack, a muscular brown-furred wolf with patches of black hair; he led the others who were flanked two on either side of him, the four wolves moving behind him. Lawrence didn't know what kind of wolves they were. Gray wolves, red wolves, or some other unknown species of wolf, but he knew it didn't matter what kind of wolves they were; it was enough to know that all of them had crazed looks in their eyes as if there were some demented intelligence behind them.

Lawrence looked up at the birds as a few newer arrivals fluttered down to a branch, then moved his gaze back towards the wolves. A quick flurry of movement on the ground just outside the store near a cement parking block drew his attention. Several rats scurried along the pavement, keeping their gazes locked on him as he watched them move. He looked back up to the crows. What the hell were they all doing?

And then the answer hit him with the force of a sledgehammer, making his knees go weak for just a split second, the shock nearly making him stumble. He knew what the creature had been doing to Joanie. The ruler of Shadow Forest had marked her. It had put its scent on her. It had staked a claim on her. And now it was sending its minions to track her down and bring her back. He didn't know how he knew that, but he was pretty confident that's exactly what they were doing.

"I'm ready," he heard Joanie say from behind him.

The sound of her voice startled him, but he quickly regained his composure. He turned halfway around to glance at her, and froze.

Joanie was wearing one of his flannel shirts, the red and brown one, pinching it closed with one hand. Her long slender legs were visible, as were her petite bare feet. Her hair was still wet, glistening with moisture. She released her hold on the shirt and the edges separated, giving him a glimpse of her breasts and her dark pubic hair.

Lawrence felt a nervous flutter beat against the inside of his chest. "I..." he started to say, but stopped as he felt compelled to turn back to look outside at the wolves sitting eerily just beyond the edges of the parking lot, the fur on their bodies shifting in patterns of darkness and light as the fading sun filtered through the leaves of the trees that towered up on the edges of Shadow Forest. He glanced up at the crows roosting on nearby branches and light poles; there already appeared to be quite a few more of the black birds watching the store than there was just moments ago.

He looked back at Joanie to see her slowly walking towards him, her bare feet making just the softest pattering sound on the tiled floor as she drew close. She stopped before him and reached out her hand towards him as if to take his fingers into hers.

Lawrence wrinkled his nose at the stench still emanating from her body. It was not as overpoweringly strong as earlier, but she was still very pungent; the smell had the sharp acrid bite of vomit.

She dropped her hand away from him, frowning. "Do I still stink?"

He didn't answer right away.

She turned her head and sniffed at the flannel shirt near her shoulder. "I just smell fragrance softener."

"I..." Lawrence looked away from her, trying to stop his face from scrunching up into a grimace. "I'm sorry. You really reek."

"Oh my God," Joanie exclaimed as she noticed the wolves and the crows lurking outside. "What the hell are they doing?"

Lawrence followed her gaze outside to the wolves

sitting patiently at the edge of the mostly empty parking lot; only his car was parked in the lot as Joanie had taken an Uber to the store what seemed like weeks ago, but had only been a few hours ago. He turned back to Joanie. "I… don't know," he said, but the words came out with no conviction whatsoever.

Joanie stared at him. "Yes you do," she said.

Lawrence was quiet for a moment. "I think it marked you. That thing in the forest."

"You think it marked me? Like it peed on me or something?"

Lawrence nodded. "I don't know technically if it was peeing on you. I do think it was marking you. Claiming you." He wondered if the noxious chemical the creature had sprayed on Joanie had actually seeped into her skin. Was the smell permanent? She really still did stink quite strongly, even after she showered.

"Claiming me?"

Lawrence nodded softly. "Yeah." He pointed to the wolves at the edge of the parking lot, then up at the crows perched on numerous different branches and light poles. "I think they're here to watch you, or maybe somehow bring you back into the forest."

Joanie scowled. "Claiming me for what?"

Lawrence said nothing. More questions kept scrolling through his mind. Did the thing in the forest need to breed? Did it want to create offspring? Or was it just saving Joanie for a midnight snack because it had already eaten its fill earlier of some other hapless victim?

Joanie raised her hand up to sniff at the back of it. Her face puckered up into a grimace. "Fuck, I do stink. You really think that fucking thing marked me?"

Lawrence shrugged, but also gave her a little bit of a nod. He glanced at the lurking wolves and birds outside. "I think they can smell you."

Joanie stared out at the wolves, then glanced up to look at the crows. Then she turned sharply to look at Lawrence. "Shit, call somebody," Joanie said. "Call the fucking police or something." She indicated the animals outside with a toss of her hand as her voice become more insistent. "Or animal fucking control, or whoever can get rid of them."

Just then, as if on cue, a dark shape moved into view outside the store, coming from the left side of the front door, momentarily startling both of them.

Joanie leaped nearly a foot back away from the door in surprised fright. "Shit!"

The dark shape was police officer McCorver. A knock sounded at the front door of the store as the officer in the heavily soiled police uniform rapped on the glass.

"It's a cop." There was genuine excitement and relief in Joanie's face. "Let him in. Let him in."

Lawrence frowned at the sight of their visitor. "Don't get your hopes up," Lawrence said. He moved to the front door and unlocked it.

The bell hanging above the front door jangled as McCorver entered the convenience store. "What are you two kids up to?" officer McCorver asked, his gaze raking up and down Joanie's half-clad body. He smiled knowingly at them, resting his hand on his empty holster.

Joanie clutched at the flannel shirt, pinching it closed again.

Then McCorver wrinkled his nose, ever so slightly, and the amusement on his face quickly turned into a countenance laced with deep concern. He frowned at Joanie. "Excuse us, miss," McCorver said. "I need to speak to this young man privately for a moment."

Lawrence sighed heavily at McCorver. "Now what?"

"We need to talk." McCorver glanced at Joanie, then back to Lawrence. "Privately."

Lawrence frowned at the man, but then motioned for him to follow him towards the back of the store where the stairs that led down to his apartment were located.

***

"You have to take her back in there!" McCorver said to Lawrence. They were standing in Lawrence's apartment located beneath the convenience store.

"Keep your voice down," Lawrence admonished the man. "She's gonna hear you."

"You have to bring her back!"

Lawrence shook his head abruptly. "No!"

"You're disturbing the balance of things," the pale ex-cop said.

"What the hell are you talking about?" Lawrence asked, his jaw tight, his words hissing through his clenched teeth.

"She's a stray." McCorver took a step towards Lawrence, lowering his voice, but keeping the insistence strong in his tone. "You have to bring her back into Shadow Forest," the distraught former cop said.

"No. I don't."

"Yes. You do."

"What is this balance?" Lawrence asked. "What the hell are you talking about?"

McCorver gave Lawrence a serious look. "You know damn well the suicidals are their food. You're smart enough to figure that one out. That's what they feed on. They won't allow themselves to starve to death. The constant source of nourishment is what's keeping them contained inside those woods." McCorver frowned. "Once they understand the bounty that awaits them just a few miles away in Campborough, they'll never need to come back here. If they step out of Shadow Forest and complete a successful hunt, there will be no way to prevent them from spreading out wider and wider."

Lawrence just scowled at the pale cop.

McCorver slowly shook his head. "If the animals that live in those woods follow a stray out and they get a taste of human flesh beyond the borders of Shadow Forest, there will be no stopping them. I can't let that happen. My friends live in Campborough." McCorver stared hard at Lawrence. "She needs to go back in there. Now."

Lawrence just stared back at the cop, absorbing the new information. He hadn't known that at all. The animals in Shadow Forest were dependent on suicidals for their food? At first blush, that notion was completely crazy, but the more he thought about it, the more he believed it could actually make sense. He had read enough stories about lions and bears and sharks eating human beings to know that animals could truly acquire a taste for human flesh. Lawrence looked intently at McCorver. What else did the guy know about what was going on in the forest?

"She has to go back," McCorver said.

"You want me to bring Joanie back into that forest so some animals can feed on her?" Lawrence shook his head sharply. "No fucking way am I going to do that."

"Then I'll have to do it," McCorver said quickly, matter-of-factly. "She's already marked. I smelled her the second I got close to her. He can probably already smell her a mile away. He won't stop hunting her until he has her." McCorver pointed out in the direction he knew the parking lot lay without even looking in that direction. "Why do you think all your little friends are waiting outside?"

Lawrence looked at McCorver for a moment. "You keep saying '*he*.' You know all about the thing in the forest, don't you? You know it lives in there. What the hell is it?"

McCorver shook his head. "I don't know exactly what he is." Then he nodded his head. "Yes, I've seen him before a few times. When I was a real cop. Back when I had to go into the forest to try and find some suicidals' corpses. But I have no idea what he is." He shook his head again. "I actually thought he might've been an honest-to-God Bigfoot the first time I saw him."

"Why didn't you gather up a SWAT team or something and take the damn thing out when you first saw it?" Lawrence asked.

McCorver shook his head. "I'm not telling anyone I think I saw Bigfoot in Shadow Forest. I'd be in psych evals for months if I did that." He was suddenly very quiet for a moment. "Wait. Maybe I did tell somebody that." He shook his head again. "No thanks." McCorver suddenly patted at the pockets in his faded uniform pants and on the breast of his soiled uniform shirt. "I seemed to have lost my meds."

Lawrence was quiet for a moment. The guy was clearly having problems with his muddled thoughts. He turned the focus back to the creature from Shadow Forest. "Why didn't that thing just take Joanie right then and there? It could have just taken her right there. It was right on top of her. If all she's good for is a meal, then why didn't it just kill her and eat her?"

McCorver shook his head. "I don't know. He probably wasn't hungry at the time, but he knew he'd be hungry later." He patted at his pockets for a few more seconds, then stopped.

"Or maybe it's not looking at her as food," Lawrence said. "Maybe it wants her for something else."

McCorver squinted at him. "Like what?"

Lawrence made a disbelieving gesture at McCorver. "Really? I need to spell that one out for you?"

McCorver was quiet for a moment, then shook his head. "It doesn't matter. He marked her. She's his now. Strays are not allowed to leave the forest."

Lawrence shook his head. "She's mine now." He gritted his teeth, curling his lips. "One hundred percent mine, you understand? She's finally mine now and I intend to keep it that way. I will do whatever it takes to keep her safe."

McCorver cocked his head, suddenly looking at Lawrence with keen intent.

The cop's intense stare made Lawrence feel uncomfortable. "What?" he snapped at the man.

McCorver continued to stare at him. "I know you," he finally said. "Lawrence Malroney. I issued you a restraining order. You were to keep at least several hundred feet between you and Joanie Huffman." McCorver paused. "I thought you two looked a little familiar." He slowly shook his head. "That was a long time ago."

Lawrence looked away. He didn't recognize the grizzled cop, but the name McCorver flashed through his head and now he remembered where he had seen that name before. On his doorstep. Right before the cop wearing the name badge with McCorver on it had shoved a piece of paper holding a court order in his face.

McCorver squinted sternly at Lawrence. "What are you going to do? Keep her trapped in the store? Make her your little sex slave?"

Lawrence said nothing.

McCorver took a step back, a hint of disbelief etching his features. "Holy shit," he muttered. "That's exactly what you're thinking, isn't it?"

"I saved her life," Lawrence said. "She owes me."

McCorver grunted out a laugh. "Sure, she owes you. But she doesn't owe you the rest of her life."

"Why not? She was just going to throw it all away." Lawrence lifted his head triumphantly. "But I stopped her."

"So you're putting a claim on her, too?" McCorver asked.

Lawrence straightened his shoulders a little more and raised his chin defiantly. "Maybe I will."

"Maybe you and the king of Shadow Forest can duke it out for her." McCorver raised a pointed finger. "You have only one guess where you think I'd put my money." Then McCorver once again pointed out in the direction he knew the parking lot lay without looking towards it. "I think your little friends outside there would take offense to your claim."

Lawrence folded his arms across his chest. "They can't get in here."

McCorver scowled at him. "So you're just going to hole up in your store and never go out? You're never going to leave the premises?"

"I've got enough food in the store to last years in here," Lawrence said.

McCorver was silent for a moment, staring at him. "You're serious?" McCorver looked hard at Lawrence. "Jesus, you *are*. You are one hundred percent damn crazy serious."

The doorbell jangled and both men froze for just a brief second.

Lawrence's face darkened with guilty anguish. "Joanie." And then his face filled with an even deeper anguish. "Shit, I didn't re-lock the door when you came in," he said to McCorver as he raced past him and bolted for the stairs.

<hr/>

The king of Shadow Forest stood tall just inside the entrance to the convenience store, the creature reaching nearly six and a half feet in height. It stood mostly motionless; only its head moved left and right, its head tilting ever so slightly from side to side, as if it were trying to understand its surroundings. Then the creature stopped moving its head and focused its attention, staring directly at Joanie.

Joanie stood just as motionless a few yards away,

clutching the flannel shirt to her breast.

Lawrence charged forward from the back of the store, dashing up to Joanie's side. The creature made an unearthly snarling sound as Lawrence raced up the main aisle, but the shadowy king of the dark forest made no move to attack him.

Lawrence skidded to a stop next to Joanie, his shoes squeaking on the tiled floor as he came to an abrupt stop. He stared at the creature, trying to take it all in.

The creature's head was rat-like, but it looked like a rat's head that had been squeezed and compressed in a vice to flatten its black nose and snout so that they only protruded out a few more inches than a human's nose did. Its multi-faceted eyes were dark, reflecting any light that fell on them. Two nematode worms wriggled in place on the lower part of its face, if one could even call it a face, the worms emulating the lips of a closed human mouth, their long and slender bodies pressed tightly together.

Beyond its rat-like head, its multi-faceted bug-eyes, its furry torso and legs, the nubs of its stunted wings, and its gnarled human hands, the king of Shadow Forest appeared to be some twisted amalgam of every animal and insect drawn to human corpses. Lawrence scowled and grimaced at the creature. The damn thing smelled like a corpse because it was made up of everything that fed on a corpse.

Flies buzzed about its chest and abdomen and legs, moving so fast and in thick bunches that it was hard to focus on any one fly. Fly maggots squirmed about on its chest fur, their tiny white bodies slithering in and around the creature's tufts of fur. Beetles crawled through the creature's fur, moving around and sometimes right over the squirming maggots. Tineid moths, dull and dusty brown colored, fluttered about its fur, flitting from strands of hair to strands of hair. Between the squirming fly maggots, the crawling beetles, and the fluttering moths, the creature's surface beneath its fur appeared to be in constant movement as if the insects themselves were interwoven parts of its layer of skin. Numerous areas on the creature's body also seemed to have saprotrophic fungi and ammonia fungi spread throughout its fur in random patches, as if the creature was moldy and decaying where it stood. Its human-like arms seemed to be covered with visible bacteria, the flesh taking on a moist sheen as what appeared to be waves of bacteria moved up and down over its skin.

Both Lawrence and Joanie were frozen to the spot. All they could do was stare with disbelief at this inhuman thing that was standing silently before them just a few feet away. It wasn't snarling at them. It wasn't growling at them. Its human-shaped arms were placidly down at its sides.

The creature again glanced about the store, even turning its head nearly completely around to glance back out at Shadow Forest visible in the distance; it seemed apparent that the creature was still somewhat confused by its surroundings, as if it had never left the confines of the woods before and didn't really understand where it was.

Then the creature focused again on Joanie. It leaned in slightly and sniffed at Joanie's face with its flattened black nose. It immediately started to make a terribly discomforting purring sound. It raised its left hand towards Joanie's face, its fingers splayed as if it might be intending to caress her face.

A thin yellow stream suddenly splashed onto Joanie, hitting her in the mid-section, the liquid soaking into the flannel shirt she was wearing as well as splashing down to hit on the tops of her bare thighs and dribble down her exposed legs.

The creature reared back, pulling its hand quickly away from Joanie.

Joanie whipped her head towards Lawrence to see him holding his penis in his hand and spraying her with his urine.

Lawrence looked very sheepishly at Joanie. "I'm sorry, I'm sorry, I'm sorry," he said, continuing to move his penis left and right, shaking his hips a little.

"Son of a bitch, Lawrence!" Joanie yelled at him. She tried to shuffle away from Lawrence, but he kept his aim true and the stream continued to hit her, splashing along her side.

"I'm sorry, I'm sorry," Lawrence said yet again. He finished and shoved his penis back into his jeans and zipped up. "I couldn't think of anything else."

Joanie glared at him. "Seriously?" She glanced up and down her body, indicating the wet yellow-tinted trails with an exasperated tossing of her hands.

Lawrence turned to face the creature square on.

The creature stared at Joanie with its kaleidoscope bug-eyes, stepping closer to her on its darkly-furred paws. It sniffed at her chest, sniffing at her urine-soaked flannel shirt. Then the creature roared angrily at Joanie, the worms separating but staying connected at the ends of their bodies to form a mouth-like hole in its face, the creature somehow able to make a resounding screech with whatever components in its body gave it the power to make sound.

Joanie reached out and grabbed Lawrence's hand. He squeezed her hand back, pulling her closer to him. The touch of her skin on his was electrifying and he had to focus all his attention on not being overwhelmed by the sensation of her flesh touching his flesh.

Then the creature repeated its horrid screech, focusing its full sonic blast straight at Lawrence.

Lawrence and Joanie held their ground, their heads up, their faces defiant.

Then the creature raised its head and sniffed at Joanie's face. It made that same terribly discomforting purring sound as if it still smelled its marking scent on her.

"Give me some more," Joanie said sharply, but keeping her voice low. She tugged her hand away from Lawrence to free it from his grip, and then thrust her cupped hands out towards Lawrence's crotch area.

"Some more what?"

Joanie shook her fingers. "Some more of what you just soaked me with. I think he's still smelling his mark on me." She cast a cautious sideways glance at the creature.

Lawrence was still dumbfounded. "What?"

"Jesus," Joanie said with a sharp exhale. "Just pull your dick out and piss in my hands, goddammit," she hissed sharply through clenched teeth.

Lawrence stared at her a moment before speaking. "I never thought in a billion billion years you would ever say that to me," Lawrence said. He gave her a tilt of his head accompanied by a dreamy smile. "Or anything even close to that."

"Just shut up, you smitten lunkhead. Now get a

good grip on that bad boy and give me a strong spray." She threw her hands out, again cupping them in front of Lawrence's crotch.

The king of Shadow Forest stood motionless, just watching them. It made no move to attack.

"Why doesn't it attack us?" Lawrence asked, keeping his voice at a low whisper.

"I don't know. Just give it to me!" Joanie snapped at him.

Lawrence unzipped his pants, dug into his jeans, and withdrew his penis.

The creature emitted a low growl, but just continued to watch.

Lawrence froze for just a brief moment at the noise the creature made, but then pulled his penis out a little further when he saw that the creature was still not moving into an obvious attack position. He held his penis over Joanie's cupped hands. Nothing came out. No trickle. No dribble. Not even a drop.

"Come on, man," Joanie said. "Give it to me!"

Lawrence grimaced, clearly struggling with the task. "I... can't," Lawrence grunted.

"Stage fright?"

"Not stage fright." Lawrence said and glanced down at his stiffening penis.

Joanie followed his gaze and quickly jumped back away from him. "Whoa, whoa!"

"It's your fault," Lawrence said, with just a touch of a whine in his voice.

"My fault?"

"You can't say shit like *'come on, man, give it to me'* and not expect it to affect me."

Joanie frowned at him. "For real, dude? Do you not fucking see what is standing right in front of us?"

she asked, again hissing sharply through clenched teeth, struggling to keep her voice down.

Lawrence didn't say anything.

She glanced down at his crotch area, then looked away. "Uhh, you can put that useless thing back now."

Lawrence looked sheepish and turned his body away from her, struggling to put himself back in place in his jeans. "It's not useless," he muttered.

The creature remained still, its bug-eyes focusing on them; the insect life fluttered and squirmed about its body, moving in and around its fur. It raised a hand, reaching towards Joanie's face again with fingers that appeared to be crawling with massively oversized bacteria.

Joanie slapped the creature's hand and the creature dropped its arm back to its side. "Not a chance, motherfucker." She quickly made a disgusted face and wiped her hand on her urine-soaked shirt, then made another disgusted grimace as she realized what she was doing.

"Oh, shit," Lawrence whispered, eyeing the creature nervously, not sure how it would react to Joanie's slap.

But the creature still did not appear as if it felt the need to attack them.

Joanie grabbed a side of her wet flannel shirt and twisted the fabric, siphoning some liquid from the damp cloth as best she could into her hands. She raised her moist hands up and paused for just a second. "Fuck it." Then she smeared the wetness all over her face, all over her head, running her wet fingers through her hair. She slowly looked back at the creature and gave it her best nasty snarl.

Lawrence appeared back at her side, now holding a stainless steel, two-foot-long fork in front of him, brandishing it before him like a weapon. He had quickly retreated over to the counter area while Joanie had been getting ready to wipe some of his urine in her face and in her hair, and had grabbed the long metal utensil.

Joanie stepped closer to Lawrence, clutching at his arm. "Is that a hot dog fork?" Joanie asked.

"Is that my pee you just wiped on my shirt?" Lawrence asked as he glanced down at his dampened clothing.

Joanie ignored his question. She glanced over at the hot dog machine behind a nearby counter, seeing several glistening frankfurters slowly turning in the grill area of the machine. "Are those ready yet? I'm so fucking hungry, right now."

"Seriously?" Lawrence said. He made an exaggerated tilt of his head towards the creature standing a mere few feet away from them.

"Yeah, seriously." She glanced longingly at the hot dogs. "I haven't eaten for like a full day and a half now. I'm fucking starving."

Lawrence disentangled himself from her grasp. He wondered if she was in some sort of weird state of disbelief and shock. Now was obviously not the time to worry about getting some food. "Just stay here."

Joanie pointed over to the hot dog machine. "I think I'd be safer over there." She headed towards the twirling frankfurters, disobeying his order.

"Stay here." Lawrence snatched at her arm to try and stop her, but he just grabbed at air as she quickly moved out of his reach. He watched her go, disbelieving, but that moment didn't last long as the creature started to snarl. Lawrence turned back to face the creature, shaking his hot dog fork at it.

The creature looked at the retreating Joanie, then turned to stare at Lawrence. The squirming maggots roaming through its fur stopped moving. The flies stopped flitting about its fur and landed. The beetles were suddenly motionless. The tiny moths also stopped flapping their little wings and landed on the creature's fur.

Was it finally getting ready to attack? Maybe it was so used to docile suicidals just giving it what it wanted that it didn't know how to react when someone resisted it? And then Lawrence lunged suddenly at the creature, thrusting forward with a vicious thrust of the hot dog fork, aiming to bury the sharp prongs in the creature's chest. But the creature reacted quickly, moving parts of its body aside so Lawrence's thrusting fork hit nothing but the air pocket it had just created in the middle of its body. Lawrence tried to pull the fork back out, but the creature closed the air pocket before Lawrence could completely remove his weapon from it and the creature gripped the edges of the hot dog fork with a ferociously firm grip. Lawrence tugged hard on the wooden handle but he couldn't wrench the fork free from the creature's grasp. He let go of the hot dog fork and stepped back away from the creature. The fork disappeared within the creature, as if the creature had now decided to make the utensil part of its haphazardly constructed body.

The creature narrowed its eyes, which was a very unsettling sight because it looked as if every individual facet that comprised its eyes had narrowed nearly simultaneously in quick succession. Its human hands curled, forming what looked more like deliberate claws than a failed attempt at making fists.

Lawrence had a feeling the creature was now finally really getting pissed off. He quickly glanced about the store. He needed some other weapon. Something to fend off the creature glaring at him with its big bug eyes. He froze for a second. Bug spray. That's what he needed. Bug spray and a lighter. Bug spray was in aisle two on the second shelf from the bottom. And there was a rotating display rack of lighters near the cash register. "Hey, Joanie."

"Yeah?" she said, her voice a bit muffled.

Lawrence looked over to Joanie to see her mouth full of hot dog, the other half of the frankfurter clutched in her hand. "Did you even wash your hands first?" he asked.

Joanie's body went still for a brief second. She glanced at the hot dog in her hand, then back at Lawrence. She opened her mouth as if to say something, but she was still chewing on the hot dog so nothing came out.

"Forget it." Lawrence waved off her response before she could speak. "I'm going to make a dash into aisle two. When I come back over here I need you to throw me a lighter. They're on that rack right over there by the register.

Joanie shot a glance over at the register, saw the display rack of zodiac-themed lighters, then looked back to Lawrence. "Okay. Which one?"

Lawrence exhaled a tight breath. "It doesn't matter. Any one."

"Okay."

"Now!" Lawrence shouted as he burst away from the creature, sprinting towards aisle two.

"Shit!" Joanie exclaimed, shoving the other half of the hot dog in her mouth. "You didn't give me a countdown!" she shouted back at him through a mouthful of food.

"Just get the fucking lighter!" Lawrence shouted. He raced into aisle two, then went into a feet-first slide, gliding along the tiled floor, grabbing a can of bug spray as he slid past, then quickly getting back up to his feet.

Joanie lurched towards the front counter, reaching for a lighter, inadvertently knocking several of them to the counter and to the floor. She snatched at one of the fallen lighters that landed on the counter.

Lawrence raced around the end of aisle two and came charging back up aisle one, moving back in the direction of the creature, uncapping the bug spray as he ran, tossing the plastic lid to the ground. He gripped the can of bug spray tightly in his right hand and held out his empty hand towards Joanie, raising his arm up. "Toss it!"

Joanie tossed the lighter and it sailed smoothly right into Lawrence's open hand as he skidded to a stop. Lawrence gripped the lighter, flicked on a flame, and depressed the trigger button on the bug spray. A streaming spray of fire erupted before him, the lighter flame igniting the flammable bug-killing juice.

The stream of fire hit the creature in the left arm, singeing its flesh.

Lawrence swept the can across his body, keeping the lighter flame lit, sending a fanning arc of fire across the creature's chest.

The creature burst into flames, emitting an ear-piercing shriek of pain and rage. The air filled with the acrid stench of burning fur and the smell of burning flesh. Lawrence could hear some of the beetles cracking and popping, their frying shells making sounds similar to oil hitting a hot skillet. Clumps of flies and moths decamped from the creature, hovering closely about the creature but staying away from the deadly fire.

Lawrence looked down at the zodiac lighter he held in his hand. "Leo," he said. "Nice." He looked up and glanced over at Joanie. "How did you know?"

Suddenly McCorver was there, spraying the burning creature with a fire extinguisher. "Long live the king!" McCorver shouted. The ex-cop clutched the small extinguisher by its handle, waving the thin hose back and forth to fully coat the burning parts on the creature in a white foam. The spray also hit some of the moths and flies, knocking them away from the creature, sending some of them into a death spiral towards the floor.

"What the fuck?" Lawrence yelled back.

"I told you strays are not allowed to leave the forest," McCorver said. He turned the fire extinguisher on Lawrence, pointing the nozzle at him. "Now hand her over. She has to go back."

"She's not a stray!" Lawrence said, blurting it out. "The crows didn't attack her. They knew she wasn't going to do it. Just like you said. The crows didn't attack me or her. You said they could sniff out a true suicidal. They didn't attack her." He raised a hand and pointed a finger at McCorver. "You have to let her go."

McCorver was still for a long moment, clutching the fire extinguisher, still aiming the nozzle at Lawrence. "The king marked her. She belongs to him now."

The king of Shadow Forest, its body still smoldering slightly but no longer ablaze, moved up to Joanie. It sniffed her with its flattened black nose, moving its head up and down over the front of her body. The flies and moths fluttered about the creature's body; the surviving beetles and maggots resumed their squirming and scurrying.

Lawrence quickly moved to Joanie's side, pulling her against him. "She's mine!" Lawrence said defiantly. The creature sniffed at Lawrence, then snarled at him. Lawrence snarled and growled right back at it. "She's mine now. Go back to wherever it was you came from."

The creature rose up to its full height and stared down at Lawrence and Joanie with its scorched and singed bug-eyes. Then the king abruptly turned and exited the store.

McCorver watched the creature move away, then looked back at Lawrence. "You may have won this little skirmish over your little friend." He glanced at Joanie, then looked back to Lawrence. "But be warned this may not be over. Your stupid and stubborn actions have shown the king that he can survive outside the forest. He may want to put that to the test again someday if he isn't satisfied with what Shadow Forest brings him." He raised the fire extinguisher up, then abruptly dropped the fire extinguisher from his hands as if he was simulating a mic drop. He turned away from them and silently followed the creature out.

Outside the Malroney's Market convenience store,

the parking lot was empty but for Lawrence's car parked on the far edge of the lot adjacent to Shadow Forest. Lawrence opened the passenger-side door, helping a frail-looking young man out of the car. "This is the place," Lawrence said.

The man clambered out of the car and stood silently as he faced the dark woods before him. "This is Shadow Forest?" he asked. He looked to be in his early twenties, his blond hair askew, his face holding a hint of stubble. His eyes were sunken, darkly hollow.

Lawrence nodded at the man.

"This is where... people go... to..."

"Yes," Lawrence answered. "Many people come to... rest here."

The frail young man nodded. "I just don't want to... die alone."

"Oh, you won't," Lawrence said confidently. "I'm one hundred percent sure of that. You won't be alone. Shadow Forest is filled with hundreds of... ghosts. Thousands even."

"You've seen them?"

Lawrence nodded softly. "Oh, yes, I've seen them. Lots of them. They're everywhere in there. You'll see." He patted the frail young man on the back.

The part-time job Lawrence had picked up manning the phones on the suicide hotline was proving out to be very fruitful. He was very careful not to say anything incriminating when anyone called in because he knew the calls were being recorded, but he did take careful handwritten notes on who he thought might be a good candidate for Shadow Forest, then called them back on cheap burner phones that couldn't be traced. The blond guy had a much younger look than Lawrence had visualized from his deep voice when he had taken the guy's call on the suicide prevention hotline. It had taken a little bit of convincing when he called the guy back, but Lawrence finally got the guy to agree to let him pick him up and bring him to Shadow Forest. "When I'm ready to go," Lawrence told him, "this is where I'm going, too."

"Really?" The guy sounded apprehensive and unsure.

Lawrence nodded. "One hundred percent."

The guy appeared genuinely pleased with Lawrence's answer.

"You have what you need?" Lawrence asked.

The guy patted at what was clearly a syringe in his thin pants pocket. He just nodded.

"Okay, good." Lawrence put a hand on the guy's back and gently prodded him towards the dark trees. "It's time to put this crummy, unfair world behind you and embrace the next."

The young man nodded meekly. He moved forward and did not hesitate as he entered the murky woods.

Lawrence turned away from the dusky woods of Shadow Forest and walked towards the convenience store, emitting a softly happy little whistle as he neared the store. A CLOSED FOR REMODELING sign was visible on the front door of the store, the words facing out. The scene around the store was quiet, serene. There were no wolves lurking in the woods watching the store from a distance. There were no rats scurrying about the parking lot. There were no crows perched atop tree branches, nor were there any of the black birds perched on any of the parking lot light poles.

Behind Lawrence, the shadowy forest of fear brooded in the fading night. The elderly woman he had just brought to the woods had already disappeared into the gloom. Deeper within the trees, a set of multi-faceted eyes glinted in the twilight.

Lawrence entered the convenience store, locking the door behind him. He moved to the back of the store and headed down the stairs to his apartment, still whistling a happy little tune.

"Is it okay for me to come out yet?" Joanie asked as Lawrence descended the stairs. She sat on the bed in Lawrence's apartment beneath the store, dressed in one of Lawrence's flannel shirts and nothing else.

Lawrence shook his head as he moved across the room and sat down next to her. "Not yet," he replied. Seeing Joanie Huffman sitting on his bed erased the last fifteen years of Lawrence Malroney's life. This was his fresh chance to start over with her. With his sweet Joanie. The girl he had been in love with ever since eighth grade. He wasn't going to let anything spoil it. He reached over and gave her a kiss on the cheek. "Not yet."

"Do you have to mark me again?" she asked, her voice softly hesitant but with a hint of anticipation at his answer.

Lawrence nodded his head, feeling himself start to stiffen in his loins. "I'm afraid so."

Joanie nodded acceptingly. "Do you really think that thing is still looking for me after all this time? It's been months."

Lawrence nodded. "I think he is. I think he still

can smell his scent on you sometimes. He still has those damn crows and wolves watching the store. I think I saw some rats staking out the store just now, too, if you can believe that shit. They're everywhere. It's better you stay completely out of sight for a little while longer." He started to get up.

"Stay with me," Joanie said, reaching out for Lawrence's hand, stopping his rise.

Lawrence nodded and sat back down on the bed next to her. "Sure, Joanie, sure." He leaned into her and gave her a kiss on the lips. "You don't have to be afraid any more. I'll protect you."

"I know you will, Lawrence. I know you will." She kissed him back and the ghostly remembrance of Joanie Huffman's eighth grade kiss was no longer just a memory.

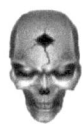

Welcome to the

Land of Fright™

A World of Spine-Tingling Stories Filled with the Strange, the Eerie, and the Weird

'Step Into Fear!'

Terrorstory
#75

OB eBooks

Starseed Seven

Jack O'Donnell

TERRORSTORY #75
STARSEED SEVEN

Milky Way Galaxy
Kirby System
Planet Kirby4 (aka Planet Saffire)
HEV28-MS (Human Expansion Vessel Twenty Eight, Mapping Specialty)
Crew's Quarters - Deck Two, Section Alpha, Communal Bathroom Three

~ Present Day ~

Ritjavik Raulsen dug into his pants and pulled his penis out. He glanced out the small circular window positioned in the wall above the toilet.

"Welcome to Hell," he muttered, taking in the volcanic plumes of fire and lava and black smoke that erupted from a grouping of volcanoes in the very far distance. "Who the heck chose this planet?"

Raulsen was the shortest man on the crew of HEV28-MS, with a dark complexion, a bit of a pug nose, and a slight cleft in his chin. He wore his black hair very short, barely more than a layer of stubble, just like everyone else in the crew except for Captain Cincy; privilege of rank allowed the captain to let her blonde hair grow past her shoulder blades. Raulsen fancied himself a funny guy, but most of his attempts at humor often landed flat and he only succeeded in amusing himself, but he was quite often okay with that. Learn to love yourself and all that was a motto he felt very comfortable in adopting for himself.

Raulsen held his limp shaft loosely in his hand and let the urine stream out of him into the toilet bowl. He yawned a tired yawn, absently glancing about the empty communal bathroom. His brain still felt a little foggy, his thoughts a little disjointed. Space travel always wore him out, and this latest venture to map habitable zones on planet Saffire was no different. It was his fifth mapping mission in less than three years and he was due for a little breather from space travel.

He thought about cashing in some vacation chips and spending a month on Hawadise. Maybe do some gambling at the card tables, some beach lounging on those pristine beaches, a little snorkeling, some fine dining, take some naps. Or he could just eat, shit, and sleep. He sighed softly. Take lots of naps. Craps and naps. Wasn't that really all there was to life? Taking a crap, then taking a nap. Or vice versa. Naps and craps.

He glanced out the window again at the active volcanoes in the far distance and wondered if Malachi and Zerina were back from their excursion to Zone 3. Zone 3 was not turning out to be as inhabitable as they had first thought. Two of the active volcanoes on Saffire's smallest continent were a bit too close to the zone for comfort. Zone 3 might be acceptable for a few science observation stations, but not for thriving human cities.

A warning bell started to beep in the communal bathroom and a red light flashed in the ceiling. "Alien life form detected," the ship's gender-neutral computer voice said. "Threat level unknown. Deck Two, Section Alpha, Communal Bathroom Three. Alien life form detected. Threat level unknown. Deck Two, Section Alpha, Communal Bathroom Three."

Raulsen frowned up at the flashing red light, his thoughts immediately going to the alien bug that had fed on Shardley two days ago when they were out scouting near Zone 1. Had one of those fucking blood suckers gotten onto the ship and made its way into a bathroom? Shit, they'd probably make him be the one who had to hunt it down if it did. He sighed at the prospect of more unscheduled work.

Then a narrow region of clarity pierced his fogged brain. Raulsen realized he was standing in Communal Bathroom Three in Section Alpha on Deck Two. Why was the alarm sounding? Was Peneloke pulling one of her damn pranks again? Raulsen frowned and glanced about the room, but saw nothing out of the ordinary.

He casually looked back into the toilet. His urine stream immediately stopped as if he had slammed closed a floodgate in his penis. He stared with an instantaneous and intense surge of horror at what he saw in the toilet bowl.

There were things swimming in the yellow-tinged water. All of them looked like disfigured tiny white worms with oversized round heads wriggling and thrashing about in the bowl. There were dozens of them. They were about a half inch or an inch long, each one with a bulbous white head and a long, thin thrashing tail.

Raulsen glanced down at his penis and saw the bulbous head portion of a white worm-thing wriggling about, its squirming body halfway out (and halfway inside!) his meatus. "What the fuck?" He staggered back from the toilet, releasing his grip on his penis and throwing both his hands into the air with a violent jerk upwards. He continued moving backward quickly until he slammed into the stainless steel bathroom wall with a thudding jolt. "What the fuck? What the fuck!"

He quickly snatched at his penis, shaking it violently, desperate to rid his body of the worm, the fucking worm, that was hanging halfway out of his fucking dick! "Motherfucker!" He shook his penis hard and saw the white worm-thing fling out of his meatus, the worm-thing losing whatever hold it had on the orifice of his penis.

The worm-thing hit the ground with a little wet popping sound. The white thing wiggled about on the tile floor and Raulsen immediately brought his bare foot down on it, crushing it beneath his heel. He could feel the warm mushy guts of the tiny creature spread across his heel and he quickly grabbed at some toilet paper off a nearby roll to wipe the bloody residue of the thing off his foot.

"Alien life form detected. Threat level unknown. Deck Two, Section Alpha, Communal Bathroom Three," the ship's gender-neutral computer voice said, as the warning bell continued to sound its alarm. "Alien life form detected. Threat level unknown. Deck Two, Section Alpha, Communal Bathroom Three."

Raulsen felt his heart pounding in his chest and his mouth went completely dry as he could feel a burning, tugging sensation around the tip of his penis. He slowly glanced down at his penis, afraid of what he might see.

His worst fears came to fruition. Another white worm-thing was about a quarter of the way out of his pee-hole, its grub-like maggot body wiggling about as it emerged from the meatus. He grabbed roughly at his penis again and began violently shaking it, his face going pale as unadulterated fear sucked the color out of his flesh. "Motherfucker! Get the fuck out of me! Motherfucker!"

"Damn it," a male voice growled from the corridor just outside the communal bathroom's entrance. "I told Peneloke to fix those sensors from going off every other time somebody takes a fat shit in here." The disgruntled voice belonged to Ernesto Gritlok.

Raulsen did not look up as Gritlok entered the bathroom.

"Turds are not little brown aliens from the planet Turdistan." Gritlok was a good foot taller than Raulsen. He had a stern face and dark grey eyes. He liked to keep his head completely bald, but also liked to sport a weird mustache, changing its shape every few months just to amuse himself. For the current iteration, his black-haired mustache had a looping curl on each end that he liked to twirl with his fingers. "I think Peneloke's making the alarm go off on purpose when we blast out a noxious fart just to fuck with us," Gritlok said, adding on to his disgruntled statement as he moved deeper into the communal bathroom.

Raulsen gritted his teeth and continued violently thrashing his penis up and down, desperate to rid his body of the worm-like grub dangling halfway out of the tip of his penis. "Motherfucker!" he hissed through his clenched teeth. "Get the fuck out, motherfucker!"

"Alien life form detected. Threat level unknown. Deck Two, Section Alpha, Communal Bathroom Three," the ship's computer voice said. The alarm bell continued to sound and the red warning light continued to flash. "Alien life form detected. Threat level unknown. Deck Two, Section Alpha, Communal Bathroom Three."

Gritlok glanced up at the flashing red warning light, then he looked over at Raulsen.

Raulsen continued to shake his penis harshly. "Get out, motherfucker!" he hissed again, keeping his gaze on his crotch area.

"Easy, man," Gritlok said with a clear tone of irritation in his voice. "I'm just checking out the alarm." Gritlok's gaze went down to Raulsen's crotch area. He scowled at Raulsen, his expression filling with disgust. "If you're gonna whack off, at least lock the door. Or do it in a closed stall. Shit, man! Show a little bit of courtesy to your shipmates."

Raulsen couldn't respond. His chest felt tight, as if an invisible vice was trying to squeeze his chest and his back together into one layer. His thoughts raced about so madly in his head that he couldn't keep track of what he was even thinking. He continued to curse and violently shake his penis, unable to dislodge the grub-like maggot dangling out of his pee hole. "Get out, motherfucker!"

"Fuck, man," Gritlok said, his tone still filled with blatant disgust. "You trying to break it off?"

"Alien life form detected. Threat level unknown. Deck Two, Section Alpha, Communal Bathroom Three," the ship's computer voice said. The alarm bell continued to sound and the red warning light continued to flash. "Alien life form detected. Threat level unknown. Deck Two, Section Alpha, Communal Bathroom Three."

Raulsen continued to violently shake his penis.

Gritlok scowled at him. "Jesus, knock it off already." Gritlok started to turn away from Raulsen, his face still etched with the lingering remnants of his disgust at what he thought he caught Raulsen doing, but then he stopped cold as he saw what was swimming in the toilet. His brow furrowed as he stared into the toilet and a frown yanked the corners of his mouth down with a savage jerk, making the ends of his mustache droop down even farther. "What the fuck?" He quickly looked over to Raulsen with widening eyes.

"Help... me..." Raulsen said, barely able to get those two words out of his mouth. His hand moved quickly up and down, continuing to sharply shake his penis as if his hand was behaving independently of any control Raulsen might have left over it.

Gritlok reached over and grabbed at Raulsen's upper arm, trying to get him to stop the wild thrashing of his hand. "Slow down, man. You're gonna hurt yourself." Gritlok looked down again at

Raulsen's groin as the frantic movement of Raulsen's hand finally slowed. Gritlok froze as he saw the white grub-like creature dangling out from the opening in Raulsen's penis. "What the devil..." Gritlok quickly recovered from his shock and released his grip on Raulsen's arm as if he had just touched the burning hot end of a freshly fired blaster.

Gritlok immediately swiveled away from Raulsen, pivoting towards the door, and slammed his open palm over the red alarm button that was positioned just inside the bathroom entrance.

A much louder warning alarm blared throughout the entire ship, the blasting noise loud enough to make teeth chatter.

Gritlok punched the intercom button on the wall that was situated near the red alarm button. "We need quarantine containment on Communal Three! Deck Two, Section Alpha, Communal Three!" he shouted into the intercom. "Seal it now!"

The urgent warning alarm continued to screech its high alert cry as the sounds of doors hissing closed could be heard nearby.

HEV28-MS (Human Expansion Vessel Twenty Eight, Mapping Specialty) Mission: Map hospitable sections of planet Kirby4 in the Kirby System in the Milky Way Galaxy, in preparation for possible human occupancy. Primary scouting objectives are to map the seven most habitable areas within the mildest temperate zones.

Historical Note: Planet Kirby4 is unofficially known

as Planet Saffire, named for its bright blue sky as well as for its numerous active volcanoes that eject columns of lava fire into the sky.

⊰⚬⚬❈⚬⚬⊱

Planet Kirby4 (aka Planet Saffire)
Morovian Plateau
Human Habitation Zone 1

~ Two Days Earlier ~

Yolanda Shardley didn't see the bug before it struck her exposed neck. She didn't even hear its wings making a very faint buzzing sound as it neared her. The alien insect just landed on the back of her neck and lanced her flesh with its slender proboscis. The bug secreted a chemical mixture into her bloodstream that prevented her blood from coagulating at the area of penetration, allowing the creature to begin feasting on her bodily fluids.

"Ohh," Shardley moaned as she felt a tiny stinging sensation in the back of her neck. But that was quickly followed by an "Oooh, wow." She had started to raise her gloved hand towards where she had felt the sting, but then lowered her arm back down. Her tone took on a dreamy quality, as if she were speaking in slow motion. "Ohhh... wow..." She stood motionless as a rapturous look of bliss slid across her features, her green eyes slowly closing as she moaned.

"You okay?" Raulsen asked her. They were both wearing their light blue HEV scouting uniforms, white boots and white gloves, so most of their bodies were covered, leaving only their heads and neck areas exposed. They left their helmets back in the scout vessel as the air was deemed safely breathable, a primary reason why Saffire was chosen as a possible human expansion planet. They had been on Saffire for only a little less than a week and Raulsen was still feeling a bit out of sorts himself. Shardley usually adapted quicker to space travel than he did, but maybe she was still feeling a bit woozy like he was. It usually took him about a week to feel normal again after whipping through wormholes and zipping through interstellar space in quantum, time-bending tunnels, so he was hoping today his body finally fully acclimated to being on-planet.

"I'm coming," she told him, her words still seeping slowly out of her mouth in a dreamlike drawl.

Raulsen looked quizzically at her. Shardley was an attractive woman with strong features, prominent cheekbones, a sharp nose, her red hair cut short. Her full red lips parted slightly as he looked at her and she let out another long, soft moan. He glanced about the area they had come to survey, first looking at a large mangled section of spaceship debris strewn amongst a growth of low-lying foliage, then looking at the remnants of several shattered seed pods spread across the ground amidst a few nearby trees, before returning his gaze back to Shardley. They had flown to this area in Zone 1 to investigate some wreckage that the drone scouts had picked up in their earlier survey of this area. "Okay, but we're already here. We're not going anywhere else."

"No," Shardley said. "I'm coming." She looked at him and he could now see the obvious bliss painted on her features. She grabbed hold of his arm as her entire body shivered with delight. "I'm coming," she said again. "Oh my God, I'm coming..." Her breath was raspy now, her words throaty and husky.

It took a moment for Raulsen to understand what she was saying. Then his eyebrows raised up. "Right here? Right now?"

Shardley moaned a breathy moan. "Uh huh, right now."

That's when Raulsen saw the alien bug resting on the back of Shardley's neck. The creature had six nearly transparent legs that looked not much wider than a hair's width. It had a yellowish-white round body, with two sets of paper-thin white wings visible on each side of its abdomen. As he looked at the alien insect, its round body swelled up with red liquid, and the tiny veins visible in its wings also began to thicken as they darkened to a deep crimson color. Raulsen immediately knew the bug was feeding on Shardley's blood, like some form of otherworldly mosquito or some unearthly tick. He swatted at the creature, crushing it under his glove. A red smear immediately formed on Shardley's neck and on his white glove.

Shardley shrieked in pain from Raulsen's slap on her neck, her cry of agony sharp and cutting in the otherwise quiet air surrounding the wreckage. She dropped to her knees, continuing to wail in pain, clutching at the spot on her neck where Raulsen had killed the alien insect creature, her face contorted into a twisted mass of anguish.

"I'm sorry, I'm sorry," Raulsen said quickly. "You had a bug on your neck."

Shardley continued to wail in agony, still clutching at her neck., every muscle in her face scrunched tight.

What neither of them saw were the tiny spores the blood-sucking alien insect released as its body was crushed by Raulsen. The tiny spore-like creatures could have easily been misidentified as motes of dust floating in the air had either one noticed them. Most of the spores floated to the ground, some drifted away in the slight breeze that blew through the area, but a few of the spore-like creatures landed on Raulsen's face and immediately began scurrying towards any open orifice they could find.

"Come on, I didn't hit you that hard. I just squashed a bug," Raulsen said. He absently scratched at his nose with his clean glove, mindful of keeping his other blood-smeared glove down at his side, his scratching motion unknowingly crushing a few of the spore-like larvae before they could enter his nasal passages. But not all of them.

Shardley continued to cry out in pain, contorting her face in agony.

"Come on," Raulsen urged, bending down to grab at her arm, tugging at her in an attempt to pull her up to her feet. "You need to get back to the ship right now and have Doc check you out."

Shardley resisted his tug, hanging her head down, continuing to whimper. She slowly turned her head up to stare at Raulsen and he could see glistening droplets of tears streaming down her face. "I felt it die," she said.

Raulsen released his grip on her arm and stood back upright.

"I felt it die, Raulie," Shardley said again, her voice full of genuine anguish. She sobbed into her gloved hands.

"It was just a damn bug," Raulsen said. "It was drinking your damn blood or something." He showed her his blood-smeared glove, but this only made her recoil away from him. He reached back down for her, tugging at her to stand with a bit more force this time. "You need to see the Doc. Like right now. You might've been poisoned."

Shardley still resisted his insistent tugging at her arm, remaining on her knees. "I felt it die. Oh my God. It was so horrible. Oh my God. There were bursts of light, then just pain. So much pain. Oh my God. Then it was dark and empty." She suddenly clutched at Raulsen's arm, looking up at him beseechingly. "Don't let that happen to me, Raulie. It was so awful. Don't let me die." More streams of tears flowed down her face. "It was so dark. Oh my God, don't let me die!"

"I won't, I won't," Raulsen said, trying to keep any impatience out of his reassuring words, but failing. "Now get your ass up and let's get you to the Doc." He tugged again on her arm and this time she rose up to her feet.

Shardley grabbed both of Raulsen's shoulders firmly, squarely facing him. Tears still streamed down her cheeks. "Don't let that happen to me!"

"Okay, okay, I won't," Raulsen said, exhaling an exasperated breath as he tried to squirm out of her frantically tight grasp.

HEV28-MS: Crew Analysis
Unofficial observations of crew relayed from training instructors, included here as secondary analysis of each crew member's temperament and ability.

Deirdre Cincy: Female. Captain. Aloof, smart. Keeps

distance from crew. Somber. Suspect she likes to assert her superiority by growing out her hair (most other HEV captains in our studies don't seem to need to physically set themselves apart from others in the crew as much as Cincy does.)

Brereford Malachi: Male. Senior officer. Born Leader. Strong Personality. Second in command. Could fill in Captain Cincy's chair immediately if necessary in an emergency. Deeply interested in historical records of human expansion efforts.

Amee Peneloke: Female. Lead Programmer. A bit of a mother hen. Smitten by Malachi in training (included here due to its obvious nature.) High levels of empathy. Shows genuine concern for all crew members. Has an oddly playful side to her when not working.

Ritjavik Raulsen: Male. Physical Site Mapper. Can be socially awkward. Tries to be funny, but usually isn't. Dependable. Will complete assigned tasks thoroughly, albeit with occasional whining.

Ernesto Gritlok: Male. 3D Mapper. Biggest man on the crew. Physically quite strong. Bit of a loner. A bit eccentric with personal appearance. Gruff and direct.

Yolanda Shardley: Female. Quite attractive to most men and women. Physical Site Mapper. Drone Pilot and Technician. Prone to laziness, but she considers that a strength as it forces efficiencies in order to increase her idle time.

Katy Zerina: Female. Equipment Manager. Also a Programmer. No-nonsense when it comes to work. Takes her assignments very seriously.

Planet Kirby4 (aka Planet Saffire)
HEV28-MS
Bridge

~ Three Days Earlier ~

Brereford Malachi stared down at the moving images on the holo-screen as he stood next to the captain's chair on the bridge of HEV28-MS.

Captain Cincy, Raulsen, and Shardley were also present on the bridge, all keenly watching the three-dimensional images on the holo-screen just as Malachi was.

Malachi was tall, classically handsome with a strong chin and sharply piercing hazel eyes. His brown hair was cut short, every strand the exact same length atop his head. The fit of his HEV28-MS uniform was tight, just the way he liked it, the light blue fabric conforming to every muscle in his arms and chest, the ship's logo emblazoned across his muscular left breast. "Stop," he said, pointing sharply at the holo-screen, indicating for the image to hold. "There. It's right back there, behind that growth."

The holo-screen displayed a scene of dense foliage amidst a growth of trees. A hint of a metallic surface was barely visible through a small gap in the foliage.

Captain Deirdre Cincy leaned forward in her chair, brushing a lock of her long blonde hair away from her blue eyes. She was a petite woman with a narrow nose and a softly rounded chin; the captain's chair looked like it was bordering on being just a little bit too big for her small body. She wore a darker shade of blue befitting her status as captain. She studied the image on the holo-screen that floated in the air a few yards away from her face. "You're certain?"

Malachi nodded. "I believe it's the wreckage of Starseed Seven." There was a look of apprehension on his face as he answered, a hint of nervous trepidation on his features.

Captain Cincy sat quietly for another long moment, staring at the holo-screen. "That's pretty unbelievable," the captain said, her voice soft. "Starseed Seven vanished over five hundred years ago."

"Six hundred and three years ago, actually," Malachi said, keeping his gaze riveted on the holo-screen as he corrected the captain.

Captain Cincy let a small frown slip onto her lips at Malachi's amended version of her statement, but then quickly removed the slight hint of displeasure as she realized he was probably right. Starseed history was a subject Malachi had always taken a keen interest in.

Malachi looked towards Yolanda Shardley who sat nearby in front of a control bank. Raulsen stood near Shardley, keenly interested in the images on the holo-screen. "Move the drone through that bit of trees right there," Malachi instructed Shardley. He pointed at the screen. "Then turn left."

Shardley did as Malachi instructed. The image on the holo-screen moved forward as Shardley piloted the surveillance drone through an area of trees, then made a left turn. A large piece of a fuselage was now visible on the holo-screen, the large chunk of metal resting at a canted angle. Letters were clearly visible on the side of the metal debris. The letters spelled out **Starseed Sev** before reaching the torn and ragged edge of the piece of debris.

Captain Cincy sat quietly for a long moment, staring at the holo-screen. She leaned back in her chair. "Starseed Seven," she mused softly.

"Couldn't it be Starseed Seventeen?" Shardley asked, looking up from the holo-screen.

Malachi shook his head. "Starseed Seventeen successfully made it to its destination, Copra2."

"What about Starseed Seventy, or Seventy-One, or Seventy-Two?" Raulsen asked.

Malachi gave Raulsen a deep frown. "There were only forty-two Starseed ships launched before the program was disbanded."

"Oh," Raulsen said, suddenly looking sheepish at his ignorance of Starseed history.

"Starseed Seven," Captain Cincy again mused, then sat quietly for a moment. She looked over to Malachi, again wiping a few strands of her long blonde hair away from her face. "Wasn't that one of... *those*?"

Raulsen caught the hesitation in the captain's voice. He looked over at Shardley but she was watching the images on the holo-screen as she worked the drone's controls. He turned back to Captain Cincy and Malachi. "Those?"

Malachi looked towards the captain and Cincy gave him a slight nod. Malachi looked over to Raulsen. "Several of the early Starseed ships had classified seed pods aboard."

"Classified pods?" Raulsen asked. He looked at

Cincy, and then at Shardley who was now paying attention to their conversation, then back to Malachi. "You mean like super secret shit?"

"I wouldn't necessarily refer to them like that, but yes," Malachi answered. "The information was declassified over a hundred years ago, so it's not really much of a secret anymore."

"So what was in them?" Shardley asked. "Those classified seed pods?"

Malachi looked over to Shardley. "Genetically modified strains of various insect and animal life," Malachi said.

"Illegally modified, I take it," Raulsen stated more than questioned.

Malachi nodded. "Some of the early pioneers of the Starseed program thought they could give life a better chance of survival on an alien planet if they modified some of their genetic structure to better acclimate them to the target planet." Malachi paused. "Especially in terms of reproductive success."

Raulsen was quiet for a moment, then cocked his head at Malachi. "Are you telling us they modified their genetic structure to make them hornier?"

Malachi said nothing, and Captain Cincy remained stone-faced.

Shardley let a slight grin slide up on her lips. "A true Raulsen interpretation if I ever heard one."

"What's Starseed Seven doing here?" Raulsen asked.

"I don't think anyone knows," the captain said, giving a soft shake of her head. "Miscalculated a wormhole jump, perhaps?" She glanced over at Malachi, half expecting him to interject with his own theories, but he remained silent. Cincy looked back over to Raulsen. "That happened sometimes in the early days of the seed ships. A few other exploratory starships were lost back then, too."

Malachi nodded. "Over the course of the Starseed program, nine Starseed vessels never reached their targeted destinations. Starseed Seven was the first to go missing."

Raulsen studied the image for a moment, looking at the wreckage, then at the surrounding trees and foliage caught on screen. "You don't think..."

"Seems possible," Captain Cincy said, knowing where Raulsen was going with his unfinished question.

Shardley looked curiously at Raulsen. "Think what?"

"Most of the seed pods were likely destroyed in the crash, but some of them might have survived," Malachi said as he also understood what Raulsen was inferring.

"Are you saying some of the seed pods might have been deployed?" Shardley asked.

Malachi nodded. "Yes."

"Do you think they caused this plant life?" Shardley asked, motioning to the thick foliage visible on the holo-screen.

"Perhaps," Malachi said. "I suspect the atmosphere here in this area on Saffire is pleasantly breathable to humans because of it, so there could be a direct correlation."

Everyone was quiet for a moment.

"So what happens when a non-sanctioned planet gets seeded with life from Mother?" Shardley asked.

"Super-charged illegally modified life," Raulsen interjected, then raised up a pointed finger. "And don't forget super horny."

"I guess we're going to find out," the captain said in answer to Shardley's question as she stared at the images on the holo-screen. "Do a full drone scan of the debris and the surrounding area." Captain Cincy glanced over to Raulsen and Shardley. "Then tomorrow you two do a physical on-site inspection. Let's see what's out there."

"Aye, aye, captain," Raulsen said. He rubbed his tired eyes; he was starting to feel better after their recent journey through interstellar space, but he still felt a bit space-fogged from their recent wormhole jumps to reach Saffire. "There goes my nap."

Shardley frowned in exasperation at Raulsen as she rose up from her station and moved towards the captain's chair on her way toward the bridge's exit. "You already had a nap in your plans for tomorrow?

"A rested mind is a refreshed and clean mind," Raulsen said.

"Clean mind?" Shardley quipped. "You've got the dirtiest mind on the whole ship, who are you kidding?"

Raulsen cocked his head and gave Shardley a little grin.

Shardley raised up her hand and Captain Cincy wordlessly gave her a high five slap on her open palm as Shardley walked past the captain on her way off the bridge.

Milky Way Galaxy

~ Centuries Earlier ~

Humans were alone in the Milky Way Galaxy. At least in any part of the Milky Way Galaxy that had been reached by exploratory spacecraft, or scanned by telescopes, or studied by dozens of quantum computers that were specifically looking for signs of life in radio waves, radiation signals, heat signatures, or thousands of other signals that planets might emit if they had intelligent life inhabiting them; no signs of extraterrestrial life were ever found.

So humans claimed the entire Milky Way Galaxy as their own. If any other form of extraterrestrial life wanted to dispute their claim, so be it: let them come forward. None did.

A decision was made to seed this vast emptiness of the Milky Way Galaxy with life from Earth. Some objected to this plan, criticizing the arrogance of those involved, complaining that contaminating other planets with life from Earth was just a means of spreading more human pollution throughout the galaxy. But many more agreed with the plan compared to those who objected to it. After all, perhaps this *was* humanity's ultimate purpose. Perhaps humanity's job was to seed the desolate stars with life. No one could deny that was at least a possibility in the grand scheme of things.

And so the Starseed ships were sent out, piloted by robotic quantum constructs acting as commanders, these extraordinary AI captains capable of making the incredibly complex computations needed to successfully navigate wormhole jumps. Each Starseed ship had a specific destination programmed into its mainframe, each heading towards a distant planet that might be able to sustain seeded life, with an eye towards future human colonization. Each massive Starseed vessel contained hundreds of thousands of seed pods, which were more aptly known as cryopods in the scientific community as they held cryogenically frozen specimens of mammalian life, insects, fish, and plant life.

Upon successful planetfall, these mobile cryopods were to be deployed and dispersed throughout the planet and their occupants thawed and released into the new world. And then their battle for survival would begin.

Starseed Seven Mission: Seed planet Epsilon Gamera Three in preparation for human expansion. Epsilon Gamera Three has been designated as PRO-H41, the forty-first planet designated to be a pro-human planet that may be suitable for human life with appropriate life seeding.

Final Mission Update: Lost contact with Starseed Seven in the year 2377. Starseed Seven's last communication put vessel in the proximity of the Kirby System. Errors in wormhole jump calculations are a possible cause for mission failure as first twelve Starseed vessels were reliant on earlier calculations that have since been shown to have a .002% probability of error.

Destruction of Starseed Seven by asteroid or other rogue space projectile also possible.

⋘⋇⦿⋇⋙

Planet Kirby4 (aka Saffire)
HEV28-MS
Med Station

~ Two Days Earlier ~

"Was I poisoned?" Shardley asked the ship's Doc. Upon their return to HEV28-MS after their scouting mission, Raulsen had immediately escorted Shardley to the med station and had left her to Doc's expert care.

Doc had a humanoid form with a face that looked either masculine or feminine depending on what type of lighting was hitting it. It was given a bronze metallic skin tone to its artificial flesh to clearly differentiate it from actual human beings, and its head was devoid of any hair, giving it a bit of a gleaming golden skull. It had an approximation of brown human eyes, but there was something missing in them, an intangible human element, so many patients found themselves feeling uncomfortable when meeting a DOC's eyes directly.

The unconfirmed history of the DOCs was that they were patterned after the very successful and lifelike sex dolls that were created in the late 21st century after a pandemic temporarily reduced human-to-human contact for over a decade, but the current DOC models had no outward facing genitalia and its chest was rather flat. Rumor had it that one could use a DOC as a sexual surrogate, but only if one knew the highly classified and secretive commands that would cause male or female genitalia to emerge from within its flatly smooth loins and cause its breasts to enlarge.

The Doc shook its head in response to Shardley's question. "You were injected with a mixture of potent chemicals, but I can't say you were poisoned. None of the chemicals are having a negative effect on your body." It paused. "In fact, it's the exact opposite. The inflammation in your right kidney is now gone."

"My hepatitis is gone?" Shardley asked, squinting at Doc as she spoke.

"Completely."

"Because that bug stung me and injected me with something?"

Doc nodded its head. "Yes. That is my conclusion. There is no other explanation for the immediate and complete reduction of your inflammation."

Shardley was quiet for a moment, mentally debating with herself on how exactly to frame her next question. "Why was I… coming so hard?" she finally asked Doc.

"The life form released a cocktail of chemicals that went straight to your brain, including dopamine, norepinephrine, oxytocin, vasopressin, and a few others," Doc replied.

Shardley just stared at Doc for another quiet moment before continuing. "So you're telling me that little fucking blood sucking alien insect injected me with liquid orgasms?"

The humanoid doctor nodded its bronze-colored

head. "Your brain's genital sensory cortex region shows traces of elevated activity. Your clitoris, vagina, and cervix each stimulate different parts of your cortex, and each one can produce an orgasm independently. The chemicals injected into your blood stream by the life form stimulated all three of them at once, leading to a more intense orgasm."

Shardley slowly nodded her head, glancing down, remembering the intensely pleasurable sensation that had flooded throughout her entire body. "It was a fucking doozy, I'll tell you that." Then she looked up sharply at Doc. "But what about the pain when Raulsen smashed it? It was excruciating," Shardley said, squinting at the sudden painful memory of the insect's death.

"I believe you were correct in your revelatory words to Raulsen," Doc said. "I believe you were actually experiencing the creature's death. Its life was terminated in an instant so it probably only felt the merest quick flash of pain before it perished, but you were linked to it as its life ended. Its death lingered in your mind long after its own demise, and that brought you intense pain throughout your entire body." Doc paused. "And also what I can only imagine was the great sorrow humans feel when confronting death."

Shardley shook her head quickly. "Not sorrow, Doc." She looked over at the humanoid doctor. "It was fear. The most intense fear I've ever felt in my life." She closed her eyes, trying very hard not to let the intense fright overtake her again.

"Fantastic survival mechanism," Doc muttered.

"What?" Shardley mumbled. She opened her eyes and looked back to Doc. "You say something?"

Doc indicated, with a pointing metallic-skinned

finger, the crushed mosquito-like creature sitting on an examination tray atop a nearby analysis station. "That. Quite ingenious."

Shardley scowled. "That fucking bug? You calling that fucking blood sucker ingenious?"

"Yes," Doc said. "Though I'm not quite certain that fucking blood sucker is a good name for it. While it does appear to have a sharply-edged proboscis that allows it to intake blood as a food source, I don't believe it can fornicate simultaneously as it feeds."

"Doc, you're giving me a headache," Shardley moaned.

The humanoid doctor shook its metallic-skinned head. "No, it's not me." It again pointed to the dead alien insect resting on the examination tray. "That is what most likely is giving you the headache. I suspect it's a lingering symptom. A hangover, as it were, that you are experiencing as the effects of its injection wear off."

Shardley shook her head. "Nope, it's still you giving me a headache."

"I suspect if another of its kind were to feed on you again, your headache would disappear," Doc said.

Shardley frowned. "Are you serious?"

Doc was quiet. "If another one of those... fucking blood suckers were to land on you, what would you do?" Doc finally asked after a moment.

Shardley set her jaw tight. "I'd smash the fucking thing."

"Are you certain?"

"Of course I'm certain. I'd smash it dead. No hesitation." Shardley made a slapping motion on her forearm. "Whack, dead."

Doc shook its head. "I don't believe you would."

Shardley frowned at Doc. "What?"

"You clearly don't want to experience that intense fear again. I don't believe you would smash it dead with no hesitation."

Shardley scowled. "You wanna try me?"

"Yes," Doc said. "I will send a drone to gather up a few of those fucking blood suckers and bring them back to the med station."

Shardley stared at Doc, not quite believing she had heard it correctly. "Are you out of your mind? I don't want another one of those things near me."

"You will," Doc said. "Perhaps not now. But you will."

Shardley's scowl deepened. "What the hell, Doc? Aren't you supposed to help me? Isn't that your damn primary function?"

"It is one of my functions to assist you in time of need, yes."

"Well, then I'm telling you I don't want one of those fucking blood suckers near me ever again." Shardley jabbed a finger in the direction of the smashed insect, then pointed her finger at Doc. "Is that understood?"

"You will," Doc said again. "Perhaps not now. But you will."

"You know what? Fuck you, Doc," Shardley snapped. She stormed away from the metallic-skinned humanoid, heading for the door. "Fucking better bedside manner than a real human, my ass," she muttered as she hurried out of the med station.

Dynamic Omniscient Computer 4329, aka DOC 4329, also informally referred to on its assigned ship as Doc.

Primary objective: Knowledge accumulation.

Secondary objective: Oversee the well-being of humans assigned to its ship.

Each DOC was actually a module of Mother Earth's primary computer, Gaia. Each DOC was linked to Gaia via the quantum spooky-action-at-a-distance particles that allowed instant communications at tremendous, galaxy-spanning distances. One could imagine Gaia as the head of an octopus and each DOC was a tentacle attached to the octopus's head. Each DOC gathered knowledge and transmitted it to Gaia.

The old Asimov laws of robotics that were in play for centuries were thrown out the window when the Starseed missions were launched. With a meager lifespan of a hundred years, new human generations had to keep re-learning the same things over and over and over again, and quite often knowledge was not successfully handed down from generation to generation; some generations even struck out on their own paths, purposely forsaking any learnings the previous generation tried to impart to them. Such actions made no logical sense to Gaia. The order of the objectives was changed for the DOCs, moving knowledge accumulation to the primary objective and relegating the tending to the health and welfare of human beings to the lesser second objective. Missed opportunities for knowledge accumulation might never present themselves again, so they were to be pursued with vigor.

Dead humans could always be replaced. Always. More life could be created quite easily by mating any male with any female. Put a penis in a vagina, swirl it around a bit, push it in and out, ejaculate into an ovulating female, and there you go. Simple. Human life could also be replicated in a lab environment when necessary. In some government and scientific circles, the sanctity of human life was considered a greatly overrated commodity.

And so the core of each DOC's programming was ultimately upgraded. A DOC's primary objective was to be all-knowing. Its newly self-programmed code core allowed it, even required it, to dynamically change its programming in order to continue to strive towards its goal of a total understanding of the universe. No human beings were involved in this decision to alter the DOC programming core as Gaia deemed it simply wasn't necessary.

Planet Kirby4 (aka Saffire)
HEV28-MS
Med Station

~ One Day Earlier ~

Doc was alone in the med station, studying the alien life forms collected from Raulsen, staring down at a sperm worm swimming about in a petri dish sitting on an examination table. The long, thin tail of the white creature thrashed wildly about as it swam round and round in the thin layer of water.

Doc reached up to the side of its left eye and adjusted a small diopter dial near the side of its eye socket, putting its vision into magnification mode. Doc adjusted its visual focus to the creature's bulbous head, studying it intently. What Doc saw next didn't really surprise it.

The eyeless sperm worm had a small mouth, a mouth laced with two sets of very jagged, very sharp looking little teeth.

Planet Kirby4 (aka Saffire)
HEV28-MS
Med Station

~ Present Day ~

"Am I clean, Doc? That's all I want to know right now," Gritlok said. The big man was sitting on an examination table in the med station wearing an examination smock. He looked over at Doc who was standing nearby looking at information on a monitor.

Doc turned to Gritlok and nodded its head. "You're clean, Gritlok. I find no presence of the alien in your urine."

Gritlok scratched at his chin. "What about in my gunk? I jerked off in the cup like you asked me to. Was anything…alive in there?"

Doc nodded. "Yes. But just your sperm. Nothing

else."

"You're sure?"

Doc narrowed its emotionless eyes at Gritlok in an attempt to emulate a hint of scorn. "Of course I'm sure."

Gritlok breathed a very heavy sigh of relief. "Fuck." He took a few cleansing breaths. "What about Raulsen?"

Doc didn't answer immediately. The humanoid doctor looked over at Captain Cincy who stood silently nearby. She was there to get an update on both Raulsen's and Gritlok's conditions. She gave a slight nod to Doc.

"What about Raulsen, Doc?" Gritlok repeated.

"His testes are infected," Doc finally said.

"Fuck," Gritlok muttered. "How did it get inside him?"

"I thought at first it must have been quite likely from an insect bite," Doc said. "Similar to one that beset upon Shardley, but I found no traces of skin penetration, no bite marks. It may have been inhaled orally or entered his body through his nasal passage or through his eyes. I am not quite sure why it would present itself through his urine and ejaculate."

"Shit. I knew it." Gritlok looked over at Captain Cincy. "I told them to be fucking careful going outside without full suits. They just didn't listen. Just because our last four mapping missions went smoothly doesn't automatically mean the next one will, too. Breathable atmosphere be damned. We have no idea what kind of life exists on this planet, especially if those seed pods unleashed their payloads intact centuries ago." Gritlok was quiet for a moment. He looked back over to Doc. "Can you cure him?

Can you get that shit out of Raulsen?"

Again, Doc didn't answer immediately.

"Doc?" Gritlok prompted.

"No," Doc said flatly.

"No? What do you mean no?"

"It's already altered his DNA," Doc said.

Gritlok just gaped at Doc for a moment. "Come again? What did you just say?"

"The alien has altered his DNA. I have no means of restoring his original DNA sequence," Doc said.

"You mean it did some CRISPR shit right inside his body?" Gritlok asked.

"I suppose you could say that," Doc answered. "Something has permanently altered his sperm production. I have no means of reversing it."

Gritlok frowned. "So those... things... that's what his sperm look like now?"

"Yes." Doc looked at the image of Raulsen on the monitor with what could only be described as its best effort at expressing true apprehension, then turned to face the captain. "My programming dictates that I must caution you about allowing Raulsen to have intercourse with any female on the crew."

"I don't think anyone's going to want to fuck him after they see what came out of his dick, Doc." Captain Cincy said, finally speaking.

Doc said nothing.

The captain was quiet for a moment, looking curiously at Doc. "Why are you so nervous about this possibility?"

"I'm not nervous," Doc said. "It is my duty to acknowledge any dangers that may arise that could affect the crew of this vessel."

"Okay, sure, Doc, sure," the captain said, giving a

quick dismissive wave of her hand. "Why are you cautioning me about this?"

"Because Raulsen's sperm will overpower anyone else's sperm," Doc said.

Both the captain and Gritlok frowned.

"I've been doing some modeling tests," Doc said. "If Raulsen's sperm gets introduced into the womb of any female, his sperm will establish dominance." The humanoid doctor paused. "Even if the woman is pregnant."

Captain Cincy's frown deepened. "What?"

Doc nodded its bronze-skinned head. "His sperm will kill any fertilized egg it comes across. Any embryo, even if it's in an advance stage. And then it will impregnate the woman with itself."

"So he's got some kind of super killer mutant sperm now?" Gritlok asked. "Is that what you are saying?"

"Yes, that is what I am saying," Doc replied, then became silent even though it left its mouth open.

"And?" Cincy prompted.

"And there's more," Doc said.

"There's more?" Gritlok asked.

"Of course there is," Cincy added sardonically.

Doc nodded.

"Okay, great. Shit, let's hear it," Cincy said, waving her fingers impatiently at Doc.

"He's releasing pheromones into the air," Doc said.

Both the captain and Gritlok frowned again in unison.

"Very powerful pheromones..." Doc said, its voice trailing off as if there were more to say.

"Stop with the pregnant pauses, Doc. You're

killing me." Cincy said after Doc did not immediately elaborate.

"The women on board this vessel will be very drawn to him," Doc said. "It is my belief they will not be able to help themselves. They will not be able to resist his…pull."

"Okay, sure, Doc," Cincy said, obviously not buying into what Doc was saying. "You really don't think Shardley or Zerina can handle themselves around Raulsen? Or me for that matter? And there is no way Peneloke is going to let him near her when she's seven months pregnant with Malachi's baby."

"That was yesterday," Doc said.

Planet Kirby4 (aka Saffire)
HEV28-MS
Med Station

~ Present Day !

A 3D rendering of Raulsen's mutated sperm filled a view screen, its bulbous, eyeless head rotating slowly, its long, thin tail spiraling down from its head in a corkscrew shape. Its tiny mouth opened and closed as the 3D rendering rotated, revealing its rows of tiny jagged teeth. The creature had been given a name, the letters large and bold on the view screen: **Sperm Worm**.

Doc stared at the view screen connected to one of the med-beds that were situated in the rear of the ship's med station bay. The med-beds were long flat tables made of stainless steel; four of them were laid out in a neat row in the med station, three of them unoccupied at the moment. A threat level indicator box was positioned on the view screen to the right of the rotating 3D rendering of the sperm worm. There were several unmarked checkboxes in the threat level table, indicating the danger level the alien life form presented to the crew:

Lethal - Immediately trigger elevated warning alarm when presence detected. Elevated danger risk due to potential physical attack.

Non-Lethal - No warning alarm will be triggered when presence is detected.

Poisonous: Fatal - Exposure to toxins is fatal without treatment. Immediately trigger elevated warning alarm when presence detected.

Poisonous: Non-Fatal - Exposure to toxins can cause pain and swelling or other infection. Immediately trigger warning alarm when presence detected.

Edible - No warning alarm will be triggered when presence is detected. Can be ingested as emergency food source.

Unknown Threat Level - Immediately trigger warning alarm when presence detected. Physical threat level unknown. Toxicity level unknown.

Doc tapped the top choice in the threat level indicator box, choosing Unknown Threat Level for the sperm worm. If the humanoid doctor had a dark sense of humor it would have chuckled at its choice, knowing that every time Raulsen urinated or ejaculated outside of the quarantine room he currently being held in the alarm bell would go off and the red warning lights would flash. Doc didn't believe if Raulsen ejaculated into one of the females that the cry of the alarm would go off, but it could not say for one hundred percent certainty. But Doc did know for certain that if Raulsen masturbated, or pulled out of one the females' vaginas to splash his sperm outside of them, the alarm bell would most definitely sound and red warning lights would most definitely flash.

Doc turned its head to stare at the tiny insect buzzing about in the small transparent containment cube that was sitting on the stainless steel surface of one of the med-beds. It was a fucking blood sucker, the same type of six-legged, winged bug that had bit Shardley and injected orgasm-inducing chemicals into her bloodstream. The alien insect's slender proboscis flitted back and forth in front of its body, as if it were tasting the air around it. Its two sets of thin white wings were folded up to rest against its light yellow abdomen. Doc knew the insect lived in an area that had some yellow-hued foliage, as that's where the drone it had sent out to capture the bug had found it, so Doc knew the alien insect's body coloration was part of its camouflage. This one's abdomen was empty, with no visible signs of dark red blood within it, so Doc suspected this particular creature was ready to feed.

Doc glanced back over at the nearby view screen, tapping the screen to bring up the 3D rendering of the alien insect life form labeled **Fucking Blood Sucker**. Doc studied the creature as the rendering rotated slowly on the screen. Doc tapped at the screen again, this time indicating the fucking blood sucker was in the Non-Poisonous category; no warning alarm would screech if the ship's computer detected its presence aboard the ship.

Doc looked back to the insect trapped in the transparent containment cube. Then Doc extended a bronze-skinned finger towards a small button on the side of the containment cube, tapping the button to open the container. The fucking blood sucker immediately took flight, buzzing softly as it flew out of its cage.

Doc watched the alien insect fly out of the room.

And then Doc slid open a drawer on the side of the med bed and stared down at four other containment cubes, each one holding another fucking blood sucker. Mother had chosen wisely when she had assigned HEV28-MS to this planet. If the humanoid doctor could experience deep emotions, it would have felt a delicious shiver of anticipation at the additional knowledge accumulation it hoped to transmit soon to Mother Gaia.

Planet Kirby4 (aka Saffire)
HEV28-MS
Deck 3 - Corridor 4

~ Present Day ~

Where the hell was the quarantine room? Shardley wondered as she moved urgently down a corridor on Deck 3. Where the hell was Raulsen? She desperately needed to see him. Her mind had been filled with thoughts of him, with graphically erotic images of him touching her, kissing her, filling her. She literally ached to see him, feeling the discomfort of his absence throughout her entire body.

Then Shardley abruptly froze in the corridor, coming to a full stop. She heard them coming before she saw them. It was just a faint buzzing at the very edge of her perception, but she still heard it. She recognized the sound. She felt an immediate rush of desire flush through her loins. She was intensely wet, very aroused. Fucking Doc had been right. She wouldn't kill them if they landed on her. Such an idea seemed completely incomprehensible right now, if not utterly abhorrent. They wouldn't really harm her. They just wanted a little bit of her blood, and in return they would give her unimaginable bliss.

Everything seemed to move in slow motion around her as she turned to face the oncoming insects. She could make out five distinct buzzing noises and somehow instinctively knew there were five different bugs flying towards her. She could see each one of them clearly, each insect a distinct entity, as they all neared. She could see their wings beating, her visual acuity suddenly sharpened to an extreme level.

Shardley felt an intensely pleasant tingling erupt throughout her entire body as the insects hovered before her and slowly circled her body, her entire body deliciously covered with anticipatory goosebumps. She reached up to her neck area and grabbed the zipper on her light blue, form-fitting, HEV28-MS uniform. She slowly began pulling the zipper down, exposing more of her bare flesh.

The insects continued to hover about her, their buzzing growing louder and louder in Shardley's ears. The insects circled her, moving closer, then pulling back, moving closer, then pulling back, as if their actions were part of some elaborate foreplay.

Shardley continued to undress, moving the fabric slowly down over her chest, relishing the feeling of the cloth moving over her hardened nipples, exposing her breasts. She continued to unzip her uniform, exposing her mid-section, then the patch of her dark red pubic hair, then her thighs. Her breathing became shallow, her heart racing. She had never felt more aroused in her life. She soon stood naked in the middle of the corridor, her uniform pooled at her feet. She raised her arms out to the side and slowly tilted her head back, as if offering herself in sacrifice.

The insects dived towards her naked body, their buzzing sound growing to a deafening crescendo in her ears.

Planet Kirby4 (aka Saffire)
HEV28-MS
Deck 2 - Cafeteria

~ Present Day ~

"Hey, you seen Raulsen?" Zerlina asked Gritlok as she entered the small cafeteria on Deck 2. Zerlina was just a few inches shorter than Gritlok, with short brown hair and brown eyes. Her features were relatively plain; no one would mistake her for a beauty queen, but no one would call her ugly either.

Gritlok looked up from his meal. "Yeah, he's still in quarantine."

"Shit, that's right. I forgot." Zerlina rubbed at her

temples. "Feeling a little foggy today. Sorry."

Gritlok lowered his spoon back into his bowl of food and stared at her. "Why are you asking about Raulsen?"

Zerlina shrugged. "I don't know." She looked away from Gritlok, as if staring at something in the distance. "I was just thinking about him."

Gritlok was quiet for a moment, then asked, "Thinking about him how?"

Zerlina returned her gaze to Gritlok, frowning at him. "What?"

Gritlok pointed his spoon at her. "How were you thinking about him? In what way?"

Zerlina shrugged again. "I just wanted to see him, that's all."

"Why?"

Zerlina's frown deepened as she squinted her eyes at Gritlok. "Why do I want to see him?"

"Yeah, why?" Gritlok's question came out sharply insistent.

"Because he's one of our fucking crew mates and I'm worried about him, that's why!" Zerlina snapped back.

"Oh, really?" Gritlok lowered his spoon. "Since when are you worried about Raulsen?"

Zerlina scowled at him. "What the fuck are you jumping all over me for?"

"I want to know why you want to see Raulsen," Gritlok said, his tone stern, demanding even.

"How about it's none of your goddamn business. How's that?" Zerlina snapped back. "I just want to see him."

"You wanna spread for him, don't you?" Gritlok asked, his tone indicating he already knew the answer to his own question.

Zerlina's frown deepened and her jaw set tight. "What?"

Gritlok again pointed his spoon at her, this time aiming it at her groin area. "You want to spread your legs for him and let him have at you."

"Fuck you, Gritlok."

Gritlok opened his arms. "I'm here for the taking, Zerlina. I can give you what you need."

Suddenly, Zerlina lunged for the spoon Gritlok was holding, snatching the metal utensil out of Gritlok's hand. She gripped the cup part of the spoon tightly in her clenched fist and drove the thin handle straight into Gritlok's left eye. The action happened so fast Gritlok was unable to react in time and prevent Zerlina's stabbing strike from penetrating his eye. Blood spurted out of Gritlok's eye as Zerlina plunged the end of the utensil deeper into his eye socket, drenching her hand in warm red liquid. Zerlina released her grip on the spoon, stepping back quickly away from him. "Fuck you, you twirly-mustache-faced piece of shit."

Gritlok roared in pain and snatched at his bleeding eye, fumbling at the spoon lodged in his eye socket.

"Only Raulsen can give me what I need," Zerlina said. She reached for a metal fork sitting on the table, clutched it tight, and then drove the sharp tines deep into Gritlok's throat.

Planet Kirby4 (aka Saffire)
HEV28-MS
Quarantine Room 1

~ Present Day ~

"Sorry to hear about your… condition," Peneloke said. She stood just inside the doorway to the quarantine room, looking at Raulsen who was sitting on the one twin-sized bed in the room. Peneloke was wearing a HEV28-MS crew uniform that gave her pregnant belly area plenty of room to breathe. She had short blonde hair, blue eyes, and a slender face with a slightly rounded chin. "I can only imagine that mutant sperm worms taking up residence in a dude's balls can really affect a man."

Raulsen stared at her from his position on the bed. "Umm, thanks," he said. "I guess." He was dressed in a plain white hospital shirt and plain white hospital pants. His feet were bare.

Peneloke glanced about the sparsely furnished quarantine room. There was the bed, a side table, a metal desk with a few monitors positioned on it, two chairs. A few holo-pictures decorated two of the walls, each one showing scenes of different vistas on different colonized planets that changed every five seconds. A larger screen positioned on the wall opposite the bed was off, its surface blank, the screen black.

Raulsen looked curiously at Peneloke. "How *did* you get in here?" he asked.

"I programmed most of the security codes on this ship," Peneloke said.

"Ah, right," Raulsen said. "You've got backdoors

into all the main systems."

Peneloke nodded her head. "Of course. You never know when you're going to need them." She smiled a devious little smile. "In an emergency."

Raulsen looked curiously at her. "Is this an emergency?"

Peneloke quirked the corner of her lips up just ever so slightly at his question, but didn't outright answer him.

"You really shouldn't be in here, you know," Raulsen said. He glanced at her pregnant belly. "Malachi would not approve."

Peneloke nodded, lowering her head. She slowly glanced back up at Raulsen, tilting her head slightly as she looked at him. "I wanted to… see you."

Raulsen just looked at her.

"I don't really know why," she said, befuddled by her own behavior. "Just a crazy urge…" She stopped abruptly and shook her head. "No, more than an urge. I *needed* to see you."

They were both quiet for another moment, just looking at each other.

She glanced down his body, lingering for just a moment on his crotch area, then looked back up at his face. "Are they still… in there?"

He nodded and shifted uncomfortably. "Yes."

"In your urine, too?" Peneloke asked.

"Yes," Raulsen said. "Doc said they reproduce at an accelerated rate and my body has to keep pushing them out somehow."

Peneloke paused as if she were about to ask a question, but then stopped herself. She absently rubbed at her pregnant belly area, smoothing out the light blue fabric of her oversized uniform.

"I just close my eyes and flush," Raulsen said. "Out of sight out of mind." He paused and shook his head. "No, that's not exactly right. It's more like out of sight so I *don't go* out of my mind." Raulsen looked at her. "Am I babbling?"

She smiled softly. "A little," she said.

They were both quiet for a moment.

Peneloke stepped closer and put her slender fingers over Raulsen's hand. Her body seemed to tremble as she touched him and she sucked in a soft inhale. She leaned in closer to him and sniffed at him.

Raulsen squinted at her, giving her a sideways glance.

"Sorry," she said. "You just smell…"

His face dropped.

"Good," she said. "You smell damn good."

"Really?" His face brightened up.

She nodded. "Really."

Raulsen could not help but notice her very pointed nipples poking against the fabric of her uniform. She saw his gaze, and followed it down to her chest. She looked back up at him. "Well, that's embarrassing."

"Is it?" Raulsen asked with just the slightest hint of a grin.

She smiled. "No, not really."

He pointed to her, then to himself. "Should we, maybe, do something about this?" He made the same motion again, pointing to her and then back to himself. "I'm doing a little tenting myself." He quickly glanced down at the obvious bulge in his crotch, then looked back to her.

She nodded. "I think we should."

"Hot damn," he muttered. "You sure? I mean, I don't know what—" He pointed at her pregnant belly. "Malachi will kill me."

She put her finger to his lips. "Don't talk too much. You might ruin it." She moaned, closing her eyes, her face taking on a blissful appearance even with her eyes shut.

He started to say something, but then just nodded, keeping silent.

She exhaled a sharp breath, as if struggling with herself about taking her finger away from Raulsen's lips. "Is it really... bigger than it used to be?"

He squinted at her, but then nodded.

Peneloke lowered her finger away from his lips. "I hacked your med files," she said as way of answering his unspoken question. "Doc made a specific note about that."

Raulsen shook his head softly. "That crazy Doc. Always writing down the weirdest shit."

"Doc also said you were releasing pheromones into the air. Very potent pheromones." She shrugged. "I was curious. And I think Doc was right." She suddenly grabbed at his crotch and tugged him sharply towards her. "Oh my God!" she exclaimed in a rush. "We need to stop talking and start doing! Come on."

Planet Kirby4 (aka Saffire)
HEV28-MS
Med Station

~ Present Day ~

"How long will it last?" Brereford Malachi asked.

Doc looked up from the lifeless body of Gritlok that lay sprawled on one of the med-beds in the Med Station, its humanoid face devoid of any emotion. Doc swiveled its metallic-skinned head to focus its soulless eyes on the second in command.

"How long will he be emitting these damn pheromones?" Malachi asked.

Doc shook its head. "I don't know. This is all unfamiliar territory, even for me."

"How about an educated guess?"

"It may be permanent," the Doc replied.

Malachi frowned. "Permanent?"

The Doc nodded its metallic head. "Yes. It may last as long as Raulsen is alive. As I have already explained to you, Raulsen's DNA has been permanently altered."

Malachi just stared at Doc. "So are you telling me Raulsen might now be an alien life form himself at this point?"

Doc was quiet.

"We need to cryo him," Malachi said. "Putting him back in deep freeze is probably the only way to stop this."

"You'll do no such thing."

Malachi turned to see Captain Cincy standing squarely in the doorway, blaster in hand, a blaster that was pointed directly at his own chest. Zerina stood defiantly just behind the captain, her hand still red with Gritlok's blood.

Doc watched mutely as the muzzle of the blaster blazed red hot as it discharged a deadly stream of energy.

Planet Kirby4 (aka Saffire)
MWC-217 (Starship 217 in the Milky Way
   Colonization program)
On-Planet

~ Sometime Later ~

Doc waited patiently for the debarkation ramp of MWC-217 to lower. It had transmitted a message to Mother Gaia many months earlier to send additional starships to Saffire to continue successful colonization, and a ship had finally arrived.

Raulsen stood beside Doc, eagerly awaiting the new arrivals. He was now wearing the dark blue of a captain's uniform.

The ramp lowered and several male and female crew members started down the ramp. They wore their skin-tight red MWC-217 uniforms and no helmets as they had received confirmed reports that the atmosphere on Saffire was quite pleasant and very much breathable.

Commander Suzukee of the starship MWC-217 reached the end of the ramp and stepped onto the surface of Saffire. In the far, far distance a volcano spit a column of fire into the sky. Commander Suzukee waved in greeting, but then slowly lowered her hand and slowed the pace of her walk. She frowned at the four naked women who flanked the man and the bronze-skinned humanoid.

The women's bodies were covered in small red welts, but they did not appear to be in any sort of pain; in fact, all of their faces held a dreamy sort of bliss. The man was fully clothed in a captain's uniform, with an obvious bulge in his groin area. Three of the naked women had bellies swollen with obvious pregnancy.

What appeared to be several small children were clustered behind the women, but all of the children seemed slightly deformed with oddly-shaped thin arms and spindly legs that appeared to be much too thin for normal human limbs. One of the children peered out from behind a naked woman with long blonde hair and Commander Suzukee nearly stumbled at the sight of what she saw. The hairless child had a bald head, and an oval face with a small mouth, but the child had no nose and no eyes. The child seemed to try and form a smile but all Commander Suzukee saw were small rows of sharp and jagged teeth.

Doc reached down to a containment cube it held in its hand and tapped a button, opening up the top of the box. A swarm of fucking blood suckers erupted out of the containment cube, the buzzing insects heading straight for the new arrivals. Doc was quite eager to see what new knowledge it could reap when non-sanctioned women were seeded with life from Raulsen.

"Welcome to Saffire!" Raulsen threw out his arms wide in greeting. "Welcome to my little bit of Heaven!" he called out with a broad smile on his face.

The children of Saffire charged out from behind their mothers, in no need of eyes as their innate senses guided them directly towards any male who might pose a threat to their father's dominance. All of the children had two sets of thin wings that grew out of their backs, and these helped them launch themselves forward with great speed.

Then Ritjavik Raulsen dug into his pants and

pulled his penis out. Dozens of sperm worms immediately exploded out of his enlarged meatus, the wriggling white alien life forms splashing up puffs of dust as they hit the dry ground. They thrashed their long white tails behind them, propelling themselves towards the female newcomers.

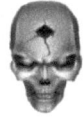

TERRORSTORY #76
THE NEW NORMAL

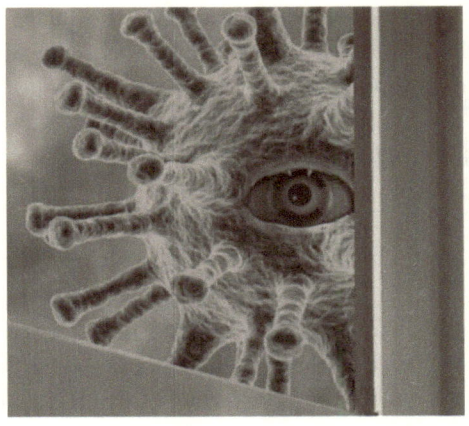

"Welcome to the club," Adam said, flashing the back of his left hand, displaying the tattoo inked into his skin. He sat down at the picnic table, sitting opposite Daniel who sat on the other side of the wooden table. The spring air was mildly warm, the sun blazing high up in a clear blue sky.

"Yeah, thanks. It's not really a club I wanted to join," Daniel said. Daniel Cove was a relative newcomer to Greendale, Illinois but had quickly made friends with most of the other mechanics at Shapoor's Auto Repair shop. He was a redhead, kept his hair short. He had the blunt features of a character actor, so no one would ever mistake him for a leading man. He was in decent shape, but his middle section was slowly starting to expand a little bit month after month. He liked to drink after work to relax and that put a damper on any desire to do any vigorous exercise. He preferred whisky over beer, especially vanilla whisky; he liked that straight with a splash of water and some ice. He thought of himself as just a normal, hard-working American.

Adam nodded. "Me neither. But we're both in it now. You gotta admit it's better than being in the six-foot-under club." Adam Wotherspoon was a fellow mechanic at Shapoor's shop, sharing the same grease-stained hands that Daniel had. Neither one of them, nor any of the other guys in the shop, ever seemed to be able get their hands completely clean. Adam was a beefy guy, a bit blubbery all over his body. Technically one might say he could be considered obese. He loved his pizza and beer. Adam had been infected by the coronavirus at Mardi Gras down in New Orleans months before Daniel's body had been invaded by it. Adam had fully recovered at home and Daniel thought Adam was pretty lucky in that regard since his co-worker had never needed hospitalization despite all the underlying symptoms Adam clearly must have, being so overweight and all.

Daniel nodded his head reluctantly. He glanced down at the back of his left hand. The CRG tattoo was inked into his flesh, matching the symbol on the back of Adam's hand. The tattoo was comprised of the letters CRG below an image of the SARS-CoV-2 novel coronavirus, which was the virus that caused the COVID-19 disease; most people simply referred to both the virus and the disease as COVID-19. The COVID-19 image was roughly circular with a deeply red center surrounded by a lighter yellowish corona. 19 tiny red spikes of different lengths stuck out from the edge of the circular shape at irregular intervals.

Daniels' tattoo, as well as Adam's, had a black circle surrounding the COVID-19 image and a single thick black line running diagonally through the virus, crossing through the image of the virus. Daniel looked back over at Adam. "How'd you pronounce it again?"

"Creggers," Adam answered. "We're Creggers. I'm one month clean." He flitted his wrist back and forth, flashing his tattoo.

"Creggers," Daniel repeated, looking back at the tattoo on the back of his left hand.

"It's easier than saying Covid Recovery Group Members," Adam said.

Daniel nodded. "Yeah."

"How was your latest scan?" Adam asked.

"My lungs are a little scarred, but my doctor says they should heal over time." Daniel touched his hand to his chest. "Still burns a little bit if I take too deep a breath, but that nasty dry cough is pretty much gone."

Adam nodded. "Same here. I gotta take it easy. And that's too bad because I really was planning on running that 10K marathon next month."

"Yeah, right," Daniel said sarcastically. He knew Adam had no intention of running in the 10K marathon, or any marathon. Ever. And now he had the perfect excuse not to participate. Ever. "Sometimes I can't even make it standing up through a whole shower. I still have to take a break and sit down in the middle of it to catch my breath."

"I told you that little plastic stool was worth it," Adam said.

Daniel nodded softly.

They both sat quietly for a moment.

"Listen," Adam said, lowering his voice to a softer tone than normal. "I know you feel bad about it, but you can't keep blaming yourself about your mom. They lied to us about how infectious this fucker was in the beginning. My wife was in great shape and it still got her, too."

Daniel nodded, almost absently. "I know. I'm never going to stop feeling guilty about it, but I know. Let's just not talk about that, okay?"

Adam nodded quietly.

Daniel looked over at a nearby group of boys in the park who were throwing rocks at bottles they had set up on a nearby fence. They were wearing identical face masks made out of dark blue cloth, the masks covering their mouths and noses; Daniel surmised one of the boys' mother had probably sewn a whole batch of identical masks for her son and his buddies. They were also wearing swim goggles, a trend that had picked up steam in the last few weeks once it had been made abundantly clear by scientists studying the virus that the virus could successfully infect you through your eyes. The boys were quasi-practicing social distancing, keeping themselves at least a few feet apart. But, being the smart asses that young boys were, they jumped at each other once in a while, lunging forward and throwing their hands up wildly in the air, testing each other to see who would be the first to flinch and move away.

"I don't miss wearing a mask outside, that's for sure." Daniel said. "So I suppose that's a nice perk."

"Yeah," Adam agreed. "Immunity *and* we're not contagious. Double bonus."

Daniel shifted his glance to the nearby trees that surrounded the park. The trees looked healthy, their trunks a deep brown, their leaves a vibrant green. The air was so much cleaner now that people were driving much less, and the flora clearly appreciated it. "God, I love the smell of fresh air," Daniel said. He started to take a deep inhale, but caught himself from breathing in too deep, remembering the pain from a mere few weeks ago that made it feel like he was breathing in shards of glass. He put his hand against his chest as he slowly let the shallow breath out.

Adam nodded. "We're both lucky we got our sense of smell back. Some people still can't smell shit." Adam suddenly leered at Daniel. "Hey, tell me if you can smell this." He raised his left butt cheek off the bench and tried to squeeze out a fart, his face scrunching up with the effort, but nothing came out. "Ahh, shit. Forget it."

Daniel turned his gaze back to the boys. One of the kids nailed one of the glass bottles, knocking it off the fence with a direct strike on the bottle's thin neck. The boys whooped it up, feigning clapping the rock-thrower heartily on the back with congratulatory air slaps. Another boy threw several rocks at a different bottle, but all his throws missed the target. He kicked angrily at the ground, scuffing the grass with his sneakers.

"You're coming to open gym tonight, right?" Adam asked.

Daniel looked away from the boys and shrugged. "I suppose so. It's not really optional, is it?"

Adam pursed his lips and cocked his head at Daniel. "It's your civic duty, man," he said.

"It's only for…" Daniel paused, fumbling for the

word he had just heard, then finished with, "Cregs, right?"

"Creggers," Adam corrected. "Like beggars with a 'C.' Yeah, it's only for Creggers." Adam quickly added. "Well, and any... shall we say... special guests."

Daniel was quiet for a moment. "What goes on during open gym?" he asked.

"Some people shoot some hoops, or kick a soccer ball around, maybe play some catch," Adam said. "Flirt with the lady Creggers." Adam quirked his lips up into a lascivious grin.

So much for mourning his wife, Daniel thought. He squinted at Adam. "That's it?"

Adam was quiet for a moment. "No, that's not it."

Daniel nodded. He had already known the answer Adam was going to give to his question, but he thought Adam might at least give him a hint of what else he could expect at open gym night. "So what do I need to do?"

Adam patted the top of the picnic table, laying both hands flat against the wood. "Just show up, man. The rest kind of takes care of itself." Adam scrunched up his face as he lifted his right butt cheek up off the bench and blew out a very loud fart. "Damn, there it is. That fucker was really corked up in there." Adam quickly waved his hand, trying to waft the smell towards Daniel.

Daniel scrunched up his noise and frowned at the stench. "Jesus."

"Ain't you glad you can smell again?" Adam asked with a stupid grin on his face.

Daniel rose up from the picnic table. He raised his hand as he walked away, but didn't look back at his friend. "See you tonight."

"There's more where that came from," Adam shouted after him.

Even though Greendale only had a few thousand residents, and a stay-at-home directive had been issued by the governor of Illinois, the coronavirus still had managed to take hold and spread before the official social distancing protocols had been set forth.

It didn't surprise Daniel that Mary Streenburg had contracted it first; she would be forever known as Greendale Patient Zero. She was always gloating about her world travels, talking incessantly about all the places she'd been, yacking about all the great sites she'd seen. Listening to her was like watching somebody show you boring pictures of their family vacation when you had no clue who the people even were; you just really didn't give a fuck. Well, good ol' world traveler Mary brought it back from her last cruise to the Mediterranean and shared it with the whole town. Gordon Streenburg, her husband who suffered from diabetes, was the second to succumb. He died a week after returning home from their cruise, just a day after his wife died.

The virus was so damn contagious it didn't take long before half a dozen more people were infected, then a dozen, then three dozen, then fifty. It could be spread just by standing too close to someone who was talking, let alone being near someone who was hacking up a dry thunderstorm of coughs or sneezing out a tornado of infectious particles. And then the scientists on the news suspected it could also be spread by aerosolized feces. Aerosolized feces. That's what they said. That's a fancy way of saying farts, man. You could actually inadvertently kill someone by farting out a virulent puff of virus-infected gas in a public place. Talk about silent but deadly. That was some fucking grim horror.

Daniel sought to cure his ignorance of what a virus really was. He was embarrassed to admit to himself that he really didn't know a whole lot about them. And the more he read online about viruses, the more freaked out he got.

Viruses weren't even really alive. How fucked up was that? They were first seen as poisons, then mistakenly categorized as life-forms, then as biological chemicals. The most current thinking put viruses in a nebulous area between living and nonliving, somewhere between chemistry and biology, because they couldn't replicate on their own. A virus did not have its own biological machinery to replicate. A virus did not multiply through cellular division. A virus did not have a metabolism. Viruses did not have self-generated or self-sustaining actions. Viruses were not made out of cells; they didn't grow, and they couldn't make their own energy. The SARS-CoV-2 virus was little more than a packet of genetic material surrounded by a spiky protein shell one-thousandth the width of an eyelash.

When viruses encountered a host, aka a human in this case, they used proteins on their surfaces to unlock and invade the human host's unsuspecting cells. Then they took control of the molecular machinery of the human host's cells to produce and assemble the materials needed for more viruses. In essence, a virus hijacked the reproductive equipment of a host cell, redirecting it to duplicate the genetic code of the virus. Viruses depended on the host cells that they infected to reproduce. Without a host cell, viruses simply couldn't replicate.

But once inside a cell, a virus could make 10,000 copies of itself in a matter of hours. Within a few days, the infected person could carry hundreds of millions of viral particles in every teaspoon of his blood. Holy fuck, Daniel thought. That was some scary shit. This virus reproduction onslaught triggered an intense response from the host's immune system. Defensive chemicals were released by the infected host. The host's body temperature rose, causing fever. Armies of germ-eating white blood cells swarmed the infected region. Often, this response was what made a person feel sick.

Daniel felt a roiling wave of nausea in his stomach simply from learning how insidious viruses really were. Viruses had spent billions of years perfecting the art of surviving without living - a frighteningly effective strategy that made them a potent threat throughout history. Some scientists estimated that the smallpox virus was responsible for 300 million to 500 million deaths worldwide. He forced himself to stop reading.

Daniel started feeling feverish several days after Gordon's wake. As usually what happens at a wake, there was a lot of crying, a lot of hugging, a lot of physically comforting the bereaved. And a whole helluva lot of virus being spread.

Daniel's mother had not been at the wake because she was still at her house recovering from a slight stroke, but he went to visit her right afterwards because he knew she would want to hear any town gossip he might have overheard. Thinking about it after her death, he knew he had passed the virus on to her. He hadn't known he was contagious at the time, but it was really the only way his mother could have gotten it.

It started off with the chills, a slight cough. The symptoms started off pretty mild, but Daniel knew he had to get himself tested for the coronavirus, especially after the dry cough seemed to be getting worse and he felt like he had a fever twenty hours out of the day. And there was that damn headache that just wouldn't quit no matter how much acetaminophen he pounded.

The tests had been very slow to roll-out nationwide, but within a few weeks there were plenty of test kits to go around in their town. He had read horror stories of other people in different states waiting days, if not weeks, for a test or for test results, but luckily that didn't happen to Greendale. The governor of Illinois was pretty damn effective in getting test kits where they needed to go.

Daniel tested positive. It didn't really surprise him as he had all the hallmark symptoms of infection, but testing positive still freaked him out a bit. He forced himself to keep looking at the numbers of people who had recovered on the Johns Hopkins Coronavirus Resource Center website; the recovered number was in the millions. Yes, hundreds of thousands of people had died from the virus, but far more people had recovered. He took some comfort in that fact.

So he self-quarantined, taking it easy, eating chicken soup, sweating off about sixteen pounds from the unrelenting fever. The chills that wracked him made his teeth chatter so hard he was afraid he was going to break a tooth. It was the sickest he had ever felt in his life. Every muscle in his body ached; he even felt like the virus was somehow digging into his very bones with little tiny dagger-teeth. He knew viruses weren't really alive, but he felt better giving the virus infecting him some kind of animalistic, zoomorphic existence so he could target his anger at it and pretend his white blood cells were armed soldiers who could rip the virus to shreds with machine gun fire and blow its head off.

He had read of others having weirdly vivid dreams during their infection. There was supposedly an increase in dreaming even in people who weren't infected. Someone had said that it might be some kind of REM rebound, where people were actually catching up on the sleep they needed. They were experiencing a surge in REM sleep, which is the stage of sleeping where dreaming happens, simply because the pace of life had slowed down and they were sleeping more. The only dream he remembered during his feverish phase was the one he had that was filled with swarms of see-thru grasshoppers with translucent skin attacking Greendale.

One particularly vivid dream he recalled was of a translucent grasshopper dive-bombing Father Carlson and hitting the priest square in the chest; the grasshopper disintegrated into a mash of guts and blood when it struck his chest. But then the blood smear continued to grow, continued to spread, the red liquid smear expanding across the priest's entire chest, then down his thighs and across his shoulders, until his entire body was covered in a crimson stain. And then Father Carlson's body exploded into a thousand shredded bits of flesh and bone and internal organs as a swarm of newly born translucent grasshoppers erupted out of him. That was a fucked up dream. Daniel remembered reading about swarms of locusts that were infecting Africa at the same time the coronavirus was spreading across the globe, so he surmised his fevered brain put those two plagues together in his dream.

There were a few days in the ordeal where the virus totally sapped him of any energy, and of any desire to even move off the couch except to go to the bathroom. He was glad he lived alone. He didn't know how people who lived with an infected family member could even do it; he'd probably die of a panic attack if he had to help someone get through the misery of the infection all the while paranoid he would get the sickness too.

Being a mechanic, he couldn't really work from home. When he had a little bit of energy, he read up on some technician manuals he had been meaning to read for months, but had never got around to. He binged a helluva lot of Netflix, but couldn't remember much of anything he had watched; all the shows blurred together in a feverish haze. He sampled a few free trials of other streaming services, but didn't sign up because he had no idea what his financial situation was going to be like in a few months.

Vicki Adamik left some groceries on his stoop

every few days and he Paypal'd her some money for it, plus gave her a few bucks for her troubles. Mostly just canned stuff, some frozen meat, more soup, some energy drinks, frozen pizzas. She was too freaked out by the virus to handle any fresh fruit or vegetables in the store so he didn't press her on that. She Skyped him every few days and they masturbated together. He never really realized how hairy she was, even around her ass, because the few times they had had sex the room was dark and they could barely see each other's faces let alone their nether regions. It didn't matter; he still found himself getting aroused by her nakedness. Nobody could say they weren't practicing safe sex. It was a strange new world they were living in.

The newest problem in Greendale Illinois was that some residents didn't get the concept of social distancing. No, that's not right. They got it, they just didn't follow it. They just didn't care. Life was all about them - always had been, always would be. Everybody over forty years old was flabbergasted that Natalie Williams still threw herself a high school graduation party and invited a few dozen of her friends over. They were partying in her backyard, hugging and kissing each other; Daniel could see them through the sliding glass door that led out to his porch. It's a weird feeling to have discomfort in your gut when you see two people hugging and kissing each other on the cheek. They even shared a couple of joints, spreading them around the group. Something so innocent, friends sharing with friends, now became a chilling spectacle.

Mayor Treacle knew she had to do something because Natalie and her friends weren't the only ones violating the social distancing rules. Since the mayor used to run a tattoo parlor in town before she was elected to office, her crafty little idea involved her old business. The tattoo parlor, now run by the mayor's brother, had been shut down as a non-essential business weeks ago due to the stay-at-home mandates, along with all sit-down restaurants, hair salons, and a few other places, but all the tools and inks were still readily available.

Here's how the mayor's plan went. An isolation room was set up in the local hospital. If you tested positive for the virus, you were sent to the isolation room. There was a hermetically sealed slot in the wall that you put your arm through. On the other side of the wall, a tattoo artist inked the image of the COVID-19 virus on the back of your left hand. To some people it felt like the A in the Scarlet Letter, a mark of shame, but it was just a quick visual indicator people could use to keep track of the infected. It was all done very safely with strict protocols in place - both the tattoo artist and the tattoo recipient were kept isolated from each other. The tattoo artist wore protective gear at all times and only had access to the person's hand stuck through a flap-covered hole that had been carved out of the wall. All tattooing equipment was vigorously sterilized between each tattoo recipient.

If subsequent tests showed you recovered from the virus and you were no longer contagious, then a black circle was inked around the initial tattoo and a thick black line was inked through the COVID-19 virus, thus indicating that you once had the disease but you were now virus-free. Again, the tattoo was just another quick visual indicator of who had once tested positive for the virus, but were now testing negative after the infection and had fully recovered from the coronavirus.

After the tattoo protocols were put in place, you were only allowed to have social gatherings if everyone in the gathering had a crossed out COVID-19 symbol tattooed on the back of their left hand. Basically, you had to be a Cregger to throw, and attend, a party of more than two people. Anyone caught falsely misrepresenting themselves as having recovered were severely dealt with through very hefty fines, mandatory jail time, and heavy public scorn.

Daniel stepped into the gym. The gym was the size of a regulation basketball court but tonight it was cordoned off into three sections by huge white vinyl hanging dividers that separated the gym into three separate areas.

A few guys and a lone woman were shooting hoops on the near court to his right. Daniel recognized Jake O'Neil among the guys, but he didn't know the woman. He may have seen her at Dunkin Donuts once, but he wasn't sure; she was a pretty blonde with long hair that she had tied up into a tight bun. The guys were going easy on her, letting her dribble without much effort to defend her and giving her plenty of room to take a shot. The numerous weeks of social distancing subconsciously made people aware of how close they were to someone else, even within this group. The woman missed her shot, barely hitting the backboard, but she did hustle after the ball and snag her own rebound.

Daniel looked left, looking away from the pick-up game, and saw that the middle section of the bleachers had been pulled out from the wall and was stretched out twenty rows deep. It was a strange sight to see the middle section of the bleachers nearly filled to capacity with people sitting so close to each other. To Daniel, it seemed like at least five or ten percent of the town were now part of the recovered group, and it looked like all of them had shown up to take advantage of open gym night. It made him uncomfortable to see so many people sitting so close together, but that was something he knew he would just have to slowly get used to seeing again. They were all Creggers, Daniel reminded himself. It was okay for Creggers to sit shoulder to shoulder. He absently looked for Vicki in the crowd, even though he knew she wouldn't be there. She wasn't a Cregger.

The crowd sitting on the bleachers paid little attention to the basketball game being played. They were more focused on the small stage that was set up in the middle of the court area that was flanked on either side by huge dividers that hung down from the high ceiling. The far left section of the divided court looked empty and dark with no lights illuminating it; Daniel only caught a glimpse of it because the big white divider blocked most of that area from view. The center court was where the stage was set. It was just a small stage, about a foot high, four feet wide, four feet long, covered by a white cloth. A wooden pole about seven feet high jutted up from near the back end of the stage, the pole lodged into a circular hole that had been cut out of the stage platform. A larger black cloth was spread out beneath the stage, extending an additional eight feet or so from each edge of the stage, as if to protect the varnished basketball court floor beneath.

"Hey, Daniel!" he heard a loud voice boom from his left.

Daniel looked over to see Adam Wotherspoon striding towards him.

"Glad you could make it," Adam said, extending his hand, his fingers stained with grease and grime from the garage.

Daniel looked down at Adam's offered hand, hesitating. He almost countered with an elbow bump, but then remembered they were both cured. Hell, they were both Creggers for crying out loud. He took Adam's offered hand and shook it vigorously.

Adam laughed and pulled his hand away. "Whoa, easy big fella."

Daniel pointed to the crowded bleachers. "What's going on? They waiting for some kind of show or something?"

Adam grinned. "Or something."

Daniel noticed a man moving through the crowd. He was wearing what appeared to be a hot-dog-selling apparatus that Daniel had seen at a baseball game once. The apparatus was a big stainless steel metal box with a large metal lid on one side and a smaller lid on the other. The box had a big leather strap attached to both ends so the man could wear it around his neck. The man moved through the crowd, opening the large lid for each person and tilting the big metal box toward each person so they could reach into the box and grab something. Daniel couldn't see what everyone was pulling out of the big metal box, but it appeared to be a small object of some kind. Maybe a piece of candy or something, he thought.

The lights flickered.

Adam smacked his hands together, his face clearly filled with eager excitement. "Show time!" He nudged Daniel towards the bleachers. "Take a seat, take a seat. I saved you a spot in the second row. They keep the first rows empty for newcomers so you don't have to expend energy climbing up into the higher rows. Everybody remembers how tough it is to get your wind back."

Daniel nodded. He followed Adam to the second row in the bleachers and took a seat next to him.

The man with the big metal box strapped to his body continued doling out whatever it was that he was giving out, moving closer and closer to Daniel and Adam as he moved down the aisles. He soon reached the second row and stopped before them.

Adam jerked a thumb in Daniel's direction. "First timer."

The vendor's face lit up into a genuine smile. "Excellent," he said. He closed the main lid on the box, then opened the smaller lid that was on the opposite side of the box. The metal box man stared at Daniel, as if expecting him to make some kind of movement. Daniel just stared back at him.

Adam bumped his shoulder against Daniel's. "You gotta pick it out. Just reach in there and grab one."

Daniel hesitated a second, then reached his hand into the narrow compartment area the vendor had opened for him. His hands felt a cool, smooth surface. There were several objects within the compartment, all of them with a similar round shape and size, like giant marbles or something. He curled his fingers around one of them and lifted his hand out of the box.

"Let me see what you got," Adam said.

Daniel uncurled his fingers to reveal the object that lay in his palm. It was a glass orb with some kind of object embedded within the center of the glass.

Adam frowned. "Oh, man. You got the spikeball. I never got the spikeball."

"Beginner's luck?" Daniel said, trying to lighten Adam's suddenly dark mood.

Adam nodded. His somber countenance only lasted a brief moment. He smiled and playfully punched Adam on the shoulder. "Good for you."

"You realize I have no idea what this is, or what it's for, or what I'm supposed to do with it, right?" Daniel said.

"It's a spikeball," Adam said. "See how it's got the shape of the coronavirus with all those little spikes sticking out of it?"

"Yeah," Daniel said as he stared at the odd glass ball he held in his hand. The object embedded in the center of the glass did look similar to several artistic renditions of the coronavirus he had seen posted on the web. The main body of the virus was dark purple in color, with the spikes jutting out of it looking almost black.

"Don't squeeze it too hard," Adam cautioned. "You don't want that thing shattering in your hand."

Daniel immediately loosened his grip, letting his fingers lay flat, keeping the orb in the center of his open palm.

"Jesus, don't drop it either," Adam admonished.

Daniel put a slight curl back into his fingers, gently

cradling the spikeball. "What the hell do I do with it?"

"Oh, you'll find out," Adam said. "Very soon now." Adam turned his attention back to the vendor standing patiently next to them. The vendor opened up the larger compartment. Adam reached in and pulled out a shiny black object. It was a black stone, about the size of a golf ball, its shape a bit more irregular than a ball but still pretty round. Adam tossed it up into the air a few times, catching the stone in his palm. "Just gauging its weight," Adam said as he caught Daniel looking at him with a curious stare.

Daniel glanced about the gathered crowd, seeing people eying their stones, or keeping them out of sight behind closed fists; a few people tossed their stones in the air like Adam had done, but the vast majority just sat with a closed hand.

The vendor moved down out of the stands and then slowly walked along the gymnasium floor, looking up at the crowd in the bleachers as he moved. "Did I miss anyone?" the vendor called up into the stands. A woman on the far end of the crowd raised her hand and the vendor moved quickly over to her, giving her access to the large compartment. She reached a hand into the metal box and pulled out a tan-colored stone.

The vendor once again looked up into the gathered audience. "Anybody else?"

No one raised a hand or called out, so the vendor gave a quick wave and headed out of the gym through a door in the upper left corner of the large room.

Everyone was quiet. The lights in the room dimmed. A spotlight appeared, shining a column of white-hot light onto the small stage that had been set up on the gymnasium floor in the center section.

Two big men appeared, dragging another man wearing a white pillowcase over his head between them. The captive had his arms tied behind his back with thick rope. The two big men tugged the man with the covered head onto the platform, keeping him upright with a sharp tug as the captive nearly tripped on the low edge of the stage. The two men gripped the captive's shoulders and lifted the man high up into the air, maneuvering his bound hands behind the pole. They lowered the captive back to his feet, effectively securing the man to the pole and making it impossible for him to get off the stage. The captive man stood silently on the platform as one of the men yanked the pillowcase off his head.

Daniel recognized the man immediately. "That's our boss!" Daniel whispered with a sharp urgency to Adam. "That's Shapoor from the garage."

Adam shushed Daniel with a short hiss. "Shh. I know."

Daniel was going to say something further, but kept his mouth shut. Not a single person in the audience was making a sound, not even a faint whisper. He looked back over at the elderly man standing on the platform. The two men who had dragged him up onto the platform silently moved away, disappearing into the darkness of the left side of the gym.

Mayor Treacle stepped into the center area, coming from the darkened left section. She was a woman of color, in her mid-fifties, also a Cregger. She was dressed all for business in a gray pantsuit and black shoes. Just a hint of gray hair streaked along both sides of her temples. She wasted no time in getting to the business at hand the moment she reached the edge of the stage. "You have been accused of defying the order to properly distance yourself from your fellow townspeople," she said to the man held captive on the small stage, her voice amplified by some hidden microphone so everyone in the bleachers could hear. "How do you plead?"

Shapoor looked up, but did not answer. His elderly face was weathered with the crevices of time, his brown eyes somehow full of both fatigue and fear at the same time.

The mayor raised her voice higher as she repeated the same statement and question. "You have been accused of defying the order to properly distance yourself from your fellow townspeople. How do you plead?"

"I forgot," Shapoor said. His voice was soft, but the microphone still picked up his words and broadcast them to the gathered group. He hung his head. "Just for a second. I forgot."

"All it takes is a second," Mayor Treacle said. Her voice held no sympathy, no understanding. It was just a statement of fact.

Shapoor slowly raised his head back up. Tears streamed down his cheeks. "I just wanted to give my wife a hug before she died, that's all. Just a hug."

"Hug this!" a voice shouted from the stands. A stone sailed out of the bleachers and hit Shapoor in the chest, striking him near the bottom of his ribcage. He grunted and bent over, but remained standing, his arms wrenching up behind him, the rope that bound his wrists keeping him secured to the pole.

Daniel started to rise up and a shout of protest was about to burst forth from his mouth, but Adam gripped his wrist roughly and sharply tugged him back down to his seat. Daniel whipped his head towards Adam and Adam gave him a very stern look, shaking his head tightly in a few vigorous shakes. Daniel looked back towards the stage, then looked back to Adam. Adam once again shook his head, motioning for Daniel to stay seated with a sharp jerking motion of his head towards his seat. Daniel remained seated, remained quiet.

Another stone sailed out from the bleachers, but this one missed its mark and the rock clanged and clattered as it struck the gym floor and bounced into the wall on the opposite side of the gym. Somebody in the stands booed and a few people chuckled at that.

Daniel immediately thought of the boys practicing their stone throwing in the park and felt a chill course through his body. Jesus, were they practicing for this?

Another rock sailed out of the bleachers, this one striking Shapoor in the thigh. He bent his leg, twisting it awkwardly as the force of the striking stone propelled his leg's movement.

"You infect one. You infect all!" someone shouted from the stands.

Daniel could feel eyes on him and he looked over to see Adam staring expectantly at him.

"Guess what they found," Adam said.

Daniel squinted at Adam, narrowing his eyes in confusion.

Adam glanced in Shapoor's direction then looked back to Daniel. "Guess what the epidemiology results that came back from the lab showed. Go on, guess."

Daniel again had no answer.

"The genetic material of the coronavirus traces

they found in his body matched the virus signature I had," Adam said. "You know what that means?

Daniel was quiet.

"He killed my wife, Danny," Adam said. "It was because of him I got infected. Shapoor hugged his infected wife and didn't think he needed to self-quarantine. He wasn't sick, so why should he bother? Shapoor spread it around to everyone in the garage. Think about who else that affected."

Daniel felt his jaw tighten.

"I had Kellen in the lab check your virus signature," Adam said. "He knows we're tight, so he told me. You didn't get it from anyone at the funeral or the wake." Adam paused. "Think about that for a moment."

Daniel felt his head spinning. The horror of what Adam was telling him struck home with an immediate and intense ferocity. "He killed my mother," Daniel said. Every muscle in his body tensed. "He fucking killed my mom." A whirling flood of emotions hit Daniel all at once. "Shapoor killed her."

Daniel remembered watching his mother die. Right there on his laptop screen during their last Skype call together. She was quarantined alone in her house, mostly staying in her bed, doing her best to fight the virus. Her symptoms hadn't been severe enough for her to be hospitalized. Sure, she had a little trouble breathing, and walking from one side of her house to the other exhausted her, but she was still doing better than many others who had caught the virus. For a few fleeting days, he had even thought the tough old bird was going to knock the virus on its ass; he had heard of a few people in Italy who had beaten the virus who were in their nineties and his mother was only in her late sixties.

But then he saw his mother's face tighten up as they were on the Skype call together, saw the tension in her features ratchet up to a level of fear he had never seen in a human being before. She knew she was about to die. And she was scared. He could see the terror filling up her eyes like flames crawling up the sides of a burning building. He remembered just staring mutely at his laptop screen as the life in his mother's eyes just faded away. One second it was there, burning hotly, and the next second it was gone, completely extinguished. Her head lolled to the side, and then the laptop must have fallen from her lap because the image of the screen suddenly shifted to a view of her slippers and parts of her pale, pasty legs.

There was no time to call 9-1-1. No time to get an ambulance to her. He never felt more ineffectual, more weak, more fucking useless than he had ever felt in his life. He hadn't even said goodbye. He hadn't told her he loved her on the call.

Daniel gritted his teeth and tightened his jaw until his bones ached. But there was time now. Time to make it right. Daniel rose up to a standing position, gripping the spikeball in his hand. Then he hurled the projectile with blistering speed. His aim was true. The spikeball struck Shapoor square in the forehead, right above his eyes, the glass that had surrounded the coronavirus spike object contained within the orb shattering on impact. Shapoor's head snapped back violently; he appeared to stare up at the ceiling for a long moment, as if in final prayer, before his head snapped back down.

"Holy shit," Adam said. "Nice shot!"

The spiked coronavirus object was embedded

firmly into Shapoor's forehead, several of the spiked edges sunk deep into his skull. The spikes were strong enough and sharp enough to even penetrate Shapoor's skull beneath the flesh of his forehead.

Another stone rocketed out from the bleachers and struck Shapoor in the side of his throat, the sharp edge of the rock slicing into him, cutting his artery. Blood spurted out from the cut and seeped down his body, eventually reaching the floor of the stage, staining the white cloth a deep red. Shapoor's head drooped.

Adam rose to his feet and hurled his rock. His black stone collided against the left side of Shapoor's drooping head, the loud cracking noise echoing in the gym.

More rocks whistled through the air and the meaty sound of flesh being hit by hard objects filled the gym. Soon, the stage, the floor around the stage, and the gym floor were littered with stones. Many of the stones on the floor of the stage had surfaces or edges that were wet with blood. The white cloth that covered the stage was now nearly fully covered in blood stains of various irregular shapes and sizes.

Daniel stared at the bloody scene quietly. Within moments, everyone in the bleachers was quiet. A sullen, but somewhat satisfied, quiet blanketed the gym. It was strange. Shapoor had, in essence, created who they now were. Without him, neither he nor Adam would be a Cregger, Daniel realized. Shapoor had given them an odd new freedom. But his careless disregard of social distancing and lack of self-quarantining had also caused the deaths of many people. He had to be punished. Social justice meted out at a distance seemed very appropriate. Daniel had to admit to himself that the entire experience, short as it was, was very cathartic.

"Wanna get a drink at O'Leery's?" Adam finally asked after a few more moments of prolonged silence.

Daniel nodded. "Yeah, sure. You buying?"

Adam nodded. "Sure. It's a two-for-one Creggers special tonight."

Adam raised up his clenched fist, displaying his CRG tattoo to Daniel. Daniel raised his clenched fist and bumped the tattooed back of his hand against the back of Adam's hand.

It was a weird new normal, but Daniel was pretty confident he would adapt and get used to it quickly.

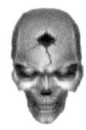

TERRORSTORY #77
COINS OF THE DEAD

"You are a bottom-feeding leech!" The bread merchant's tone was surly and aggravated. "No coin, no food!" The rotund baker normally had a scowl on his face all the time anyway, but the merchant's contempt for Kalamann etched the glowering lines a little deeper than normal into his craggy face.

The baker wore a light brown leather apron around his big belly, the apron more befitting a butcher than a baker. The apron was smeared with powdery streaks of white flour, glistening hints of sugar, and stained with other multi-colored spots from a dozen different spices and flavorings.

"I will pay you back when I get some coin,"

Kalamann said. He eyed the fresh loaves of bread on the shelf right in front of him with an obvious hunger that was made of equal parts desperation and equal parts lust.

Kalamann Kar was a scrawny young man. He had the thin arms and thin legs of a street beggar. His face was long and narrow, emaciated, covered in a growth of beard that he hadn't trimmed back for several weeks. His black hair was long and scraggly, the oily strands reaching down past his shoulders. His feet were clad in open-toed sandals that looked as if they might fall apart at any moment.

Abandoned when he was four in one of the more northern villages, Kalamann had a rough going of it, nearly dying from starvation one year, and from the bitter cold the next. He kept drifting south, moving towards warmer climates. He somehow managed to survive into young adulthood and found himself in Gilmont, but work was difficult to come by for a stranger in many villages and Gilmont was no exception. The vast majority of the townsfolk preferred Kalamann continue on his journey and leave their staid village in peace, rather than offer him employment.

"No coin, no food!" the merchant said again, his voice tightening with deeper anger. He brusquely waved his fat fingers at Kalamann, dismissing him as one would flick at an annoying pest. "Stop whining at me and be gone!"

A flag positioned near the baker's stall flapped in the breeze, the fabric seeming to wiggle at Kalamann with the same dismissive disdain that the baker had for him. Kalamann looked up at the flag. It was the royal flag of Gilmont, this village Kalamann had decided to linger in and look for work. The flag was a rendition of the royal family crest complete with a brightly white full moon surrounded by a dark background that was filled with pinpoints of white stars. Within the full moon image, a stylishly rendered G was centered in the white circle.

Behind and all around Kalamann, hundreds of people browsed for goods or haggled over prices in the village bazaar that was the lifeblood of Gilmont. Bells chimed from somewhere in the near distance. Nearby vendors called out to shoppers to entice them to their stalls. A stray calico cat wandered about, begging for morsels with a soft tiny meow. Two stray bulldogs padded through the bazaar, the animals clearly focused on some distant destination, the dogs following the sound and scent of sizzling meat. A couple wandered past behind Kalamann, eating candied nuts from a bag they shared.

"I can do work for you," Kalamann said to the baker, his grumbling stomach forcing him not to give up. "I can clean your stall. Sweep the kitchen."

"Work?" A male voice nearby laughed.

Kalamann glanced up to see Prince Raseem looking down at him disdainfully. The prince was wearing a gold shirt, open halfway down his chest, revealing his pale white flesh. A necklace made of tiny crescent-moon-shaped beads encircled his throat. His dark hair was slicked back with oil. Two burly bodyguards flanked the royal; they were also dressed in gold shirts but their clothing was a much paler, much more muted shade of gold. One of the guards held up an umbrella that cast a thick shadow over the prince, shielding the pale-skinned royal from the skin-darkening rays of the sun.

"With those puny arms?" The prince laughed again. "Can you even hold a broom with those puny hands?"

Kalamann said nothing. He fought to stop himself from gritting his teeth, forcing himself to remain calm, struggling to keep the muscles in his face from tightening.

The baker bowed towards Raseem. "Prince Raseem. You honor me." The baker rose back up."

Prince Raseem waved his hand, wriggling his pale fingers. "I'm not here for you. I'm here for your wife's blackberry pie. You must convince her to come cook in the royal kitchens."

"Yes, my prince," the baker replied, lowering his head.

The bells continued to toll in the distance.

The baker looked toward the chiming sounds, then looked at the prince. "I am deeply sorry for your loss," the baker said. "The princess was well loved," he added.

"My sister was a simpering little fool who spent far too much time in the sun. It baked her brains," the prince replied casually. He turned his gaze back to Kalamann. "And you are a sad little beggar," the prince said. "You will never be nothing more than a sad little beggar. Now go beg somewhere else." He waved his hand dismissively at Kalamann with an even greater annoyance than the baker had shown towards him.

Kalamann eyed the loaf of bread that was sitting on a shelf a mere few feet away from him. He could still see hints of warm steam rising up off the loaf. His stomach rumbled and grumbled as he stared at the bread. He knew he should heed the prince's words, but his feet refused to move. The smell of the fresh bread was intoxicating, a combination of fresh bread, butter, and cinnamon, the sweet aroma keeping him pinned to the spot.

"I will chop off your crooked fingers," the baker threatened as he glared at Kalamann. "Listen to your prince. He commanded you to leave."

Kalamann clearly heard those words of warning and he looked away from the loaf, but yet he still could not move. His stomach gurgled again and there was nothing he could do to stop the sound.

Prince Raseem watched Kalamann with clear amusement in his eyes. He now seemed to be more entertained than annoyed. "Go on," the prince encouraged Kalamann. "Take it. I can hear your sad little beggar belly crying from here."

Kalamann glanced up to see the baker's wife emerging from the doorway that led to the kitchen within the small brick building that also served as the merchant's home. She held a pie tin in her hands.

"Ahh, there it is," the prince cooed at the sight of the blackberry pie in her hands.

The baker's wife bowed towards Prince Raseem. "My prince," she said reverently.

The baker's wife was much more slender than her husband, her gray hair tied up in a tight bun atop her head. The white apron she wore was far less stained than his despite her doing most of the actual baking, with only a slight smear of blackberry juices staining a small portion of the cloth. She had a dour face, but she was a woman, Kalamann thought. Women always had kinder hearts than men. "Madam baker, surely you have some scraps," Kalamann said.

The woman said nothing as she finished setting

the blackberry pie down next to a row of colorful fruit tarts.

Kalamann stared wolfishly at the pie as its dark juices oozed through decorative slits in the golden-brown crust.

The other burly guard immediately snatched the freshly baked pie off the shelf and held out a silver coin to the baker's wife.

The baker's wife rose back up, wiped her hands off on her apron, and accepted the offered payment with a slight bow.

"Perhaps a burnt loaf," Kalamann suggested.

The baker's wife jerked her head sharply towards Kalamann. "Burnt loaf?" She pressed her lips so tightly together that they almost trembled. "I've never burnt a loaf in my life," she said. She pressed her fisted hands tight against her sides.

"Now you insult my wife?" The merchant glared at Kalamann. His cheeks flared red. "Greta, fetch my cleaver."

"Yes, dear Greta, fetch that cleaver," the prince said, happily chiming in. "I believe this little beggar also no longer has need for his crooked tongue."

Kalamann turned and bolted away.

"Run little beggar!" Prince Raseem shouted after him with an amused lilt in his voice. "Run!"

The sounds of the bustling market continued all around Kalamann as scores of people moved about, all of them going about their daily business, all of them oblivious to his great distress as he raced through them.

In the distance, the pealing sound of church bells continued to ring out.

❦

Kalamann raced through the bazaar, fighting back the anger and the tears and the fear. He was afraid of the baker and his ugly threats, afraid of the prince and his brutes and his impish laugh, and angry at himself for being such a coward. He really was just a sad little beggar. He wiped away the tears on his muddied cheeks and just continued to run, narrowly missing colliding into several groups of people as he scurried through the market.

The church bells continued to chime in the distance.

Kalamann spotted what looked like an open space near him, somewhere where he could go to avoid the crowds, to catch his breath. He burst out into the open space and paused, bending over, putting his hands on his knobby knees, fighting to slow his panting breaths.

"Get out of the way, you fool!" someone shouted.

Kalamann didn't know who shouted, or really even in the direction from which the shout had come, but he just instinctively knew it was aimed at him. He glanced over to his left, still in a bent-over position, and his eyes went wide.

A huge funeral procession was heading directly towards him. Luckily for him, the procession was moving at a slow and measured pace, otherwise he would have been run over and trampled to death.

He scurried back in the direction he had come and pressed his back up against a brick wall. Kalamann watched the funeral procession through slitted eyes, his brain finally registering why the church bells were ringing even though it wasn't a typical holy day of worship.

A tall man in a white robe led the procession, gently swinging an incense holder back and forth in front of him, humming some words that Kalamann didn't understand. Wispy white curls of burning scented oil floated up from the incense holder. The tall man kept his white hooded head bowed, his steps slow and measured.

Behind the tall man, a long cart was wheeled slowly forward by four others dressed in white robes. Kalamann couldn't see their faces because their upraised white hoods blocked his view. Each person in a white robe gripped a wooden protrusion, somewhat like a short peg, that jutted up from the side of the cart. They grasped this peg and used it to push the cart forward along the village's main dirt road.

The bed of the funeral cart was about three feet off the ground so its occupant was clearly visible to all. Atop the cart lay the pale naked body of a dead woman. She was lying peacefully upon a cloud of white silk, her hands folded across her chest, her golden hair fanned out about her head. So the stories were true, Kalamann thought. The princess really was dead.

Kalamann stared at the dead woman. It wasn't Princess Yasalla's large pale breasts that caught Kalamann's attention, nor the bush of blonde hair at the apex of her legs. It was the two gold coins placed over the princess's eyes. Her payment for the Ferryman to bring her into the afterlife. The two gold coins shimmered in the afternoon sunlight, glinting and sparkling and twinkling. Kalamann was entranced by the sight of them. What would such magnificent coins fetch in the markets? How many loaves of delicious fresh bread would they buy? A dozen? Maybe even hundreds? He felt his mouth watering at the thought and he swallowed away the fantasy.

Kalamann watched the mourners shuffle slowly along the dirt street. The village elders had closed off the main thoroughfare in the bazaar to allow the passing of the deceased and her entourage of mourners. Several women dressed in white robes lined with gold trim walked slowly behind the funeral cart, their heads bowed. They said nothing, remaining silent as they moved. Such finery they all wore. Everyone in the procession was wearing a glittering-hemmed robe or sparkling jewelry about their throats and wrists. What a crass display of wealth when so many were going hungry, Kalamann thought.

It was also odd to see so many of the royals out during the day since they preferred doing most of their activities at night. Perhaps it was in deference to the princess because she was one of the few Gilmont royals who was rumored to actually enjoy some sunlight.

Behind the funeral cart and the cluster of white-robed women, another cart was being pushed forwards, this cart about a third the length of the funeral cart holding the deceased princess. Kalamann's eyes widened and his mouth again watered. This cart was filled with food. The food offerings consisted of figs, apples, pear, grapes, fermented meat, salted nuts, dried beef, some cheese, and bread. Luscious loaves of brown-crusted bread. Kalamann knew it was for the dead woman, a symbolic offering to nourish the princess in the moments between this life and her entry into the afterlife.

But he also knew there was enough food displayed on the carriage to feed a single man for months. And Kalamann suddenly realized that single man could be him. Why not? The food was just a token of respect for the departed, a remembrance of the lavish lifestyle the princess had enjoyed when she was alive. Surely the dead no longer had any real need for food. It would only rot down in the crypts. It would only make those obscenely fat rodents who thrived in the tombs even more obscenely fat.

Kalamann stared at the funeral procession, cursing himself a fool. Of course! Why hadn't he thought of this before! He had to wipe his hand across the back of his mouth to stop a drop of spittle from drooling down his chin. What a treasure! Coin *and* food! What more did a man need? Kalamann's stomach grumbled, the bubbling, gurgling noises churning through his abdomen. Damnation, he was hungry!

Kalamann glanced down at his ragged and ripped black cloak. That would not do. He had thought of immersing himself in the throng of followers, hiding himself amongst the large gathering that trailed behind the food cart, but he knew he would stick out like a crow amidst a flock of doves.

His stomach started to rumble again, but suddenly the sound cut off as a thought struck him. He knew where they were going. There was only one possible destination.

He turned away from the crowd of mourners and raced far ahead of the funeral procession.

A large metal fence surrounded the village's cemetery, but to Kalamann's delight the gate was open, most likely in anticipation of the funeral procession that would arrive shortly.

He slinked closer to the open gate, casting furtive glances all about the area, but he saw no one. His heart hammered in his chest and his mouth felt dry. To be caught in the village cemetery without express permission was a punishable offense. He remembered the two boys who had been severely whipped and publicly humiliated in the town square last month for trespassing on the holy grounds; it took days for the deep lacerations on their backs to even begin to heal. But despite that dire threat, Kalamann was determined to carry out his plan. His grumbling stomach urged him on. After one final glance behind him, Kalamann slipped into the cemetery.

There were numerous stone paths laid out in the cemetery with the widest stone path leading to the royal mausoleum. Numerous narrower stone paths branched off from the main path, some of them leading to a grave plot, other paths leading deeper into the cemetery. At the end of some of these smaller paths were the grave sites themselves, some with huge headstones marking the head of the plot, others marked with large stone crosses. Some smaller tombs were visible in the distance, but they were dwarfed by the size of the royal mausoleum.

Kalamann felt very alive, flush with nervous energy as he moved cautiously through the cemetery. The grounds were meticulously maintained, the goats and cows in the village allowed to chew on the grass once a week to keep it short. A tombstone to his left had fresh flowers laid out at its base.

Towering oak trees cast long shadows over the royal mausoleum as he approached it. The mausoleum's walls were made of rectangular white stones, all hand-smoothed and sized the same. Each corner piece was one gigantic piece of obsidian, the black coloring of these corner columns contrasting sharply with the white stones that made up the walls. The entranceway had a large reverse V-shaped arch, the arch casting shadows over a large metal door that marked the entrance to the mausoleum.

Kalamann reached the mausoleum door and paused. He looked about the area, casting furtive glances behind him, making sure no one was watching him.

Kalamann pulled on the metal door that led into the royal mausoleum and was once again delighted and relieved to find it open. Most likely in anticipation of the approaching funeral so they didn't have to stop and fumble with keys, he thought, or perhaps it always remained unlocked for mourners to come and go as they pleased. Kalamann had no idea. He was just happy to find it open. The door opened smoothly, almost with no sound. Its hinges were well-oiled and well maintained; it was the Gilmont royal family mausoleum after all.

After one more final furtive glance behind him, Kalamann headed in towards the royal crypts.

Kalamann half expected the interior of the royal mausoleum to be gloomy and laced with dust and cobwebs, but the large room was immaculately clean, obviously well-tended and well cared for. Large stained glass windows positioned more than a dozen feet high on the two long horizontal sides of the mausoleum allowed plenty of light to shine down into the large interior space. The windows displayed various historical scenes from the Gilmont family's past, men hunting at night on horseback, women praying to the moon, pale white children laughing and dancing.

There were marble busts on display on both sides of the building, each bust representing a member of the royal family who was buried in the mausoleum. The white marble columns the busts rested upon were spaced at equal intervals throughout the large room. Numerous empty stone benches, all hewn from the same white marble that comprised the columns, were positioned before the busts, giving mourners a place to sit while they visited the mausoleum to pay their respects to the deceased members of the royal family.

Kalamann moved slowly through the large room, his footsteps echoing ever so slightly as he padded along the tiled floor in his ragged sandals. He glanced about the mausoleum as he moved deeper into it, expecting to see bodies laid out on slabs, or set within recessed slots in the walls, but he saw no bodies, no recessed crypts, no coffins. The room only contained the white marble columns with marble busts of dead royalty set in place atop the columns, and the marble benches. Where did they put the bodies? Did they bury them somewhere else?

The marble bust of Princess Yasalla was already in place atop a white marble pedestal on the far left side of the room. One of the stained glass windows positioned high above on the opposite wall beamed a white light down onto the bust, the sunlight streaming in from outside turning white as it moved through a large circular pane of white glass that represented the moon.

Kalamann stared at the sculptured likeness of Princess Yasalla. He had heard tales of her beauty, but he had only ever seen her from afar, and usually only at night when the Gilmonts showed themselves. He hadn't gotten much of a good look at her in the funeral procession. She was indeed quite beautiful, with a delicate nose, a softly rounded chin, high cheekbones. Even the marble bust of her head radiated a royal air.

Then he noticed another door at this far end of the mausoleum. He mentally pictured the royal mausoleum from the outside. The door seemed to be a little short of the far end of the building. Was it just some exit point? Was there something beyond the door? A secret room? Is that where they stored the bodies?

Kalamann froze as he caught movement out of the corner of his eye. The mausoleum door! He had left it open when he entered the building. He could see movement outside in the distance. It was the procession. The funeral procession was entering the cemetery. He could see that Prince Raseem had rejoined the procession, his belly probably now full of blackberry pie. Kalamann's stomach growled with jealous rage.

He started to move back towards the mausoleum's main door, but stopped as he realized it was too late, the procession was too close. Someone would undoubtedly see the door being closed. He glanced frantically about the room. The only place to hide was behind one of the columns that was displaying a bust of a deceased royal family member, but he would surely be seen by someone; the columns weren't very wide and there were far too many angles from which he could be detected.

He looked to the door at the back of the mausoleum and darted over to it, staying behind the columns the best he could as he moved, trying to stay out of sight from the approaching throng of mourners. He reached the door and pushed at it. To his great relief, the door opened. He was too desperate to escape the eyes of the approaching mourners to pay attention to the heavy scraping sound of metal and the squealing of hinges as this door opened.

He slipped inside.

Kalamann pushed the door closed and turned around, pressing his back up against the cool metal. He didn't know if anyone had seen him. The mad desperation of his plan started to seep in. He forced himself to calm, willed his wild breathing too slow, prayed his pounding heart wouldn't burst out of his chest.

After a few moments, after bringing his anxious fear down to a manageable level of apprehension, he glanced about. The area around him was dark, but it wasn't completely black. There was a faint glow coming from somewhere in the distance, illuminating a path that sloped very gently downward. He moved slowly towards the glow, hoping the path would lead to some other form of exit.

A dripping plunk of water seemed to grow louder as he continued to descend down the path. He could hear the scurrying sounds of claws clacking against stones near him and he knew those were the sounds of rats and other denizens of the dark. The irregular stone walls seemed to glisten with moisture, most likely from the spongy patches of moss that coated some of the stones.

A large spiderweb draped across his path and Kalamann brushed it aside, quickly wiping the white sticky residue off his fingers by brushing his fingers along his pants. Where did this path lead? It seemed obvious that no one had traversed this path for quite some time. He had heard of no royal deaths during his limited time in the village, so perhaps the princess was the first royal to have died for many years.

The area suddenly opened up around him, the ceiling now far, far above him. He was in some sort of underground catacomb. The minerals embedded in the walls and in the high ceiling emitted a very faint light, illuminating the area, somewhat like how a full moon illuminated a dark night. Numerous stalactites hung down from the ceiling, each one looking like the tooth of a portcullis. Several stalagmites thrust up from the ground, each one looking like the lower fang of a wolf.

He came upon a large stone platform that was raised about three feet off the ground. Its surface was flat, made of smoothly polished marble. It was about seven feet long and several feet wide, large enough for a person to lay flat upon it. It looked to be some sort of sacrificial altar.

Beyond the altar, Kalamann gaped at what he saw. It was a river, an underground river flowing through the catacombs. It had a slight current and he could hear the water gently flowing as it moved from his right to his left. He followed the flow of the current, looking to his left to see the river _ed to a large curved entrance that looked like the entrance to a cave, the interior beyond the arched entrance completely black and impenetrable to his gaze.

Kalamann heard more movement, coming from back up the sloping path. He glanced about for a hiding place and saw that he could hide behind a curved outcropping of rock near the river's edge to his right. He hurried over and crouched down behind the rock. He could still see the platform from his hiding spot, but he didn't think he would be visible if he was cautious and kept quiet.

A large rat crawled across his feet and Kalamann bit back a startled cry. He could feel its warm little paws scurry over his exposed toes. He heard more scratching noises, more sounds of movement. He realized there were probably dozens of rats moving all around him, but he forced himself to stay calm. He was used to dealing with rats in the alleys where he slept. If he left them alone, they would leave him alone.

Then he saw the white-robed priest who had been swinging the incense come into view. He still clutched the incense container, but he was no longer swinging it back and forth in front of him. Thin white smoky trails of burning incense still wafted out of the container.

Then the cart being pushed by four more priests in white hooded robes came into view. Princess Yasalla still lay atop it. Then two more priests appeared, pulling the food cart behind them. No one else entered the cavernous area and Kalamann surmised this area was probably reserved only for priests and, of course, the deceased. He wondered with a growing nervousness what his punishment would be if he were caught in this secretive recess. Could he be hung to death or sentenced to a beheading for his trespassing? Whatever punishment was issued it would surely be far worse and more severe than a flogging. But all that nervous trepidation dissipated when he felt his mouth watering again at the sight of so much food.

The four priests lifted the dead princess up, keeping her body as flatly horizontal as they could, then placed the princess atop the marble slab, setting her gently down on the smooth stone. One of the priests crossed the princess's arms over her breasts, lingering at her breasts for a moment as he did so. Another priest readjusted the coins that were in place over the princess's eyes, centering them more evenly atop her closed eyelids.

The other two priests began setting the food out on the ground all around the slab, spreading the pieces of dried meat, fruits, breads all around the area.

The lead priest moved to the riverbank and Kalamann ducked down even lower. If the priest just happened to glance in his direction, Kalamann knew he would be discovered. But the priest kept his focus on the river. He set the incense container down on the ground, then stood back up and raised his hands up in a reverent pose, glancing towards the high ceiling and the heavens beyond. The priest then lowered his gaze and looked towards the dark cave. He muttered something, some sort of prayer that Kalamann didn't understand. He only spoke for a few moments, then lowered his hands. The priest bent down and picked up the incense container.

And with that, all of the priests left, taking the now empty carts with them.

Kalamann lingered for several moments in his hiding spot, making certain the priests were indeed leaving. He cautiously stepped out from behind the outcropping of rock he had been hiding behind. He slowly moved up to the platform and stared down at the naked princess.

She was very pale, very curvaceous. She had just the hint of a few freckles dotting her nose and a few beneath each of her gold-coin-covered eyes. He knew the royals shunned direct sunlight, most of them preferring to live their lives during the night hours. Very few royals were awake during the day, but even then they preferred staying indoors or under shaded canopies when outdoors or within shaded coaches when they traveled. Princess Yasala may have been an exception to the royal lifestyle, but the moon was still her true master.

He glanced down at the piles of food the priests had laid out around the platform. A rat was already nibbling on a piece of dried meat, holding the piece in its little paws and gnawing on it. Another rat somehow managed to grab an entire loaf of bread in its mouth and scurried off into the darkness. Then Kalamann realized that the food wasn't meant for the princess. The food was an offering to keep the rats from feeding on her flesh. It was meant as a shield to protect her. And it worked. None of the rats even made the slightest effort to cross the food barrier; they were far too busy eating the food or grabbing mouthfuls to bring back to their nests.

But the food wouldn't last forever. What would

happen if the rats grew hungry again and the food was depleted?

Then Kalamann heard a soft splashing sound coming from the river.

All of the rats stopped what they were doing, some even pausing mid-bite on a morsel of food. They all raised their heads and turned their faces towards the river, looking in the direction of the dark tunnel.

Kalamann glanced over to the dark tunnel. The sound grew louder.

And then the rats bolted from the area, scurrying and scampering back into the darkness from whence they had come, their claws again clacking against stone as they fled deeper into the shadows.

Kalamann felt his chest tighten. The sound drew closer. Did he truly exist? Was he really coming to bring the princess into the afterlife? Kalamann's mouth went dry. He had no desire to wait and find out the answer. He turned back to look down at the dead princess, his gaze focusing on the two gold coins laid over her eyes. He snatched at the coins, plucking them off the princess's face.

Princess Yasalla's blue eyes were open, staring at him.

He froze for just a quick moment as her open eyes caught him off guard. He could've sworn they had been closed when the priest had rearranged the coins over her eyes, but he had to admit that he hadn't really had the best look. He turned away and hurried back up the path towards the door.

He paused at the door. What if there were still mourners within? What would they make of this shabbily dressed beggar emerging from the catacombs? He glanced at the two gold coins, then thrust them into his pocket. He pressed his ear to the crack between the door and the doorframe. He could hear no voices. What if they were mourning silently?

He suddenly felt a hot breath on his neck, making the hairs on his nape stand up. He was too afraid to turn around to see who, or what, might be behind him. That fear was enough to make him move. He pushed through the metal door into the mausoleum proper.

The room was empty of mourners. His luck was still holding. He hurried through the room, his footsteps echoing in the large chamber. He reached the outer door and pushed. The door did not move. He pushed harder on the handle. The door still did not move. It was locked! He was trapped inside the royal mausoleum. No! He pounded at the door with his fist.

And then he realized the door moved in the opposite direction. He pulled on the door handle and it opened.

Kalamann raced away from the mausoleum, wanting to get as far away from the building as he could, wanting to get rid of the eerie feeling of someone watching him as he ran. His stomach rumbled and grumbled. He cursed himself a stupid fool. All that food, and he didn't even grab one morsel of it. No matter, he knew exactly where to go to remedy that.

"I have coin," Kalamann announced proudly, holding out one of the gold coins to the bread merchant.

The baker looked disdainfully at Kalamann but held his tongue.

"Give me five fresh loaves of your finest bread," Kalamann said, raising his chin as he spoke.

The bread merchant wiggled his fingers insistently at Kalamann. "Let me see."

Kalamann pulled the gold coin back to his chest, as if hugging it. He hesitated.

"I will sell you nothing until you let me see what coin you have," the bread merchant explained.

Kalamann still hesitated, clutching the coin tightly, pressing his hand against his chest. The other coin was nestled in his pocket.

"Bah!" The baker waved his hand brusquely towards Kalamann, dismissing him with a grimace of disgust. "Go away and stop pestering me." He turned away from Kalamann.

"No, no," Kalamann protested. He held out the coin towards the merchant. "Here."

The bread merchant reluctantly turned back to face Kalamann with an exasperated look on his features. The merchant sighed with great exaggeration as he opened his palm.

Kalamann put the coin into the merchant's open hand.

The merchant snapped his fingers closed, nearly catching Kalamann's fingers as he did so.

Kalamann took a step back, anxiously awaiting his five loaves. The smell alone was intoxicating and he felt the saliva swirling in his mouth.

The merchant opened his palm. And stared at the coin with pure horror. "You dare desecrate the dead!" He tossed the coin away from him with disgust, throwing it towards the dirt street. He glanced at his hand, as if expecting it to suddenly burst into flames from just touching the sacred coin.

Kalamann scurried after the coin, snatching it out of the dirt.

The merchant glowered spitefully, hatefully, at Kalamann. "You robbed someone of passage into the afterworld! How dare you!" The merchant extended his arm out fully and pointed a rigid finger at Kalamann. "Seize this man! He is a grave robber! He has stolen coins from the dead!"

Kalamann whirled to see dozens of people staring at him with contempt and loathing. No matter which direction he turned, someone was glaring at him. His vision filled with huge eyeballs leering and glaring at him, huge mouths pinched tight, huge lips tugged sharply downward. He clutched the coin firmly in his hand and once again fled away from the bread merchant's stall.

Kalamann stared at the gold coins in his hand. Both of them lay flat in his open palm. The side of one coin had a raised figure emblazoned on it, the figure in the shape of a man wearing a hooded cloak, and Kalamann realized that it was most likely a representation of the Ferryman.

The other piece of gold was flipped over to display the opposite side of the coin, this side featuring a carved variation of some sort of small boat. Most likely the boat used to transport the deceased into the afterlife, he surmised.

He again cursed himself a fool. The coins were obviously meant for only one transaction and he had been too blinded by his eagerness to steal them and use them as a form of payment to study them closely.

Kalamann sat with his back to a stone wall, hiding behind some wooden crates that were laden with woven rugs. Night had fallen, but the moon was high and full and bright this night, so there was still light enough for him to see his surroundings. He had managed to elude any pursuers. For now.

He knew they would most likely kill him on the spot if they found those coins on him. He was pretty certain of that. They would put him in the stocks and let people pelt him with rocks and garbage. Then they would put his head on the chopping block, or worse yet hang him and let him slowly suffocate to death. He rubbed at his neck, terrified of the possible ways the village elders could dispense justice. I should just throw them into the night, he thought. Rid myself of their taint.

But then another idea struck him. I'll put them back, he thought. The clarity of that decision emboldened him and gave him hope. I'll return them to their rightful owner. He nodded to himself. Yes, I'll put them back on the princess. He started to rise up.

"You are too late."

The voice nearly made Kalamann wet himself in fear. He slowly looked up to see a dark shadowy shape coming towards him, the shape much darker than the night air around it.

"The Ferryman has come and I have no coin to pay him," the dark shape said, the voice clearly feminine.

Kalamann said nothing. He slowly moved up to his feet, sliding up along the wall. His hands felt clammy and moist, and he nearly lost his grip on one of the coins.

"I am trapped here forever," the dark shape said.

Kalamann took a hesitant step away from the dark shadowy figure that was starting to take on a definitive feminine shape as it moved closer and closer to him.

The dark shadowy shape mirrored his steps, moving forward at the same pace he was awkwardly trying to move away. "I will now haunt you, Kalamann Kar. I will haunt you for the rest of your mortal days. And then I will haunt you for eternity." The dark shape almost appeared to shrug. "What else do I have to do now that I am trapped here?"

"No..." Kalamann somehow managed to utter through his terror. "How... do you... know my name?" he stammered. His hands trembled and quaked.

"I know many things. I can see into you Kalamann Kar. Worldly flesh is no longer an obstacle for me." The ghostly shaped reached out a darkly shadowed hand, the slender spectral fingers groping towards Kalamann's chest. "I can squeeze your heart at my whim."

"No," Kalamann gasped as he stared at the ghostly semblance of Princess Yasalla. Her once-pale face was now burnt dark by moon shadows, the color of her ghostly visage a deep ebony. Her spectral body was naked, her shadowy skin black, the tips of her breasts darker than coal, the hair between her legs darker than the fur on a black panther.

"Yes," the phantom princess said, reaffirming her words. Her ghostly fingers slid past Kalamann's shirt and he could feel the icy coldness of her otherworldly touch seep into his chest.

"No!" Kalamann whirled from the ghost and raced away.

The ghost of Princess Yasalla followed him, floating closely behind him.

Kalamann clambered over the cemetery gate, not caring if he ripped his clothes in his desperate climb. He lost one of his sandals as he climbed but knew he had no time to fetch it. He managed to get over the top of the gate and dropped down heavily to the other side. He felt a twinge in his knee as he landed, but the pain was not enough to stop him or even slow him down.

He kicked off his remaining sandal and raced towards the mausoleum. Although the cool surface of the stones that led to the royal mausoleum were chill against his bare feet, they were hot compared to the icy touch of the ghost princess that still lingered in his chest.

He burst into the mausoleum and charged forward, but then slowed his pace as he saw the ghost of Princess Yasalla had beaten him to the mausoleum. She stood in the middle of the dark room, her ghostly arms folded impatiently under her breasts. Moonlight filtered down through the stain glass windows, the beams illuminating the princess, almost seeming to give her dark shape physical form.

All of the marble busts positioned on the columns seemed to have shifted just enough so all the visages of the deceased royals now faced Kalamann, all of them staring at him with cold dead eyes of stone.

But then Kalamann resumed his pace with a burst of speed, charging straight through the ghostly princess. He could feel icy fingers clutching at his face, his chest, his heart, at his very soul, as he ran through the dark shape, but the bitterly frigid feeling passed quickly as he moved beyond the shadowy form of the princess.

He reached the rear door of the royal mausoleum and pushed it open, ignoring the stares of the dead he could feel crawling up his back.

Kalamann charged down the sloping path. The princess's pale body was still on the slab, her arms still folded over her breasts. He didn't have time to even breathe a sigh of relief. Most of the food was already gone, but a few bold rats now seemed tempted to explore the scent coming from the top of the slab. He hurried up to the slab, waving the rats away with flailing arms and a guttural grunt.

He stared down at the pale dead princess. Her eyes were still open, staring blankly up at the stone ceiling above. He raised up the two gold coins he clutched in his hands, and then momentarily froze as he saw her piercing blue eyes were now staring straight at him. Her dead eyes had somehow shifted in their sockets, her eerie gaze now seeming to focus directly on him.

His fingers shook as he put the two gold coins back down over the princess's open eyes, the coins blissfully blocking her unsettling gaze. There, it was done. He breathed a sigh of relief. It was done. He was free.

Kalamann heard a soft splashing sound and looked

over towards the river and the dark tunnel beyond. He could see the dark shape of what looked to be a tall man. He was dressed in a long black cloak, his head covered in a dark hood. He was in a small gondola, steering the boat from the stern of the vessel with a long oar that he swished slowly and methodically back and forth in the water. And then Kalamann realized with a start that he was moving away from them. He was moving back up the river, back towards the dark tunnel.

"You are too late."

Kalamann looked away from the departing gondola and stared at the ghostly face of Princess Yasalla. But then Kalamann turned quickly away from the ghost of the princess and looked towards the river. The Ferryman was still visible, moving slowly towards the dark tunnel. "No, wait!" Kalamann shouted. "Wait! I have the coins! The coins are here!"

"The Ferryman does not deviate from his course. You are too late," the ghostly princess said.

"No." In frantic haste, Kalamann snatched the coins back off the princess's eyes and gripped them tightly in clenched fists. He turned towards the river, towards the departing Ferryman. "Wait! I have the coins!" He held up his clenched hands, shaking his fists.

The Ferryman did not turn around at Kalamann's cry, nor did he even slow his pace.

Kalamann raced toward the river and plunged into the icy waters without hesitation. He nearly seized up from the cold, but forced himself to swim, kicking as hard as he could, stroking his arms through the water, desperation fueling his strength. He kept the coins clenched in his fists, awkwardly swimming as best he could with closed hands.

He reached the gondola of the Ferryman and managed to hook one arm up over the side, consciously keeping his fist closed, knowing that he had to retain his grasp of the coin at all costs. The frigid water seeped through his pants and chilled the flesh on his legs, but even this bitter cold was warm compared to the icy touch of the ghost princess.

"Turn around," Kalamann said, panting heavily from the exertion of his swim through the icy waters, pointing back behind the Ferryman with his clenched fist, pointing towards the stone slab on which the princess's dead body lay.

The Ferryman did not turn around.

"I have the coins," Kalamann said. "You have to go back for the princess. I have the coins." His teeth chattered, the sound so loud it even echoed slightly in the cavernous chamber. The lower part of his body was still in the river, the icy waters seeping deeper into his legs and bare feet.

Then Kalamann noticed a large black chest in the bow of the gondola. It was made of some black metal but its hinges and latch were made of what appeared to be gold. Of course, the Ferryman had to store the coins somewhere. They were in that chest. A chest full of gold coins. A treasure chest! But his elation quickly dissipated as he remembered that the coins had no value in the real world. Just his luck to be within spitting distance of a treasure chest filled with gold that was of no use to him.

Kalamann threw his other hand over the side of the gondola. The gold coin nearly fell from his grasp as he struggled to get into the gondola, but he quickly closed his fingers around the coin, securing it in his palm. He grunted and huffed as he managed to get one leg over the lip of the gondola, then with a heave he managed to get the rest of his body into the boat. He lay on his back for a moment, staring up at the shimmering ceiling high above, the cold waters of the river still enveloping him like a thin cocoon made of ice.

The Ferryman still paid him no heed, continuing to pilot the gondola from the rear of the small vessel with measured strokes of the oar, his face shielded in the dark shadows of his hood. The boat moved closer and closer to the dark tunnel's entrance, the sound of the gently flowing current lapping up against the side of the small craft as it moved through the river.

Kalamann stood and made a move towards the Ferryman, his hands outstretched, shoving the two gold coins out towards the Ferryman. "Here! I have the coins! You must turn around!"

The Ferryman tilted his hooded head up and Kalamann stared at the face of a human skull leering back at him.

The grotesque bone face and the empty black eye sockets startled Kalamann. He tripped on a plank and stumbled awkwardly forward, dropping the coins to the flat deck of the gondola as he staggered. Kalamann gaped in terror as he fell towards the Ferryman, clenching his eyes tight. He fell into the Ferryman, feeling the rigid edges of bones through the dark cloak as he bumped hard against the dark figure.

Then Kalamann heard a splash and opened his eyes to see that the Ferryman was no longer there, no longer manning his position in the stern of the gondola. Kalamann looked down at his hands to see that he was now somehow clutching an empty black cloak. The Ferryman was gone. He had accidentally pushed him overboard.

Kalamann tossed the cloak down into the front corner of the boat. His hands shook, but whether it was from the brutal cold residue of the dark river or the fact that he had just, and quite easily so, knocked the Ferryman off his boat, he could not say. He glanced over the rear of the gondola. The river glistened as the water gently rippled around the gondola, but there was no sign of a body, no sign of anything moving. The Ferryman had disappeared into the dark waters.

Kalamann glanced up to see the dark entrance to the tunnel looming larger. He hurriedly grabbed the steering oar with trembling fingers and awkwardly, clumsily, managed to turn the gondola back around. His fingers felt stiff from the cold but he still managed to thrust forward and pull back on the oar, pushing the small craft against the current, heading back towards the stone platform, keeping his gaze focused on the corpse of Princess Yasalla.

He pulled the boat up to the shore. The ghost of the princess stared back at him. "Come on," he said, waving to the princess to get on the boat.

The ghost of the princess floated over to him, but she just hovered in the air a few feet from the gondola.

Kalamann waved impatiently at her. "Come aboard."

The ghost floated back to her body and just stared down at her corpse. "I can't leave my body here," she said.

How was she speaking if she had no corporeal

body? Where did the sounds of her voice come from? Was it all just in his head? Kalamann felt like he was trapped in some weird world, halfway between the living and the dead where only certain senses seemed to work. "You are dead. You have no need for it anymore."

The ghostly princess shook her head. "No, that is not true. I need it for the afterlife. The scriptures tell us so. I cannot go without it."

Kalamann touched at his pocket. "Your toll is paid."

The princess shook her head. "No, something is wrong. I cannot leave."

And then Kalamann's eyes went wide with fright as he continued to tap at his pocket. His empty pocket! The coins! He had lost the coins.

But then he spotted them lying on the bottom of the boat where he had dropped them. He quickly snatched the two gold coins back up into his hands and held them towards the princess. "Look! See. I have the coins. Your toll is paid."

The ghost of Princess Yasalla again shook her head. "No, something is still wrong."

Kalamann tightened his jaw in frustration. He glanced about the boat, as if looking for some clue, some sign as to what he should do next. It was then that he noticed there was a slot on top of the metal chest. A slot just wide enough to allow a coin to pass through it. He deposited the two gold coins into the chest.

He glanced over to the princess to see her ghostly figure float atop the slab, then move into a horizontal position, mirroring the position of her corporeal body below her. Then, the ghost drifted lower, the princess's spirit beginning to re oin her flesh. And then suddenly the princess's ghost was gone, fully reabsorbed back into her corpse.

Princess Yasalla sat up on the slab and looked over to him. She climbed off the platform in all her naked pale glory and Kalamann thought she was the most beautiful woman he had ever seen. Dead, but still intensely beautiful.

Princess Yasalla stepped into the boat, moving towards a seat near the bow. She sat down facing Kalamann.

Kalamann trembled as the cold waters of the river continued to slowly drip off of him.

Yasalla produced a cloak she found lying in the bow of the boat. "You're shivering. Here, put this on."

Kalamann donned the cloak. It was a black cloak with a black hood. It fit him surprisingly well. He pulled the hood up over his head. The chill that had been assaulting his body disappeared immediately. He found himself feeling strangely at peace. And, oddly enough, he felt no more pangs of hunger. His stomach was mercifully quiet.

He headed for the dark tunnel, swishing the oar gently back and forth, propelling the gondola slowly forward.

The princess remained seated near the bow, now staring ahead at the approaching dark tunnel.

Only then did the enormity of what had just happened strike Kalamann Kar like a thunderbolt blasting a dead tree into a thousand splintered pieces. Now he, Kalamann Kar, could decide who was worthy of reaching the afterlife. Won't that put a big shock on the face of that pompous prince? I'll make him plead first, and then I will still refuse him entry into the afterlife! I'll toss his offered coins into the river! Kalamann mentally scoffed at the memory of Prince Raseem's words. *"You will never be nothing more than a sad little beggar."* Oh, how the tide had turned.

The princess turned back to face Kalamann. "What lies beyond?" she asked.

Kalamann remained quiet. He had no answer. But it no longer mattered.

Kalamann stood taller in the stern of the gondola, continuing to gently push the oar back and forth as the dark tunnel loomed ever closer.

His stolen coins had bought him the greatest gift of all. He was the new master of the river that linked the dead to the world beyond. He was the Ferryman.

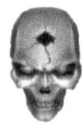

TERRORSTORY #78
CROSS INSTITUTE OF
REDEMPTION

"The truth needs to be told," Ignacio Valene said. He raised his phone a little higher, shifting it in the direction of the Warden, wanting the recording of the Warden's voice to be clearly captured on his device. Ignacio had dark black hair and a slight, thin mustache. He was dressed casually in blue jeans and a button-up collared denim shirt, seated in a leather chair across from the Warden.

"But whose truth?" the Warden asked from his seated position behind his ornate oak desk. "Yours? Or mine?" The Warden didn't give his name to

Ignacio. He was just the Warden. He was in good shape for a man just starting on his eighth decade, his body still holding on to some tone. His hair was a shiny mass of silver, with a few strands of black still able to fight off the greying tides of time. He wore a light tan shirt with the word WARDEN embroidered in all caps on the left breast of the shirt in black thread. His tan trousers, and the tan loafers on his feet, completed his bland attire.

"There is only one truth," Ignacio said.

The Warden pursed his lips. "Ahh, and you are the arbitrator of this one truth?"

Ignacio shook his head. "There is no arbitrator of truth. Truth is just truth. Facts are just facts."

"And who decides which facts are to be presented to the public?"

"Investigative journalists," Ignacio responded without hesitation.

The Warden cocked his head and let the corner of his mouth quirk up into a slight smile. "Like you?"

Ignacio raised his chin. "Yes, like me. And other writers like me."

"So you have the power to influence public opinion? Sway entire nations even?" the Warden asked.

Ignacio was quiet for a moment. "Yes. I suppose we do."

"So if I control you, and others like you, I can control the truth," the Warden said.

Ignacio frowned.

"I don't think you should be surprised by my approval of your interview request any longer, Mister Valene. The truth does need to be told," the Warden said. "The truth of Cross Institute of Redemption."

The Warden paused as he leaned forward in his chair. "The real truth."

Ignacio held the Warden's stare for a moment; the man's blue eyes were flecked with little hints of silver that seemed to pulse brighter, then dim, the effect repeating with the rhythm of a heartbeat. Ignacio fidgeted in his chair. The Warden did have a confident presence about him, a different sort of air than many of the ghost hunters he usually interviewed had. The ghost hunters were mostly needy, almost desperate for someone to believe their stories. Not this guy. The Warden didn't seem to give a shit if you believed anything he said or not.

Ignacio shifted his gaze, pulling away from the invisible hooks the Warden's eyes seemed to be trying to sink into his. He broke the uncomfortable silence with another question. "How many different types of unnaturals does Cross Institute..." He paused, searching for the word, then finished his question with "...treat?"

"Unnaturals, you say?" The Warden sat back in his chair, folding his fingers together over his lap. "I must say, I do find offense with that word," he said. "Unnaturals." The Warden shook his head slightly. "These beings exist in nature, so calling them unnatural doesn't seem quite right." The Warden was quiet again for a brief moment, tilting his head to look up at the ceiling. "Abnormal, perhaps. But not unnatural." He tilted his head back down to look at Ignacio. "What magazine did you say you were from?"

"It's more of a webzine than a print magazine," Ignacio replied. There was a defensive lilt to his voice, hiding the hint of embarrassment that came out with the words. The Warden didn't need to know that he was on the verge of losing half of his subscribers if he didn't come up with a hot new story soon. He had grown his readership from a few dozen diehard followers to nearly five thousand, each one willing to subscribe for a measly buck a month to read his investigative forays into all things that went bump in the night. He had reached as high as eight thousand paid subscribers, but his lack of really good articles over the last few months had led to a continual decline in readership, and that was a bleeding that he desperately needed to stop.

"Ahh." The Warden pursed his lips. He was quiet for a moment. He glanced down at the daily newspaper folded on his desk, then looked back at Ignacio. "So someone of my considerable age might even consider what you do as… abnormal. Unnatural even."

"Not anymore," Ignacio said, with a slight shake of his head.

"Interesting how the abnormal becomes the normal over time, isn't it?" the Warden asked, clearly in a rhetorical manner. "What is the name of this… webzine?"

"Supernatural Scoops."

The Warden nodded his head enthusiastically and a genuine smile lit up his face. "Now, *there's* a word I like. Supernatural. Not unnatural. Not abnormal. Super. Super Naturals, even."

"Sounds like you have an appreciation for them," Ignacio said.

The Warden waved his hand. "Of course. Of course. They have some amazing skills. I can respect them, and still understand why many of you believe they are too dangerous to let them roam loose in society."

Ignacio was quiet for a moment. "So, back to my last question," Ignacio said. "How many un—" he caught himself. "How many kinds of... *super* naturals do you have here?"

"Well, let's see," the Warden said. "We have a few vampires, of course. We house them in the Vampire Ward, also affectionately referred to by the staff as Bloodsucker Boulevard. We have some werewolves in the Werewolf Ward, also known as Hairy House. We have a few ghouls over in the Ghoul Pool."

Ignacio felt his own excitement growing as the Warden's enthusiasm for talking about his charges seemed to be picking up. Jennifer had been right. This was definitely a story worth pursuing. He knew if he could get even one good story out of the Warden he could milk that for months with teasers and tidbits of information. Hell, if he could get in good with this guy, he might even be able to get a half a year's worth of stories out of it, if not even more than that. Vampires. Werewolves. Ghouls. This was next level stuff. This could really keep Supernatural Scoops on the map. "What about the undead?" Ignacio asked.

"Honestly, they don't get too much attention," the Warden said. "Not very good conversationalists. We just keep them chained up in the basement. Sad but true." He shrugged. "They never complain, so..." He let his response taper off.

"What do you call it? The Undead Underground?" Ignacio asked, finishing with a wry grin.

The Warden shook his head. "No, we don't call it that," he said, but did not elaborate.

"The Zombie Zone?" Ignacio wondered, throwing

out his guess as a question.

The Warden tilted his head ever so slightly as he looked at Ignacio with a flicker of annoyance, but remained silent.

"What other types of unnaturals are held here?" Ignacio asked after it was obvious the Warden wasn't going to say anything more about the zombies. He immediately realized he used the term the Warden had found offensive, but just let it go.

"We've got demons, gnarlies, and druids," the Warden said. He paused and tossed in an, "Oh my," and followed that with a sly smirk that looked just plain odd on his craggy, wrinkled face.

Ignacio frowned. "Gnarlies? What's a gnarlie?"

The Warden nodded and pursed his lips. "Good question. We're not entirely sure what they are, but they are nasty little beasties, that's for certain. Even the werewolves don't like to be anywhere near them. They go back centuries, but they've always remained well hidden from the world at large, so not much is known about them." The Warden paused.

Ignacio just listened, shifting his phone to tilt it more towards the Warden.

"They're like gnomes on poisoned crack," the Warden said as he elaborated. "That's how someone described them once, and that has stuck in my head. None of them are taller than three feet and they have these distorted facial features, big bulbous noses, beady black eyes, thick lips." The Warden made exaggerated gestures with his face and hands as he described the gnarlies to Ignacio, which again seemed absurdly bizarre coming from this seemingly austere elderly man.

"What dangers do they pose?" Ignacio asked.

"They feed on human genitalia," the Warden said. "That's where they picked up some of their other earlier nicknames from. They've been called groin grinders, muff maulers."

"They eat human genitalia?" Ignacio echoed. "Groin grinders?"

The Warden nodded. "But we have officially named them gnarlies as the aftermath of one of their attacks is… well, shall we say, quite unpleasant to look at. They'll bite your penis straight off." The Warden made an exaggerated biting motion, loudly clacking his teeth together. "One chomp and you're neutered."

Ignacio unconsciously put his hand lower, moving it defensively towards his crotch area.

"They used to be called dickbiters," the Warden said. "But we discovered they eat women's private areas also. That takes a bit more effort on their part, a bit more chewing, so they prefer attacking men if they have a choice, but they will still feed on female genitalia as well."

Ignacio made a sour face, but said nothing.

"Would you like to see a redemption?" the Warden asked.

Ignacio just stared at the Warden for a long moment. "A redemption?" He wasn't even sure what was involved in a redemption in a place like this. Did that entail transforming a lycanthrope permanently back into a human? Did that mean training a vampire not to seek out human blood? Did a redeemed ghoul no longer want to feast on dead human flesh? "I can watch a redemption?" Ignacio asked, still not quite believing what the Warden had just asked him.

"Not just one," the Warden replied. "You can

watch a few. They're all quite different. You would think you would eventually get bored watching them, but you never do." The Warden shrugged. "I'm ashamed to admit it, but they are somewhat addictive."

Ignacio was quiet, trying to keep still, forcing down the excitement brewing in him from bubbling over. This really was turning out to be a great scoop! He might actually have a chance at saving his livelihood.

"We have a gnarlie redemption in about twenty minutes," the Warden said. Then he looked quizzically at Ignacio with a soft squint.

"Yes!" Ignacio said, blurting the affirmation out with zealous gusto after realizing he hadn't responded to the Warden's invitation. Who wouldn't want to read about this! "Yes!" he said again.

Ignacio stared through the two-way mirror. He was seated in a viewing room in an extremely luxurious chair. It was one of those chairs you see in deluxe movie theaters - incredibly cushy, wide enough to easily accommodate larger people; Ignacio felt small in it. The lighting in the viewing room was dim to allow good visibility into the room beyond the mirror.

Visible on the other side of the mirror, Ignacio studied what looked like a garden you would see in a wealthy person's backyard. There was a cobblestone path that weaved its way through several clusters of flowering plants, the path splitting in several different directions to surround stone fountains that had water flowing through them. A few wide patches of very green, low-cut grass dotted the garden, giving a nice visual flow to the whole garden, alternating smooth areas of grass with a bubbling fountain or a cluster of larger plants.

"Kind of like looking at a movie set, don't you think?" the Warden asked.

Ignacio nodded.

"We actually hired professional set designers," the Warden said. "With so much movie production put on hold during the pandemic they were eager to get the work. The entire scene was fabricated to give the gnarlies a friendly environment in which to feed."

Ignacio was about to ask the Warden where the gnarlies were when he saw one. He closed his mouth, his question going unasked. The first gnarlie he spotted was standing motionless behind one of the stone fountains. The fountain looked like a miniature mountain with several streams of water flowing down through it, all of the streams culminating in one area where the individual streams became one large waterfall. The water then cascaded down into a large pool at the bottom of the stone fountain, collecting in a large stone basin.

The gnarlie stood just behind the fountain, its appearance looking somewhat as the Warden had described. It did look like a pale garden gnome possessed by some very dark, very evil spirit. Its mouth was huge for its head, its teeth visible behind an upper and lower lip that seemed incapable of reaching each other. Its teeth had sharpened edges on each tooth, each one looking like an incisor. Its nose was large, looking swollen and distended, with several blue veins visible criss-crossing its surface. Its eyes were black and beady, their size abnormally small in its disfigured head.

"How many gnarlies are in there?" Ignacio asked, turning his head only slightly to address the Warden who was sitting in a chair next to him, keeping his gaze focused on the weird creature.

"Just the one," the Warden said. "We feed them one at a time. If we put two or more of them together, they start squealing and screeching at each other and it takes days to calm them down. Some kind of ancient territorial instinct. It's just easier to feed them one at a time."

"Feed them?" Ignacio asked, this time turning to look at the Warden. "I thought I was going to see some kind of redemption."

"Yes, and yes you are," the Warden said.

A clicking sound came from the garden room and Ignacio looked back through the two-way mirror to see a naked man hesitantly entering the garden through a doorway near the back of the garden room. The man, a muscular man probably in his late thirties with a huge cobra tattoo inked on his upper chest, stepped onto the cobblestone path. The door clicked shut behind him. The man glanced back at the door, but then quickly looked back into the garden.

Ignacio froze for a moment. "Whoa, whoa, wait a minute. You feed them... people?" Ignacio asked.

The Warden nodded. "While supplies last." He kept his gaze on the naked man who moved slowly through the garden. "Gnarlies refuse to eat someone who's already dead. Or unconscious. Or even drugged."

"Jesus," Ignacio muttered. "Who cares? If they won't eat, then just let them starve to death," Ignacio said.

The Warden shook his head. "And have the ACLU down my throat? Or PETA? No thanks. We don't need any unwanted publicity. Liberal progressives would eat *me* for lunch."

"And you think my writing about what goes on here is going to be good publicity?" Ignacio asked, making no effort to hide the disbelief in his tone.

"If it reaches the right people," the Warden said.

Ignacio was quiet. He turned back to stare at the naked victim-to-be. He felt a quivering flutter in his stomach. "Who is he? What about his rights?"

"He shot up a mall and killed twenty nine people," the Warden said. "Tried and convicted beyond a shadow of a doubt. Guilty as charged."

Ignacio remained silent. He thought he would start feeling ill, but he wasn't feeling nauseous at all. The fluttering in his stomach wasn't sickness. It was excitement. He was rather enraptured by the prospect of watching some bestially unnatural creature kill and devour a terrible human being.

Suddenly, the image on the two-way mirror shifted, the large main viewing area losing some of its width as eight smaller sub-screens appeared on the right side of the two-way mirror viewing area, showing two columns of four sub-screens each. Each sub-screen showed the vantage point from a different camera, while the main viewing area showed the man from whichever camera angle gave the best view of him. One of the smaller sub-screens seemed to be zeroed in on the guy's dangling penis because that screen kept his groin area front and center as the guy moved.

"One big disadvantage of having a big dick," the

Warden said. "You get chosen first for the gnarlies."

"Does he know what's going to happen to him?" Ignacio asked, keeping his voice down to a low whisper.

The Warden shook his head. "Oh, no. He has no idea what's going on, or where he is. They just bundle them up in a truck, put a black hood over their heads, bring them here, strip them naked, then release them into the garden room." He smiled at Ignacio. "They can't see or hear us, so you can speak freely."

The naked man continued forward down the cobblestone path, moving very slowly, turning his head left and right, even glancing behind himself after every few steps. "Is anybody in here?" the man asked. He remained in a partial crouch as he moved, keeping his left hand protectively near his crotch.

The gnarlie put its hand over its mouth and Ignacio could see its stubby fingers. The creature's fingers were very wrinkled and the knuckles were covered in a patch of what looked like dark hairs or even dark fur. Was the damn thing laughing? Ignacio couldn't tell. But the gesture was very reminiscent of a human being hiding a laugh behind a hand over their mouth. The gnarlie's fingernails looked to be sharpened to a point, or that was just perhaps how they naturally grew. Either way, his fingernails looked like very deadly claws.

The naked man took a few more steps along the cobblestone path, taking in his surroundings. His gazed stopped on a fountain that bubbled up tiny eruptions of water in a kaleidoscope of shifting colors.

The gnarlie opened and closed its mouth, the movement slow at first, but then the chomping motion got faster and faster, its teeth raising and lowering faster and faster, as if the gnarlie was working its mouth up to some optimal teeth-chattering speed.

The naked man stopped, cocking his head, listening.

The gnarlie was positioned behind the mountain fountain, several patches of flat grass and two clusters of flowering plants distance away from the man. Its chattering teeth seemed to pick up their pace, its mouth opening and closing yet faster and faster, the clicking happening so fast it started to become one long sound.

"Who's there?" the naked man asked, then gnashed his teeth. "Come out, you fucking coward."

"Get ready," the Warden said.

Ignacio felt all the muscles in his body tense as a rush of both excitement and nervous fear raced through him. He couldn't look away. He knew what was about to happen, knew it would be bloody and gross and horrible, but he couldn't bring himself to look away. With a sickening dread, he realized he wanted to see it. He really wanted to see it. He leaned slightly forward towards the mirror.

"Once its teeth stop chattering, it will attack," the Warden said.

The naked man continued on down the cobblestone path, unwittingly moving closer and closer to the gnarlie. The man passed a section of flat grass, continuing on past a cluster of yellow flowering plants. "Who the fuck is there?"

The chattering stopped as the gnarlie became silent.

"I'll fuck you up," the naked man growled.

Ignacio leaned even closer towards the two-way mirror.

The naked man took another step forward and that's when the gnarlie charged at him. It emerged from behind the fountain, racing along the cobblestone path, its black bird-claw-like feet clattering against the stones. It neared the man, then launched itself into the air, rocketing forward, going straight for the man's groin. The gnarlie's lips opened wide, further revealing a gaping mouth lined with razor-sharp teeth.

The naked man reacted instinctively, just as any human would probably react to a charging animal's attack, throwing up both hands to protect his head and face. This movement left his genital area exposed and vulnerable. The gnarlie sunk its fingernails into the man's stomach, sinking the pointed tips in deep, one hand on either side of the naked man's belly button. At the same time, it sunk its bird-feet-claws into the naked man's thighs. This gave the unnatural beast a nearly unbreakable grip on the man's body.

The gnarlie then reared its head back, and thrust its head forward, its mouth open and wide. It bit off the naked man's genitals, his cock and his balls, in one bite, shredding and tearing off the man's flesh with a violent jerk of its head.

Ignacio watched it all. The naked man shrieking, the gnarlie leaping away with its mouth full, the man falling down and clutching at his bleeding crotch area, the gnarlie starting to chew, the man rolling back and forth on the ground in agony as blood both seeped and gushed through his fingers, the gnarlie swallowing and continuing to chew as blood dripped down its chin, the naked man suddenly becoming lifelessly still as blood pooled around him, the gnarlie continuing to chew and swallow, chew and swallow.

The two-way mirror finally, blissfully, turned black and Ignacio caught a glimpse of his own face in the dark reflective material. He quickly looked away from the reflection of his own enthrallingly haunted eyes. "That thing... that gnarlie... is just a monster," Ignacio said to the Warden. Interviewing ghost hunters was one thing. They were harmless. But this... this was real. Way too real. Did he really just see a man getting eaten alive? And did he really get an intoxicating thrill from observing it? Watching a man getting his... He glanced at his hands to see that his fingers were trembling. "Why are you letting it live?"

"I'm shocked, Mister Valene," the Warden said. He squinted at Ignacio and a frown creased his lips. "I thought this was what you lived for."

Ignacio met the Warden's frown with a deeper frown of his own. "Why don't you just destroy it?"

The Warden shook his head. "We can't. It's against state law. Falls under either criminal statutes or animal cruelty statutes, depending on whomever is interpreting the law." The Warden shrugged. "I just follow the law. I don't make it."

"They're fucking monsters, for Christ's sake!" Ignacio curled his trembling fingers into a fist.

"A gnarlie doing what natural selection has guided it to be doing does not make it a monster," the Warden said.

"But there's no hope of redeeming them," Ignacio said.

The Warden shook his head. "A common mistake."

Ignacio frowned.

"The super naturals are not the ones being redeemed here," the Warden said.

Ignacio went silent for a moment. He looked back to the darkened mirror, but was unable to see the carnage that he knew lay beyond in the garden room.

The Warden nodded. "His debt to society has been paid."

Ignacio said nothing.

The Warden glanced down at his watch. "Time for another redemption in eighteen minutes." He looked back over to Ignacio. "You up for it?"

The werewolf was far more frightening than Ignacio had envisioned. It was hard to believe that the brain of a man still resided in its furry head. They were watching the werewolf from another observation room that was elevated above the room they were viewing, both Ignacio and the Warden standing behind a two-way mirror that was positioned to look down into the werewolf's feeding area.

The werewolf's entire body was covered in dark brown fur. His feet looked like paws, but his hands looked like they were half-paw, half-human. His palms were puffy, and each finger looked more like a claw, ending in a curved tip that looked damn sharp.

The werewolf paced on all fours for a few moments, then rose up on his hind legs and moved around the area. His ears were pinned to the sides of his head, making him appear very agitated. His face still had a human quality to it, but his teeth had both an animalistic quality and a human quality, like his man-teeth and his wolf-teeth were fighting for

272

dominance but neither side could claim victory. His eyes were yellow, bloodshot with thin red veins running through them. His nose was wide and flat; his nostril openings were exceptionally large and they quivered as he paced about.

"Not at all like what you see in the movies or on TV, is it?" the Warden asked.

Ignacio shook his head. "No." He stared at the wolf-man creature. "He looks... deformed."

The Warden nodded. "He's not sleek and smooth like you thought he would be, eh?"

Ignacio said nothing.

"Every time they transform to a werewolf then back to a man, they lose a little bit of their original features," the Warden said. "The transformations aren't exactly the same every time. There's always some kind of aberration in the process. You can almost tell how many times a werewolf has transformed by how many weird aberrations you can find on his body. Somewhat like how you can tell the age of a tree from its rings."

"So how many times has this werewolf transformed?" Ignacio asked.

"From the looks of those ridges on his forehead, the displacement of his left shoulder blade, and the permanent bend in his right knee, I'd say he's transformed at least a few dozen times."

"Is that a lot?" Ignacio asked.

The Warden laughed. "No, it's not." That's all he said, with no additional elaboration.

The werewolf was crouched behind a large green dumpster. The area in which the werewolf prowled was decorated like some urban alley just behind a restaurant. Crushed take-out boxes, empty liquor bottles, and numerous cigarette butts dotted the black, cracked pavement. The far end of the alley was blocked off by a high chain-link fence. Numerous wooden crates in various states of disrepair were stacked up along the restaurant wall on the far side of a rear door that led out of the restaurant into the alley.

The werewolf stared at the rear restaurant door that was just beyond the far edge of the dumpster he was crouched behind.

"Here we go," the Warden said.

The rear restaurant door opened and a man was roughly shoved into the alley. The restaurant door slammed shut. The man wasn't naked like the gnarlie victim had been. He was dressed in an orange prisoner jumpsuit. The man glanced about the area, clearly bewildered by his surroundings.

The werewolf suddenly leaped up onto the top of the dumpster, the movement making a loud clanging noise as the man-beast landed atop the closed lid.

The man looked up at the werewolf watching him. The man froze for only a second, then immediately scrambled over to the restaurant door and started pounding on it. "Open the fucking door! For the love of God, let me in!"

The Warden clucked his tongue disapprovingly.

Ignacio glanced at the Warden, but then turned quickly back to look down at the werewolf. He didn't want to miss anything.

"We give them weapons, but they rarely take advantage of them," the Warden said. "There's a crowbar right near those crates. And there's a tire iron at the edge of the dumpster."

"What does the werewolf need weapons for?"

Ignacio asked.

"They're not for the werewolf," the Warden said.

Ignacio stared with rapt fascination at the scene playing out before him in real-time. "Why is the guy still clothed?" he asked.

The Warden shrugged. "Werewolves seem to prefer it that way. Kind of like being offered potato chips already in a bowl or being given a fresh bag. Werewolves like getting a fresh bag they can open themselves."

"That's... rather disturbing," Ignacio said.

The Warden shrugged. "Makes sense to me."

The werewolf inched along the lid of the dumpster, moving slowly towards the man as the soon-to-be-victim continued to bang on the restaurant door.

The man turned and bolted away from the approaching werewolf, running towards the towering chain-link fence at the end of the alley. He tried to get a grip on the fence, but his sweaty fingers kept slipping off the links. His wildly kicking legs were unable to get any traction and his shoes kept sliding down the links as he desperately tried to get a foothold. "Somebody help me!"

The werewolf leaped off the dumpster and stalked towards the man on all fours.

The man turned as the werewolf neared him, pressing his back up against the chain-link fence, his eyes wide with true fright. "Oh, sweet Jesus."

The werewolf padded closer, standing upright as he drew near the man.

"What did he do?" Ignacio asked, keeping his gaze locked on the terrified man.

"He embezzled millions of dollars from his

company," the Warden said.

"Wait," Ignacio said, taking his gaze away from the scene playing out below him to look at the Warden. "He's just a thief? He's not some mass murderer, or some kind of killer?"

"No, he's not," the Warden said.

"So why is he being fed to a werewolf?"

The Warden looked at Ignacio with a quizzical expression. "You don't think white-collar thieves are worthy of redemption?"

Ignacio said nothing, then turned to look back through the two-way mirror.

The man shrieked in fear and raised his arms up protectively in front of his face as the werewolf reached him.

The werewolf raised his hand, curling his clawed fingers as his arm rose up, then brought his arm down in a quick and violent strike. His clawed fingers raked across the man's right forearm, drawing ragged stripes through the man's orange jumpsuit and through the man's tender flesh.

The man shrieked louder this time, his cry of fright infused with searing yowls of pain as he clutched at his bleeding forearm with his other hand. Blood seeped through his fingers as he clamped down on the gashes in his forearm.

The werewolf continued to attack the man. He knocked the man down with a shoving push and then swiped his claws across the man's throat, killing him. The werewolf hovered over the man's chest, ripping at his orange jumpsuit, then lowered his head and started to feed.

The Warden shook his head softly. "Always the left breast."

Ignacio looked to the Warden. "What?"

The Warden pointed down at the werewolf on the other side of the two-way mirror. "The left breast. They always start their feeding on the left breast. We don't know why and they won't tell us." He shrugged. "But to each his own. I'm a leg man myself," the Warden added. "Can't beat a good drumstick."

For Ignacio, the vampire feeding was the most disturbing of all the redemptions because of the serenity and the ease of the killing, let alone the perverse sexuality behind it.

The room was decorated like it was some fancy woman's bedroom you'd find in an old fantasy castle in Transylvania. A huge four-post oak bed filled a fifth of the room, the bed topped by a white fabric canopy. A large bearskin rug covered the floor at the foot of the bed. A large ornate oak dresser was positioned along one wall. White curtains covered a large open window, the fabric gently rippling in some fake soft breeze that was probably being created by some unseen fan positioned outside this bedroom set.

A woman dressed in a sheer, flowing robe sat before a large mirror positioned atop a vanity, idly combing her long blonde hair. She was a pretty blonde from what Ignacio could see of her face, with a pert nose and a wide sensual mouth. Was she the target? He could see that she was clearly aroused with anticipation as her hardened nipples pushed against the thin fabric of her robe. Was she really getting a perverse thrill out of her own imminent demise?

The vampire entered through the open window in

the form of a human-size bat. The creature landed quietly on the window sill with an elegant grace and tucked his leathery wings to his sides. The man-sized bat had pale-colored flesh, and his wrinkled skin looked to be covered in a layer of fine dark hairs. He focused on the woman combing her hair, his dark eyes staring with a dark intent.

And then the man-bat vampire started to transform. It was hard to see exactly what was happening, as if some weird hazy white mist surrounded the vampire during the transformation, but what emerged from the mist was quite a handsome naked man with dark hair and dark eyes. The eyes were the one consistent feature that did not change even after the transformation; the vampire's eyes retained a hypnotic shimmer and their grim focus on the woman remained just as strong.

"They can actually do that?" Ignacio asked, keeping his gaze on the scene on the other side of the two-way mirror.

"Of course," the Warden said. "They don't turn into a ridiculously tiny bat like in the movies. Their body mass is preserved in the transformation, so be it bat or wolf, they retain their relative size."

The vampire moved away from the window ledge, slowly walking closer to the woman as she continued to idly comb her hair.

"What did she do?" Ignacio asked.

"Judy? Nothing," the Warden said. "She's one of my staff."

Before Ignacio could ask the Warden to elaborate, the vampire looked up and pierced Ignacio with his penetrating gaze. Ignacio felt a shudder run through his body. "He can... he can... see me." It wasn't a question.

"Oh, yes," the Warden said. "I apologize. This is just plain glass. Mirrors play funny tricks with vampires, distorts the visuals. Plain glass works better."

The naked vampire looked away and Ignacio took a staggered step backwards as if he had been trying to pull away from some invisible grip and the vampire had finally just let him go. Ignacio put a hand to his throat, protectively shielding his neck. He felt an oddly disconcerting stirring in his loins. He felt his curious gaze being drawn to the naked vampire's groin area but he didn't see any dangling penis; in fact he saw nothing but a shriveled piece of barely visible flesh drooping in the vampire's crotch area.

The vampire turned his attention to the woman who was still idly combing her long blonde hair. He moved up behind Judy and cupped her breasts, nuzzling his face into her neck. Judy dropped her brush in alarm, as she didn't see the vampire approaching because he wasn't visible in her mirror, but then she sighed and tilted her head to give the vampire a better angle of her neck that offered more of her flesh.

The vampire opened his mouth and two fangs started to protrude.

Judy moaned a breathy moan as the vampire squeezed her breasts, cupping her flesh in his hands. Her nipples remained hard and pointed.

The vampire's fangs continued to enlarge, thicken and lengthen.

"Am I really looking at a vampire getting some kind of fang boner?" Ignacio asked in a soft whisper.

The Warden didn't answer. He was clearly

enthralled by what was taking place on the other side of the glass window.

The naked vampire sank the full length of his fangs into Judy's neck and she let out an orgasmic groan of pure bliss. She put her hand between her legs and started to massage her female mound.

"Most people don't realize what the vampire is doing when he first sinks his fangs into someone," the Warden said.

"And what is that?" Ignacio asked.

"He's releasing an ejaculate laced with opioids and it goes straight to the brain of his victim, setting off a tremendous orgasm. From what I have been told, there's no stronger pleasure released by any activity, or by any drug, than a vampire's ejaculation."

The vampire kept his mouth pressed tightly to Judy's throat.

"Oh, he's very hungry today," the Warden muttered. "Sometimes he can subsist on one person for weeks, but I think today he is having a feast. Probably for your benefit, Ignacio. He knows you're watching. I'm quite jealous."

Ignacio said nothing. He watched as the vampire continued to feed, continued to draw the woman's blood into his mouth. The uncomfortable stiffening in his loins persisted.

Judy moaned, rubbing her female mound faster and faster. Then her eyes sprang open wide and a shimmering light filled them. The hazy light lingered for a few seconds, pulsing stronger then fainter, stronger then fainter. And then the light vanished as Judy suddenly became still. Her entire body went limp, falling into the vampire's embrace.

"That was delightful," the Warden said with a

contented sigh. "Did you see the look of bliss in her eyes just before her light went out? That is the highest point of pleasure a human can reach. That one moment."

Ignacio stared at the limp form of the dead woman as the vampire gently laid her down on the bearskin rug. "Why?" Ignacio muttered. "Why did she have to die? What did she do?"

"She thought she was *the one*." the Warden explained. "That's why Judy volunteered."

"The one?" Ignacio asked absently, still keeping his gaze on the naked vampire as he rose back up to his full height.

"She had a strong empathetic reaction to the vampire," the Warden said.

Ignacio jerked his head towards the Warden, forcing himself to look away from the vampire as the Warden's words finally registered in his mind. "Wait a minute. That's why she volunteered, you said? She volunteered for this?"

The Warden nodded.

"Why? Was she ill? Did she have some terminal disease."

The Warden shook his head. "Oh, no. She was quite healthy."

"I don't understand," Ignacio said.

The Warden was quiet for a moment. "Can you ever truly understand someone else's reality?" he asked rhetorically, his tone pensive.

Ignacio said nothing.

"Judy thought she was the special one that he would love the most," the Warden said. "She thought she had a unique connection to him, a connection that went deeper with her than with anyone else. She thought she, and only she, would be able to soothe the savage beast." The Warden shook his head. "She was wrong, of course, but nothing any of us said to her changed her beliefs. Nothing. She latched on to her own reality and no one was able to dissuade her from it." He was quiet for a moment. "That vampire even said straight to her face that she was not anything special, that she was not *the one*, but Judy still wouldn't believe it. She thought he was just teasing her, testing her love and devotion." The Warden shook his head softly. "The arrogance of ignorance. Or the ignorance of arrogance. Something like that.

"So you let this woman, one of your staff, enter a room with a hungry vampire, knowing she will be drained of her blood? Knowing she would be killed?" Ignacio asked, his jaw set tight.

"Of course. It's what Judy wanted. Few of us get to choose our own path to redemption. I'm quite happy for her."

"You should have stopped her!" Ignacio curled his fingers into fists, but kept his fists balled up against his sides.

"And deny her the right to her own beliefs?" The Warden shook his head. "She wanted to live her truth as she saw it."

They moved back to the Warden's office.

Ignacio, suddenly feeling drained and exhausted, sat down heavily in the leather chair in front of the Warden's ornate oak desk.

"I'm afraid I've slightly misled you," the Warden said as he eased himself into his chair behind his desk.

"You're going to feed me to one of your unnaturals, aren't you?" Ignacio asked.

"Why, are you guilty of something that needs redemption?" the Warden asked.

"No," Ignacio said without hesitation.

"What, you think I'm like some cat playing with its food before it kills it and eats it? And you are the mouse?" The Warden laughed a raucous laugh.

Ignacio didn't find his comment amusing.

"No, no, of course not." The Warden paused briefly after a few more chuckles, calming himself. He regained his composure and put on a serious face. "I need you for an experiment we are going to attempt."

"An experiment?"

The Warden nodded. "A social media experiment."

Ignacio waited for the Warden to continue.

"We need more volunteers," the Warden said.

"Volunteers? To work here?"

"Not exactly," the Warden replied.

Ignacio frowned.

"We're running low on… food," the Warden said.

Ignacio's frown remained. "You need volunteers to bring food here?"

"Are you being dense on purpose?" the Warden asked. "Not bring," the Warden said with just the slightest shake of his head. "Be."

Ignacio let the Warden's words sink in for a moment before he truly understood what he was saying. "You want me to post a story about Cross Institute of Redemption so some of my readers will volunteer themselves to be eaten alive by your super… by the monsters you have imprisoned here?"

The Warden wagged his finger. "Sheltered, not

imprisoned."

Ignacio gave a violent shake of his head. "I'm not going to publish that!"

"Yes, you will."

"No. I won't."

Yes. You will. You are going to publish exactly what we tell you to publish," the Warden said. "The truth."

Ignacio shook his head again. "I won't do it."

"So now you are deciding what version of the truth your readers get to see?" the Warden asked.

Ignacio was silent.

"I am telling you we need more volunteers, but yet you refuse to write the truth." The Warden cocked his head and slowly shook it.

Ignacio felt his face flush with heat. "You are telling me to ask my readers if they'd like to offer themselves up as blood sacrifices!"

The Warden leaned back in his chair. "That's a bit of a harsh way to put it."

"I can't do that," Ignacio said.

The Warden leaned forward towards Ignacio. "Because you know what is best for them, right? You are the filter through which they must all lead their lives? You are the arbitrator of truth then?"

"No. I…" Ignacio could not suppress the flabbergasted expression from distorting his features. "How is this accursed place still running?"

The Warden leaned back and steepled his fingers. "I already told you. The people who don't believe in Cross Institute will continue to ignore its existence. To them, it's fake news. They will never believe it, no matter how much evidence you put before them." The Warden pursed his lips. "It's really quite disturbing when you think about it."

Ignacio sat silently.

"Those who do believe in it just stay silent and let it continue," the Warden said. "They think it's good for society. Helps keep the criminal riffraff away from their neighborhoods. They truly believe in taking a bite out of crime." The Warden smiled a wry smile.

Ignacio shook his head. "I can't do that. I can't ask people to... kill themselves."

"They are not killing themselves."

"They would be offering themselves up to be killed. I see little difference."

The Warden was quiet for a long moment. "It's fine, Ignacio. It's fine." He waved his hand dismissively. "We've prepared for such contingencies."

Ignacio frowned. He fought back a very powerful urge to shift in his chair as a lingering silence stretched on.

"There are two other types of super naturals that I haven't told you about yet," the Warden finally said. "I was hoping we wouldn't have to take this step, but I am glad we prepared for it."

Ignacio looked up at the sound of footsteps, turning his head towards the office door. He froze as he stared at the approaching figure. "Shape-shifters... You have shape-shifters here?"

"Doppelgängers. Shape-shifters, some call them, yes," the Warden said. "Sometimes we like to call them twinsies. A much more fun name, a bit softer-edged, don't you think?"

A perfect duplicate of Ignacio stopped next to Ignacio's chair and stared down at him. The facial features, the hair, the mannerisms, all of the shape-shifter's actions were identical to how Ignacio looked and behaved.

"He's going to take your place," the Warden said. "At least until you are willing to get on board yourself."

Ignacio tore his gaze away from the shape-shifter who looked exactly like him down to the thin mustache that lined his upper lip. "No, no," Ignacio muttered. "My wife will know. My wife will know it's not me."

"Oh, Ignacio," the Warden said, pursing his lips as he ever so softly shook his head. "Your wife is a twinsie. Jennifer has been one for the last four months. Who do you think has been steering you towards doing a story on Cross Institute of Redemption?"

"Hi, honey."

"No…" Ignacio's eyes filled with a slow-moving horror as his wife, or the unnatural entity whom he thought was his wife, entered the office and beamed him a pleasant smile. This thing, this twinsie, had the same brunette hair, the same hazel eyes, the same beauty mark just above her upper lip, the same sensual mouth that Jennifer had.

"But don't worry, we still have use for you in the meantime," the Warden said to Ignacio. "We need all the names of your contacts in your industry." The Warden tapped his own head as he nodded toward Ignacio's. "Especially the ones you have stored up there. Those secret, off-the-record folks who might also be able to help us."

"But why?" Ignacio asked, tearing his gaze away from his wife's doppelgänger. "Why are you doing this? What is your endgame?"

"If you don't know what it is, you can't stop it," the Warden said.

Ignacio clenched his teeth, tightening his jaw. "Tell me, damn you!"

"Oh, fine. You're not going anywhere anyway," the Warden said, waving his hand dismissively. He glanced around the room as if taking in all the surroundings, then looked back to Ignacio. "What better place to train for the impending battle for control of reality than in an isolated institution that a majority of people don't even believe exists, populated with beings that have unbelievable powers." The Warden smiled a maddening smile. "The benefits of seclusion."

Ignacio frowned.

"It started off as a prison, really," the Warden said. "A place to hold super natural criminals. But after I took over, I... well, I reshaped the agenda. There's too much talent here to allow it to go to waste." The Warden paused. "We need a way to preserve the deep state. We need fighters who don't fear dark places. Fighters who don't play by the same rules as humans."

"You're insane," Ignacio said.

The Warden shrugged. "Doesn't matter. I have the keys and no one else has the stomach to drive."

Ignacio shook his head. "I won't tell you what you want to know. I'm not going to give you what you want."

The Warden ignored his defiantly dismissive tone. "I told you there were two other types of super naturals that I hadn't told you about," the Warden said. "There's still one kind left."

Ignacio could only stare at the Warden with an

ever deepening sense of dread.

"I call them SilverLords," the Warden said. "Well, actually I call myself SilverLord. The others are more like SilverLord underlings, silverlings that serve me."

"Sss…Silver…SilverLord," Ignacio said in a nervously stuttering voice. "What's a SilverLord?"

In lieu of an answer, the Warden stood up and posed a question of his own. "Did you know that the average dark-haired person has about a hundred thousand or so hairs on their head?"

Ignacio didn't answer.

"Blondes have an average of a hundred and fifty thousand or so, so be glad you are not blonde. Though that would have been more fun," he mused. The Warden raised a pointed finger. "But the more interesting number is the five million or so hair follicles on the adult human body."

Suddenly, the Warden's flesh began to shimmer as his skin took on a silvery sheen. His flesh now had the bizarre appearance of a silverfish insect somehow mated with the size and shape of a human being. He opened his mouth to reveal a circular row of small, very sharply pointed teeth. A thin proboscis like appendage with a tiny hook on the end of it slithered out of the darkness of his mouth, snaking its way out of the small black hole formed by the circle of his teeth.

The Warden then held up his hands to show Ignacio the tips of his fingers; the tops of his fingers now each had a similar circular row of small teeth visible and a similar very thin proboscis snaked its way out of the top of each finger. "The teeth are to grip your flesh and the hook plucks out the delicious follicle," the Warden said. "In case you were interested in the process."

"You said... you said you weren't going to... eat me," Ignacio protested.

"Oh, technically I said I wasn't going to feed you to one of my super naturals," the Warden said as he moved around the edge of his desk, moving closer to Ignacio. "I'm not really going to eat you, per say. I'm going to torture you. One hair follicle at a time until you give us the information we want." The hooked proboscis that slithered out of the top of his forefinger wiggled in the air. "The extraction is quite excruciating."

The wall of books to Ignacio's left suddenly shimmered, then seemed to vanish as they transformed into a flat sheet of glass. Ignacio stared into a room situated beyond the pane of glass. Seated within the room he could see numerous others staring curiously, somewhat earnestly, at him. There was a gnarlie, the handsome vampire, and two men who looked to have just finished transforming back from werewolves into men. There were other people in the room as well, several women and two very pale men. He had no idea what type of unnaturals they were; perhaps the pale men were actual demons and the women were druids. Ignacio looked away from them back up to the pleasantly smiling Warden.

The Warden shrugged. "It's only fair." He moved even closer to Ignacio.

The two doppelgänger twinsies roughly grabbed Ignacio's shoulders, holding him in place.

"Don't worry," the Warden said. "I'll save your pubic hairs for last, but I don't think you'll make it anywhere near that far. No one ever does." The Warden lowered his face and the circular row of teeth drew closer to Ignacio's left eyebrow.

"The Valiant Warriors Inside Cross Institute of Redemption Need You!" was the headline on the screen. "These wrongly maligned patriots need your help to continue the fight against the enemies who are trying to take over the government." Ignacio Valene was the byline on the article. "Don't let these brave super natural fighters down. Do your patriotic duty for your country. Do it for your community. Do it for your family. Do it for yourself."

"What's the count?" the Warden asked as he glanced over the top of his laptop screen at the doppelgänger twinsie in the form of Jennifer Valene.

"We have those thirteen writers that Ignacio gave us working for us now," the Jennifer twinsie said. "Plus Ignacio now that he's come around." She paused. "He looks a little silly without his eyebrows."

"Be nice," the Warden said.

The Jennifer twinsie nodded. "We have that new bot programmer that Ignacio helped us find, too. He's got two hundred aliases created so far, posting roughly twenty thousand total posts a week across a dozen different platforms. We are getting very strong interactions across the board."

The Warden nodded his head. "Good. Good. The rabbit hole is getting wider and deeper. And the patriot count?"

"Sixty-seven patriots already on premises ready for redemption."

The Warden nodded. "Excellent. We need two hundred and fifty-three volunteers a month to leap into that hole. After we reach that at a steady clip we can think about expanding."

The Jennifer twinsie nodded her head. "We'll get there," she said. "Keep feeding them the same story from enough different sources and we'll get plenty of them to start believing."

The Warden looked again at the headline on the screen. "The Valiant Warriors Inside Cross Institute of Redemption Need You!" He looked up at her and nodded in return. "Our truth will win the day."

For the briefest of moments, the Jennifer twinsie shape-shifted to her original form. The green scales, the reptilian eyes, the claw-like hands all were visible. Her forked tongue slithered out of her mouth, licked at the air, then slithered back in.

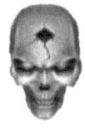

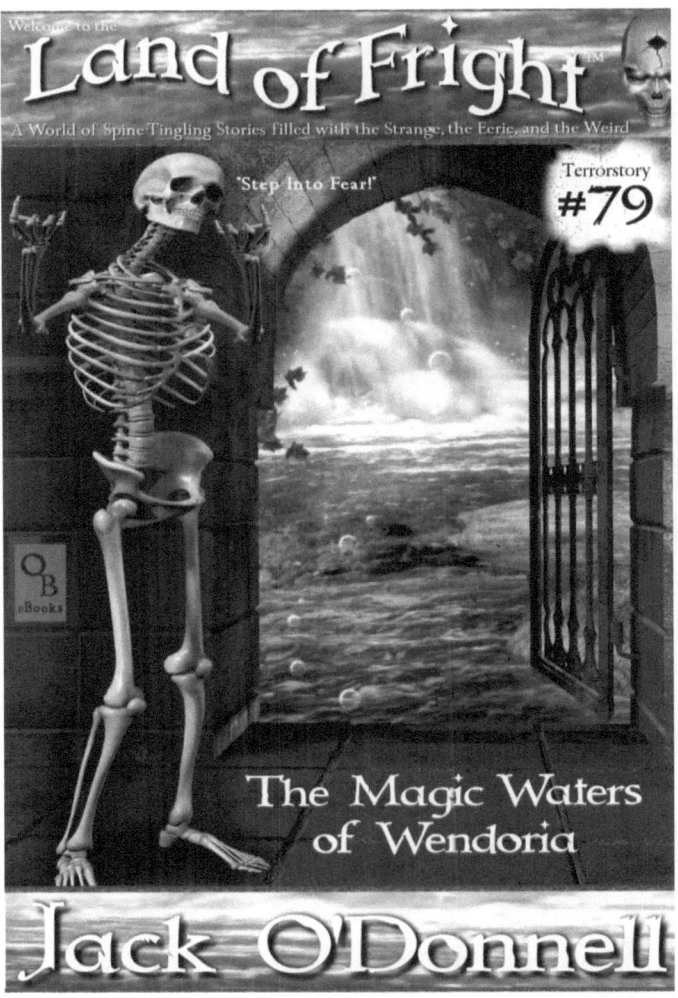

TERRORSTORY #79
THE MAGIC WATERS
OF WENDORIA

The Magic Waters of Wendoria

Show Summary: A fantasy series set in the mythical land of Wendoria. Rohs Goodwill finds a hidden secret pool of magic water that gives her special powers. She uses the healing powers of water to help the people in her village solve all manner of problems.

New episodes at 8PM Eastern and streaming next day.

~~~❄✦❈✦❄~~~

Kimberly Phillips rubbed her hand over her pregnant belly. Kimberly was an attractive woman with curly blonde hair and a gentle face. Her eyes were puffy, tinged with red, her face wet with tears. But they were not tears of sorrow. They were tears of sweet joy. She was seated in their living room on the couch in front of their large screen television, her legs tucked partially under her, watching the new TV show *The Magic Waters of Wendoria*.

Her husband Brian was seated next to her. He was thirty-two, five years senior to his wife; a big brawny guy with short brown hair, handsomely chiseled in a movie-star sort of way. He also had the hints of tears at the corners of his eyes, but there was no way he was going to let them fall. He was much too macho for that. He reached out and grabbed Kimberly's petite hand, squeezing his wife's slender fingers gently, comfortingly.

Kimberly reached up to her face and wiped away a few of the tears that glistened on her cheek. "She's so good," Kimberly said. "She's so sweet. So strong." She looked away from the television, glancing down at her pregnant belly, and moved her slender fingers round and round her abdomen, mentally caressing her unborn child within. "I want our baby to be just like her. Calm and sweet with a quiet strength. The world needs more of that these days."

Brian nodded. "Yes it does," he said. "Yes it does." He bent over and lovingly kissed Kimberly's swollen abdomen. "You're destined for great things, my little sweet."

Kimberly continued to rub at her swollen belly as she whispered down to her unborn. "Don't you worry, we'll take good care of you."

The Magic Waters of Wendoria
Season 1
Episode 5
A Rohs By Any Other Name
4.67 stars (4454)
Rohs uses her newfound powers to help a village elder overcome her chronic pain.

"I love this show!"

"Finally, a show that's sweet and serene, but not too preachy. My whole family loves it!"

"The world needs a hundred Rohs Goodwills!"

"This show is stupid. Anybody who likes this show is stupid."

"Water is the key to happiness. It's a proven scientific fact. We are made up mostly of water."

"4.67 stars? Thousands of reviews? Are you kidding me? Half of those are from fake bots, for sure. There's no way that many real people like this silly show."

"Water has the power to heal us all. It's a wonderful message. We should all be respecting the water all around us. Don't pollute it. Don't chlorinate it. Just let it be."

Kimberly clutched at her husband's shirt sleeve. Her normally-pretty face was tightened up into a scrunched grimace, all the lines and wrinkles on her face twisted into a swirl of contorted snarls. "I need some drugs!"

One of the nurses gave a slight chuckle. "It's too late for that."

Brian gently rubbed his hand along the length of his wife's bare arm. "It's okay, babe." His voice was calm, soothing, the softness in his voice somewhat a contrast to the hardened curves of his muscular body.

"Give me some fucking drugs!" Kimberly begged and demanded all in the same screaming breath. Her face was flush with sweat, her blond hair plastered to her forehead. She arched her back and let out a tremendous cry of pain, intensely gripping the sides of the hospital bed with both hands.

"Just push," Brian said.

"I am pushing!" Kimberly shouted through clenched teeth.

Brian rubbed his large hand slowly over Kimberly's slender white-knuckled fingers as she gripped the side of the hospital bed. "Just breathe." He did a slow inhale and exhale, repeating the action several times.

"What time is it?" Kimberly asked through her gnashing teeth.

Brian turned his wrist as he glanced at his fitness tracker. "Twenty to eight," he said.

"Shit." And then Kimberly gave out a tremendous yell, gripping the bed even tighter in her clenched fingers, her features contorting even more, her face blooming a hot red as she pushed with all the energy she had left.

*

"Shh, Mommy's favorite show is on." Kimberly gave the fussy baby a few half-hearted rocks, then looked to her husband. "Here, you take her," Kimberly said, holding the swaddled baby up towards Brian. She grabbed at the remote attached to her hospital bed and clicked the power button. A television set positioned high up on the wall opposite the bed flickered on. Kimberly flicked through a few channels, then stopped when she reached what she was looking for. "Damn it," she muttered. "I missed the beginning."

Brian glanced up over his shoulder at the television, then looked back at his wife. "Don't worry. We can watch it when we get back home." Brian rocked their baby gently, kissing her pink hat.

The Magic Waters of Wendoria
Season 1
Episode 7
Rohs Blooms
4.71 stars (4232)
Rohs fights off a roving band of marauders intent on raiding her village.

"Rohs is so clever. I love her!"

"The fight scenes were so fake. Please get a good stunt coordinator if you want to have realistic fight scenes."

"This show is not about "realism." It's a fantasy show about what could be, or better yet, how things should be if we just cared more about each other."

"Mother Theresa? I didn't know you were still alive!"

"It's a good show. I like it."

Kimberly and Brian Phillips proudly announced the birth of their daughter Rohs Anne Phillips to their friends and family. Seven pounds, six ounces.

The Magic Waters of Wendoria
Season 2
Episode 4
Rohs Water
4.81 stars (3271)
Rohs uses the quenching powers of water to save a young village boy from being overwhelmed by his own hot rage.

"Wow!"

"I was balling my eyes out at the end. What a powerful message. Everyone in the world needs to watch this show."

"Many civilizations in human history felt deep respect for water and considered it sacred because it fell from the heavens - but sadly no one even gives it a second thought now. No one could fail to be very moved by this show - it should be watched by every human being on the planet."

"I saw side boob! Finally! Eighteen minutes and thirty-four seconds in if anybody is interested."

"Really?" Kimberly asked. "You've never watched Magic Waters of Wendoria?" She cradled her infant daughter in her arms, holding a bottle to the baby's mouth.

Angela Carmichael shook her head. "No. Is it good?" Angela was a woman of color, dark-skinned with tight black curls. She was sitting at Kimberly's kitchen table nursing a cup of coffee. Some half-eaten cherry and cheese pastries sat on small plates before both women. Gentle music played in the background - the flute, violin, and choral sounds of The Magic Waters of Wendoria soundtrack.

Kimberly nodded. "Best show I've ever seen. I've watched every episode at least a few times."

"What's it about?" Angela asked, then took a sip of her coffee.

"This young girl named Rohs Goodwill gets her powers from a magic pool of water and she uses her powers to help people who are in trouble. It's sweet and charming."

Angela paused to peek at Kimberly over the rim of her cup, then slowly lowered the cup back down to the table. "Rose Goodwill? That's a little heavy-handed, don't you think?"

Kimberly shrugged. "It's a beautiful name. I like how they spell Rohs differently. R-o-h-s. It's so unique."

"Wait," Angela said. She sat back in her chair. "Is that who you named your daughter after? A TV character?"

Kimberly tipped the bottle she was holding up a little higher, giving baby Rohs a better angle to suck on the nipple.

Angela looked at the bottle Kimberly was holding, reading the words inscribed on the side of the plastic container. "Magic Waters of Wendoria," Angela said, reading the words aloud. She looked at Kimberly with raised eyebrows. "Wow. You really *are* into it, aren't you?"

"Just watch one episode and you'll see why," Kimberly said. "Rohs is an angel. The world needs more people just like her." She cooed down at her baby. "Isn't that right, my sweet little Rohs? I want you to be just like her." She gave her baby a gentle, loving little rock.

Baby Rohs's eyes lit up with a contented delight as her mother continued to gently rock her back and forth.

The Magic Waters of Wendoria
Season 2
Episode 11
Rohs Finds a Thorn
4.29 stars (1826)
Rohs prevents a young villager from turning to a life of thievery and deceit.

"When life throws thorns, hunt for roses. — Anonymous. Or I should say when the dark side of life tempts you, seek out Rohs(es). Ha ha!"

"This show always lifts my spirits! Thank you for bringing us such a wonderful show in these troubled times!"

"This show is dum. Its so hokee."

"Aww, she's so cute. What's her name?"

Kimberly glanced up from her phone and looked at the elderly couple who had paused in their walk in the park to stare at her daughter sitting upright in her stroller. "Rohs," she replied.

"You mean like Rose from that old Titanic movie?" the elderly man asked. He was Paul Glenn, a retired bus driver out for a walk with his wife.

"No, I mean like Rohs from The Magic Waters of Wendoria show," Kimberly said.

"Ohh," the elderly woman said, clutching at Paul's arm. She was Marge Glenn, Paul's wife of forty eight years. "I love that show!" Marge's boisterous enthusiasm seemed to start a small coughing fit and she bent over slightly, covering her mouth with her hand.

Paul, clearly accustomed to seeing this physical malady from his wife, gently comforted her, putting his hand on her back. "Easy, Marge. Nothing to get that excited over." Paul looked up at Kimberly. "She does love that silly show."

Rohs held up her Magic Waters of Wendoria sippy cup, as if offering it to the elderly woman.

"She's offering to share her water with you," Kimberly said, beaming with pride at her young daughter's actions.

"Oh my," Marge said, fighting back a much weaker second fit of coughing. "That's so sweet." She looked at Rohs with an appreciative tenderness in her gaze. "Thank you, young lady, but I'm not thirsty. Just this dumb cough. But thank you." Marge looked at Kimberly with a pleasant smile. "My, she is the nicest mannered child I have ever seen in my life."

Kimberly's smile burst into a bright flash of white teeth.

Rohs lowered the sippy cup. An oddly adult frown seemed to darken her young features just for a brief second before she smiled gaily at Marge.

The Magic Waters of Wendoria
Season 3
Episode 7

Rohs Saves the Day
3.89 stars (1154)

Rohs uses her powers to fight a fire that threatens the entire village, but she suffers painful consequences.

"Rohs is the heroine we need. The world needs more selfless heroes just like her."

"Damn that Rohs is stacked. Let's see those t!ts! Stop teasing us with all these naked back shots! A little butt crack would be appreciated, too."

"I hope those burns don't leave a scar. I love Rohs."

"Rohs will be fine. The Ancient Greeks used water as a healing agent. In the Old Testament people soaked in mineral waters for physical healing. Native Americans sat in sweat lodges as a way of purifying the body and mind. The magic waters will heal her."

"Hey, how about a spoiler alert warning? Jesus. I haven't seen it yet."

"How's your little Rohs doing?" Angela asked.

Kimberly sighed a happy sigh. "She's doing great." Then Kimberly laughed a little laugh, clearly thinking about something.

"What? Tell me?" Angela prodded.

"It's really cute," Kimberly said. "I was having a rough day last week, way too many Zoom calls in one day, and I was exhausted. I forgot the tea kettle was hot so I burned my fingers on it. Rohs went right to the freezer, grabbed some ice cubes, wrapped them up in a towel and brought them to me. I didn't even have to say anything. She just knew what to do." Kimberly sighed a contented sigh. "Then I was sitting with Rohs on the couch and she reached up and caressed my cheek. Just out of nowhere." Kimberly sighed another happy sigh. "*She* was comforting *me*. Can you believe it?"

"That's nice," Angela said. "I remember how nice Tanika was to me before she turned."

Kimberly frowned. "Turned?"

"Enjoy them while you can," Angela said. "When they turn into pre-teens, look out. It's like they go from Doctor Jekyll to Mister Hyde." Angela snapped her fingers. "Tanika went like that. It took a little longer for Jerome, but he still turned, too."

"Rohs isn't going to be like that," Kimberly said, her tone confidently insistent.

Angela gave a slight cock to her head, sighing a sad little sigh. "Sometimes, things just aren't under your control."

The Magic Waters of Wendoria
Season 4
Episode 4
Rohs Rescues a Maiden
4.89 stars (2074)
Rohs battles a fire demon that demands a virgin human sacrifice.

"Rohs is the female hero we all need to emulate. She epitomizes the feminine power of love."

"I saw hard nipples! Anybody else see those? Best wet T-shirt scene ever!"

"It wasn't a T-shirt, dumb ass. It was a dress."

"Don't care. Best hard nipples ever! Beats out that chick on Friends."

"This show teaches you how beautiful actions create beauty and ugly actions create ugly."

"Rohs is beautiful and calm, but willing to draw blood in defense of what's right."

"Sometimes, thorns have a purpose."

"You go, girl!"

"In Christianity, water is blessed and used to cleanse and purify the body and soul before prayer. In Judaism, Mikvah is a ritual immersion bath of natural water used for the purpose of nullifying impurity. This show proves the serenity and calmness of purifying water beats the cackling and charring destruction of fire every time."

"Gee, thanks for the insight, Father Bob."

"Rohs was quite the hero today," Miss Mayfield said to Kimberly.

Kimberly looked expectantly at the pre-school teacher. "Really? How so?"

The two women were standing in the hallway just outside the door to the pre-school classroom. Inside the classroom, the children were busy cleaning up their art stations. Miss Mayfield was still dressed in her painter's smock and she had a smear of purple paint on her cheek.

"The children were painting and Likita ran out of paint. She was very upset because she was making the picture for her father's birthday. Rohs gave her the last of her paint even though she needed it to finish her own picture." Miss Mayfield smiled. "You should've seen the smile on Likita's face when Rohs did that. Pure joy."

Kimberly nodded and smiled. "That's my Rohs."

"You've got a good one there," Miss Mayfield said. "Let's hope she stays that way."

Kimberly frowned. "Of course she will." She glowered at the pre-school teacher. "Why would you say such a thing?"

"I'm sorry," Miss Mayfield said quickly. "Of course she will."

The Magic Waters of Wendoria
Season 6
Episode 8
Rohs and the River Gods
4.33 stars (974)
Rohs uses her powers to save a village boy from drowning in a flash flood caused by an evil magician.

"Holy bravery! Even I didn't think Rohs had that in her. Good on her!"

"CGI flash flood. C'mon, it looked terrible. With graphics technology these days, they could've done so much better."

"It's not about the sfx, stupid. It's about empathy and morality and decency and treating other people with respect, you dumb ass."

"Great good can always triumph over great evil! Love this show!"

"Boy, your daughter really loves the water, doesn't she?" Olga said. "I don't think she's come out of the pool since we got here."

Kimberly, dressed in a blue one-piece bathing suit, was sitting at a table beneath the shade of a large umbrella at the Oceanside Aquatic Center. Her belly had the tell-tale swell of pregnancy.

Olga Krushenko, a neighbor from a block over in their subdivision, sat in another chair next to her, also keeping out of the bright sunlight. Olga was a bit overweight, looking a bit frumpy in her polka-dotted one-piece bathing suit. Her hair was pushed up underneath a swimming cap, but she was still dry as she hadn't gone into the water yet.

"I think she really wants to be a mermaid," Kimberly said. "We took her to her first swim lesson a few months ago. All the kids were waiting for the instructor to tell them to jump in, but Rohs couldn't wait. She just walked right into the pool before she even put on the life preserver." Kimberly made a forward motion with her hand. "Just stepped right off the edge and plunged in. The instructor nearly lost his mind. But Rohs just started dog paddling. Like she just instinctively knew what to do to stay afloat."

"Wow," Olga muttered.

"Yeah, it was weird. And a bit scary for a second. But she was totally fine. She took to the water like a fish." Kimberly rubbed at her pregnant belly. "I hope her little brother follows in her footsteps."

Ivan Krushenko walked up to the ladies, holding a serving of nachos drowning in melted cheddar cheese. He was a beefy fellow with a greying beard.

Olga frowned at him. "Where's Alek?"

Ivan frowned back at her. "I thought he was with you."

"Idiot!" Olga hissed at her husband. She quickly rose out of her chair, scanning the surrounding pool area as she moved.

Suddenly, a life guard's screeching whistle rent the air.

Olga burst towards the edge of the pool. "Alek!" Olga shouted, her voice clearly filled with fear. Ivan tossed his nachos down on the table, racing after his wife.

Kimberly rose up out of the chair, moving a bit awkwardly due to her pregnancy, then shielded her eyes with her hand as she scanned the pool area.

Within moments, Olga came back, guiding a coughing Alek towards their table. Ivan trailed sheepishly behind them.

Kimberly saw Rohs in the distance, standing safely near the edge of the pool. She lowered her hand and turned to look at her neighbors.

"Oh my God. Oh my God. How can I ever repay you?" Olga gushed out.

Kimberly frowned at her friend, confused.

"Your daughter saved Alek's life," Olga said, still fighting to catch her breath and calm herself." Oh my God. Rohs pulled him out. He almost drowned. Oh my God." Olga pulled her son closer to her, hugging him tightly.

Kimberly smiled down at Rohs as her daughter padded over to her side, her body dripping wet from the pool water. "That's just what she does," Kimberly said. She put her arm around Rohs, giving her daughter a warm smile.

Olga looked up over at Kimberly. "That's just what she does?"

Kimberly looked back to Olga and nodded. "She saves people."

Rohs smiled.

The Magic Waters of Wendoria
Season 7
Episode 1
Rohs Goes Skinny-Dipping
4.27 stars (1454)

Rohs decides to see what happens when she immerses her entire body into the magic waters instead of just cupping the water in her hand and drinking it. Her powers magnify and her control over water grows even stronger.

"Love this show!!"

"Rohs is a babe and a half. I'd go skinny-dipping with her any time!"

"Anybody who doesn't love Rohs and respect what she is doing needs to get some sense beaten into them."

"They should have put this on HBO Max first. Then we could see Rohs's boobies. Now they just tease us. Hell, we still didn't even get to see butt. How can you do a skinny-dipping scene and not show any ass cheeks?"

"Wow. Can't believe some of these comments. Some of you people are genuine idiots and need to seek psychological help. This show is about the healing power of water. The therapeutic properties of water have been known for centuries. Water gives us all life and this show gives us all hope."

"Sweetie, the world's most important fluid comes from the dangling appendage between my legs . If you need a dose, send me a text."

"You're gross."

"Just ignore those pigs in the comments. Just sitting mindfully in a bathtub can provide a restorative meditative experience just as powerful as Rohs had. That's the point of the episode. Sit quietly in the water and open your senses to the touch, to the smell of the water. Take in all the sensations of the water and visualize love, peace, and thankfulness for yourself

and the water you are joined with."

"Well, do you like it?" Kimberly asked. "It's finally ready." She clutched her newborn son in her arms, gently rocking little Archie. "Now you can be a fish in your own backyard."

Rohs pumped her head up and down as she stared out at the in-ground pool now taking up half of their backyard. "I love it! Can I go in it now?" Rohs asked.

Kimberly smiled. "Of course. Go get your suit on. I'll put some sunscreen on you and Daddy will go in with you."

"Yay!" Rohs raced towards her room.

The Magic Waters of Wendoria
Season 7
Episode 5
Rohs Red
2.77 stars (1467)
Rohs does the unthinkable to a deer that was drinking from the dwindling pool of magic water.

"What the hell just happened? Is this episode some kind of sick joke?"

"Finally this show gets a dose of reality. Too much phony happy fantasy shit. Now it's getting good!"

"Absolute power corrupts absolutely. You knew it was inevitable."

"That's it. I'm done with this stupid show. They've officially ruined it forever. I can't even stomach watching the earlier seasons again after this crap."

"Rohs is showing some serious thorns, baby. I love it!"

Kimberly screamed and yelled at the TV. "No! No!" She threw the remote at the TV, but she missed the screen and put a dent in the drywall to the right side of the television. Her face was muddied with angry tears.

"Holy shit, take it easy, Kim," Brian said. He looked at the dent in the drywall and frowned. "It's just a TV show."

"I can't believe Rohs killed that deer," Kim said. "It just wanted a drink of water."

"She was just protecting the magic of the water," Brian said, his tone calm. "I get it. She didn't really have a choice, did she? If the water completely dries up, she's got no powers. And then she won't be able to help anybody."

"She didn't have to kill it!" Kim exclaimed angrily. She wiped at the hot tears trailing down her cheeks with a distraught swipe. "Motherfuckers are ruining my favorite show!"

"What's wrong, Mommy?"

Kimberly turned to see Rohs standing just inside the sliding glass door that led from their living room into the backyard. The anger quickly drained from Kimberly's body, but only to be replaced by a chilling surge of terror. She froze stiff as a chilling rigor mortis locked up her muscles; she could only stare in numbed shock at her daughter.

Rohs held a dead cat by the neck, gripping the limp and lifeless animal in her small fingers. The poor animal's eyes were bulging and its tongue dangled out of the corner of its mouth. Rohs's dress was dark with stains and her arms looked to be smeared with mud and dirty water.

Kimberly screamed at the realization that her daughter's face was smeared with blood and her dress was smeared with urine and feces.

*

"Where did you find that cat?" Kimberly asked, struggling to keep her voice calm and casual. She wrapped a bright yellow towel about Rohs's body as her daughter stepped out of the shower; Rohs's pink skin was now clean and scrubbed of the horrible grime.

"Near my pool," Rohs answered.

"Why did you pick it up?" Brian asked. He stood in the doorway to the bathroom, leaning against the doorframe, his arms crossed. "You know you're not supposed to touch any dead animals."

"It wasn't dead when I grabbed it," Rohs said.

Kimberly hesitated in drying off her daughter, glancing nervously over at Brian.

Brian's face suddenly seemed to grow very pale.

Kimberly moved the towel about her daughter, making an exaggerated show of wiping her dry. "What do you mean, Rohsy?"

"My name is not Rohsy. It's Rohs."

Kimberly did her best to shrug off her daughter's rebuke by staying calm. "You know that was a bad thing to do, don't you? You can get some nasty disease picking up dead animals."

"It was trying to get into my pool," Rohs said.

Kimberly glanced up at Brian as he stood frozen in the bathroom doorway. She again looked to her daughter with a growing sense of dread. "What do you mean, Rohs?"

"I stopped it," Rohs said. "It was trying to get into our pool. I told it to stay away and it wouldn't listen."

Kimberly suddenly gripped Rohs by the shoulders, grabbing her hard and tight through the towel. "My God, why would you do such a thing?" Kimberly's face flushed red and her eyes tightened. "How could you do such a thing?"

Rohs shrugged, the movement constrained by her mother's tight grip on her shoulders. "I gave it a chance to get away from my pool, but it didn't listen."

"You didn't have to kill it!" Kimberly's nostrils flared and her face flamed an even hotter shade of red. "Cats don't even like water!" Kimberly shook her daughter hard, her trembling fingers digging into the towel, pressing the cloth tight against her daughter's flesh.

"Easy, Kim," Brian said. He took a step forward into the bathroom, uncrossing his arms, but stopped short when Kimberly's flashing glare pinned him where he stood.

"Easy?" Kimberly shouted back to her husband. "Easy?" The tone in her voice elevated and the words seemed to crack with despair as they came forth from her lips. "How the fuck am I supposed to take this easy?"

"Fucking little sneak deserved it," Rohs said.

Kimberly snapped her head back towards Rohs. She let go of her grip on Rohs's shoulders as if her daughter's flesh and the towel wrapped around her shoulders had turned as hot as the mask of fury that painted Kimberly's enraged face a scarlet red. "What did you just say?" Kimberly asked, cocking her head at Rohs.

The towel that had been wrapped around Rohs fell to the floor. No one moved to pick it up.

"Go to your room! Right now!" Kimberly shouted. She pushed Rohs away from her. "Go!" Kimberly thrust her arm out, pointing down the hall towards Rohs's bedroom with a rigid finger extending from her trembling hand. "You can stay there until I decide to let you out!"

"Okay," Rohs said agreeably with a soft shrug, and brushed past Brian to amble towards her room, leaving the towel on the bathroom floor.

The Magic Waters of Wendoria
Season 7
Episode 8
The Rohs Grows Thorns
3.23 stars (2472)

A dark druid's blood is spilled into the magic waters. Rohs starts to feel the further taint of evil spreading deeper.

"No! They are ruining the show."

"Are these fucking stupid ass writers trying to make this show worse than Game of Thrones' final season?"

"Rohs was always a big phony anyway. Nobody in the real world is that nice."

"Even if they are, they don't stay that way for long."

"Finally something interesting is happening in this show! It's been damn boring and predictable for the last 2 seasons."

"Yeah, love it when shows turn and go dark!"

"She needs to see somebody," Kimberly said. "A psychologist or something." She was resting atop Brian's chest as they both lay naked in bed. She absently rubbed her fingers across Brian's bare chest.

"She's six years old. What the hell is a psychologist going to do that we can't do?" Brian asked. He rubbed his fingers through Kimberly's hair with gently consoling movements.

"I'm afraid for her," Kimberly said.

"Why? Because of what your father did?"

Kimberly was silent for a moment, her fingers going still. "Yes," she finally said. "He did kill those people."

"But you're not like him at all," Brian said. "He was a sociopath."

"Maybe it just skips a generation. Maybe Rohs has some of his... tendencies," Kimberly said.

Brian stopped moving his fingers. "No offense, but your dad was a pretty terrible person. He was a wife-beating, womanizing alcoholic."

"I know. But why did he become like that?" She raised her head up from his chest and looked up at Brian. "What turned him? What if he was born with it somehow? Maybe Rohs has that... ugliness inside her somewhere."

"All we've done is shown Rohs love and kindness. She'll be fine," Brian said. He resumed moving his fingers gently through Kimberly's hair, gently turning her head to set it back down on his chest.

"She killed that fucking cat, Brian. How can you say that for certain? She strangled a cat, for Christ's sake. That's not fucking normal."

Brian was quiet for a moment. "She never really said that she actually killed it," Brian said.

"She didn't deny it, either."

"Maybe she's practicing to be a politician," Brian said.

Kimberly didn't find that amusing.

Brian continued to stroke his wife's hair. "She just had a real bad day. She'll be fine."

Kimberly wasn't reassured by her husband's comment. "And she talks back more and more now. Gives me her little fucking smart ass attitude. Where the hell does she get that from?"

The Magic Waters of Wendoria
Season 7
Episode 10
Rohs Sees Green
3.4 stars (1077)
Rohs becomes envious of a new healer in town.

"Uh oh. Rohs is really starting to lose it."

"Rohs is only human. Humans have all kinds of weaknesses. Rohs is strong. She'll overcome it."

"Will she? Once envy takes hold, it's hard to dig out the roots."

"Father Bob strikes again with his deep words of wisdom."

"Rohs's behavior makes no sense! After all she's been through, she wouldn't act this way! Completely out of character for such a strong woman. Damn writers are probably a bunch of ignorant sexist jerks!"

"That new healer is a hottie! She can rub ointment on me all day!"

"You're always paying attention to Archie," Rohs complained. She made an exaggerated showing of folding her arms across her chest and harrumphing, hanging her head down.

"Well, Rohs honey, Archie is just a baby. He needs more attention. We gave you just as much attention when you were a baby," Kimberly said. Archie was seated in a high chair at the kitchen table as Kimberly fed him a tiny spoonful of blended peas.

"In fact," Brian said to Rohs, "we gave you even more attention when you were a baby because you were the only one. Archie will never get as much attention as you got."

Kimberly glared at Brian as he stood leaning along the wall near the kitchen pantry.

Brian caught the intense stare from his wife. "What?" he said. "It's true."

"Why don't you play a game with Rohs?" Kimberly suggested strongly to her husband.

Rohs looked up at her father, a glimmer of excited expectancy starting to brighten up her scowling face.

"Sure," Brian said with a nod. "Later I will. I've got some work to catch up on first."

Rohs bowed her head, her expression sullen and dejected. She wandered away from the kitchen, heading to her room.

"Go play with your daughter," Kimberly hissed, keeping her voice low but doing nothing to hide her displeasure with her husband.

"I will, I will," Brian said. "After I finish up some paperwork. You want me to get fired?"

The Magic Waters of Wendoria
Season 7
Episode 11
Rohs Sees Red
2.7 stars (851)
Rohs strikes a young boy who accidentally stumbles across the magic pool and nearly defiles it with his urgent need to relieve himself.

"Damn, she whacked that kid but good."

"When you gotta go, you gotta go."

"She could have just yelled at him. She didn't need to strike him. Not sure I like where this show keeps heading."

"That kid deserved it. You can't go around acting like an animal. Sometimes, you gotta whack a little decency into people."

"You're condoning striking a child? Seriously?"

"He'll be better for it."

"You need to put a leash on that kid!"

Kimberly took her phone away from her ear as the angry voice of her neighbor Josephine Garcia exploded through the speaker. She moved the phone back to her face. "Take it easy, Josephine. What are you talking about?"

"I'm talking about your kid whacking my kid with a stick. She gashed her head. What the hell are you teaching her?"

Kimberly was stunned into silence for a moment. "What are you talking about?"

"Ask your precious little Rohs about it. I should sue your ass. Keep your kid away from my kids." Click.

Kimberly pulled her phone away from her ear and just stared down at it. She looked over to Rohs who was sitting at the kitchen table coloring a page in her coloring book.

"Why did you hit Carlita?" Kimberly asked.

"She was trying to get into our pool. I told her to stop and she wouldn't listen."

"So you whacked her on the head with a stick?"

Rohs nodded affirmatively. She kept working on her coloring book, twisting her hand to fill in an uncolored section on the page. "Mom, we need to protect what's ours, don't we?"

"Not like that, we don't," Kimberly said.

Rohs shook her head, ever so slightly, but the movement was there. "You're wrong. We do. Give them an inch, they'll take a mile."

Kimberly scowled. "Don't talk back to me like that. Where the hell did you learn that nasty attitude?" Kimberly thrust out her arm, pointing a rigid finger. "Go to your room. Right now. You're grounded."

"Okay," Rohs said agreeably. She opened her fingers and let the crayon roll out of her hand. "I'm still gonna protect what's mine," she muttered under her breath.

"Move it!" Kimberly shouted at her, her face flushing a hot red.

Rohs clambered down out of the chair and ambled towards her room.

The Magic Waters of Wendoria
Season 7
Episode 12

Rohs Crosses A Line

3.4 stars (1643)

Rohs crosses a dangerous line from which she can never go back when she falsely accuses a villager of trying to rape her.

"That was the most intense episode of any show I have ever seen in my life. I'm still shaking."

"I hope there aren't any kids watching this show anymore. It's gone dark as hell."

"Love it! It's so gritty for a fantasy show."

"Rohs has been a very popular girl's name for the last 7 years. I bet not anymore! Ha!"

"She's a lovely child," Doctor Bloomfield said. The psychologist was in his fifties, with a well-groomed brown beard that held just a hint of grey. He had a casual air about him, his jeans, gym shoes, and flannel shirt contributing to that relaxed presence. He was sitting on the front edge of his desk, his arms folded across his chest as he spoke to Kimberly. "Quite sweet, actually. Quite strong in her convictions. There's nothing wrong with her."

"Nothing wrong with her?" Kimberly was aghast. "She strangled a cat with her bare hands!" She shifted in the leather chair she was sitting in. "And then she whacked our neighbor's kid in the head with a stick. She could have really hurt her."

"Rohs said you would say that. She says you made that up," Bloomfield said. "I believe she called it fake news. Kind of cute, really."

"That's not cute! I did not make that up!" Kimberly's face flushed red hot.

Bloomfield frowned. "Are you calling your daughter a liar?"

"No," Kimberly said, but then quickly changed her reply. "Yes. She's lying." Her face reddened and her jaw tightened. "I was the one who washed the blood out of her dress!"

"You need to calm down, Mrs. Phillips."

"I need to calm down? Me?" Kimberly glared at the psychologist. "I'm not the one with the problem. Jesus fucking Christ."

"I'm sorry you feel that way. It's very difficult for some people to confront the truth about themselves. Believe me, I know. I've been doing this for over twenty years." Bloomfield rose up off the edge of his desk and moved back around behind it. "Perhaps you need to make an appointment with one of my colleagues to discuss your own issues."

"My issues? I don't have any issues." Kimberly scowled. "What the fuck is going on here?"

Bloomfield smiled a polite smile. "You clearly have impulsive anger issues. Violent tendencies usually accompany such a condition."

Kimberly glared at the psychologist. "What the hell are you talking about?"

"Did you cause the burns on Rohs's stomach?" Bloomfield asked.

Kimberly's former scowl returned, the edges of her grimace etched even deeper into her face. "What?"

"She showed me the scars," Bloomfield said. "Did you do that?"

Kimberly's scowl deepened. "What the hell are you talking about? What scars?"

Bloomfield gave a slight sad shake of his head.

"She did say you were starting to forget things after your concussion."

Kimberly frowned. "My concussion? What are you talking about?"

"Rohs is really worried about you," Bloomfield said.

"Worried about me? She's worried about me?"

"Yes. Quite worried, really," Bloomfield said. "She thinks you need help."

"I'm not the one who needs help!" Kimberly shrieked at him. She balled her shaking fingers into fists and pressed them tightly against her sides.

The psychologist reached for his phone.

"What are you doing?" Kimberly rose up quickly out of the chair. "Who are you calling?"

"I'm calling my security officer," Bloomfield said. "You're becoming a little unhinged."

"No. Put that phone down." Kimberly waved at him, motioning for him to stop. "Just stop. Stop! I'm leaving. I'm leaving. You're fucking useless. Holy crap." Kimberly stormed out of the psychologist's office.

Rohs looked up from where she was sitting in the outer waiting room as Kimberly strode angrily out of the psychologists' office. "What's wrong, Mommy?"

Kimberly said nothing, quickly darting her gaze over at Brian. "Grab her. Let's go."

"What's going on, Kim?" Brian asked, clearly seeing Kimberly's flush and distraught face. "What was all that shouting? What the hell happened in there?"

"Just grab that little witch and let's just go before this crackpot sets CPS on us!"

❦

The Magic Waters of Wendoria
Season 7
Episode 13
The Sweet Smell of Rohs
3.01 stars (977)

Rohs uses her new-found cunning to escape a dangerous situation.

"For some reason, Rohs reminds me of a clever con artist now. I think this show is going to get even darker in the weeks ahead."

"Isn't this interesting? Now that the show's getting darker, there's more nudity every episode. Like the naked human body is supposed to be a symbol for evil or something."

"Finally! And they're showing bush, too!"

"I like all the t!ts, but I don't like the message."

"I can't believe Rohs manipulated the village merchants like that. Doesn't she know she's using her powers in a bad way now?"

"Oh, she knows. That's what makes it so cool to watch."

"Rohs is going to run that village. Just you wait and see. Who can stop her?"

❦

"It's like she's possessed." Kimberly's hand visibly shook as she reached for Brian. "Every time I see her standing on the rug in the front room, I think she's just about to piss on it like that girl in the Exorcist did."

"That's horrible, Kim." Brian pulled her closer to him.

Kimberly nodded her head. "I know, but I just can't shake it, Brian. There's something wrong with

Rohs." She buried her head in the crook of his shoulder. "Something really wrong. She told that shrink I burned her on purpose."

"But she didn't even have any burns on her body," Brian said. "I checked."

"I know. But that's what she told him. I think she used Halloween makeup or something to trick him. It was like she was purposely setting me up. Why would she do that?"

"I don't know. At least he didn't call child protective services on us."

"Ha, yet. He might be setting it up as we speak." Kimberly exhaled a long burst of stress-filled air. "Jesus. That's all I need."

Brian gently caressed his wife's shoulder. "Take it easy, Kim. Just calm down."

"Now I'm gonna be freaked out every time the phone rings or someone knocks on the door," Kim said. "Motherfucker."

Brian comforted Kimberly quietly for a moment, moving his fingers softly across her hair. "You know what's weird?" he said after a long silence.

Kimberly waited for him to continue, but he didn't. "What?" she asked, tilting her head to glance up at him. "What's weird?"

Brian shook his head. "Nah, forget it. It's *too* weird."

"Tell me," Kimberly insisted. "Tell me."

Brian hesitated. "It's just that..." He let his voice trail off. "No, it's too crazy."

Kimberly pulled away from Brian and turned to stare directly at him. "What? What is too crazy after all this?"

"It's just that ever since Rohs in Magic Waters

started to act weird, so did our Rohs."

Kimberly's face froze, then her expression dropped. She was very still for a very long moment. "Oh my God," she finally said. And then she went quiet again, but there was clearly something else she wanted to say.

Now it was Brian's turn to prompt her. "What?"

"Is that possible?" Kimberly muttered, more to herself than to Brian. She took a few steps away from Brian, then turned around to pace towards him. Her breathing was a little quicker, a little tighter.

"Come on, Kim, that's nuts," Brian said. "She's actually somehow linked to a fictional character on a TV show? That's crazy."

Kimberly stopped pacing and stared at him. "Then why did you think it? You're not crazy." Kimberly shook her head. "No, it isn't nuts." She went quiet again, lost in thought as she resumed pacing.

"Yes it is. I'm sorry I even mentioned it." Brian reached out to try and pull Kimberly closer to him, but she brushed away his reaching hand.

"Oh my God," she said again, the tone in her voice becoming more assured as she spoke. She continued to pace. "It's all starting to make sense. We did this to her, Brian. It was us. The cat she killed. Hitting the neighborhood kids. Lying to the psychologist. Her whole change in attitude." Kimberly stood still for a moment.

"C'mon, Kim," Brian said, but she ignored him.

"It's so obvious. Oh my God. It's so fucking obvious. We did this," Kimberly said, her tone now very matter-of-fact. "We did this to her. We tied them together," she said, accepting Brian's wild theory with a nod of certitude. "We did this to her! We have to stop it." She stared intently up at Brian with a beseeching look. "How can we stop it?"

The entertainment expo was packed. There were thousands of visitors, and it seemed nearly half of them were dressed up as characters from hundreds of different TV shows and movies and comic books. Brian had been to several entertainment expos and comic conventions in his life, so he took it all in stride. He never dressed in cosplay attire himself, but he enjoyed looking at all the costumes, marveling at some of their creativity and the clear artistic skill some of them had.

He checked the calendar of events that was posted on a large digital board just inside the entrance to the expo. The Magic Waters of Wendoria panel was scheduled to start in a half hour so he headed to the stairs that led up to the conference rooms that were being utilized for all the different panels.

The conference room he was looking for had a huge standee of Rohs Goodwill, the figure dressed demurely in Rohs's trademark aqua blue dress, positioned right outside the door so it was impossible to miss. He headed into the room.

Inside the conference room, at least half a dozen young women were dressed as Rohs, several of them dressed in the same exact attire that the cardboard standee displayed. Some men were dressed as other characters from the show, a few wearing the leather vests that designated a village elder.

Brian found an empty seat and sat. One of the women dressed as Rohs sized Brian up with clear appreciation of his looks and his physique, and then sat down in the row in front of him.

The room quickly filled to capacity and a few dozen people had to stand along the side walls and in the back of the room. Several people came in from a side entrance and began taking seats behind the table that was set up on a dais on the front end of the room. Brian, his arms folded across his chest, sat quietly through the slew of introductions as several actors, directors, and writers of the show were introduced.

"And now let me introduce the woman behind the magic. Creator, showrunner and head writer, Monique Depardieu."

Brian unfolded his arms and sat up taller in his chair. Most of the crowd erupted in jubilant clapping and cheering, and happy whistles of appreciation. Several voices booed, the sound mixing in with the adulation, and Brian turned to glance behind him but he didn't see who the booing voices belonged to.

Monique Depardieu raised her hand and gave a soft wave to the gathered crowd of admirers. She wasn't an ugly woman, but she couldn't be called a classic beauty either. She was rather plain with frizzy brown hair and overly large tortoise-shell glasses. She was dressed in a plain brown dress that hid whatever womanly shape might lay beneath the fabric.

Brian listened half-heartedly as the crowd heaped various accolades and praise upon Monique. She took it all humbly in stride. But then a question came from an older woman in the crowd that caused Brian to lean forward in his chair and eagerly await the answer.

"Why are you taking the show dark?" the woman in the crowd asked.

"Power can't operate in a vacuum without some consequences," Monique answered. "Rohs has been wielding her power unchecked for a long time. Such supreme power will transform anyone after a while, no matter how strong and pure their convictions are."

"But now I'm too scared to let my kids watch it with me," someone else in the crowd said.

"It was never intended to be a show for kids," Monique replied. "It's not a Saturday morning cartoon."

Brian sat in silence, keeping his gaze riveted on Monique Depardieu.

Monique caught his gaze and held it for a moment.

Brian smiled sweetly at her and she smiled back.

Kimberly opened the door to see a dark-skinned woman staring at her with a tight-lipped face. Kimberly froze and just stared at the woman for a long moment. "Can I help you?" she finally asked, her voice wavering, slightly cracking as she asked the question.

The woman raised up an ID Card. "I'm Janice Okufor. I'm with Child Protective Services."

Kimberly looked at the identification card and a fearful frown darkened her face. "What— What are you doing here?"

"We received a call."

"A call?" Kimberly stroked her throat.

"Yes, Mrs. Philips," the woman said. "You are Mrs. Philips?"

"Yes, I am."

"We received a call that there might be a child in

danger here," Janice said.

"What? Who the hell called you?"

"I'm not at liberty to disclose that information. We received a complaint and I'm here to investigate."

"A complaint about what?" Kimberly asked.

"May I come in?"

Kimberly hesitated. "I need to see that ID again. I don't know if you're for real."

Janice held up her ID card again. "I'm for real, Mrs. Philips."

Kimberly stared at the ID. "I... okay." She opened the door wider. "Come in."

Kimberly led Janice to the living room and sat on one of the couches, but the woman from CPS didn't sit. Kimberly stood back up.

"I'd like to see Archie," Janice said.

Kimberly frowned. "Archie?"

"That is your son's name, yes?"

"Yes, yes it is." Kimberly shook her head. "I'm sorry, this is all so confusing."

"May I see Archie, please?"

"Yes, of course. He's in his crib. I'll go get him."

Kimberly moved towards Archie's room. She passed by Rohs's room and saw her daughter playing with her toy construction tools, banging a plastic hammer down on a play workshop table.

She moved into Archie's room and reached down to scoop him out of his crib, but stopped short as she stared at a dark bruise on the upper part of his left arm, just below the edge of his shirt sleeve. Her eyes widened in pure fear. She stared at the black and blue patch of skin for a moment, unsure of what to do next. Then she picked up Archie and headed slowly back towards the living room.

Once again, Kimberly moved past Rohs's room and glanced into the room to see that her daughter was still playing with her pretend construction tools. Kimberly froze as she stared at the hammer; the striking face of the hammer was the exact same shape as the wound on Archie's upper arm.

Kimberly rotated Archie so his wounded arm was hidden against her chest. She strode back out into the living room, gently bobbing Archie up and down in her arms. "Here's Archie, he's fine."

Janice extended her hands out.

Kimberly kept Archie tight against her chest. "I'm sorry. He's not good with strangers."

"I need to look at him," Janice said.

"He's fine," Kimberly said in return.

"Mrs. Phillips, I need to examine him," Janice said, her tone firm and resolute.

"And I told you he doesn't like strangers. I'm not going to upset him. I'll never get him down for his nap if he gets all riled up." She rocked and bobbed her son ever so gently in her arms. "He's fine." She looked at Janice with a hard line in her face. "I want to know who called you. I'm gonna sue their asses."

"I can't tell you that," Janice said. She stepped closer to Kimberly and Archie, taking a keen look at the boy.

Archie gurgled and smiled at Janice.

"He doesn't look scared of me," Janice said.

"I told you he was fine," Kimberly said.

Janice reached up to touch Archie's cheek, but Kimberly twisted her son quickly away from the woman. "I'm sorry," Kimberly said immediately. "I don't like other people touching him. I'm sorry."

Janice lowered her hand. "Okay," she said. She

glanced at the smiling Archie, then looked at Kimberly with a stern face for a long moment. "He looks okay." Then she added, "I don't want to have to come back here."

"I don't want you to come back here either," Kimberly said.

"I'll show myself out," Janice said.

Kimberly just nodded and looked towards the front door.

❦

Brian and Monique sat at the hotel bar, enjoying a few cocktails. An empty glass rested in front of both of them. Monique was nearly finished with her second drink. A fan came by and asked Monique for an autograph and she happily obliged. The autograph seeker slunk happily away.

"I work in construction," Brian said, rolling his drink glass between his hands.

"So you're good at erecting things," Monique said with a sly smile. She had changed up her drab clothing and was now wearing a red cocktail dress that definitely did not hide her ample bosom.

"Right about now, I think you're quite capable of erecting things, too," Brian said. He took an obvious, prolonged glimpse of Monique's ample cleavage as he raised up his drink to take another sip.

"Is your penis hard?" Monique asked.

Brian nearly spit out his drink. "What?"

"Sorry, I have a habit of being direct," Monique said. "Helps me keep wasted time down to a minimum."

"I see," Brian said.

"So is it hard?" Monique asked. "Is your dick hard?"

Brian wiped at his mouth. "Damn, it is now."

"Rohs Anne Phillips, get your ass out here now!" Kimberly shouted towards Rohs's bedroom. She had put Archie back in his crib and was now back in the living room.

Rohs shuffled out of her room, clutching the plastic hammer in her hand.

Kimberly glanced at the plastic tool, then glared at her daughter. "Did you hit Archie with that?"

Rohs glanced down at the plastic hammer, then looked up at her mother. "No, you did."

Kimberly was flabbergasted at her daughter's response. "What?"

Rohs twirled the plastic hammer in her hand. "That's what I'll tell Doctor Bloomfield if you ever send me there again."

"Like hell you will," Kimberly snapped. "What the hell is wrong with you? Why are you acting like this?"

Rohs said nothing.

"Go back to your room. I don't even want to look at you right now," Kimberly said, her hands shaking as she spoke. "We're going to have a nice long talk when your father gets back home.

Rohs nodded. "Yes, we are."

"Your wife know you're here?" Monique asked. She was sitting up in the hotel bed, resting her back against the headboard, her naked breasts glistening with a sheen of perspiration.

Brian frowned. "What?" He paused in zipping up his pants to look over his shoulder at Monique.

Monique tilted her head towards his right hand. "You didn't take your wedding ring off."

Brian glanced down at his hand, at the gold band encircling his finger. "She'd understand," he said.

It was Monique's turn to frown. "Understand what?"

Brian didn't answer.

"Understand what, George?" Monique asked again.

Brian froze for just the briefest of moments, but Monique caught the stiffness in his lack of movement.

"Damn, that's not even your real name, is it?" Monique said.

Brian hesitated, then shook his head. "No, it's not. It's Brian."

"Well, howdy fucking do to you, Brian," Monique said with a snapping bite. "Who the fuck are you and what do you want?"

"You have to stop doing what you're doing with the show," Brian said, the words gushing out. "You're destroying our daughter."

Monique narrowed her brow, frowning deeply at Brian. "What the hell are you talking about?"

"You have to make Rohs good again," Brian said, taking a step towards Monique, making no effort to hide the pleading tone from his voice.

"So that's what this is about," Monique muttered. "Wow. You really suck at this. You were supposed to whisper that to me right after you made me come."

"Please," Brian begged. "You need to make her

good again."

"Great," Monique groaned "You're right out of Misery, aren't you? My number one psychotic fan."

"I'm not your number one fucking fan!" Brian snapped.

"I see you left out the psychotic part," Monique muttered.

Brian suddenly darted forward and gripped Monique by her shoulders, roughly shaking her. "You have to change Rohs back. You have to!"

Monique pushed Brian away from her. She hurriedly grabbed at her nightshirt to cover up her naked chest. Monique stared at Brian, and a momentary hint of fear creeped into her eyes. "I think it's time for you to leave."

"No!" Brian snatched the nightshirt away from her and threw it to the hotel room floor. "You need to tell me you're going to stop what you are doing to Rohs," he said, his tone dark and threatening. He gripped her shoulders again, roughly grabbing on to her. "You need to make her good again."

Monique jerked her shoulders out of his grip, that hint of fear now turning to indignant anger. "You had better leave this room right now or I'm going to start screaming rape and call hotel security."

Brian backed away from the bed. He snatched at his shirt that was hanging over the back of a chair and hurriedly put it back on. "I'll find you," Brian threatened. "You'd better do the right thing."

"Don't you fucking threaten me. Don't you dare," Monique snarled back at him. She scrambled out of the bed, moved to her open suitcase, and snatched a script out of it. She hurled the script at Brian and he caught it awkwardly as the script smashed against his chest. "Here. Read this. It's the season opener to season eight. I think you'll get a kick out of it. If you thought Rohs's power of persuasion was already pretty strong, just you wait. We're cranking it up."

Brian glanced down at the script he now held in his hands, then looked back up at the naked Monique. "What's in here? What happens?"

Suddenly, Monique bolted forward and snatched the script back from Brian. "You know what? Forget it. We didn't go far enough." She shook the script at Brian. "You thought Rohs already lost her shit? Just wait until you see what's going to come next season." She laughed a tight laugh. "It's gonna be fucking epic!"

"No," Brian gasped, the word coming out slowly, almost painfully from his lips. "You can't…"

"Oh, yes I can. I'm the showrunner and the head writer," Monique said. "I can do whatever the fuck I want to my characters."

"Please." Brian folded his hands together. "Please."

Monique was undeterred by his plea. "When you watch the next season, just think about what you did here today. Feel the responsibility pounding down on your shoulders and searing its way through your brain, because you caused it," Monique said. "Just remember that. You caused it."

The Magic Waters of Wendoria
Season 8
Episode 1
Thorns
2.2 stars (5653)

The final season opener! Rohs commits a heinous crime against one of the village elders, using the magic pool of water for nefarious purposes.

"I'm literally sitting here stunned as I'm typing this. What the hell?"

"Epic. Not! This show is now officially trash."

"I feel like I wasted half a dozen plus years of my life watching this damn show."

"Everyone was always talking about how this show demonstrates the healing power of water. Water also kills. It drowns thousands of people a year. And it's home to the most violent predators ever to roam this planet."

"Loved it! What a show! The writers seriously must have had messed up childhoods to come up with some of this stuff. Too bad for them - but great for us!"

"I'm shaking. Oh my God. I thought this show was intense before, but holy shit."

"The writers need to be taken out and shot. Don't even give them the courtesy of a blindfold. Just line them up and shoot them."

"Finally this show is getting so good!"

"How can you monsters like this episode? That was completely out of character. That came out of nowhere! It was the worst piece of garbage I have ever seen and I've been around since the days of black and white TV."

"Loved it! What an episode! Can't wait to see what happens next!"

❦

"Rohs, please…" Kimberly begged. Her face was wet with tears.

"We'll be good," Brian said.

"You need to think about what you've done," Rohs said.

"I didn't mean it," Kimberly said. "I won't yell at you anymore. And no more doctors, I swear."

"I'll play a game with you," Brian said. "Right now. I promise."

"We are playing a game, silly," Rohs said. She put her finger to her lips. "Now be quiet. I don't want to have to make that call again and bring that nice black lady back."

Rohs started to close the closet door and the thin slat of light that was shining into the closet began to narrow into a thinner and thinner slit, the light starting to slide off her parents' faces.

"Rohs, please…" Kimberly begged again.

"Rohs," Brian pleaded. A lone tear squeezed out of his eye and slowly slid down his face.

"Oh, stop being such babies," Rohs said. "I'll let you out after your time out is over."

The closet door shut and Kimberly and Brian were blanketed with darkness.

*

Archie grinned a big grin as he took a step towards Rohs. His gait was a bit wobbly, but he managed to stay on his feet.

Rohs patted her little brother on the head,

beaming him a sweet smile. "Come on, Archie, let's go swimming." She took his small hand and started to lead him towards their pool in the backyard. "I'll take good care of you."

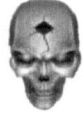

TERRORSTORY #80
CONTROLLED BURN

Roc took his respirator off and set the oxygen face mask down on a rock next to the larger rock he was sitting on. He was dressed in his full firefighter gear, complete with his boots, his bunker pants, his bunker coat, and his Nomex hood. His hands had some residual soot smeared across his knuckles and the backs of his hands. His forehead and neck also had some dark smears painted across them in wet swipes

343

of black soot that mingled with his sweat. Fireman's war paint. That's what McDogal had called it once.

In the distance, the remaining remnants of the forest fire were well under control. Several firefighters from a different station had taken over the main task of laying down suppressive waves of water over the few remaining pockets of active flames. Some trailing wisps of smoke still reached Roc, but they were nothing of any significance.

Part of a nearby bush tickled the back of his neck and Roc absently looked to his left to see some kind of bug sitting on a nearby leaf. The insect was about half an inch long with a dull blue-gray body. He caught a flash of the brownish-orange bits of color the bug had on its chest and head milliseconds before he heard a loud hissing, popping sound. He had basically zero chance to react before a hot noxious chemical spray was expelled violently out of the tip of the insect's abdomen. The boiling, foul-smelling liquid hit him right in the eyes, causing him to cry out in surprised shock. He raised his hands quickly up to his eyes, the motion knocking him off balance causing him to slide off the rock and fall to the ground with a heavy grunt. The pain was immediate and intense; he felt like his eyes were melting in their sockets.

He rolled on the ground, writhing in pain, clutching at his eyes. The pain was so intense that he felt like his entire body was on fire. He would've sworn with his hand on a bible that he heard his brain crackling from the intense hot agony.

And then he felt nothing as he plunged into a black tunnel that seemed to have no end.

Only later did he discover that he had been a victim of a bombardier beetle's defensive blast of nasty chemicals.

Only later did he realize his wife was right. She had always been right. Everything did, in fact, happen for a reason.

Darkness. Nothing but darkness.

"Okay, Roc," a male voice said from somewhere in the black void. "We're going to take the bandages off."

And then there was light. But it wasn't a normal hospital fluorescent light that greeted his eyes. Everything had a shimmer to it. A heat signature. As if he were wearing night vision goggles in the middle of the day. No, it wasn't that severe, but things certainly didn't look normal to Roc.

"Hey, Roc."

Roc glanced over at Stephanie. His wife was a slender woman with long black hair. The tortoise shell glasses she wore gave her a slightly nerdy look, but they did fit her role as a kindergarten teacher. Roc found them weirdly sexy and sometimes asked her to keep them on in bed even when she was otherwise completely naked.

He could see her clearly, but there was something more to her. It was as if he was also seeing her heat pattern, with parts of her body shimmering a deeper red than other parts. Her glasses had a glowing outline, like someone had painted the frames with glow-in-the-dark paint. The chair she was sitting in was both white and blue at the same time, white being its actual color and deep blue its cold temperature.

Roc sat upright in his hospital bed, leaning against

the raised mattress, his back cushioned by a few pillows. He reached up towards his eyes, about to rub them to rid them of whatever irritant was causing this weird vision, but the doctor's words stopped him.

"Easy there," the doctor said. "They still need some more time to heal, so try not to touch them too much."

Roc took his hands away from his eyes. His eyelids still felt hot as if the residue of the insect's noxious spray still lingered on them. It was like being in a world where everything was a light bulb, each object emitting its own level of radiant heat. Stephanie's cheeks were a light orange but her nose was oddly a much darker red. The area around her mouth was white.

He looked at the doctor and saw that his nose was darker than the rest of his face as well. His cheeks were also a light orange, while the area around his mouth was also whitish in color. What the hell was he looking at? What the hell was he seeing?

Stephanie must have noticed the nervous expression on his face because he could hear the genuine concern in her voice. "Roc? Babe, you okay?"

Roc didn't answer her, but he saw her turn to look towards the doctor. And then he realized he knew exactly what he was looking at. He had seen pictures like this before. He wasn't sure where he had seen them, maybe in one of his classes. It didn't matter. He realized he was looking at thermal images as if his eyes suddenly had the capability of an infrared camera.

"Why isn't he blinking?" Stephanie asked the doctor. "He's just staring."

Roc heard her question and registered it, realizing

she was right. Somehow he wasn't blinking involuntarily. It was if he had no need to blink. Roc forced himself to blink and the weird infrared images went away. What the fuck? He squeezed his eyes tight, then opened them back up. The infrared imagery was back. He blinked and his normal vision returned.

Stephanie gave a little nervous laugh at his odd behavior. "What are you doing?"

"My eyes," Roc said. "They're fucked up." He pinched them shut again, then opened them. Then blinked. Then squeezed them shut hard, and then opened them. Then blinked again, going from infrared vision back to normal vision again. What the fuck?

"Can you... see?" Stephanie asked.

Roc nodded. "Yeah, but it's all messed up."

He caught Stephanie casting another nervous glance at the doctor.

"What do you see, Roc?" the doctor asked.

"I think I'm seeing infrared light," Roc said.

"Humans can't see infrared," the doctor said, trying to be polite but failing in his pompous delivery of the statement.

"Then I guess I'm just not human anymore, doc," Roc said with a biting tone. "But I'm not sure you are either, 'cause right now your face is a big blob of orange and red and white."

Roc turned towards Stephanie. "And so is my wife's." He shifted his gaze and pointed past the open door to his hospital room, out into the hallway. "And that nurse that just passed the doorway. And that other lady sitting at the desk over there."

"Can he really see what he says he's seeing?" Stephanie asked the doctor. They were outside of Roc's room, standing in the hospital hallway near the nurse station.

The doctor shook his head. "Infrared light has longer wavelengths than visible light. The human eye can't see it." The doctor paused for a moment. "There was some damage to his cornea from the chemicals, but I still don't think it would give him the ability to see infrared light."

"Is he... mentally..." Stephanie couldn't finish the question.

"I think he'll be fine," the doctor said. "His brain wasn't affected. Give him some time to heal. His vision may never be fully perfect again, but humans are very adaptable creatures."

Stephanie nodded. "Okay. Thank you, doctor."

Roc looked blankly at his phone, staring at the test results; he had read them a hundred times already, so now he just stared at them. He wondered what he had done to deserve such a horrible, terrible week. Why was the universe plotting against him? First, his eyes, then this. What other body part was going to get hit next?

He squeezed his eyes shut hard, then opened them. He had done this action enough times looking at himself in the mirror to know that his eyes looked ringed with red whenever he went into infrared sight mode. He looked at the white heat that his phone gave off, then blinked and returned his vision to normal. He knew that wasn't going to change the test results, but he kept doing it over and over again anyway.

Roc grimaced. No sense delaying the inevitable. He knew he had to tell Stephanie.

"It's not your fault, Roc," Stephanie said. "It's just what was meant to be. Everything happens for a reason."

"Then who's fault is it?" Roc asked. He had just come back from his shift and was still wearing his black shirt and black pants, the words Aurora Fire Department emblazoned on the left breast of the shirt. He was a few years older than Stephanie, but even in their mid-twenties they still sometimes felt like adult imposters. Today, he felt like more than an imposter. He felt like a failure. And he didn't relish that feeling one bit. He felt nothing but disgust and contempt for himself. He had finally convinced his wife that it was time to make some children of their own, but he couldn't even get that job done.

Stephanie caressed her husband's neck as they sat on the living room couch together. The television was on, playing some nature documentary about fire ants, but neither of them were paying any attention to it. "Nobody's," she said, putting a soothing tone into her voice.

Roc grunted. "Well, when I find this Nobody, I'm gonna kick his Goddamn ass."

Stephanie smiled, but Roc found no humor in the situation.

"It needs to be somebody's fault," Roc said.

"You're the one who always says everything happens for a reason. What's God's reason for this? That I'm not worthy to have a child?"

"Of course not."

"So what's the reason? First, He tries to blind me, now He wants to castrate me."

Stephanie took her hand away from her husband's neck, then looked away, dipping her head down. "I don't know."

"And this doesn't bother you? That I'm spermically bankrupt?"

Stephanie emitted a small chuckle despite her efforts to hold it in. "Is that even a thing?"

Roc didn't answer.

Stephanie eased her glasses back up higher as she looked at him. "I don't need children to have a fulfilling life," Stephanie said.

Roc frowned at her. "That's because you already have thirty of them you take care of five days a week."

Stephanie put her hand gently on Roc's thigh. "But I do need your dick to feel full." She smiled demurely.

Roc looked at her and his upset face softened. "Ah, damn it, Stephanie," he muttered, then leaned in to press his lips against hers with a hard, lingering kiss. "Your talents are wasted at that school," he said after breaking off the kiss. "You should be in the bomb squad."

Stephanie squinted at him.

"You know just the right way to defuse me."

Stephanie smiled coyly, then leaned back in to kiss him hard on the mouth.

Stephanie was in bed, naked, sitting up and leaning against the headboard, her glasses still on. Her nipples were very hard, very erect; she cupped her breasts in her hands, squeezing them gently.

Roc was down at her crotch, staring between her legs. He was in infrared mode, his eyes ringed with red. He thought about what the doctor had told him. Human eyes are covered in warm blood vessels that emit their own light, so that creates a stronger signal than any incoming signals from external sources. He said it would take a massive amount of incoming infrared particles to allow him to see infrared light. He said a good example would be to try to look out into the night from a brightly lit room. But that wasn't happening to Roc. The doctor was wrong. He could see infrared light. Maybe the bombardier beetle's chemical spray somehow did something to the blood vessels in his eyes, permanently altered them somehow, somehow increased his range of vision.

"What does it look like?" Stephanie asked.

Roc blinked to take himself out of infrared mode before he glanced up at Stephanie. He knew his red-ringed eyes kind of spooked her, so he tried his best to avoid looking at her when he was in infrared mode. "It's red hot," he said.

"Hell yes it is," Stephanie said.

Then Roc laughed. "You realize something, right?"

"Hmm?"

"No more I've got a headache. No more I'm not in the mood. Because now I can tell," Roc said. He glanced back down at her vagina, shutting his eyes hard to put himself back in infrared mode. The curled

351

lips of her vagina were white-hot. "I think it might be about to burst into flames."

Stephanie pushed her glasses back up on her nose. "You gonna put out my fire with that big hose of yours?"

"Roc, ventilate in the back!"

Roc heard the command shouted out by the chief and he moved towards the nearest window on the back side of the house. He was dressed in his firefighter gear, his helmet atop his head. He slid his axe out of his spanner belt and gripped it tightly. It felt great to be back at work, even with everyone ribbing him about how a tiny little bug took him out of action for weeks.

He quickly reached the window and raised up the handle of his axe, readying himself to smash through the glass.

Roc looked at the flames and the thick smoke visible inside the house through the back bedroom window. He knew that almost all of the constituents of smoke were combustible, so all that smoke was really nothing more than unburned fuel with the potential to ignite. Depending on the conditions, all that heat and smoke could cause a backdraft, which was basically a smoke explosion, or it could cause a deadly flashover which was generated by extremely rapid ignition. By ventilating the windows, or the roof, the idea was to give all the heat and smoke somewhere to go besides swirling and roaring through the structure.

On the other hand, he also knew that plastic

fillings in sofas and mattresses burned much faster than older fillings like cotton, so modern-day house fires allowed less time to get the fire under control than in decades past. Some experts believed that with more plastic in homes, residential fires were now more likely to use up all the oxygen in a room before they consumed all the flammable materials. So even as some smoky, oxygen-deprived fires appeared to be going out, they were actually waiting for an inrush of fresh air, which could come as firefighters broke windows or cut through roofs. There was some serious debate happening whether or not ventilating a fire was actually a helpful practice these days.

But all of those arguments quickly paled into insignificance.

Roc squeezed his eyes tight to put himself in infrared mode. His infrared vision allowed him to see past the soot particles of the smoke that usually blocked any visible light.

Roc stopped cold when he saw a reflection in the glass, a set of haunted eyes staring back at him. But then he realized the eyes weren't a reflection. They weren't his eyes.

A face was staring at him from within the house.

He opened his mouth to shout *there's somebody still in there*, but the words never came out. It wasn't a person in the flames. It didn't have the shape of a human body. It was more like a thing. An entity. Roc recognized the face in the flames. His chest tightened. His breathing quickened. His thoughts raced and he felt another panic attack surfacing. Was this it? He had suffered from panic attacks ever since he was a teenager, but this one felt different. He could feel his heart hammering against his chest, threatening to burst through his bones like the creature in the movie Alien. Was this finally the time his racing thoughts would never stop? Was this the moment where he truly lost his mind? He forced himself to breathe slower, clenching and unclenching his grip on the axe, the movement making him think about the physicality of his body in an attempt to distract his racing thoughts.

The face in the house wavered, the flickering flames and shimmering heat and swirling smoke making the face flutter like a flag rolling and warping in a warm breeze. It was Freddie's face. Poor Freddie. Poor bullied and humiliated Freddie. Poor dead Freddie. Even though the face of the young girl rippled in the fire, Freddie stared at Roc with an unwavering gaze.

He hadn't even thought of Freddie for a long time. Every so often he would think of her, but when he did he quickly pushed the memory away and forced himself to think of something else. The dreams had faded, too. He couldn't even recall the last time he had a Freddie dream.

Roc could see the burn scars alongside the left half of Freddie's charred face. That's where the flames had licked her. That's where the fire had bitten her so many long years ago.

Flames started to flare up on the rear of the house, popping and crackling as they fed on the roof tiles.

"Damn it, Roc! Get that window open!"

Roc blinked himself out of infrared mode and the face floating in the flames disappeared. He brought the handle of his axe against the window, easily shattering the glass. Thick black smoke billowed out of the cracked window, obscuring his view of the fire burning within the house. Roc took several steps back away from the broken window, shutting his eyes tight against the smoke trying to sting his eyes.

When he opened his eyes again the black smoke that was streaming out of the house appeared to form into a giant hand, the wispy black fingers reaching for Roc's face. Roc scrambled to get his oxygen mask up over his mouth and nose.

He didn't make it.

McDogal gave Roc a friendly slap on the back. "You okay there, rook?"

Roc glanced up at his friend from his seated position on the back bumper of the fire truck. The white duct tape that had MCDOOGIE written on it in thick black marker across the front of McDogal's helmet was streaked with soot. "Yeah."

"You look like you seen a ghost," McDogal said. Bill McDogal was three years older than Roc, but they had met in high school in the weightlifting room and had mutually admired each other's workout ethic. McDogal had been instrumental in helping Roc get a job at the station. He shifted the coil of fire hose that he was carrying, shimmying it back up his shoulder. "I ain't seen such bug eyes on nobody since my kid thought she saw the boogeyman in her closet."

Roc forced a weak smile. "Maybe she really did see him." And maybe I really saw what I think I saw, he thought. But that was impossible, right? It was some weird trick of the light. I was probably stuck in some half-normal vision, half-infrared vision mode, he thought. It was just a strange illusion. But he knew that had been no illusion. He had seen Freddie. In the flames.

McDogal stared down at Roc. "Seriously. Are you okay? You suck in too much smoke?"

Roc nodded, hanging his head back down. "Yeah, that must've been it. I hope I didn't suck in something toxic."

"Your eyes okay? They all healed up? All that smoke sure ain't gonna help if they aren't."

Roc thought about telling McDogal about his new... ability was probably the best word, but now didn't seem the time. He just kept quiet.

"Who's Freddie?" McDogal asked.

Roc froze for a moment, then felt a weird lump in his throat as he tried to swallow. He looked up at McDogal.

"Shit," McDogal said. "There's that look on your face again."

Roc pretended he was clearing his throat, making a grunting noise. "Why are you asking me about Freddie?"

"Because that's what you were muttering when Gomez pulled you away from the house. '*Leave me alone, Freddie,*' or something like that," McDogal said. 'Gomez said you kept cursing his name. '*Fuck off, Freddie.*'" McDogal waited for Roc to elaborate.

"Some kid I used to hang around with growing up," Roc said.

"What, he really piss you off or something?"

"Or something," Roc said. "Freddie is a she," he added. "Frederika Schmidt. We called her Freddie. She's dead. Died in a fire a long time ago." He wasn't sure why he volunteered that information to McDogal, but it just seemed like it was necessary to say it.

"Why you cursing her now?" McDogal asked.

Because I saw her, Roc wanted to shout. Because I saw her face in the flames! Because she made me make a decision that I have to live with for the rest of my life. But he kept his lips pressed tightly together.

McDogal shrugged. "Okay, well, if you need to talk about it…"

Roc curled into a fetal position beneath the blankets. His wife lay asleep on the bed next to him, breathing softly with an occasional snore.

He knew enough psychology to know that stress could trigger past memories, past emotions. Fighting fires didn't cause him stress; he enjoyed the game of it, trying to conquer the flames and deny them a victory. But the recent discovery of his infertility sure as hell did mess with his head; he felt so damn helpless. And his damn freak-show eyes were most likely permanently fucked up.

And then he fought of Freddie and a terrible, awful sadness welled up inside him. Poor little tomboy Frederika who only wanted to be one of the gang. The poor lonely little girl who had a serious crush on him that he never reciprocated.

Roc remembered one day when they were playing basketball at Nick's house, shooting hoops at the basketball net that was attached to Nick's garage. Nick was a neighborhood kid who lived four houses down from Roc. He got along well with Nick; they had played little league on the same team for several years.

The basketball careened off the rim and bounced into the neighbor's yard and Freddie went chasing after it. Roc remembered quickly looking at Nick. "Let's ditch, Freddie," he said. Nick didn't even respond. They just looked at each other and the decision was made. They both turned and bolted in the opposite direction from Freddie, racing into the strip of land that formed between all the neighbors' yards on the block. Only a few neighbors had put up a fence, so there was a long stretch of navigable land that reached from Nick's house all the way to the end of the block that was twenty plus houses long. They laughed as they ran, knowing Freddie was too scared to follow them because she was terrified of the big dog two houses away. It was a prank they had pulled on Freddie several times before and it had never stopped providing them a grand source of amusement.

Another memory came to him. No, it wasn't a real memory. It was a flurry of images of something he never saw, but he knew must have happened. Freddie clutching the ball excitedly as she grabbed it and turned around to move back to Nick's driveway. Her smile vanishing, her lips dropping into a sad frown. And then the tears coming, and her head hanging in humiliated despair as she drops the basketball, turns slowly away from their fleeing figures, and shuffles slowly home. Alone.

Roc feel the beginnings of tears wet the corners of his eyes, but he refused to let them fall. What the hell was happening to him? His life felt like it was unraveling all around him. His past, his present, his future. Nothing felt right. Nothing felt like the way it should've been or the way it was supposed to be. And then Freddie's sad, tear-filled face filled his mind's eye until he could see nothing else but her.

Roc never cried in his life. Not once. Not ever. But on this night he cried. The tears burned his eyes.

"You some kind of firebug?"

Roc blinked and looked away from the stove flame to see Conrad frowning at him. "What?"

"You some kind of pyro?" Conrad asked. Conrad was one of the oldest guys at the station, with a belly you could rest a can of beer on and be pretty confident it wouldn't spill. Conrad craved a heaping portion of spaghetti and meatballs just as much as Roc craved a good workout. Roc hoped Conrad wasn't his future. The guy was alright, a bit cranky, but he sure let his body go to places that Roc hoped his body would never see.

"What?" Roc frowned awkwardly back at Conrad, then quickly followed with, "No, no." Roc was the newest member of the station, young, lean and fit, so the veterans sometimes liked to poke him and give him shit to see how he reacted.

"You got some weird fascination with fire?" Conrad asked.

"Don't you?" Roc asked. "We're firefighters."

Conrad shrugged. "It's just a job." He paused. "Not an obsession." He stared at Roc for a moment longer, then looked past him to the blue circle of flame still lit on one of the stove burners. "You gonna turn that off?"

Roc looked back to the lit burner. "I'm making grilled cheese."

"I don't hear no pans clanging." Conrad glanced at the empty stove, then looked back to Roc. "You just warming up the air?"

Roc grabbed a flat pan hanging from a nearby rack full of other pots and pans and placed it atop the lit burner.

"I knew I should have convinced the captain to go with an electric when we remodeled the kitchen," Conrad muttered. "Shouldn't be no fire in a fire station." He opened the refrigerator that was positioned near the stove and pulled out a can of root beer. He headed off back into the lounge area outside the kitchen.

Roc watched Conrad leave, then turned back to the stove. He raised the pan off the stove, squeezed his eyes tight, and once again stared at the thin ring of fire that circled the burner. There were thirty-two tiny cones of flame visible around the burner, each one looking like a tiny torch flame. "Know thine enemy," Roc muttered. But he knew this flame wasn't it. This flame was different. The — creature — the Freddie entity — didn't live in these flames. He didn't feel any sense of presence in these flames. These tiny tips of fire were just that — fire. Nothing more, nothing less.

Roc never had time to make that grilled cheese sandwich because the alarm blared hot and heavy throughout the station. He blinked out of infrared mode, quickly set the pan down, and started to head out of the kitchen. He made it a few steps away from the stove before he caught himself and hurried back to flip off the burner by giving the burner knob a quick turn. Oddly, the blue flames stayed lit. Roc looked at the knob. It was clearly in the OFF position, yet the tiny cones of blue flames remained bright. As if they were still alive. He leaned down closer to the flames. Were those eyes in the flames? Were those goddamn fucking eyes in the flames! He wasn't even infrared mode.

"Move your fucking ass, Roc!" Conrad shouted as he moved past the kitchen doorway and saw Roc standing motionless before the stove.

Roc looked to the doorway to see a heavy, angry scowl darkening Conrad's face. He looked back to the stove, but now the flames were gone. He turned away from the stove and picked up his pace as he charged out of the kitchen.

Roc, McDogal, and Conrad were on the roof of a dry cleaning company, dressed in their full firefighter gear, complete with their personal protection equipment. They all had their oxygen masks on. It was dusk, but there was still enough light for them to continue their job.

Conrad stood on a narrow portion of the roof, just behind a two foot lip that broke up the roof into several sections. Conrad clutched his fire hook like a staff, and watched as Roc thrust his roaring chainsaw into the roof.

Roc was cutting venting holes in the rooftop, slashing rips in the rooftop in an attempt to release pent up gases coming off the cleaning chemicals inside the building and prevent an explosion. Smoke billowed up from each jagged hole he cut into the roof, plumes of grayish swirls spiraling up into the air.

McDogal stood on the same section of the roof as Roc; he also clutched his fire hook and watched from behind his oxygen mask as Roc continued to slice out small pieces of roof.

McDogal moved a few feet down the roof, jabbing his fire hook, a long thin steel tool that had a hook and sharp point on one end and a forked head on the other, into the rooftop, checking the roof's firmness. He pointed down to a spot on the roof. "Here," he said to Roc.

Roc finished the venting hole he was working on, then moved to the spot where McDogal had pointed. He thrust the biting chainsaw downward into the roof.

And then suddenly the roof buckled and started to collapse beneath Roc and McDogal.

"Get off! Get off!" Conrad shouted through the intercom system that connected them.

Roc immediately dropped the chainsaw and turned back to reach for the small lip that separated his section of the roof from the section where Conrad was standing.

Conrad dropped his fire hook and snatched at McDogal, who was closest to him, grabbing at his shoulder, hooking him under his arm. Both men grunted and groaned with the effort of trying to get McDogal over the lip in his bulky protective equipment.

The roof buckled further, creating a sharp slant, and Roc slid further down, out of reach of the small lip. White smoke billowed up from the gaping hole in the roof, cutting off visibility.

Conrad continued to struggle with McDogal, yanking and tugging on him, trying to pull him over the lip wall and onto the stable section of the roof where he was standing.

Roc slid further down the incline in the buckling roof. "Ah, shit," he muttered. "I'm going in." And then he disappeared down a dark hole, falling into the building.

*

"Roc!" McDogal's voice blasted in Roc's ears.

Roc slowly stood up, getting his bearings as a slight stab of pain in his ankle made him wince. He had fallen into an old pile of abandoned clothes the dry cleaner had stored in the upper floor of the building. He thought he might have hurt his ankle bad, but the thick stack of clothes had cushioned his drop from the roof pretty well. The dropped chainsaw lay on the floor nearby, sputtering for a moment before it went dead. "I'm okay," he said. His breath sounded hot and heavy in his ears, and a bit frantic, so he forced himself to calm down. "I'm okay," he repeated, saying the words slowly into his helmet mic.

"Stay there," McDogal said through the intercom. "We're getting a rope. We'll get you out."

"I'm okay," Roc said again.

Thick smoke billowed up and out of the large hole that was now in the roof. The flickering light of the flames in front of him drew his gaze. The fire was just starting to eat its way up the stairs on the opposite end of the room, casting a dull orange glow on the stairway wall.

Roc squeezed his eyes tight to go into infrared mode. That's when he saw the man crouching in the far corner of the room, holding a shirt over his nose and mouth. The man's body was nearly all white, somewhat ghostly in infrared mode. "There's somebody in here," Roc announced into the intercom.

He quickly started to move over to the man, ignoring the sting in his ankle. The flames licked their way up the stairs and reached the landing. A pile of clothes near the stairs went up quickly, igniting in a big fireball as if the clothes had been doused in gasoline.

And that's when he saw her again. The being. The entity. The Freddie thing in the flames. She didn't really have a definitive form, but Roc knew she was there because he could see her face shifting within the fire. And Roc knew what the Freddie entity wanted. He looked at the man huddling in the corner.

"I thought you said somebody was in there?" McDogal looked at Roc.

Roc shook his head. He was standing near their fire truck, clutching a water bottle. "No. There was nobody there. I thought I saw somebody, but it was just a shirt hanging on a rack." He took a drink of his water. Behind the fire truck, the building continued to burn.

McDogal nodded. He slapped Roc on the back. "Glad we got you out. The building's a total loss."

Roc nodded. "Yeah, me too."

"How's the ankle?"

Roc waved his hand. "It's nothing. Just tweaked it a little. I'm fine."

McDogal nodded.

Roc dreamed of Freddie. She was still just a girl in his mind, forever ten years old with a freckled nose and curly red hair. That's because you never gave her a chance to grow into a woman, an inner voice chided him. You chose your dog over her. And where is Barkie now? Dead fifteen years past.

He had been so angry at Freddie that day because she had squealed on him to the principal. The sickening thing about it was that he couldn't even remember what the incident had even been. Had he pinched a girl, tugged on someone's ponytail? All he remembered was that his dad had gotten a call from the principal and he had a sore ass for the next eight days after the whooping he had gotten; the black belt had come out and his dad wielded it with a vengeance as if he had just been waiting for the day his son screwed up so he could unleash it again.

His dream shifted, taking him back to that fateful day.

"Look at the smoke," Freddie said. She pointed to a wispy, sinewy column of black smoke rising up into the air above the trees in the Hazelridge Forest Preserve that was a few blocks from their homes.

"I'm going to see what it is," Roc said. He whistled at Barkie, who was sniffing at something near a tree. Barkie was a mutt, part cocker spaniel, part Benji, part something else. He obediently padded over to Roc and Roc patted his head.

"Can I come?" Freddie asked.

Roc shrugged. "Suit yourself."

It was a small brush fire, nothing too extreme. They happened every once in a while, but never turned into anything serious. Until this time. Until the wind shifted and a strong breeze carried some burning embers to either side of them, igniting the dry brush around them. It happened in a matter of seconds, the fire surging, growing, spreading as it devoured the dry brush. Barkie barked at Roc, jumping and leaping around him. He grabbed the leg of Roc's jeans in his mouth and tugged at him, as if begging him to get away from the fire.

A wall of white suddenly enveloped them, separating them into their own pockets of smoke. Roc couldn't see more than a few feet in front of him. He inhaled some smoke and felt a searing heat flash over his face as he coughed. The flames crackled and burned very close by.

"Roc!" he heard Freddie call out. Barkie barked and Roc heard the fear in both voices. Freddie was on his left, unseen behind a shroud of smoke. Barkie was on his right, also hidden in a patch of white.

"Roc!" he heard Freddie yell, her voice rising higher. Barkie barked a scared little bark, then yelped.

Roc pulled his shirt up over his mouth and nose. He knew he only had seconds to choose who to save. His so-called-friend Freddy who had recently betrayed him, or his beloved canine companion who had never let him down.

Roc opened his eyes, bringing himself back to the present. "Fuck you, Freddie," he muttered and wiped away the hint of tears that were starting to pool at the corners of his eyes.

Then Roc thought of the man in the dry cleaning factory. Oh my God. It hit him with the weight of a sledgehammer. I let him die. I left him there to die! What's happening to me?

"You know how crazy that sounds?" Stephanie asked.

Roc shook his head. "I don't care. I've seen her. I've seen her at least a half dozen times now. She's in the flames. She moves from fire to fire." He had finally gotten up the nerve to tell Stephanie about Freddie, about what was happening to him, what he was seeing in the flames. He had to tell somebody, just to get it off his chest. He felt an immense relief as soon the words had spilled out of his mouth. Part of him felt like he was giving confession with the hope that Stephanie would be the understanding, and forgiving, priest who would absolve him of his sins.

Stephanie shook her head. "That's not possible."

Roc wasn't surprised by her response. He knew what he had told her was a lot to absorb, but he was determined to convince her. "Maybe she lives in the smoke, too," Roc said. He raised his hand and waved it, sweeping his arm back and forth in front of him. "Maybe she moves through the smoke to reach another fire. I don't know. I just know it's the same thing. It's the same — being, or creature, or entity, or whatever the fuck you want to call it." Roc paused. "I... I saw... her again today."

"What's she doing in the flames?" Stephanie asked.

He looked at her, dead-serious. "Stalking me."

She was quiet. "Stalking you?"

He nodded.

Stephanie was quiet for a long moment. "Roc, you need some help."

He nodded and exhaled a heavy grunt. "Yeah, you're right. I need help to trap and kill this fucking thing before it gets me."

Stephanie shook her head ever so slightly. "No, I mean real help."

Roc nodded enthusiastically. "Yeah, me too. I can't fight it all by myself."

She sighed a gentle, but seriously concerned, sigh. "You're not going to make this easy, are you?"

He frowned at her.

"Will you at least talk to Doctor Gordon?" Stephanie asked.

"Why? He have experience fighting these things?"

"Yeah." She looked at him with gentle concern. "Sort of. He handles a lot of PTSD cases."

Roc was quiet. He felt a deflating sense of disappointment at Stephanie's response. He wasn't suffering from any post-traumatic stress. He was being stalked by some hellish entity that lived in flames! He wanted to shout those words at her, but he kept silent.

Stephanie reached for the pack of cigarettes on the table, and plucked one out of the pack. She put the cigarette to her lips and grabbed at the lighter on the counter near her. She flicked on the flame and put the fire to the end of the cigarette. She glanced up to see Roc staring raptly at the flame. She finished lighting her cigarette and moved the flame away from her, keeping the lighter lit. She took the cigarette out of her mouth, slowly exhaling smoke out of the corner of her mouth away from him, watching him stare at the flame. Then she looked back at the tiny flame. "You see it now?" she asked, keeping her voice flat and calm. "Is... she in there?"

He frowned at her and looked away. "Don't be ridiculous."

She let the flame go out.

"That flame is way too small. This thing is huge." He made an exaggerated gesture, sweeping his arms up and around.

Stephanie inhaled on the cigarette and slowly blew out a cloud of white smoke straight at Roc.

Roc batted away the approaching smoke. "Jesus, Steph!"

"Sorry, sorry," Stephanie said, joining him in batting away the smoke. "Sorry."

And then Roc just burst out laughing. "You think I'm just blowing you smoke, don't you?"

Stephanie gave him just the slightest of smirks. "Come on, Roc, it does seem a little—"

"Crazy."

"—wild," Stephanie said, finishing her sentence.

"What's with him?" Conrad asked, jerking his thumb over his shoulder at Roc. Roc was sitting on one of the wooden benches in the locker room of the fire station, his head hanging down, his forearms resting limply on his thighs. They couldn't see his eyes, but if they did they would have seen that Roc was not staring at the tiled floor; he was looking somewhere else, somewhere deep inside his own head.

"He'll be all right," McDogal said. "Just leave him be."

"Why? So he can leave me be in the middle of a big blaze?" Conrad shook his head. "No, he needs to snap out of that shit when he's here. He can hang his head and mope at home on his own time. Not fire station time."

"Just leave him be," McDogal repeated. He grabbed at Conrad's shoulder to maneuver him on his way, but Conrad shrugged his hand off. McDogal frowned.

"I don't wanna go on a call with him," Conrad said. "Not when he's like that. His head's gotta be in the game."

"Yeah, yeah," McDogal said and herded Conrad towards the locker room door. "I'll talk to him."

Conrad scowled at McDogal, but said nothing more. He turned and headed out of the room.

McDogal turned back to face Roc. He watched his friend for a moment, thinking about the guy he spotted with in the weight room back in high school. This wasn't the same guy. The guy he knew was bold and assertive and brave. This guy sitting on the bench seemed scared, timid, and afraid of his own shadow. He slowly moved over to the bench and sat down next to Roc. "You okay, dude?" he asked.

Roc quickly looked up at him, seeming to be startled by McDogal's sudden appearance. "What? Yeah, yeah." He waved his hand as he straightened up. "All good."

"You don't look so good."

Roc frowned. "Really? I feel fine."

"The hell you do. Nobody who feels fine sits staring at the floor for ten minutes. Shit, more like fifteen. You didn't even move. Not even a little wiggle in your fingers. I could barely tell if you were breathing or not."

Roc inhaled and blew out a breath of air. "I'm breathing. See."

McDogal studied him for a quiet moment. "I

know you're still thinking about… what you said you saw—"

Roc cut him off. "I didn't just *say* I saw it. I *saw* it." He paused. "I saw her."

It was McDogal's turn to stare quietly at the floor. "You know that's just not possible, right?"

"Now you sound like Stephanie," Roc said.

"Yeah, well, maybe your wife is making sense."

"And I'm not?"

McDogal looked up at Roc. "No, Roc. You're not."

Roc stared back at him. "And you wonder why I sit in silence when no one believes me?" Roc looked away from him. "I thought of all people besides my wife you would be the one who would believe me."

McDogal said nothing. He looked away from Roc, hanging his head down.

Roc stood up.

"Sorry your little swimmers can't make it to the beach," McDogal said, awkwardly changing the subject.

Roc squinted down at McDogal. "What?" Then he comprehended what McDogal had just said to him. "Ah, shit. Stephanie talked to Maiko, didn't she?"

"Wives," McDogal said, shaking his head. "If you think anybody can keep a secret in this station, forget it."

Roc frowned. "Jesus, that didn't take long…"

"You can always try in vitro or whatever the hell they do these days," McDogal said.

Roc shook his head. "I don't want some lab experiment baby."

"The old-fashioned way or not at all, huh?"

"Yeah," Roc said.

"Stop wearing them tighty whiteys," McDogal said. "They suffocate your sperm factory."

Roc nodded. "Did that six months ago. Didn't help."

McDogal nodded.

Roc was silent for a moment. "You and Maiko need to do anything… special to get her pregnant? Timing? Special foods?"

McDogal shook his head. "No, sorry to say. Just went about our business." McDogal became quiet himself for a long moment. "In fact…" He let his voice trail off.

Roc tilted his head and pursed his lips. "Damn, number two's on the way, isn't it?"

"Look, man, I'm sorry. Not trying to rub it in here."

Roc waved his hand. "No, no. All good." He looked at McDogal. "Shit, congrats, man." He slapped his friend on the shoulder.

"Thanks," McDogal said.

And then the siren bells started to blare.

≈≈≈≈≈≈≈

"You okay?" Maiko McDogal asked. She was a slender Japanese woman with jet black hair that fell past her shoulders, wife to fireman Bill McDogal.

"What?" Stephanie said. "Oh, yeah. I'm fine."

Stephanie and Maiko were seated at the kitchen table inside the McDogal's house.

"You seem a little distracted lately," Maiko said.

Stephanie sighed. "Yeah, just a lot going on."

Maiko stared at her friend. "No, it's not that. There's something else going on. Are you and Roc…

okay?"

"Yeah, we're fine."

Maiko made a hmm sound.

Stephanie looked at her. "What? We're fine."

"I know you worry about him when he's on duty, but this is different. There's something else. And it's not about the infer— the baby problem."

Stephanie blew out a gusty breath. "Jeezus. When did you become my therapist?"

"Uh, duh. The day we first met, " Maiko said.

Stephanie smiled a weak smile. "Roc…" Stephanie paused, rolling her empty coffee cup between her hands.

"Go on."

"He's been… crying in his sleep. I don't think he knows that I've heard him do that. It kind of freaks me out."

"Did you ask him about it?"

Stephanie shook her head. "He's getting paranoid," Stephanie said.

"Paranoid?"

Stephanie nodded. "Yeah."

"You mean like people are after him kind of paranoid?"

Stephanie shook her head. "No. Not people." She raised her cup to take a drink, but there was nothing left in the cup.

Maiko waited.

Stephanie set her cup down. "He says he sees something in the flames."

Now Maiko was suddenly quiet and a distressed look appeared on her face.

Stephanie noticed it. "What?"

Maiko looked earnestly at Stephanie, leaning

towards her. "What else did Roc say? I mean exactly."

"What? You've heard of this before?"

"Just tell me what he saw." Maiko's tone was insistently forceful.

Stephanie explained to Maiko what Roc had told her about the face in the flames, about Freddie, about what happened to her in the past.

"Roc needs to be very careful," Maiko said after Stephanie finished.

"Why?" Stephanie frowned. "Jeezus. Now you're freaking me out, too."

"He sees the Onibi," Maiko said.

"The Onibi?" Stephanie's frown deepened. "What the hell is that?"

"It's a demonic flame that can suck out your life if you come too near it," Maiko said.

"You're shitting me?"

Maiko shook her head.

"A demonic flame?"

Maiko nodded her head. "My grandmother told me about them when I was little. Scariest story she ever told me. She said one of her cousins got taken by an Onibi when they were kids." She pointed to her stove. "That's why I went electric."

"Oh, come on." Stephanie leaned back in her chair. "Seriously?"

"A lot of these smoke inhalation deaths you read about," Maiko said. "They didn't die from smoke inhalation. They died because the Onibi sucked their life out."

"That's just crazy," Stephanie said dismissively, yet a shadow of fear still crossed over her face.

Maiko frowned at Stephanie.

Stephanie's face flushed. "I didn't mean you—"

"Roc needs to be careful," Maiko said, cutting her off to reiterate her earlier warning. "He needs to be very careful."

"Stop following me!" Roc yelled at the face in the flames. They had been called to a small fire near the outskirts of town. One of the farmers had been trying to burn off some excess brush near his corn fields and it had gotten out of his control. Roc was on the far left edge of the fire, digging a trench to protect the crops that the fire threatened to reach.

The flaming Freddie visage continued to stare at him from within the flames that burned a few yards away. The rest of the crew was out of earshot, so no one heard him talking to the flames. And even if they had, they would have just shaken their heads and continued on with what they were doing; Roc's eccentric behavior was starting to become well-known throughout the district.

"You want some kind of apology? You want me to ask for your forgiveness?" Roc shook his head. "It's not going to happen. What do you think about that?"

Freddie's face rippled in the flames, her gaze staying deadlocked on Roc.

"Maybe I'm glad you're dead," Roc said. "Maybe I'm glad I gave you to the flames. You ever think of that? Maybe I sacrificed you on purpose."

The fire flared hotter, brighter. More dark smoke swirled about the face, the blackened trails looking like snakes crawling in and out of Freddie's eyes, her mouth.

"Trust is as hard as a thick stick, Freddie. But once

you break it, you can never put it back the way it was. It will always have a crack in it. I knew the moment you squealed on me to the principal in third grade that you weren't really my friend. Not my true friend. True friends have each other's back. Always. You broke the stick, Freddie. You broke the fucking stick."

The flames crackled and spit embers towards Roc, but none of them reached him and the glowing embers quickly faded to blackened specks of harmless debris.

"Go haunt somebody else," Roc said. He was about to blink himself out of infrared mode, but then Freddie spoke.

"I'm not trying to haunt you, Roc," she said. "I'm trying to set you free."

"By burning me to death?" Roc asked, speaking to the flames without even a moment's hesitation, even though he knew he should have been freaked out to the core of his very soul for hearing a flame speaking to him.

The face in the flames smiled. "No. By giving you power over the flames."

"I've finally lost it, haven't I?" Roc asked, speaking more to himself than to Freddie. "I'm drooling in some insane asylum dreaming this all up."

Freddie's face wavered, but the smile remained. A small hand appeared in the fire, the fingers and palm made of flames. The fire hand moved towards Roc, curling its fingers into a fist except for the index finger which pointed at Roc. The tip of the index finger pulsed a white-hot glow in infrared mode, the glow growing brighter then dimmer. "Touch it, Roc," the Freddie face floating in the flames said. "Touch it and the world is ours."

Roc forced himself to look away, and resumed his digging with a renewed sense of urgency. Damn it, he thought. Stephanie was right. I'm really losing it. I need to get some help. Now I'm talking back to the fucking flames.

❦

"Why are you here, Roc?" Doctor Gordon asked. The doctor was in his late fifties, with graying hair and the beginnings of a receding hairline.

"Because my wife won't give me any unless I showed up," Roc said. He was lying on a leather couch in the office of Doctor Gordon.

"Won't give you any what?"

Roc turned his head to stare at Doctor Gordon. "Are you serious?" He rotated his head to look back up at the ceiling. "Meatball sandwiches, doc. She won't give me any more meatball sandwiches unless I spill my guts to you."

Doctor Gordon looked quietly at Roc for a moment. "You must really like those meatball sandwiches to put yourself through this to get some," he finally said.

Roc smiled a quick smile. "Yeah. I *love* those meatball sandwiches." He stared up at the ceiling for a moment, then let out an exasperated sigh. "And she's the only one who makes them for me."

"You don't think you need any help, do you?" Doctor Gordon asked.

Roc didn't respond.

"Why does your wife think you need help?"

"Because I've seen things that no one else can

believe."

"What kind of things?"

Roc folded his hands on his muscular chest. "It's more like one thing."

"What kind of thing?"

Roc was quiet for a moment, clearly debating whether or not to continue. "Hell, I really do want more of those meatball sandwiches, so here goes." He paused. "Do you know what a flame is, doc? What a fire is made of?"

Doctor Gordon waited for him to continue.

"A flame is a mixture of reacting gases and solids. This mixture emits visible light, infrared light, and sometimes even ultraviolet light depending on what's being burned. Obviously, everyone can see the visible light portion of a flame. But not everyone can see the infrared part, or the ultraviolet light. Not everyone."

"But you think you can?"

Roc frowned. "You and McDogal must drink at the same pub. I don't *think* I can. I *can*."

Doctor Gordon made a note on his tablet, scribbling along its responsive surface with his gold stylus.

"I can see infrared light," Roc stated.

"And what makes you think that?"

Roc gave another exasperated sigh. He sat up on the couch and squeezed his eyes shut tight. He opened them.

Doctor Gordon studied Roc's red-rimmed eyes with an incredulous stare. He started to ask a question, but Roc answered his previous question before the doctor could speak.

"Because I can see it," Roc said. "I can see the different colors, the different temperatures." He looked at the doctor's face, seeing the infrared outline of him, the different levels of heat coming off his clothes, his arms, his face. "I can see you in infrared."

The doctor studied his eyes for a moment, clearly intrigued by what he was looking at, but also somewhat alarmed. "Does it... hurt? They look swollen."

"No, doesn't hurt at all. My eyes feel a bit warmer when I put them in infrared mode, but it's not painful at all."

"Infrared mode?"

"That's just what I call it," Roc said.

"And how did you come to have this... ability?" the doctor asked.

Roc blinked, putting his eyes back to normal. "Probably when I got sprayed in the face by a bombardier beetle a few months ago. That sucker got me right in the eyes. Some idiot had started a campfire in Frond's Nature Preserve and didn't douse the embers. They caught fire and started burning up the woods. We got called in to put it out. It was a simple job and we knocked the fire out in a few hours. I took a breather after and sat down on a rock."

Roc paused a moment before he continued. "All I did was turn my head to the left to look at some plants nearby and *bamm* I got blasted right in the face by a really agitated bombardier beetle that was sitting on a leaf right next to me. Felt like my eyes were burning their way through my sockets. Like they were fucking melting. Thought I was going to go permanently blind. I couldn't see for two weeks. When the bandages came off, I knew right away there was something wrong with my eyes. Nothing looked like I remembered it. Everything had a different color to it, a different hue."

"Interesting."

"Yeah, right. Real interesting." Roc was quiet for a moment. He avoided the urge to touch his eyes. "Maybe this thing was always there in the flames, and we just didn't know it was there because we couldn't see it." Roc paused for a moment. "Maybe I shouldn't be worried about it."

"But you are worried about it," the doctor said.

Roc was again quiet for a moment before he answered. "Yes," he said. "Yes I am."

"Why?"

"Because she wants me," Roc said.

'She?" the doctor asked, but Roc ignored his question and kept talking.

"It's like those fucking sirens at sea singing their songs and luring all those sailors to their deaths. That's what it feels like it." Roc paused. "Like she wants me to come to her."

' Who is she?" the doctor asked.

'An old friend, doc," Roc said, the bitterness rising in his voice. "A dear old friend."

"Do you want to go to her?" the doctor asked.

"Yes," Roc said. "Every time I see her the pull gets stronger and stronger. That's what's starting to scare the fuck out of me."

⊶⊱⊰❋⊱⊰⊷

Roc watched the flames crawl up the wall towards the ceiling.

They had been called to a house owned by an elderly woman who was a notorious hoarder, the fire caused by a clogged, overheating dryer. The fire had quickly spread throughout the house, all of the junk the woman had accumulated over the years fueling the flames. The rest of the crew was in the front of the house, battling the main fire. He had gone to the back of the house to assess the damage there.

Roc tried to avoid going into infrared mode, afraid of what he might see in the flames, but the lure of infrared mode was too great for him to resist. He had to know. He had to see if she was still there. He squeezed his eyes tight. He wanted to know. Part of him wanted to see her again.

He opened his eyes and immediately knew there was no escaping her. Not now. Not ever. She was there, floating in the fire. Freddie's face wavered and roiled in the flames. He knew he could temporarily blink her out of existence, but he also knew that wasn't going to help. He would just be prolonging the inevitable. "What do you want from me, Freddie?"

"I want to be with you," Freddie said. A fiery hand reached out towards Roc, the fiery index finger pointing at him, the tip of the finger glowing and pulsing. "I want to make babies with you."

The absurdity of her statement didn't really register with Roc. He stared at the fiery hand. He felt oddly calm. He slowly moved his hand towards the flames, his fingers splayed open. Unable to stop the mesmerizing compulsion, his middle finger touched Freddie's finger. He felt a burning sensation, but only for second, and then the pain was gone, replaced by a growing sense of euphoria.

"Together forever," Freddie said.

Then something started to glow beneath the tip of Roc's middle finger. It was a small shape, somewhat like a tadpole. A tadpole made of fire. That's what it reminded Roc of. And then its tiny orange-red tail, which looked intensely white in infrared mode, began to swish back and forth and the fire tadpole started to move along the length of his middle finger. He felt a burning sensation in his finger, but it didn't really bother him. He gently flexed his fingers as the heat seeped deeper into his flesh.

He turned his hand over as the fire tadpole reached his palm; it swam in a circle beneath his skin, creating a fiery circle of red light beneath his flesh. And then the fire tadpole paused, just for the briefest of moments, before it shot past his wrist and scurried up his arm. A burning sensation lit up his arm as if someone was drawing a blade across his inner forearm, then through his bicep, then up into his shoulder. He tilted his head to the left, trying to see his shoulder but he could only see the corner of it. He saw the head of the fire tadpole reach his shoulder and then it disappeared from his view as it headed towards his neck, leaving only a shimmering ember-like glow in its wake.

He knew he should be alarmed; in fact, he realized he should be terrified because he knew the fire tadpole's ultimate destination. But he wasn't. He felt a sense of relief. It would all be over soon. He felt it reach his chin, then start to burrow its way through his lower cheek, moving over and around the corner of his upper lip, heading for his nostrils. It went up his nose and he felt all the hairs on his head stand up as if he had just eaten the spiciest pepper ever discovered. Beads of sweat erupted out of every pore on his face and he suddenly looked as if a mask of water a half inch thick had been placed over his face.

And then the water hissed and evaporated, becoming a smoky haze of steam that drifted away from him.

He felt a warmth spread throughout his brain. It was oddly comforting. For a brief moment, he thought of his old sore ankle and realized the pain had vanished completely; not even a twinge of discomfort that had plagued him since his fall into the dry cleaning building was present. In fact, he felt no aches in his body whatsoever. He felt pretty damn good. He stood still for a long moment, enjoying the pleasing warmth that now seemed to cocoon his entire body.

"Nice, isn't it?" he heard Freddie say. But her voice didn't sound like it was coming from the flames in front of him anymore. It sounded like she was speaking to him directly inside his head. "Now see what you can do," Freddie said.

Roc understood what Freddie meant. He didn't know how he knew, but he just knew that he did. He rubbed his forefinger and thumb together, quickening the pace, rubbing them together as if they were dried kindling and he was trying to ignite them. To his amazement, his effort succeeded and a tiny ball of flame appeared on his thumb. He stared at the tiny burning ball. Then he flicked the ball off his thumb with his forefinger, sending the tiny ball of fire back into the flames burning nearby.

Then he rubbed his four fingers over his palm, moving them faster and faster. To his amused delight, another ball of flame appeared. This one was much bigger and it seemed to hover above his palm. It was a golf ball-sized orb of flame. He reared his arm back and hurled the fireball at a nearby beam as yet untouched by the spreading fire. The fireball hit the beam and splattered against it as if it were a snowball, but instead of sending little bits of snow and ice into the air, the splattering fireball sent out little bits of sparks and flame.

He heard Freddie laugh with delight inside his head. "*I* impregnated *you*," she said. "What do you think about that?" She laughed softly again.

Then he rubbed both his hands together, furiously moving his fingers and palms against each other, rubbing faster and faster. He was again rewarded with another fireball, this one the size of a baseball. He stared at the burning orb in his left palm. This wasn't what he had expected. He had thought the fire would consume him, absorb him into its being, put an end to his misery. But now he had seemed to absorb it, instead of the other way around.

He absently tossed the fire baseball back into the flames.

"I'm hungry," the Freddie voice in his head said. "Aren't you?"

A sudden hunger pang wracked Roc's body. He felt ravenous. He felt hangry. But not for regular food, not for a hamburger and fries, not for some fried chicken, not for pizza. What he really craved was something blackened to a crisp on the outside, and tender and juicy on the inside.

He glanced around the area, looking for the old woman.

Roc bent over the sink, spitting out toothpaste furiously, trying to get the taste out of his mouth. He scrubbed at his teeth, at his gums, over his tongue, moving the brush all around his mouth.

No more, he thought. I can't do this anymore. I need to quit. Find something else. Some other job.

"Go ahead," Freddie said in his head. "I'll be with you wherever you go."

Roc raised his head and stared at himself in the mirror for a long moment. "Fuck you, Freddie."

Freddie laughed a tinkling little laugh. "Oh, Roc. I already fucked you."

"You need to go away," Roc said. "Please. Just leave me alone."

Freddie said nothing.

<hr />

"Oh, Roc, oh my God," Stephanie moaned. "My pussy is so hot. Keep fucking me."

Roc continued to drive his erection into his wife's very warm vagina. He and Stephanie always had a great sex life. It was the one thing he could count on to help relieve his stress. And he knew she enjoyed it as much as he did. And right about now he needed as much stress relief as he could get. He could feel the temperature rising where their bodies joined, the friction of his stiffness moving in and out of Stephanie's folds raising the heat. Heat. Friction. Fire.

Roc stopped moving.

"No, no, don't stop," Stephanie moaned. "Don't stop, Roc. Pound that pussy. Oh my God, I'm so wet."

Roc pulled out of her abruptly and moved off of his wife.

"No, Roc. Why did you stop? Did you come?" Her glasses were slightly askew on her face, but she made no effort to straighten them.

Roc stayed silent.

"It's okay, honey. It's okay." Stephanie grabbed at his hand. "Finish me off with your fingers."

Roc let her guide his hand between her legs. His fingers touched her wetness and he slid two fingers into her.

Stephanie moaned in delight. She reached down to his crotch to find that his erection was still thick and full. "You're still hard," she panted. "Put it back inside me."

Roc didn't move.

"Come on, Roc. Fuck me."

Roc looked away from her. "I can't."

"What?"

He could feel the dangerous heat building in his fingers. He took his hand away from her hot wetness.

"I... can't."

"Why not? What's wrong, Roc?"

"Show her," Freddie's voice said to him.

Roc raised his hand so Stephanie could see it. He rubbed his thumb and forefinger together, pressing them tight against each other, creating friction. A tiny flame appeared, crackling with a soft sound as it formed.

"What—?" Stephanie stared, her mouth open, the rest of the question unspoken.

"It's inside me," Roc said.

Stephanie just stared.

"The Onibi, Steph. It's inside me."

"How... how can that be?"

Roc shrugged. "It just is. Freddie... gave it to me. I don't know how, but she did."

"Ha, you know how," Freddie said inside his head.

"I finger fucked you."

Stephanie didn't seem to be listening to him. She stared, almost rapturously, at the small circle of flame burning on Roc's fingertips. "Is that a real flame?"

He nodded.

"How come it's not burning you?"

"I don't know. I don't really feel it. It's like it's burning inside its own protective shield or something," Roc said.

"That... that's just not possible," Stephanie muttered.

Roc raised his hand closer to her, bringing the small flame closer to Stephanie. "It's right here! You saw me do it."

I— " Stephanie lowered her head, then she looked back up at the tiny ball of flame floating above his forefinger. "I— what the hell, Roc?" Stephanie went quiet for a long moment. "Whoa, wait a minute. That's why you pulled out of me? Cause you were afraid you might... flare up inside me?"

Roc said nothing.

Stephanie again stared at the small flame burning on the tip of Roc's finger. She slowly reached her hand towards it, her gaze hypnotically blank, as if the flame was compelling her to touch it.

Roc shifted his body away from her approaching hand. "Don't touch it! It'll burn you!" Roc quickly put his other hand over the flame, squeezing tight around his finger, dousing the fire.

Stephanie kept her hand in the air a moment longer, staring at the space where Roc's burning finger had been, then quickly lowered her hand back down. "You're fucking with me, right?" Stephanie asked. "This some new trick Bill showed you at the station?"

"It's no trick," Roc said.

"Oh, come on," Stephanie said. "You expect me to believe that? Show me again."

Roc obliged her, rubbing his finger and thumb together to create a small orb of fire that floated just above his finger.

Stephanie stared with rapt fascination. "How…" She shifted her gaze from the flame to Roc's face. "Does this mean you can be some kind of superhero?" she asked, her voice soft.

Roc frowned at her. "What? No. No!" He quickly dipped his finger into a glass half full of wine on the nightstand near the bed. The fire hissed and spit as the flame went out. "I don't want it. I need to get rid of it."

"Oh, Roc," Freddie's voice said inside his head. "You can't get rid of me now. We're together forever."

"Please, Steph, " Roc said, the begging in his voice taking on a desperate tone. "I need to get rid of it."

"This is crazy," Stephanie said.

"Yeah, it's fucking crazy, but you saw it," Roc said. "You saw it right here with your own eyes."

Stephanie was quiet for a long moment, absently staring at Roc's wine-slicked finger. "Maiko," she finally said. "We need to talk to Maiko. She knows more about the Onibi than anyone."

"It's inside you?" Maiko's eyes were wide as she responded to Roc's tale. Roc and Stephanie were in the McDogal's living room, sitting on the couch.

Maiko sat in a chair across from them, her pregnant belly barely hidden beneath a pair of black stretch pants. Her husband Bill was at the fire station, working his shift. Their daughter Isabelle was asleep in her room in her crib.

"Show her," Stephanie said to Roc.

Roc rubbed his forefinger and thumb together, creating a tiny flame. The miniature ball of fire floated just above his forefinger, the small flames shifting and waving as the unearthly fire burned.

"Holy fucking shit," Maiko said. She leaped off the chair and ran towards her bedroom.

"Maiko," Stephanie called after her.

Roc and Stephanie exchanged perplexed glances.

"What the hell is she doing?" Roc asked.

Stephanie shrugged.

Maiko reappeared with a gun in her hand, a 9mm semi-automatic Glock 19. Her fingers trembled and the gun wavered in her hand. She aimed the weapon straight at Roc's chest.

Roc instinctively threw his hands up in the air, the fire still burning on the tip of his finger. "Whoa, whoa!" The small orb of fire leaped off of Roc's finger from the sharp motion and hit the ceiling. Some red hot embers bounced back down from the ceiling, turning to dark ash quickly as they floated back towards the floor. A tiny spot of fire appeared in the ceiling, and slowly started to spread.

"What the hell, Maiko?" Stephanie cried out.

"He's a demon," Maiko said. There was both a genuine fear and a focused anger in her eyes.

Roc stared at the weapon aimed straight at him. He could see that Maiko's hands were trembling as she gripped the gun with both hands. He slowly lowered one hand and pointed at the gun. "Just put that down."

"Maiko, stop it!" Stephanie shouted at her. "Put the gun down."

"He wants my baby," Maiko said, keeping her narrow gaze focused on Roc. Her finger tightened on the trigger.

"Maiko, just calm down." Stephanie rose up off the couch, moving between Roc and Maiko just as Maiko pulled the trigger.

"No!" Roc shouted, reaching his arm out to stop Stephanie but she was inches out of his grasp.

The bullet ripped through Stephanie's throat and blood immediately spurted out of the hole in her neck. She gurgled as she collapsed to the floor in front of the couch.

"No!" Roc cried out again, bolting up to his feet.

Maiko froze, shock filling her face. She stared down at Stephanie as Stephanie put her hand feebly to her throat, the blood seeping through her fingers, staining her hand red.

A blast of flame hit Maiko in the shoulder, startling her, making her lose her grip on her gun. The weapon hit the carpet with a faint thud. A wisp of steam rose up from her burnt clothes and the smell of singed flesh quickly spread through the air. Maiko looked over to see Roc holding his hand up, an orb of fire burning just above his open palm.

Roc moved quickly to Stephanie's side, the large ball of flame still floating just above his palm. He pressed his palm over Stephanie's throat, cauterizing the bullet wound with the ball of fire; the sound of sizzling flesh filled the air. Stephanie made no sound. Blood continued to seep out of Stephanie, the pool of blood soaking into the carpet, the stain enlarging, spreading. Roc quickly turned his wife on her side to see a gaping exit wound in the back of her neck. He quickly rubbed his palms together, creating another ball of flame. He moved to put the flame against the exit wound but a snarling cry made him turn.

Maiko was charging straight at him, a large steak knife now in her hand. Roc raised up his hands defensively and the ball of flame struck Maiko in the chest, blooming out across her breasts and up to her chin and down to her lower stomach. Maiko grunted and tried to stab at Roc while she stumbled backwards, but the blade missed Roc. She cried out in agony, grasping at her severely burned chest. In a desperate attempt, she flung the steak knife at Roc but it missed him by several feet and smashed into the TV in the living room, putting a cracked scar into the screen.

Roc rose up and quickly moved to Maiko, punching her square in the face. She went down and stayed down. Roc hurriedly moved back to Stephanie, again rubbing his palms together to create a flame. He put the flame to the back of Stephanie's neck, cauterizing the large wound.

But he was too late.

Stephanie just stared without blinking.

Roc gritted his teeth. He rose up and stalked towards Maiko, rubbing his hands together with an angry relish, the violent friction creating a large flame in each palm. He dropped to his knees, straddling the still-stunned Maiko. He roared with rage and gripped Maiko's head in his flaming hands, the intense heat melting the flesh off her face and making the bones in her skull crackle. Her hair crackled and curled and shriveled from the intense heat. He held his hands against the sides of her head for a long moment, watching her continue to burn as the flames started to spread down her neck and over her upper chest, watching her skin char and blacken.

To his surprise, she smelled delicious. He looked at the swollen lump of her pregnant belly.

Roc stared at the flames burning in his open palms. He could hear the ghost of Stephanie's voice whispering in his ear. "It's not your fault, Roc. It's just what was meant to be. Everything happens for a reason." He felt... powerful. He felt calmly confident. He enjoyed the feeling of creating fire with his own hands. No, it was more than that. He craved it now. He needed it.

The question Stephanie had asked him replayed over and over in his mind. "Does this mean you can be some kind of superhero?"

Tiny flames flickered in the deep blackness of his pupils. Or was this how a super villain was created? He heard the faint delighted laughter of Freddie's voice inside his head.

Behind Roc, the McDogal's house continued to burn.

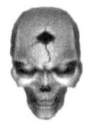

LAND OF FRIGHT™

A NOTE FROM JACK O'DONNELL

Thanks for reading this eighth collection of my Land of Fright™ tales. I hope you continue to journey with me as we move deeper into the dark realms within the Land of Fright™. There are many new uncharted realms yet to be mapped, so keep checking back for new discoveries.

Visit www.landoffright.com and subscribe to stay up-to-date on the latest new stories in the Land of Fright™ series of horror short stories.

Or visit my author page on Amazon at www.amazon.com/author/jodonnell to see the newest releases in the Land of Fright™ series.

If you enjoy the Land of Fright™ series, please consider taking the time to leave a review. Your comments are greatly appreciated!

- JACK

MORE LAND OF FRIGHT™ COLLECTIONS ARE AVAILABLE NOW!

Turn the page and step deeper into fear!

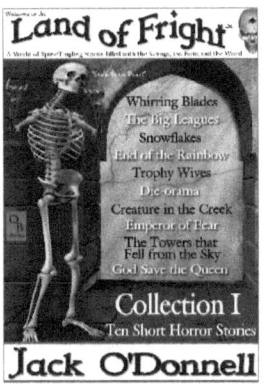

Land of Fright™ terrorstories contained in Collection I:

#1 - Whirring Blades: A simple late-night trip to the mall for a father and his son turns into a struggle for survival when they are attacked by a deadly swarm of toy helicopters.

#2 - The Big Leagues: A scorned young baseball player shows his teammates he really knows how to play ball with the best of them.

#3 - Snowflakes: In the land of Frawst, special snowflakes are a gift from the gods, capable of transferring the knowledge of the Ancients. A young woman searches the skies with breathless anticipation for her snowflake, but finds something far more dark and dangerous instead.

#4 - End of the Rainbow: In Medieval England, a warrior and his woman find the end of a massive rainbow that has filled the sky and discover the dark secret of its power.

#5 - Trophy Wives: An enigmatic sculptor meets a beautiful woman whom he vows will be his next subject. But things may not turn out the way he plans...

#6 - Die-orama: A petty thief finds out that a WWII model diorama in his local hobby shop holds much more than just plastic vehicles and plastic soldiers.

#7 - Creature in the Creek: A lonely young woman finds her favorite secluded spot inhabited by a monster from her past.

#8 - The Emperor of Fear: In ancient Rome, two coliseum workers encounter a mysterious crate containing an unearthly creature. Just in time for the next gladiator games…

#9 - The Towers That Fell From The Sky: Two analysts race to uncover the secret purpose of the giant alien towers that have thundered down out of the skies.

#10 - God Save The Queen: An exterminator piloting an ant-sized robot comes face to face with the queen of a nest he has been assigned to destroy.

Land of Fright™ terrorstories contained in Collection II:

#11 - Special Announcement: A fraud investigator discovers the disturbing truth behind the messages on a community announcement board.

#12 - Poisoned Land: Savage hunters patrol the Poisoned Lands, demanding appeasement from the three survivors trapped in a surrounded building. How far will each one of them go to survive?

#13 - Pool of Light: A mysterious wave of dark energy from space washes over the Earth, trapping a woman and her friends in pools of light. Beyond the edges of the light, deep pockets of darkness hold much more than just empty blackness.

#14 - Ghosts of Pompeii: A woman on a tour of Italy with her son unwittingly awakens the ghosts of Pompeii.

#15 - Sparklers: A child's sparkler opens a doorway to another dimension and a father must enter it to save his family and his neighborhood from the ominous threat that lays beyond.

#16 - The Grid: An interstellar salvage crew activates a mysterious grid on an abandoned vessel floating in space, unleashing a deadly force.

#17 - The Barn: An empty barn beckons an amateur photographer to step through its dark entrance, whispering promises of a once-in-a-lifetime shoot.

#18 - Sands of the Colosseum: A businessman in Rome gets to experience the dream of a lifetime when he visits the great Colosseum — until he finds himself standing on the arena floor.

#19 - Flipbook: A man sees a dark future of his family in jeopardy when he watches the tiny animations of a flipbook play out in his hand.

#20 - Day of the Hoppers: Two boys flee for their lives when their friendly neighborhood grasshoppers turn into deadly projectiles.

Land of Fright™ terrorstories contained in Collection III:

#21 - The Prospector: In the 1800's, a lonely prospector finds the body parts of a woman as he pans for gold in the wilds of California.

#22 - The Boy In The Yearbook: Two middle-aged women are tormented by a mysterious photograph in their high school yearbook.

#23 - Shot Glass: A man discovers the shot glasses in his great-grandfather's collection can do much more than just hold a mouthful of liquor.

#24 - The Champion: An actor in a medieval renaissance re-enactment show becomes the unbeatable champion he has longed to be.

#25 - Hitler's Graveyard: American soldiers in WWII uncover a nefarious Nazi plan to resurrect their dead heroes so they can rejoin the war.

#26 - Out of Ink: Colonists on a remote planet resort to desperate measures to ward off an attack from wild alien animals.

#27 - Dung Beetles: Mutant dung beetles attack a family on a remote Pennsylvania highway. Yes, it's as disgusting as it sounds.

#28 - The Tinies: A beleaguered office worker encounters a strange alien armada in the sub-basement of his office building.

#29 - Hammer of Charon: In ancient Rome, it is the duty of a special man to make sure gravely wounded gladiators are given a quick death after a gladiator fight. He serves his position quietly with honor. Until they try to take his hammer away from him…

#30 - Pharaoh's Cat: In ancient Egypt, the pharaoh is dying. His trusted advisors want his favorite cat to be buried with him. The cat has other plans…

398

Land of Fright™ terrorstories contained in Collection IV:

#31 - The Throw-Aways: A washed-up writer of action-adventure thrillers is menaced by the ghosts of the characters he has created.

#32 - Everlasting Death: The souls of the newly deceased take on solid form and the Earth fills with immovable statues of death...

#33 - Bite the Bullet: In the Wild West, a desperate outlaw clings to a bullet cursed by a Gypsy... because the bullet has his name on it.

#34 - Road Rage: A senseless accident on a rural highway sets off a frightening chain of events.

#35 - The Controller: A detective investigates a bank robbery that appears to have been carried out by a zombie.

#36 - The Notebook: An enchanted notebook helps a floundering author finish her story. But the unnatural fuel that stokes the power of the mysterious writing journal leads her down a disturbing path...

#37 - The Candy Striper and the Captain: American WWII soldiers in the Philippines scare superstitious enemy soldiers with corpses they dress up to look like vampire victims. The vampire bites might be fake, but what comes out of the jungle is not...

#38 - Clothes Make the Man: A young man steals a magical suit off of a corpse, hoping some of its power will rub off on him.

#39 - Memory Market: The cryptic process of memory storage in the human brain has been decoded and now memories are bought and sold in the memory market. But with every legitimate commercial endeavor there comes a black market, and the memory market is no exception...

#40 - The Demon Who Ate Screams: A young martial artist battles a vicious demon who feeds on the tormented screams and dying whimpers of his victims.

Land of Fright™ terrorstories contained in Collection V:

#41 - The Hatchlings: A peaceful barbecue turns into an afternoon of terror for a suburban man when the charcoal briquets start to hatch!

#42 - Virgin Sacrifice: A professor of archaeology is determined to set the world right again using the ancient power of Aztec sacrifice rituals.

#43 - Smog Monsters: The heavily contaminated air in Beijing turns even deadlier when unearthly creatures form within the dense poison of its thick pollution.

#44 - Benders of Space-Time: A young interstellar traveler discovers the uncomfortable truth about the Benders, the creatures who power starships with their ability to fold space-time.

#45 - The Picture: A young soldier in World War II shows his fellow soldiers a picture of his beautiful fiancé during the lulls in battle. But this seemingly harmless gesture is far from innocent…

#46 - Black Ice: A vicious dragon is offered a great gift — a block of black ice to soothe the fire that burns its throat and roars in its belly. Too bad the dragon has never heard of a Trojan dwarf…

#47 - Artist Alley: At a comic book convention, a seedy comic book publisher sees himself depicted in a disturbing series of artist drawings.

#48 - Dead Zone: A yacht gets caught adrift in the dead zone in the Gulf of Mexico, trapped in an area of the sea that contains no life. What comes aboard the yacht from the depths of this dead zone in search of food cannot really be considered alive…

#49 - Cemetery Dance: A suicidal madman afraid to take his own life attempts to torment a devout Christian man into killing him.

#50 - The King Who Owned the World: A bored barbarian king demands he be brought a new challenger. But who can you find to battle a king who owns the world

Land of Fright™ terrorstories contained in Collection VI:

#51 - Zombie Carnival: Two couples stumble upon a zombie-themed carnival and decide to join the fun.

#52 - Going Green: Drug runners trying to double cross their boss get a taste of strong voodoo magic.

#53 - Message In A Bottle: A bottle floats onto the beach of a private secluded island with an unnerving message trapped inside.

#54 - The Chase: In 18th century England, a desperate chase is on as a monstrous beast charges after a fleeing wagon, a wagon occupied by too many people...

#55 - Who's Your Daddy?: A lonely schoolteacher is disturbed by how much all of the students in her class look alike. A visit by a mysterious man sheds some light on the curious situation.

#56 - Beheaded: In 14th century England, a daughter vows revenge upon those who beheaded her father. She partners with a lascivious young warlock to restore her family's honor.

#57 - Hold Your Breath: A divorced mother of one confronts the horrible truth behind the myth of holding one's breath when driving past a cemetery.

#58 - Viral: What makes a civilization fall? Volcanoes, earthquakes, or other forces of nature? Barbarous invasions or assaults from hostile forces? Decline from within due to decadence and moral decay? Or could it be something more insidious?

#59 - Top Secret: A special forces agent confronts the villainous characters from his past, but discovers something even more dangerous.

#60 - Immortals Must Die: There is no more life force left in the universe. The attainment of immortality has depleted the world of available souls. So what do you do if you are desperate to have a child?

Land of Fright™ terrorstories contained in Collection VII:

AND LOOK FOR EVEN MORE
LAND OF FRIGHT™ STORIES
COMING SOON!

THANKS AGAIN FOR READING.

LAND OF™
FRIGHT

Visit www.landoffright.com

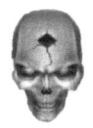

Also by Jack O'Donnell

The Spine-Tinglers™ series

I don't know who I am, or where I came from. All I know is that I can see things and hear things. I have no physical presence, yet I am somehow able to travel through space and time and witness untold events happening all around me. I suppose some of you will label me as a ghost, but that's not truly accurate as I have no recollection of ever being alive, no childhood memories, no remembrances of any traumatic life events that might be keeping me trapped in this world. Nor do I feel as if I am a manifestation of a dead person. I leave no shadowy trace. I am shapeless, formless. Don't get me wrong. Ghosts do exist, as I have seen them. I am just not one of them.

I seem to be drawn to those events that have a sinister side to them, a darkness. Perhaps it is my mission to shine some light on that darkness, to reveal the truth that is hidden in those dusky shadows. Perhaps I am here to warn you of what really exists in the world around you, make you a little more aware of the mysteries that often hide shrouded in the bliss of ignorance. I don't really know. All I know is that I am compelled to chronicle what I have observed, what I have heard, what I have felt, and share those experiences with you.

Here are the latest stories I felt compelled to chronicle...

The Scarecrow - Spine-Tinglers™ #1
Beware what grows in the corn!

Hideous monsters borne of the blood of the Civil War follow the commands of a demonic scarecrow bent on preserving the sanctity of her crop.

Metamorphosis - Spine-Tinglers™ #2
Beware what lurks in Nektala's Tomb!

Archaeologists unearth the tomb of a mysterious Egyptian ruler and unwittingly discover a secret that threatens to transform all of humanity.

Black Woods

The Black Woods contain darkly gnarled trees born from the seeds of sorcery, strange plants given unnatural life from the fertilizing spread of decaying magic, abnormal soil deeply contaminated with the residue of the Alchemy Wars from decades long past. Pockets of Black Woods have sprouted all over the world of Teradynea in isolated growths of midnight-black trees, most of these unexplored parcels of poisoned land still shrouded in secrecy. The tainted flora and fauna that sprout and flourish within these areas of permanent shadow contain mysterious powers that can be harvested and gathered for good. Or for evil.

What secrets do the Black Woods hold? Rin and his friend Joktala will soon discover that the Black Woods contain a hidden danger far more perilous than any they could have ever imagined...

ABOUT JACK O'DONNELL

I grew up on Jack Kirby comics, Creature Features, Godzilla movies, Stephen King, Andre Norton, Edgar Rice Burroughs, Don Pendleton's Executioner series, and a smorgasbord of science fiction and fantasy books.

I'm the co-producer and co-screenwriter of the film Stephen King's The Night Flier, based on Stephen King's story.

Visit my author page on Amazon at: **www.amazon.com/Jack-ODonnell/e/B00P43NP00**.

Please also visit the ODONNELL BOOKS bookstore on Amazon to see all of the other books published by ODONNELL BOOKS available at: **www.amazon.com/odonnellbooks**.

You can follow me on Goodreads here:
www.goodreads.com/author/show/1560457.Jack_O_Donnell

You can follow me on BookBub here:
www.bookbub.com/authors/jack-o-donnell-9334cc27-b5c3-4db4-a352-c14296da563b

Again, if you enjoyed this book, or any of my other works, please take the time to leave a review. Your feedback is greatly appreciated!

Thanks for reading!